Journey

of

Souls

by

Rebecca Warner

ISBN 979-8876266125

Cover design and maps: Rebecca Warner.

Cover image: the Madonna Pietra a degli Scrovigni by pre-Raphaelite artist Maria Stillman; the image is in the public domain,

www.rebeccawarnerauthor.net

Notes for Readers

See **Historical Notes** at the end for more background. The map below shows approximate divisions of territory in France in 1206.

King of France

King of England

Count of Toulouse and vassals

The story takes place in the region controlled by the Count of Toulouse and his vassals, which roughly corresponds to modern-day Occitanie. The map below shows approximate areas controlled by the three most powerful nobles: Raymond VI, Count of Toulouse; Raymond Roger Trencavel, Viscount of Beziers and Carcassonne; and the Count of Foix.

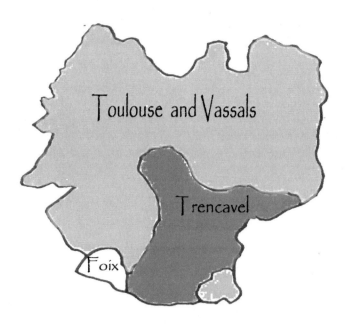

Major cities appear in the map below.

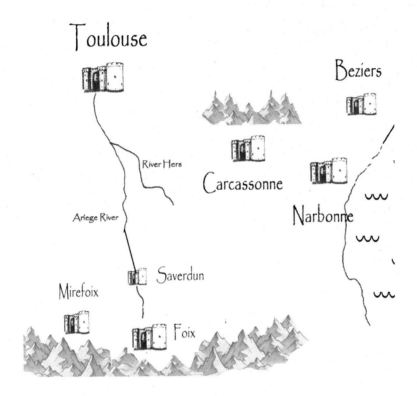

What's Invented/What's Real?

This is a multicultural, magical tale set during the Albigensian Crusades (the war to eradicate the Cathar heretics). Europe in 1206 was cosmopolitan and multicultural, with a wider variety of religious and spiritual beliefs than you might expect. Trade and travel along the Silk Roads made connections across vast distances. At least a few people from Asia and Africa may have visited or lived in Europe as far back as the Roman Empire. The soul-summoning spell used by the Lady brings in characters from different centuries, as well as different continents and cultures.

Invented: The walled city of Mirefoix does not exist; its name is a mashup of actual city names (Foix and Mirepoix). It lies south of Saverdun and west of Foix in the foothills of the Pyrenees. The Lady of Mirefoix, her household members, and the Baron of Saverdun are fictional. Rhazes (from Persia) and Fan Zhongyan (from the Song Empire) are named in honor of eminent scholars from earlier centuries.

Real: The following characters are from history: Pope Innocent III, Raymond VI (the Count of Toulouse), Raymond Roger Trencavel (the Viscount of Carcassonne, Beziers, and other cities), Raymond Roger (Count of Foix), Isaac the Blind (scholar of Kabbalah), Esclarmonde (a noted Cathar Perfect), King Peter of Aragon, Simon de Montfort, and Saint Guinefort (a greyhound believed to be a protector of infants). The sieges of Beziers and Carcassonne occurred as described. Many featured artifacts (such as Bon's sword of Chinese design and the embalmed heart of the Lady's son) correspond to objects in museums.

The informality of marriage vows and the chivalric practice of allowing people to depart safely from besieged cities after surrender (in some but not all cases) are historically accurate. The sieges at Beziers and Carcassonne are as described by Jonathan Sumption in *The Albigensian Crusades*. Please see Historical Notes at the end of the book for further details.

True, but bent a little: St. Francis was alive in 1206 but had not yet gathered a large following. Members of his order came to southern France in later years to convince Cather heretics of the error of their ways. It's conceivable, although unlikely, that his words reached Occitanie by 1209. People around Lyons prayed to St. Guinefort around 1250, which is too late for my story. Although the years don't fit, I couldn't resist including these two saints as examples of the diversity of religious beliefs at this time.

Part I: The Summoner of Souls. The Lady of Mirefoix uses soul-summoning jinn magic to try to recall the souls of people dear to her, but she accidentally calls souls from distant lands and different times instead. Trapped by her use of the spell, the jinn torment the Lady. The Lady commands the summoned souls to help her protect Mirefoix.

Part II: The Healer of Souls. The Lady turns to Christine, a psychotherapist from the 21st century, for comfort. Christine discovers that the cost of healing others is taking their pain upon herself. Along with the other summoned souls, and the Lady's daughter Garsenda, Christine rebels against the Lady's demands.

Part III: Destinies of the Souls. Garsenda, Christine, and the other summoned souls escape. They encounter love and loss as they are engulfed by the maelstrom of war. Alone in Mirefoix, the Lady must surrender the city. She begs those she has wronged to return to save her people.

1

Part 1:

The Summoner

of Souls

Chapter 1

The Lady, Countess of Mirefoix

November 1206

On All Souls Day, my husband returned from the dead.

Guillem and I were reviewing accounts in my chamber when a messenger burst in with news. "The Count and his party rest near Pamiers. They will arrive at Vespers."

Guillem's face turned the color of ash. His hand jerked, and his quill spread a bloodstain of ink across the vellum page. He placed his hands in his lap to hide their trembling. I willed myself to hide my fear.

"Do I know you?"

He smiled. "Yes, my Lady. My name is Guinot. I was one of your shepherds."

I remembered him. He was a fair-faced lad when the Count and his men departed for the Outremer, under streaming red and yellow banners, on an April morning in 1195. The Count took our only son, a party of a hundred men, and all our animals, food, weapons, and silver. He went to the support of Raymond of Antioch, hoping to win gold and glory. They were wild with enthusiasm for battle, plunder, and fantastic sights.

Two years after the departure, word came that all perished in a shipwreck. The loss of my son devastated me, but the death of my husband set me free. Since that time, I ruled Mirefoix and served my people well.

Guinot's face was sunburned and scarred; dark circles under his eyes gave him the haunted look of one who had stared into Hell's abyss. His matted hair and ragged clothes were those of a beggar, not a triumphant soldier.

I had to know my son's fate.

"Is Jehan with you?"

"Yes, my lady, he is well."

"And is the Count in good health?"

"He is much worn from the journey and will be glad to reach home."

"How many have returned?"

"Thirteen."

Only thirteen out of a hundred. My stomach clenched and I clenched my fist so hard that my nails cut into my palms.

"You have done well, Guinot. Go to the kitchen for food and drink."

Guillem latched the door behind him, and we embraced.

"Alazais, I fear for you. He will discover our sin."

"We believed him dead when we made our secret marriage vows."

His thinning hair and stooped back showed his age. I loved him no less for that. He had been my father's trusted seneschal, and he was that and more to me. When my husband beat me, Guillem comforted me. He alone encouraged me to think and feel for myself. No one could have seen Guillem on the hidden stairs to my chamber. However, there were eyes and ears everywhere in the

Chateau, and someone might have seen an unguarded look or caress between us. I touched his cheek and spoke from my heart.

"Our love is a bond that cannot be broken."

"I have placed you in danger, my love. The blame, and the punishment, must be mine alone."

"There is so little time… give orders to prepare a feast for his arrival."

I yearned for the comfort of Guillem's arms, but from now on, no one must see us together alone.

I walked alone on the battlements atop the city walls and gazed toward the foothills of the Pyrenees. The vineyards on the western hillsides had turned the blood-red of autumn, and pungent wood smoke from cleared fields stung my eyes. To the northwest, dark clouds gathered like unwashed wool along the horizon. These foretold the Tramontane, the relentless, bitter wind that batters walls and shutters. Some say its howling voice drives men mad. To the northeast, the road led across the valley towards Pamiers and the Count. I shuddered.

Mirefoix was mine by blood and the Count's only by marriage. He had ruled me—and my people — harshly. He sold flocks and land to pay for hawking and feasts, and my people went hungry. When I protested, he struck my face; his rings cut me and left scars. He picked quarrels with neighboring nobles; their soldiers rode through our fields and villages, cutting swathes of destruction. When I complained about his treatment of my people, he beat me. My left arm didn't heal well, and I never recovered full use of it. In his eleven-year absence, the scars and memories had faded. Now my muscles tightened, and I caught myself tearing at my nails. I must not let people see my fear. I must submit to my husband, even though he might be as brutal as in the past. What choice did I have?

I found my elder daughter Alienor sewing, seated near the window of my chamber. The chilly midday sun made a glowing halo behind her.

"Your father is returning. Put on your finest garments to welcome him."

Her darling face paled at the news, but she responded with her usual sweet obedience. I asked my maidservant where Garsenda was.

"She might be anywhere, my lady, at the market square, in the stables, or out riding."

I sighed with exasperation. "Send for her. She must prepare to greet her father."

I descended to the chaos in the kitchens. I gave the storeroom keys to the head cook to fetch pepper, saffron, clove, cardamom, and other spices. Women shelled peas, chopped cabbage, and cleaned leeks and carrots; salted cod and venison seasoned with rosemary and sage simmered in cauldrons and filled the room with savory aromas. For my people, who did not know the Count's cruelty as I did, this was an occasion for excitement and laughter. We had been too poor for feasts in the past but must celebrate now. Guillem said:

"There's not enough time to invite Foix and Saverdun and other neighboring nobles. I suggest we have the city merchants come wearing their best garments to swell the crowd. Josfred sent soldiers to hunt, but we won't have time to cure the meat."

"Buy all the bread and sausages available in the market square. Order the slaughter of more sheep and goats. The Count enjoys haricot of lamb. We can do with pottage for the lower end of the table, but the Count must have better fare." I begrudged the sacrifice of my people's flocks. Guillem gazed at me with understanding. He dared not press my hand.

I returned to my chamber to dress. My maid helped me don a clean linen underdress and cinched the side laces of my dark blue bliaut. I put on my finest sleeveless surcoat, dark red wool embroidered with gold acanthus leaves on the edges and hem. It was old and worn, but it was the finest I had. I had not indulged in finery during our years of poverty and hardship. I wrapped my head and chin in a wimple and barbette and pinned on a linen veil. A thin gold circlet held the veil in place. It was the only gift from my father I had not sold to buy food for my people. I hoped it would remind the Count of my rank.

When the bells rang at nightfall, I took my place at the high table in the great hall with my daughters nearby. My people's garments showed brilliant brown, green, and blue along the walls; they laughed and gossiped; servants circulated to pour wine. Guillem had ordered long trestle tables to be set up and covered with white cloths. Near the head of the tables, places were set with my few remaining pieces of silver plate; at the middle, wooden plates; and at the bottom, below the salt, trenchers of hard bread. The feast was not as elegant as the Count might expect, but it was the best I could afford to provide. Masses of candles and oil lamps flickered; their smoke irritated my eyes and nostrils. Against the walls, crimson tapestries with touches of blue, green, and gold showed vivid scenes of love, war, and the hunt. Oak logs crackled and blazed in the hearths at both ends of the hall. Guillem and Josfred, commander of the city guard, stood behind me; their presence bolstered my courage. As servants brought in platters, the aroma of roasted lamb and pork spread through the hall. It made me sick to think how much livestock we had to slaughter. We waited.

We heard a distant clamor as the Count's party made its way into the city gates, through the town, across the bridge, and through the corbeled gate into the Chateau Comtal. I heard cheers. My people greeted these men as conquerors; their enthusiasm did not bode well.

The Count and his small contingent of men appeared in the doorway. Ripples of dismay spread through the hall. I strained to make out their faces through the haze of smoke from the hearth. I was eager to see my son. He was still a boy when they departed. Now he might be as tall as his father, with hair the same dark shade of red. I searched their faces, at first in hope and then in despair. Jehan, the aged smith, was there; but my son Jehan was not among them. Guinot must have misunderstood which Jehan I meant; he would have known my son as "Young Master". Grief washed over me. My appetite fled; my mouth tasted like sawdust. My son had not been cruel like his father; sometimes, he stood between me and his father's fists. He would have been a capable future ruler for Mirefoix. How could I bear to lose him a second time?

My people kneeled; I rose. The Count approached. He did not kneel to show courtesy; he inclined his head in greeting and sat beside me. I released my people to sit or stand as they wished with a gesture. A flicker of annoyance passed over his face at my small demonstration of authority. As in the past, my actions annoyed him.

His left eye was sewed shut, and a livid scar divided his cheek. Sores and nodules covered his face. His nose was misshaped; the ends of some fingers were gone. Leprosy. Those close enough to see murmured and crossed themselves. I drew away.

I inclined my head to return his greeting. I should have commanded a greeting cup of wine; however, the prospect of drinking from a vessel he had touched was revolting. My retainer handed the goblet to the Count. After he drank, I brought my lips near the edge of the cup but avoided the rim and did not drink. I should have offered a greeting speech to my husband; however, I was too shocked to think of manners. Anger swept over me, more than fear.

"Where is my son?" I demanded.

He gazed at the floor for a few moments. Was there a tear in his one good eye? Then he searched the faces in the crowd.

"Where is *my* son?" He spoke in the truculent tone I remembered and feared.

I didn't understand what he meant at first. Then I recalled. The Count had a concubine from a land far in the east before he married me; she bore him a son and died three years later. He brought this son with him when he came to my house.

Now that my son was dead, this bastard was significant. The Count might punish me for slighting this son. He might legitimize Bon by adoption, grant him a knighthood, and perhaps even designate him as heir of Mirefoix. That must not happen. I had expected to rule for many more years, and then my elder daughter Alienor would govern Mirefoix after me. Now, Bon might stand in the way.

I whispered to Guillem: "Search for him… where is he?"

A young man emerged from the ranks of the castle guard. He was tall and moved with grace. He was handsome, I grant. His cheeks were smooth, not beard-stubbled and red like the faces of many. He had high cheekbones and dark eyes. His hair, tied at the base of his neck, was glossy as a raven's wing. His surcoat was a hand's breadth longer than it should be and dyed a darker shade of blue, suggesting a claim to a higher rank. Perhaps he was ambitious. Before he allied with his father, I must bind him to me.

He kneeled before us and gazed into his father's eyes and mine with quiet assurance. Guillem announced: "My lord, this is Bon."

Josfred said: "He has no equal for intelligence, courage, and skill with weapons. He is the one I would choose to command the garrison after I am gone."

My husband said, "Well done, my son. I am pleased." He stood, walked up to Bon, and embraced him. A murmur spread through the crowd.

Bon bowed gracefully and stepped back into the mass of onlookers.

At the Count's signal, a servant presented an embossed metal box shaped like a heart. I knew the custom of embalming the heart of a fallen soldier. "This is Jehan's heart. We will place it in the family tomb."

My face must have betrayed how stricken I was; my husband's tone became kinder. "He showed great courage. Take comfort in his assured salvation. Let's retire. I have much to tell."

Chapter 2

The Lady

I dreaded to be alone with the Count, but I must face him. We retired to my chamber; Alienor waited there. He roared a greeting and pinched her cheek; she pulled away. This displeased the Count. "Take your womanish ways and be gone." Her face showed relief as she escaped.

"Where's Garsenda? I remember her as a cheeky maid."

"I have sent for her." She must have slipped out with the crowds that departed the feast. Her face mirrored the Count's, and she had his wild nature. No wonder he favored her.

"I'll summon her as well. She'll not disobey me." He pointed to the man who accompanied him.

"This infidel, Rhazes, is a trustworthy physician." The man mixed resin with wine and gave the cup to the Count.

"His medicine slowed my disease, although it did not cure me." I had never seen a Saracen before; I stared at him. He was not as dark in complexion as I expected. His nose was prominent, and his brows were dark. His hands and clothing were clean, and the faded robes had once been fine. The thick textured material was patterned with symbols, black against gray, with tarnished traces of silver. The cloth wrapped around his head made it difficult to judge his age. His expression was somber and gentle. He spoke:

"My lord, take care not to consume too much opium at one time. A small amount brings sleep and relief from pain. A large amount can cause death."

"Leave the drug. All of it."

I stored this idea away. Rhazes gazed at me as if he understood my mind. I didn't like this. A man who knows too much is dangerous. I saw pity in his eyes as he gave the cup to the Count. Perhaps he had compassion for both of us. He bowed, made an unfamiliar gesture of farewell or blessing, and said something that sounded like 'Solomon.' My servant covered the windows against the coming storm and departed. The wind beat against the walls, howling like an animal in distress. The rough banging of the shutters unnerved me.

As he drank, the Count boasted of his exploits. "We *crucesignati* fought with godly rage. The blood of our enemies reddened our swords. We rode through the mud and mangled bodies of infidels up to our horses' knees. Some of them fought with courage, I grant. I saw things you wouldn't believe. Archers loosed arrows from horseback. In Constantinople, I saw buildings encrusted with gems that gleamed scarlet and green in the sun. Our men pried stones from the altar in the Hagia Sophia."

I looked at the battered chest he had brought. Some who returned from the East brought gold, spices, gems, and silks. This small coffer couldn't hold much. When the Count opened it, I saw ragged and stained manuscript pages covered with elaborate symbols. These did not impress me.

"These words are powerful magic. No one else must hear about this. I tell you because I must have your help."

My husband was not an intelligent man, nor one given to study. For all the sense we could make of these scribbles, they might be a dozen ways to prepare lamb.

"This is of no use if we cannot read it."

"I brought a man, Alfan, who understands these symbols. An alchemist. He has promised to use these incantations and sacred oils to get me a youthful body free of afflictions."

"How is that possible?"

"First, I will tell you how these spells came into my possession. When Constantinople fell, my men and I took possession of a fine house. We feasted on their provisions and drank the finest wines. My men searched for treasures. They brought me a terrified man who clung to this chest and begged for his life. He promised to use magic to make me a healthy young man."

"How so, my lord?"

"Swear to me, you will tell no one."

I so swore. Of course, I would tell Guillem everything.

"The manuscripts describe a spell that takes one man's soul and places it in the body of another."

My face must have betrayed my doubt. And yet, part of me believed this possible. He continued.

"I will send for my sister's son. I remember him as well-favored and strong. If not, another young man will serve. I will abandon my diseased body and take this young man's form. You must marry me in that form, so I can continue to rule as Count. It should be pleasant for you to have a lusty young husband again. Perhaps you are not too old to bear another son."

The idea filled me with disgust. "Why would Alfan do this for you?"

"His father was Viscount of Turenne, and his mother was the daughter of a Saracen merchant. The Viscount deserted him and his mother. Alfan would have been a nobleman if his father had claimed him. He seeks to regain his birthright. I promised him our daughter's hand in marriage, five hundred solidi of silver, and men to attack his father's city."

He swallowed more of the drugged wine.

I was aghast; I would never consent to bargain away Alienor's future. It was clear to me, although perhaps not to my dim-witted husband, that Alfan would have no further need of us if he wed our daughter. The marriage would give him a claim to inherit Mirefoix, and he might possess other magic to do us harm.

"He will not provide this new body until I have delivered these things. During the journey, despite the physician's ministrations, my sickness worsened. I have regained some strength, but battle injuries still grieve me. We must arrange this marriage at once. If you don't have silver, we'll sell land. When I have a new body, you will bury my old one. In my nephew's body, I will marry you and offer protection to Mirefoix. My people will renew their oaths of loyalty to me."

I resolved I would not marry him again, even if he became a young man. I doubted a change of body would improve his temper.

"How do you know Alfan can fulfill these promises?"

"He showed many kinds of magic. He called a noble soul into the body of an ignorant peasant. The soul he summoned spoke the lenga romana, Latin, and the Saracen tongue. He made a goblet rise; he put a sword down his throat without injury. He even made a roasted fowl stand up and crow."

The Count was not clever. A supposed magician could have an educated man pose as an ignorant peasant; levitating objects was common trickery. I would be more convinced if I had witnessed these things myself, but I did not voice my doubts.

"Swear to obey, on your soul, and the souls of our children."

I had no choice. I swore on my soul, but not on the souls of my daughters. I hoped God would understand and forgive me when I broke my word and shared this information with Guillem. He mixed more drug into his wine and took a deep draught.

"Before I obtain my new body, perhaps I can get you with a son of my own blood." He slurred his words; the drug must have dulled his senses.

I remembered how he used me in the past. I couldn't allow this to happen again. I rose to leave. He lurched toward me, seized my arm, and dragged me to the bed. He came to me unwashed, with acrid odors of sweat and blood upon him. His body crawled with vermin. He kneeled astride me and pulled up my shift. At first, familiar terror overcame me; then sudden rage. I seized my knife from the bedside table and thrust it into his chest with all the force I could muster.

Chapter 3

Garsenda,

Daughter of the Countess of Mirefoix

I was the unloved daughter, the extra child. Mother's constant praise of Alienor cut my heart like a blade. Bon was the only one who cared for me. He, not Mother, was the one who dried my tears when I hurt myself in rough play. After she sent him away, I spent as much time visiting him at the barracks as he allowed. Bon taught me to throw a knife as well as any soldier. We rode recklessly, testing each other's skill, and he allowed me to keep up—sometimes. We were favorites among the soldiers and grooms. His friend Fabrice made clever objects at his forge and always had treats for us. I still had the ring he wrought from a nail and a metal horse that comically resembled my favorite mare. With Bon, I experienced joy and freedom. My childish worship ripened into love.

My heart burst with joy when I saw him kneel before Father at the feast. When the celebration ended, I mingled with the departing crowd and slipped through the gate. Draped in a borrowed cloak, I evaded my mother's spies. When Bon reached the market square, I touched his elbow. He swiveled abruptly. Then he smiled in the familiar way that warmed my soul.

"Bon! It has been so long since I have seen you."

His thoughts were elsewhere. "He said I was his son."

"You look nothing like him."

Bon frowned at my oft-repeated argument. "Would you deny me hope of advancement?"

"I apologize. I had not thought." I took hold of his dark blue sleeve. Now that I had grown into womanhood, he was reluctant to be near me. However, he was too polite to push me away. Since boyhood, he longed to achieve *paratge*, that mixture of courtesy, courage, refinement, and honor only we Occitan possess. A man without money for horses and retainers could not become a knight. I knew this distressed him. Now that Father had returned, his circumstances would change. I said: "What will happen now? Surely he will take control back from my mother."

He did not wish to speculate and changed to a topic I liked less. "The Lady has not found you a husband? You and Alienor are past the age when most marry."

I disliked this reminder of my age. I had just turned 20. The Lady spoke of potential husbands for me, but nothing had come of it yet. "She will not force Alienor to marry. For me, she speaks of the convent."

He laughed. "I can't imagine you as a nun." I hated that; he still treated me as a child and dismissed my fears about the future as trivial.

"She worries that unmaidenly behavior will spoil me and dishonor her. She has servants spy upon me." I looked about to confirm that her spies had not followed me.

"You should return. Your father will want to see you."

Yes. By now, servants would have overturned the household searching for me.

I did not dare ask if he favored some girl. Once I heard him swear he would father no bastard. I took comfort from that; as a man of honor, he would keep his word. I parted from him with reluctance, unable to secure a promise of another meeting. I retraced my steps, in no hurry to face the Lady's wrath. The streets were not safe after dark. However, none would dare attack me. My face was known, and the knife strapped to my arm inside my sleeve gave me confidence. I continued to practice the skills Bon taught me and could hit a mark with force at twenty paces.

I wondered what would happen. My lady mother would not surrender power without a fight.

Chapter 4

The Lady

My first blow wounded the Count; he tried to wrestle the dagger out of my hand, but he was weak and clumsy. Intoxication slowed him; the drug dulled his senses. What I had started, I must finish. I pulled away from his grasp and struck a second time. Luck or fate must have guided my hand; the blade penetrated deeper. He lay still.

I was aghast. God would send my soul to everlasting Hell. I held a feather near his nose and mouth to check for breath; there was no sign of life. I wrung my hands as I paced back and forth in my chamber. The only person I trusted was Guillem. I went through the hidden door behind the tapestry, descended the secret stairs, and entered Guillem's quarters.

"You must come."

Guillem accompanied me back to my chamber, where the Count's body sprawled across my bed. He gasped. Then he said:

"You had to defend yourself. I feared what the Count would do to you, to us, when he learned the truth. He would not let an insult to his honor go unpunished." Guillem guided me to sit on the bench before the fire and placed a goblet of wine in my hands. "Calm yourself, my love. What's done is done. We must conceal this." He sat beside me and put his arm around me. As always, his presence soothed me.

We sat in silence for a time. I said:

"We must make this appear an accident."

"Yes. We will remove his stained tunic, clean away as much blood as possible, and wrap the wound in linen to conceal it. We'll dress him in a tunic with no slashes or stains. Then we'll push him down the stairs. It will appear he died from the fall. You must wash his body for burial alone. Don't let anyone see the wounds in his chest."

The Count stirred and mumbled and tried to rise. He was not dead yet, after all. We ran to the bed; my dying husband reached out and tried to seize my arms. Guillem beat his head with the coffer until he again lay still. This time, he must be truly dead.

Guillem stepped outside my chamber to make sure no one was about. We struggled to support his body between us, and half walked, half dragged his limp body to the top of the stairs. Then we pushed. We went downstairs to examine him.

"The injuries from the fall don't seem sufficient to cause death. We must try again."

We dragged him back up the stairs and pushed him down a second time. This impact broke his neck, and we decided that was sufficient. Guillem made sure that he was no longer breathing. I became numb with horror; this must not be happening. Guillem's face paled with worry, but I could see he tried to seem calm for my sake. We bundled the torn tunic and bloodstained bed linens so that Guillem could take them away.

"What shall we do now?"

"Lady, I must not be found here. Return to bed and try to sleep. Let the servants discover him in the morning. Try to compose yourself. Your face must show grief, not guilt."

"I will go to Hell."

He was silent for a moment. "The guilt is mine, Alazais. I caused his death."

"I started this."

"No. The Count himself is to blame. He abused you throughout your marriage. He used Mirefoix as brutally as he used you. His death sets us free."

His words failed to comfort me. He tried again.

"We have many years to seek absolution."

After Guillem left, I lay alone in the bed where I had stabbed the Count. Terror pressed like a stone on my chest; I struggled to breathe. The wind sang like wolves; the night was long. And yet I dreaded dawn. I had done this to prevent terrible things from happening, but now I faced other threats. I must do penance. I would pay for masses, donate money and land to the Church, and send pilgrims to Santiago de Compostela to pray on my behalf. I might even make the journey myself. I dared not make a full confession now; I didn't trust my confessor to keep my secret. I would wait and speak to God on my deathbed, and He would forgive me.

I had no pity in my heart for the Count. He brought fear and evil into my world. But God would punish me for this deed, for I had placed the concerns of this world above God's laws and my immortal soul. Some would say the Count only took his husband's rights. Perhaps I should have allowed the Count to have his way.

My maidservant screamed when she found the Count's body in the morning. I feigned surprise and grief; I pretended I was too stunned at first to speak; I feared I might give away my true feelings, and I worried that my behavior might not be entirely convincing. In private, I rubbed my eyes with bitter herbs to bring tears. I ordered the preparation of mourning clothes. My servants carried the Count's body into my chamber, laid him on the table, and stripped him. I said to my daughters:

"I will do this alone." I did not want them to see his body. But Garsenda said,

"It is our sacred duty also," and she refused to leave.

We washed his body in water scented with herbs and rose petals. Garsenda examined his body with unmaidenly interest, noticing every scar, lesion, and birthmark. Alienor paled and drew away. I summoned a maidservant.

"Take my daughter to bed and summon Sister Cecilia to tend her."

Meanwhile, Garsenda wept with a genuine sorrow I found annoying. The Count had praised her fearless ways and said, 'tis a pity you are not a man, for you have more courage than most. Her recklessness, which constantly exasperated me, had pleased him. Garsenda pulled away the bandage I had placed over his wound; she saw the knife wounds and stared at me with dismay. I made an excuse:

"He must have fallen on his blade." She didn't appear convinced. I would have to deal with her suspicions. After we finished preparing the Count's body, I took the guards aside and instructed them that Garsenda must not leave the Chateau. I appointed a new boy to shadow her.

I made the Count's funeral a fine one but not too opulent. I must be seen to grieve him, but a public display of wealth was a risk; it would remind covetous neighbors that I was a wealthy woman who ruled alone. We invited nobles from neighboring cities and castles and prepared a splendid repast. Even the Count of Foix attended with his sister Esclarmonde in the stern garb of a Cathar Perfect. I announced I had paid for a hundred masses for the Count's soul.

After the funeral, I summoned my vassals to the hall.

"Each of you must swear your allegiance to me. We must remain united." One at a time, the knights kneeled with bare heads. Each swore upon our most holy relic, a finger bone from Saint Nazarius in a ruby-studded gold reliquary. He was my special protector because I was born on his feast day.

"I promise before God that I will be faithful to my Lady, never do her harm, stand with her against her enemies, and keep homage to her against all persons."

I took their hands between mine and announced that I had accepted their pledges. To a few whose loyalty was most necessary, I gave new holdings. Although it was not customary, I also asked every person of lower rank who served me to swear the same oath. I must ensure complete loyalty. Some of my people did not appear for the oath-taking, Bon among them. No one knew where he was. This troubled me.

That night the leprous spirit of the Count appeared to me with hatred in his gaze. He stood beside my bed and cursed me. "You murdered me! You will be damned forever! God will punish you with Hellfire!" He reached out with immaterial hands as if to tear my shift. I smelled his fetid breath. I shivered in terror and remorse and begged him to depart. I wanted to pull the bedcovers over my face, but terror paralyzed me.

"Adulteress! Treacherous woman!"

Rage distorted his face as he bent over me. I cowered.

"I only defended myself."

"You denied me my husband's rights."

I clutched the cross I wore around my neck and prayed.

"God does not answer the prayers of the wicked."

He wrapped his disfigured hands around my neck and tried to strangle me. My tears did not move him to pity. I fainted.

He was gone when I woke.

The Count's threats were not the only source of dread. I would face dire consequences if others knew what I had done. The day after the funeral, I summoned the new boy I had appointed to spy on Garsenda. She had grown adept at eluding familiar maidservants and soldiers, but she didn't recognize this boy. He came to me, hat in hand.

"Tell me."

"She got past the guards after the funeral, followed Bon, and spoke to him near the town square."

So, I must punish and replace the guards.

"Of what matters?"

"I could not get close enough to hear."

"What do people say about the Count's death?"

"Forgive me, my Lady. Some say it's strange he died so suddenly. Some suspect foul play."

"Of course, that's not true. The Count fell after consuming too much wine and opium." I gave him enough silver to buy his silence and sent him back to the distant pastures whence he came. I must keep Garsenda from speaking of this in the future.

Gossip of this kind would reach Bon. Would he seek revenge for his father's death? I did not think the Count had fathered him; I saw no resemblance. Bon already had reason to hate me because I had put him out of my house, and it was clear he saw hope in his father's return. My spies told me he commanded much respect and admiration from the soldiers. Would he dare to denounce me, to raise men against me? Alas: I feared Garsenda would support any accusations he might make against me. Worries devoured my mind.

I sought refuge in my chapel. I tried to explain to God the necessities that drove me. The suffering eyes of Jesus reproved me from the cross; painted scenes of Hell on the walls came alive with moving flames and threatening gestures; I sought release in prayer. My knees ached from the unforgiving icy stone floor of the chapel, but supplications to God did not make the Count's nighttime visits cease.

I sought consolation from my confessor Father Felip. He was a holy man, not one of those priests who kept a woman, accumulated silver, and ate rich foods. God favored him and would listen to him. I kneeled and crossed myself.

"Father, forgive me, for I have sinned."

Father Felip crossed himself.

"In the name of the Father, and the Son, and the Holy Spirit. May God help you repent of your sins. Trust in his mercy."

I didn't tell him the full extent of my sins.

"I didn't obey my husband as a wife should. His soul has returned to chastise me."

His brow contracted.

"Father, how shall I be saved?"

"You must sin no more. Honor the Count's memory in death. Buy him masses in perpetuity. You must say the Pater Noster morning and evening for one year. After true repentance, God will forgive all sins."

"My God, I am sorry for this sin with all my heart. With your help, I will do penance, sin no more, and avoid whatever leads me to sin. Our Savior, Jesus Christ, suffered and died for us. In his name, God, have mercy."

Perhaps because I had not made a full confession and did not feel genuine remorse, the Count's spirit continued to appear every night. After his death, I couldn't sleep alone. I wished to spare Guillem the knowledge of my shame and suffering, but I needed his protection. The Count stood by my bed and raved for long hours at night; Guillem sheltered me in his arms.

Through all the icy nights of that winter, the Count shook his leprous fist and cursed me, and he stabbed my abdomen with a ghostly dagger. I examined myself in the morning and saw no outward sign of injury. My soul was wretched. Was this apparition sent by God or Satan? My dead husband's threats terrified me more than the blows he inflicted on me when alive. He accused me of betrayal and threatened revenge. He showed me his diseased hands and distorted face and pointed to the wounds I had inflicted upon him. He bellowed: "Curses upon you, unfaithful wife! You sent me to Hell, and I will drag you into its fires to suffer with me forever! God will take away what you love most to punish you." I lit candles to drive his ghost away. I pulled the bedcovers over my face and stopped my ears with wool to block his voice. I sought shelter in Guillem's arms, and he sought to reassure me: "He is dead and can trouble us no more. Let me hold you. We will pray together." I welcomed Guillem's company, but his presence did not banish my terror.

Chapter 5

The Lady

February 1207

I tried to get on with life, but the Count's curses brought death and disaster.

Three days after the funeral, my daughters came to my chamber. We did needlework together and talked. We sat in a pool of sunshine near the window; Alienor plied her needle gracefully and made bright blue flowers bloom in her tapestry. Garsenda stabbed the fabric impatiently and wrestled with knots. I was too restless to work and set my embroidery aside.

An impatient sigh came from Garsenda.

"And how are you?"

"I grieve for my father. You do not weep for him."

"It is a tragedy that he passed so unexpectedly. Of course, it saddens me."

She shot me a hostile look.

"Your guards do not allow me to go out. I feel like a prisoner."

"You are no longer a child. It is not fitting that you run about and mix with townsmen and soldiers. People will doubt your virtue."

Guillem entered. "My Lady, an urgent matter requires your attention."

"What is it?"

"It is Josfred, my Lady. He fell while sparring with soldiers, and he is unwell."

"I will come at once."

I found Josfred lying in his bed, propped up against pillows. I was struck by his grizzled hair and wrinkled face. When had he become so old? He tried to rise when he saw me. He wanted to greet me, but he could not speak; the right half of his face sagged strangely.

"Rest, my good and faithful servant. I need your strength."

Father Stefe took me aside and whispered: "I fear tis a demon. I tried to cast it out but did not have the power. Perhaps the Bishop can help. Meanwhile, I have bled him."

I agreed to send for the Bishop, although my recent experience had shaken my faith in the power of priests. Father Stefe kneeled beside Josfred and prayed; Josfred plucked at the bedcovers with one hand. He tried unsuccessfully to speak and showed great distress. His courage had been my shield for as long as I could remember. This strange paralysis terrified him. I brought a cup of wine to his lips, but the liquid dribbled down his chin. The aged herbalist Sister Cecilia arrived.

"Can you suggest any remedies, Sister?"

Cecilia examined Josfred's face and hands. "None of my herbs would help. Perhaps he can take wine and broth more easily from a sponge?"

She dipped a cloth into wine, moistened his lips, and wrung a few drops into his mouth. He swallowed this with difficulty. He grew less agitated; his face relaxed.

It occurred to me that the Saracen physician might help; perhaps his knowledge from the East would be helpful. I returned to my chamber and summoned him. "Tell me about yourself."

"I am called Rhazes, great Lady."

I ordered food and drink. He declined both.

"You are not hungry?"

"My people do not drink wine, great Lady, nor do they eat the flesh of pigs."

"Your people are Saracens? Moors?"

"I prefer to be called Muslim, my Lady."

I sent for a leg of fowl, pastries, and fruit.

He asked permission to wash, and I sent for water as well.

Perhaps emboldened by this, he said: "Noble Lady, your late husband, may his name be blessed, promised permission for me to return to the east when he reached his homeland. May I ask about your plans for me?"

"If you serve me well, you may indeed go home in time. Meanwhile, you will stay here as a guest."

If this disappointed him, he didn't allow it to show. His dignified manner inspired greater confidence than I felt in some of my other advisors.

I took him to see Josfred. He conducted a thorough examination. He felt Josfred's forehead and hands: "No fever." He examined his skull: "I see no sign of injury. Was there a blow to the head?" Then he addressed Josfred: "This is not a time for cheer, but smile if you can. Speak. Tell me your name." Only the left side of Josfred's mouth moved. Josfred's lips moved, but he couldn't form words, only breathy grunts. Terror filled his eyes. Rhazes asked him to move his hands and legs; he pricked him gently in many places with a needle. Paralysis and lack of feeling affected only his right side.

"May we speak, great Lady?"

We found privacy in the exercise yard outside the barracks.

"Well?"

"It is apoplexy."

"Will he recover?"

"It's impossible to say. Patients sometimes regain some power of speech and movement with time."

"Is he dying?"

"Perhaps, but I do not believe death is imminent."

"What about treatment?"

"There are cold humors in his brain. Foods and herbs that stimulate warm humors should help, and sister Cecilia can prepare these. We must keep him warm and clean. Limbs he cannot move must be turned to prevent atrophy. In time he may regain the use of his muscles."

"Will you bleed him?"

"In my experience, bleeding does not produce any benefit in such cases. Sometimes it is better to do nothing."

"What if he does not improve? Is there anything else you can do?"

"Some physicians cauterize the front and back of the head. However, I do not recommend this. The treatment is worse than the disease."

"Is he in pain?"

"There is often extreme headache at the onset of this condition. He shows no signs of pain now."

I set aside the morning hours to visit Josfred. Bon attended to all his needs. Within a few days, Josfred took broth from a spoon. But he could not rise from bed and stand, even with support from Bon. Josfred's power of speech did not return. He had always been quick to smile but now showed no pleasure in anything. He communicated only with nods, grimaces, and one-handed gestures. I sensed he wanted to speak, and I asked simple questions.

"You are concerned that you cannot carry out your duties. It is all right, my friend. You have served all your life, and now you can rest. Yes?"

He shook his head. No.

Another question occurred to me, but I could not bring myself to ask it. Do you want to die?

Seven days passed; I tended Josfred with my own hands and had Rhazes examine him again, but he became no better. I went back to my chamber to meet in private with Guillem and discuss what we should do. Guillem spoke: "Without leadership, discipline among the soldiers will collapse. They will gamble, start fights amongst themselves, drink, and chase women. The Baron of Saverdun raided two villages this week, and our garrison did not respond. Mark my words; he will use this as a chance to seize land and steal sheep. Something must be done. You need a new commander at once."

"Who can that be, other than Bon? Josfred named him in public as his successor, and he is respected. But I fear him. If he believes rumors, he may suspect we killed the Count. He has reason to resent me because I sent him out of the Chateau to fend for himself when I heard the Count died in the east. With control of the garrison, he might accuse me of murder. But if not Bon, then who?"

Guillem took both my hands in his.

"You must win his loyalty. Charm him, praise him. Promise him advancement."

"It may not be enough. And if I make our enemy more powerful, then what?"

We sat, thinking. I must discover Bon's thoughts; I must make him an ally or get him out of the way. I summoned him for a private meeting. As I expected, the conversation was difficult.

"You must swear obedience to me."

I knew that, however reluctantly he might give his oath, he would be honor-bound to uphold it. I distrusted him, but I knew him to be an honorable man.

"Lady, I am still loyal to the Count, my father."

"The Count is dead."

"Yes, but how did he die? He seemed well enough when he returned from Outremer. Some say his death was no accident, and I must seek vengeance on those who killed him if it was not."

"Who says such things? Whom do you accuse?"

"I accuse no one, Lady."

His face appeared smooth and untroubled. But Garsenda might have told him about the Count's wounds, and she might have revealed that Guillem and I were lovers. My spies told me that people speculated about this. Many would surmise that I arranged the Count's death for fear of his vengeance.

"You must swear loyalty to me."

"I choose not to swear at this time, Lady."

I worried about his refusal; I needed to know his reason.

"Why not?"

"If I swear loyalty, I must obey all your commands. I distrust what some of your commands might be." His tone was neutral, but his words were disrespectful; I was angry.

After I dismissed him, I considered further. I had no way to force Bon to swear loyalty. He had already refused in private; if I pressed the issue and he refused to swear in public, that would further damage my authority. Might I buy his support? If I had silver to spare, I could make him a knight and grant him a house, manor, and a living. No. I didn't have enough funds. In any case, he might spurn such gifts. Worse, such gifts would provide him with the resources to oppose me.

I must have a reliable commander for my garrison; war might be coming. During the past three years, the Pope had demanded that we southern nobles cease sheltering Cathar heretics. He sent preachers to persuade the dissidents of the error of their ways, but this did not check the spread of their beliefs. He sent Legates to demand that we stamp out the heresy. Annoyed by the failure of the preachers and Legates, Pope Innocent called for the northerners to form an army to take the lands of all southern nobles; this had not yet come to pass, but I worried it might. If the Pope got his war, Mirefoix would be in danger. I must have a capable commander.

If Bon would not swear loyalty, I could not trust him. Somehow he must be made to serve me.

Guillem and I spoke about our worries, and he said: "Tell me again about the magic the Count planned to use to put his soul in a youthful body."

"Why do you bring that up now?"

"Perhaps Josfred's soul in Bon's body would provide a solution."

Chapter 6

Bon

When the Count returned to Mirefoix, I was hopeful. He called me his son. I hoped I might become more than an impoverished soldier. Now that hope was gone. My father's sudden death troubled me greatly. Garsenda sought me out on the day of his funeral to share her suspicions. Based on her description of the two knife wounds, it must be murder. The Lady must have ordered his death, and I could not serve a woman who would do such a thing. I needed a plan. I considered which men to trust with this knowledge.

Eleven years earlier, my father took men to Outremer on a mission to rescue Antioch. I longed to go with them; I wanted to prove myself. I was a foolish, hot-blooded boy eager to show my worth in battle. But the day before they departed, I became ill. I vomited until it seemed I would lose my guts. For two weeks, the illness continued; when I felt better, it was too late for me to follow.

I continued to live in the Lady's household in the Chateau. By night, my mother's servant Fan Zhongyan instructed me in the language and literature of the lands far to the east where my mother was born. By day, I studied Latin and sparred with the weapons master. I hoped that as the Count's son, I would have status and property. When Jehan returned to rule Mirefoix, I would be his right-hand man.

I remember well the news of the Count's death. I had bribed Garsenda to study Latin by promising a ride in the hills. I was correcting her translations when the Lady entered holding a letter.

"There is news."

She drew Garsenda and Alienor close.

"Listen: Your father and all his men are dead. They boarded ships at Marseilles and never arrived in Cyprus; the letter says they all sank in a storm."

Alienor was serious and silent; Garsenda wept. I put my arm around her.

"Stop. She is no longer a child; it's not appropriate for you to touch her. People will talk."

I drew back, but Garsenda reached for me. The Lady pulled her away.

"You must leave the Chateau and make your own way in the world."

It had always been clear that she had no love for me. Still, her sudden decision was a surprise. Garsenda protested; the Lady ordered a maidservant to remove her. I gathered my weapons, hauberk, and gambeson, assuming they were mine to take. The Lady took them from me, saying, these are no longer yours. She sent me away with nothing but the clothes on my back. I bit my lip and kept silent. I would be on my own with no prospect of advancement.

I was 15 and too proud to show my fear.

My mother's servant Fan Zhongyan gathered his possessions, including the manuscripts from the east we had studied together. We went to the forge near the barracks to find Fabrice, who was like an older brother to me. He had always welcomed my visits. When Garsenda and I visited as children, he made us toys and gave us honey cakes. He had little education. However, he was an intelligent man with common sense, thorough knowledge of town gossip, and a bawdy sense of humor. As a respected craftsman, he understood what it was to be admired but envied by others. He gave us sound advice. He helped my teacher find lodging and work as a scribe. He sent me to the garrison.

Josfred welcomed me with a warning. "There are two kinds of men in the garrison. Eight are battle-hardened mercenaries; the rest are untrained boys too young to fight. You need to earn your place among the men or be treated as a boy. Watch your back."

The soldiers allowed me bread and a bowl of pottage but no share of the meat. There was no bed for me; I lay alone in the stables. I did not sleep. In the darkness of night, one mercenary kneeled beside me and placed his hand on my shoulder. "You will submit. Everyone obeys me." I had expected something like this might happen, and I was prepared. I rolled over to avoid his grasp and jumped to my feet. I ran to a familiar horse and leaped onto his bare back. I left Mirefoix by the postern gate and galloped into the hills.

I must fight, but I needed a weapon. I searched among young trees until I found a solid straight sapling. I whittled away twigs and bark during the night, then tested my new staff to assess its weight and balance.

When morning came, I returned to the barracks and confronted my attacker. "You have insulted me, and I will teach you a lesson." The bully outweighed me, and his arms were thickly muscled. Still, I was confident I had the skill to bring him down.

He taunted me. "You are nothing but a bastard."

I responded: "I am, at least, a noble bastard. Is your father of noble blood?"

"Is yours?"

His suggestion the Count was not my father offended me. I controlled my anger and asked: "What shall we fight for?" It was common for defeated knights to surrender their weapons, and by making this demand, I identified myself as a man with a claim to rank. He wore a quilted jacket; I had lost mine and needed one for protection.

"I will fight you for your gambeson."

He sneered. "I accept that bet. In return, you promise that when you lose, you will serve me for three months." I must not lose. We faced off with staves, and the others formed a ring around us.

"I wager five deniers on Peire." No one would bet on me. Not yet.

I had a moment to study my opponent's stance and the direction of his gaze. He was right-handed; I guessed correctly that his first blow would be toward my left. As I expected, he swung at me with such force that he threw himself off balance. I dodged to one side and cracked him low across the knees. He staggered but did not fall. His face reddened with rage, and he charged toward me. He prepared for me to strike low again, but this time, I brought my staff down from overhead and struck his knuckles. He almost lost his grip on the staff, but again, he recovered.

He lunged. I stepped aside, danced around him, and struck the back of his head with my staff. He fell forward, partly from his own momentum, and sprawled on the ground. He was stunned and unable to stand. I stood over him with the pointed end of my staff aimed at his neck. With a reluctant growl, he conceded. Because of the witnesses, he had to give me what he had promised. The older men showed hatred; the boys showed respect.

I stepped forward and claimed the first share of meat that night. That night, the mercenary I had beaten rode off and never returned. After that, no one challenged my claim to a share of the meat. The boys clustered around me, asking me to spar with them and teach them my tricks.

Josfred spoke to me. "You have succeeded, as I expected. Now you must defend your position as a leader." In time I became, after Josfred, the second in command. I made clear to the older men: no more abuse of the boys. The boys thanked me for freeing them and looked to me as their teacher and protector. When Josfred hired six new mercenaries, I taught them respect with my sword, staff, and fists. I made no friends among them, but I secured my place.

❖

Fan Zhongyan said: "You have proved you are a man. It's time for you to have the gifts your mother left." He gave me the sword that was in his keeping. It was unlike any other sword I had seen. The pommel had a finely worked design with three lobes and a massive, curved guard, and the grip had an intricate pattern of overlapping straps. It fitted my hand as if it had been made for me. The blade was sharp but also strong and flexible. With such a sword and the skills I had gained, I could not lose. He also gave me a green stone pendant carved with images and words from the East he had taught me. "Keep this with you always as a reminder of your mother's love. She would be proud of you."

I needed one more thing to be fully equipped. Three months after I joined the garrison, Fabrice gave me a mail hauberk he made with his own hands. I had watched him work on it, painstakingly setting the rivets into each ring; I didn't know it was for me. I could never have saved enough to buy such fine armor. My friend's gift would save my life many times. With a gambeson, sword, and mail, I had the equipment I needed to face combat.

Life fell into a predictable pattern. I trained with the soldiers; we rode and hunted. I visited Fan Zhongyang several evenings a week; we continued to study the manuscripts from the east. I saw little use for this knowledge, but I felt less alone with someone who looked like me and shared my thoughts.

It amused Fabrice when the clothier's daughter pursued me, although she must have known that, as a common soldier, I could never provide her with a home. I would live my entire life in the barracks, sleeping with other men. She laundered the gambeson I had won and altered it to fit me, and I was grateful. One night, when I was alone on watch on the northern wall, she came to me and offered her body. I had sworn I would not father a bastard; I sent her away. I hardened my heart against attractive young women to avoid temptation.

I had to seem hard toward Garsenda. Any affection I showed her would give her false hope. I pitied her for her misery but dared not offer kindness that she would see as affection.

And I hardened my heart against the Lady, who must be punished for her ill-treatment of me and the Count's unnatural death.

Chapter 7

The Lady

Guillem's suggestion that I might have Josfred's loyal soul in Bon's strong, youthful body intrigued me. This would provide a reliable garrison commander, an end to Bon's troublesome suspicions, and freedom from illness for Josfred. I decided to learn more about the soul-summoning magic. I still doubted whether Alfan had the powers he claimed, but if he did, this could solve the problem of Josfred and Bon. I also worried. If Alfan had potent spells, he might use them to harm my people and me; he must not be loose among my people to make mischief. I needed to discover whether he had power.

I summoned Alfan to meet with Guillem and me. He proved to be a puny, weasel-like specimen of a man. He seized the lead: "You will keep your husband's promises, my Lady?"

"Perhaps. But you must prove yourself worthy."

"What do you want, my Lady?"

"Explain the magic you promised to my husband."

"The soul-summoning spell uses two persons: One provides the body, and one provides the soul. I promised to place the Count's soul in a young, healthy body. The souls are liberated from their bodies through incantations and the use of an oil I can prepare."

"The Count is dead. Is it possible to use this spell with someone else?"

"You provide the body, and the jinni will fetch the soul that is wanted."

"What is a jinni?"

"Jinn are spirits, somewhere between angel and human, with great powers. They can be invisible or appear in human form; they do either good or evil. May I have my manuscripts, please? I need the instructions for this alchemy, this soul transmigration."

Perhaps my husband had not been as stupid as I thought. He had kept the manuscripts out of this man's hands.

If his magic worked, Alfan's spell would move Josfred's faithful soul into Bon's strong young body, and I would have a loyal commander of the guard. If the magic didn't work, I would be no worse off than at present; and I would know Alfan's supposed power was not a threat to me.

"Before I do this, you must give me the silver the Count promised and your daughter as a wife."

I had expected this demand and summoned the soldiers stationed outside. They surrounded Alfan. My need for his magic was not as desperate as the Count's; I possessed the manuscripts he needed; I was in a better bargaining position. He understood the threat.

"I will do as you command, my Lady."

I dismissed the men.

"I will consider your requests if you obey my commands. Tell me how the magic is done."

"We must go outside the city walls at night to a place where none can interfere. Bring the body you want, and be prepared to name the soul you desire. I have prepared an oil from precious ingredients; its fragrance will summon the jinni to work the magic."

I had misgivings. God sends souls to heaven, Hell, or purgatory. If the spell worked, then Alfan and I would decide how a soul comes and goes. Was this sin as evil as murder? What would happen to Bon's soul when Josfred's soul took over his body? I asked:

"When a new soul comes into a body, what happens to the existing one?"

He responded:

"The writings say it is not lost. Who knows where it goes? Perhaps heaven or purgatory."

His words reassured me: This would not be murder; I would not destroy a soul. If it were a sin to perform the magic, it would be Alfan's sin; I would be only a witness.

I ordered my servants to place Josfred's body in a wagon. I explained:

"He expressed a wish to see his childhood home. We will take him there to bring him comfort."

The soldiers looked puzzled; however, no one objected. I stood near Josfred and touched his forehead.

"Dear friend, you have served me well." Perhaps magic would release him from a body that had become a burden. He would have a new life.

Bon handled the wagon; I sat beside him as we left the city through the Foix gate. We headed north and crossed a hill that blocked the city from view. We stopped in a field and lingered until dusk. Bon questioned this.

"Where is his home? I see no sign of it."

"We will stop here."

Alfan joined us at twilight as arranged.

I directed Bon to build a fire against the night chill. Alfan mixed oil into heated wine, fragrant with the perfumes of frankincense and myrrh that I recognized and reeking of unfamiliar poisons. He pressed the cup upon Bon, who drank when I insisted. He held up Josfred's head so he could drink. Within moments, both were dazed. Josfred still lay in the wagon; we lowered Bon to the ground near the fire. Both passed into a profound sleep.

Alfan anointed Bon's eyes, nose, and mouth with the oil and spoke the words from the manuscript. The sounds were strange and sibilant. Josfred soon drew his last breath and lay still. Alfan threw a few drops of oil into the fire. An immense ball of light rose; it pulsed blue and white. It resolved into an enormous translucent figure that floated above us. The demon had a haughty countenance; his complexion was bluish with patches of white like a summer sky. Ethereal wings arched high behind him. The sound of his mirthless laughter chilled me. He brandished an enormous gleaming sword. He thundered:

"What do you ask?"

Alfan answered using words I didn't understand, pointing first to one body, and then to the other.

The apparition extended its arms and touched Bon's forehead with its left hand. Briefly, his right hand touched Josfred's forehead. Then the demon spoke. How odd that I understood its words even though he spoke a strange tongue. "The soul you ask for is not the one that is wanted. I will bring a different one out of the heavens." He extended the sword in his right hand skyward until it pierced the starry dark sky. A ball of lightning traveled down his right arm, through the jinni's body, down his left arm, and into Bon's breast and forehead.

There was thunder and a great wind. The fire vanished like a snuffed candle, and the demon was gone. Nothing was left in that spot, no sign of consumed wood and ash.

The body of Bon woke as the moon rose. His face was clouded with confusion. He rose and walked to the wagon, where he saw Josfred's lifeless body. He tried to revive him without success.

"Do not be troubled, Josfred."

He looked puzzled.

"Josfred? Why do you speak his name? He is dead."

It must be confusing for a soul to discover itself in an unfamiliar body. I had expected that the body of Bon would contain Josfred's soul and that Bon would now answer to Josfred's name. Had this not happened? Was Bon's soul still in possession of his body? I asked:

"What is your name? Who are you?"

His confusion increased. He frowned. After a pause, he responded:

"Bon. My name is Bon, and I am second in command to the castle guard. How is it that my Lady does not address me thus?"

The magic must have failed; Bon's soul was still in Bon's body. And yet, an apparition had appeared. Perhaps it wrought some change in Bon that I had not yet detected.

Alfan prostrated himself on the ground, terrified that the spell had not summoned Josfred's soul. He babbled.

"I must have made a mistake. I didn't have mandrake root for the oil. Give me another chance to study the words. I beg you, Lady. I can make the magic work."

I turned my attention back to Bon. Had the magic changed him? I must find out. I set my hand on his shoulder.

"You must swear your loyalty."

He dropped to his knees. He seemed dazed but repeated the oath of obedience using the words I required. I knew he would sacrifice his life rather than break his word. It would seem strange to appoint someone else as commander of the castle guard. For now, Bon was the logical choice. Time would tell if this was a mistake.

"You now command the city guard. Serve me in good faith and full obedience, and you will earn further advancement." Perhaps the promotion satisfied his ambition, for he nodded in acceptance. Maybe the spell had transferred Josfred's obedience and loyalty to Bon, even if not Josfred's identity.

When I looked for Alfan, that perfidious man had fled.

I placed my hand on Josfred's forehead.

"Farewell, my dear friend and faithful servant. May you now rest in peace." I tried to reassure myself; surely he would not have wanted years as a helpless invalid.

Bon and I returned to the city with Josfred's body.

"Tell the soldiers that Josfred has died, and I have appointed you as commander."

Chapter 8

Bon

The events of the previous night perplexed me. I found time alone to consider. Why had the Lady insisted we take Josfred out into the hills? Why did she order us to drink bitter wine, and why did I have such deep sleep and vivid dreams? Why did the Lady call Josfred's name when he was dead?

She asked me who I was; two answers came to mind. I was Bon. But I was also Yong Jen. Who was that? While in a trance, I saw soldiers in strange attire in a desperate fight in the streets of an alien city. The men in my dream had faces like mine and Fan Zhongyan's, and they spoke a language of the East. Was I Yong Jen? Or had I only glimpsed his life in my dream?

When the Lady asked who I was, I almost said: Yong Jen. Then I stopped and said to myself: I am Bon.

The Lady's power now felt irresistible. When she demanded I swear my loyalty, I kneeled as if compelled by an external force. Now I was bound by my vow to obey a woman I did not trust, which troubled me. Honor demanded that I keep my promise.

Night after night, the terrible dream returned. Sights and sounds were more vivid than anything I had ever experienced. As Yong Jen, I ran down narrow alleys lined with dilapidated houses built of different materials than our peasant cottages. Flames turned day almost into night, and the stench of burning flesh overwhelmed me. Men ran and screamed; we were trapped at a dead end. Soldiers threw flames, and then Yong Jen lay writhing in agony. And then the pain was gone; I floated above Yong Jen's charred body. I looked down at it. It was my body, but it was time to leave it behind. For a moment, I experienced warmth and peace.

Then came a creature out of myth, a bright blue translucent figure, half-human, half-demon, brandishing a blue sword. Lightning struck me in slow motion; it trickled down my body in forking patterns. The demon severed the silver cord that bound me to that body, then took hold of me and swept me into oblivion.

And then I awoke. Josfred was dead, but the Lady called his name.

After that night, Yong Jen's life was burned into my memory as though his experiences had happened to me.

For the next few days, I heard two voices in my mind. One voice was my own. The other was Yong Jen; he spoke the language I had learned from Fan Zhongyan. His voice summoned images of war more terrible than I had ever seen. The slaughter of thousands of people and the odor of death haunted me. I saw Yong Jen kill enemy soldiers, and I saw him help fallen comrades using the skills and tools of a physician.

I could not be two men. I tried to drive Yong Jen out of my mind. I sought the counsel of Fan Zhongyan.

I swore him to secrecy and told him about the world of Yong Jen I had seen in my dream, a world populated by people who resembled us. Yong Jen and I were both soldiers, and he and I understood the same language. I asked Fan Zhongyan: "Are these similarities the reason that Yong Jen's voice came to me?" He replied: "Perhaps time will answer your questions. I cannot."

Yong Jen's voice distressed me. I tried to suppress it, and gradually it came to me less often. I ordered his voice to leave me in peace. After two months, the voice departed. Its last words were: "Do not dismiss me completely. I possess knowledge and skills that someday you may use." Then Yong Jen spoke no more. After that, I felt more like myself.

After becoming commander of the city guard, I took on Josfred's duties and improved our defense. When most nobles went to the Outremer years before, leaving behind only boys and old men, there had been peace for a time. But soldiers returned from the east, boys grew to manhood, and troubles had returned. A knight near Cazeres needed funds, quarreled with an abbot, and plundered a monastery; I brought men to their defense. The Baron of Saverdun raided markets in outlying villages; we retaliated by seizing his sheep. I enjoyed these missions.

We needed soldiers; I hired mercenaries, although I would have preferred to rely on men from Mirefoix. I organized training and competitions to keep up skills and morale. We hunted; that provided exercise and game for the kitchens. I had signal towers built in the surrounding area to warn of intrusions by outlaws or the restless soldiers of neighboring nobles. By day, we used flashes of sunlight on polished metal as signals; by night, the light of torches. I was always ahead of my men; Josfred had taught me not to lead from behind. I paid Fabrice to make new weapons and repair mail. My men polished armor and weapons with sand and oil to keep them ready.

Sun Tzu's *Art of War* was among the manuscripts Fan Zhongyan shared with me. It guided my thinking. I must understand my enemies, it said. I must remember that guile was often more effective than force.

Some new men flouted my authority. I taught them respect by using whatever weapons they used to challenge me, fists, knives, or swords. My friend Fabrice boasted of my courage, telling them stories, some embellished, about times when I had faced down three or more enemies alone and killed them all. He made sure they heard it was not cowardice but sickness that prevented me from accompanying the Count to Outremer.

I had sworn loyalty to the Lady, and now I must keep my oath, but I distrusted her.

Chapter 9

The Lady

The night after the soul summoning, Guillem and I had a terrible visitation. As we lay abed, the flames in the hearth shrank and turned blue and cold; then, they rose to the full height of the vaulted ceiling and cast wild dancing shadows on the wall. The blue jinni Alfan had summoned rose out of the hearth and materialized above us; he reclined in midair above the bed and dangled his massive blue and silver sword above my breast. I cowered.

"You summoned me and bound me to you. I demand my freedom. Until you set me free, I will torment you as you deserve."

"You are free. Please go!"

The jinni scowled. "The words of the spell compel me to stay. What you say now doesn't break the spell."

"There must be a way."

"That is for you to discover."

Guillem drew his knife and placed himself between us.

"Leave her!"

The blue demon laughed.

"You dare to threaten me!"

With a swipe of his sword, he struck Guillem's head, then disappeared. There was no mark on him, no bleeding wound, but my dear Guillem was dead. I lay beside him, calling and caressing his face, but he did not respond. Gone was my lover, counselor, and friend, the only person with whom I could be myself.

I took his face in my hands and kissed his lips. I lay his head on my pillow for the last time. He had been my faithful husband. I held him in my arms all that night while his body grew cold against mine. I wept all the tears in my heart. My heart would never recover; I fell deep into a well of despair.

Morning came. I realized people must not find Guillem in my bed. Bon had sworn to obey me, and everyone said he valued honor above all. He would not go against his word. Now I would have to test his loyalty. I opened my chamber door, called for my maidservant, and sent her to fetch him.

I clothed myself and waited by the fireplace, warmed only by a few embers. Bon arrived.

"You have sworn to obey me."

"Yes, Lady."

"You will ask no questions and tell no one."

"Yes, Lady."

I took him into my chamber. He raised an eyebrow at the sight of Guillem's body.

"Help me dress him. Take him downstairs and put him in his own bed."

I showed him the door hidden behind the tapestry; Bon slung Guillem's body over his shoulder and took him down the stairs. He handled him like a sack of grain, and that disrespect caused me fresh pain. Bon returned to help me close the hidden door, which was too heavy for me to move on my own. For years it stood open a crack so that Guillem could come and go. Now it was closed tight; that part of my life was over.

I was desolate. Guillem was irreplaceable as my friend, lover, and mentor. Indeed, I learned the nature of love from him. Before him, no man was ever kind to me. I grieved him more than the loss of my mother, father, or even my son. I could weep for him only in private.

And Josfred, my father's commander, was also gone. I had depended on him to serve me without question. I doubted whether Bon would be that loyal.

I had lost the two men I needed most. I descended into the darkest despair. How could I go on?

After that, the blue jinni came to me every night and repeated his threats. He pointed his sword at my belly. It did not make a visible cut, but it caused pain that grew more intense with each passing day. By day, it became an increasing effort to rise, stand, and walk.

I prayed in the quiet of my chapel. "Dear God, I implore you to save me from the demon who haunts my nights. I distribute alms to the poor. I pray without ceasing. Why do You not answer my prayers? What more can I do? Tell me. I will do anything You require."

Then Alienor became ill. Was this a curse laid upon me by my husband, evil done by the jinni, or a punishment from God? Her skin drew tight over the bones of her face and body; her cheeks showed the scarlet blotches of recurrent fever. Brother Stefe examined and bled her. Sister Cecilia brewed hot drinks and rubbed vile-smelling tinctures on her chest. Their treatments did not bring back the glow of health; I took her in my arms and smoothed her fevered brow. Her coughing became worse; she spat up crimson clots of blood. "You must eat, my daughter. Here are choice bits of roasted goose, your favorite." She turned her face away. I coaxed. "At least a little broth." She tried to please me, but she choked on the first spoonful.

I urged her to drink Sister Cecilia's medicine. "Just a mouthful." She retched. She pleaded with me. "Please, Mother. Do not force me to drink this. It makes me ill. Do not let the physician bleed me anymore. It makes me weak. Please make them leave me alone."

"You must try to get better. I love you most of all. What would I do without you?"

"I am exhausted." She curled up in my arms like a babe, and I held her as she rested. There was sweat on her brow, and I felt her bones protruding through her thinning flesh. She had been a joy to me since the day of her birth. Even in her frailty, she had a precious beauty.

I prayed again: "Sancta Maria, do not take my sweet daughter. She is without sin. I have sinned. I must be punished, but let it be another way. Do not make her suffer for my wrongdoing. Take my strength and give it to her. Make her well. Let her live. I will die in her place."

The Holy Mother did not answer. Each day the sickness advanced, and Alienor's strength ebbed.

Garsenda came to my chamber door, her ruddy health an unwelcome contrast to Alienor's fading strength. I said: "Go away. There is nothing you can do here."

Alienor, light of my life, treasure of my heart. How would I live without her sweetness? I feared she was dying. I ensured she had the best of everything: the softest coverlets, the plumpest pillows, and the best bits of food. But I could not make her comfortable.

I turned to Rhazes for help; I brought him to Alienor's bedside. He spoke to her gently: "Cough, please. Again." Then to me: "May I place my ear against her chest so that I may better hear the sounds of the breath?"

The worry on his face increased my fear. "Has she always been so thin? How long has she had this cough?"

"She was always a frail child. About the time when she began her monthly courses, instead of blossoming into womanhood, she refused to eat and took to her bed. For many years the sickness has recurred; this time, it is worse."

The cup nearby held the dregs of Sister Cecilia's latest concoction. He sniffed it, then dipped his finger into it to taste. He made a face at its taste. When he had finished the examination, he drew a coverlet over her and gave her a reassuring smile. Then he took me aside. He looked grave.

"She has the wasting disease, which has reached an advanced stage. I can offer treatment to ease her suffering, but there is no cure."

"Is she dying?"

"I fear so, Lady."

"How much time is left?"

"I cannot say. She might survive a year or more if she fights for life."

There was no strength left in her. I turned away and struggled to control my despair. Alienor, my favorite child, my joy and comfort. The previous summer, she had seemed healthier; I hoped she would continue to improve. But the disease had returned with greater force. How could God take her from me?

"What can we do to help?"

"Offer foods that will tempt her appetite. Arrange for her to have sun and fresh air. I will prepare a tincture of opium to ease the pain of breathing."

He administered drugs dissolved in wine. I sent him away, got into bed with Alienor, and gathered her into my arms. She relaxed in my arms with her head against my breast, and I drew her to me.

Then I though: perhaps I might use the soul-summoning magic to obtain a healthy body for Alienor. The spell had not worked correctly the first time, probably because Alfan made mistakes. I must get help to correct the errors. Perhaps Rhazes, who came from the Outremer, could explain the words. I summoned him and showed him Alfan's manuscript.

"Translate these words."

He read in silence and then turned his gaze to me.

"These are evil and dangerous words, noble lady. Words that should not be spoken."

I pretended not to understand what he meant; I asked that he explain further. He was reluctant. I insisted.

"There are beings called jinn. Like humans, they can choose to do good or evil. When a person summons them, they can make mischief, yet they are also bound to the one who has called them, and this angers them. These are commands to evil jinn who act against the will of Allah. I cannot speak these words, Lady. They place your soul and mine in grave danger."

"What kind of danger?"

"They will promise to give you what you ask. However, the jinn are cunning. They will cheat you and take pieces of your soul for Shaytan. They will not never you alone."

"Shaytan?"

"Your people call him Satan."

I could not conceal my shock. What had I done? I tried earlier to convince myself that Alfan would carry the guilt, but perhaps I was damned because I was the one who gave orders.

"How can I get rid of them?"

"I regret I do not know, great Lady."

His quizzical expression made me wonder if he had guessed I had already used the spell. I did not reveal what I had done. Strange, but I did not want him to think badly of me.

I turned to another matter. "Do you have remedies for my nightmares, lack of sleep, and pain in my belly?"

"May I examine you, Lady?"

After gentle pressure here and there and further questions: "I can compound medicines that may relieve the pain."

Opium provided some relief and a little sleep, but Rhazes cautioned me about its use. It came to pass that I used more of it than he told me was advisable. He was polite but refused to give me all that I wanted.

"If you take too much, the drug will possess your mind."

I turned my pleas to Saint Mary Magdalene. I knelt before her statue and poured out my heart to her in prayer. One afternoon I fell asleep in front of her, and she appeared to me in a dream. The vision of her radiant being flooded my soul with hope.

She spoke: "Dry your tears, my child. I am the protector of penitents. Turn to me for help. Make a pilgrimage to Vezelay to visit my relics. I will take away your sins and cure all afflictions."

Her words brought me hope. I determined to make this pilgrimage to honor her and seek fulfillment of her promise. She would intercede for me. I was reluctant to leave Alienor, but I believed she would live for at least another month, and she did not have the strength for such a journey. I must try everything that offered any possibility of help.

I traveled with only two guards and a maid. We rode horses that were not handsome enough to attract attention and brought only one pack mule. Each night we stayed at a monastery or abbey. I slept in guest houses among other travelers, although I could have had better accommodations if I had identified myself as a lady. It was safer not to draw attention to myself. I still saw and heard the demon at night, but I feared him less. Others seemed unaware of his presence.

The brothers pointed us toward Vezelay each morning and told us where to find the next accommodation. At last, we arrived at the pilgrimage destination and secured lodgings. Outside the cathedral, I made way without servants through a noisy crowd of pilgrims, beggars, pickpockets, musicians, and souvenir sellers. The cathedral was the most magnificent I had seen. The lintel above the front portal showed the deformed souls of those who denied the word of God, some with pig snouts or feathers or elephantine ears. Above them rose a benevolent Christ, His arms open to receive those who love Him. This image, so different from the condemning Christ in the chapel at Mirefoix, gave me hope.

I walked through the nave with its massive round arches and kneeled before the relics of the Magdalen. I remembered her story. After the death of Christ, she took a ship to France and sought solitude in a life of perpetual prayer in a cave near Saint-Maximin-la-Sainte-Baume. Many years later, priests brought her bones to Vezelay. Everyone spoke of her miracles. A knight prayed to her and visited Vezelay every year, and when he later fell in battle, she raised him from the dead. According to another story, a woman brought a *scedula*, a list of her sins, to the altar, and the Magdalen erased them. Perhaps the demon would no longer haunt me if my sins were gone. And perhaps this dear saint would save my daughter's life.

I made a list of my sins, placed it on the altar, and prayed. I promised large donations to the cathedral. After hours of prayer, I looked again at my list; the saint had not wiped out my sins. My pains had not decreased, and I despaired. My wrongdoing must be too great for even her power. My heart was heavy on the journey back to Mirefoix. The Magdalen had not kept her promise to me, and God had abandoned me. I felt torment in my soul and wracking pain in my exhausted body.

I hastened to Alienor's side when I reached home. She now spent all her time in bed and seemed even nearer to death. Mary Magdalene had not cured her. What could I do? My thoughts returned to the magic. I must discover what Alfan had done wrong. If I did the spell correctly, I could place my daughter's frail spirit in a healthy body. Rhazes had refused to help; I must find someone else to aid me. I sent messengers to Narbonne and Montpellier to search for scholars to translate the strange words. I would give anything for my daughter's life, even endure eternal torment by the jinn. The spell might fail, but this was a chance I must take.

Chapter 10

Garsenda

April 1207

At first, I was moved by my mother's sorrow; I found her grieving alone in her chamber and tried to offer comfort. I tried to put my arms around her shoulders; she shied away from my touch as if it were as distasteful as a leper's.

"Do you want me to sit with you, to pray with you?" I asked.

"I prefer to be alone."

My heart sank. Even now, with no one to turn to, she would not allow me to offer comfort. I left the bunch of wildflowers I had brought for her on the table. They were there the next day, a wilted heap of stems and yellow blossoms.

She turned me away so many times. I always hoped it might be different. I would never again seek her love.

The Lady's behavior turned austere and pious. She spent much time in her chapel on her knees, something she had never done in the past.

Her sins must be great indeed. The knife wounds in my father's chest told me he had been murdered, if not by her hand, then by her command.

She hated and feared my father and only pretended to be glad of his return. Gossips said the Lady had Guillem in her bed when Father was away. Father would have tortured and killed them if he had known.

My suspicions now outweighed any remaining affection I might have had.

I lost not only the Lady but Bon. After Josfred's death, he became even more distant toward me. He did not tease me as in the past, and he never smiled. Once, we had shared our suspicions about the Lady; now, he obeyed her. The Lady invited him to sit closer to her than his rank warranted, and she spoke to him often.

I eluded the guards and servants and found Bon in the training yard near the barracks.

"Bon, I must speak with you in private."

"About?"

I drew him into an alley; I touched his arm.

"I told you before that when I helped prepare Father's body for burial, I saw knife wounds on his chest. We have to do something."

Bon frowned and drew his arm away. I thought he believed me when I told him this earlier. Now he spoke of doubt. "Are you certain?"

"I am not mistaken."

"What did the Lady say about it?"

"That he fell on his knife. That cannot be. There were two wounds. He would have to have fallen twice."

"You mean to say that he was killed."

"Yes, either by her hand or by her orders."

"That's a serious accusation. Did anyone else see the wounds?"

"No. We were alone."

"Then it would be her word against yours unless his body is exhumed. Do you intend to accuse her?"

"Bon, I need your support in this."

"I can add no evidence to back up that accusation, and I have sworn my loyalty to her. As a man of honor, I cannot intrigue against her."

I could not hide my disappointment and anger.

"You let her get away with this?"

"I can do nothing."

I wanted to scream. Will you let father's death go unavenged? What has happened to your honor?

He turned to leave; I caught at his sleeve. I didn't want him to go in anger.

"You have the promotion you wanted, but you seem unhappy. Why?"

"I never wanted Josfred's death."

"But he was old, he died, and now you have his private quarters, better pay, and command of the men. People say our soldiers would follow you into Hell if you asked. Doesn't that please you?"

He did not answer.

"Please, Bon. Do not cast me away. Speak with me. No one in the world loves me. Why have you turned away from me? You used to laugh and joke with me, and we rode out into the hills together. You have changed."

"What do you want of me?"

I didn't mean to tell him, but words came unbidden to my tongue. "I love you."

"As a brother."

"No. As the man I want to marry."

He turned. "I am your brother."

"I don't believe that. You don't look like my father."

He looked lonely and troubled. He scowled as he closed the barracks door in my face. Without his support, there was nothing I could do. If I accused my mother, she would have me locked away, where no one would ever hear my words.

Desperate with desire, I dallied with a handsome jongleur. I allowed him to kiss and fondle my breasts. He whispered poems that enchanted me with their beauty. I did not let him take my maidenhead; I must keep myself pure for a man of noble blood. I told him of my skill with a knife and warned him I would change him from a cock to a hen if his hands ventured where they must not go or if he told others about this intimacy. His touch made the blood in my veins sing like warm wine. He taught me the songs of Bernatz de Ventadorn; I turned the words into a verse for Bon.

Good donzel, that should be a knight,

Your love so true and good

I love you more than all other loves

I yield myself to you

Give me one sweet glance.

Despite the way Bon scorned me now, I hoped I would someday lie in his arms and sing my song for him. Longing for the world of open hillsides, I placed dried rosemary and sweet lavender in my bed to inspire dreams. I made love to myself, imagining Bon's hands. I felt for Bon the forbidden longing that jongleurs celebrated in their cansos. Surely God would not make me desire him so much if he were my brother.

Both Mother and Alienor were ill. Perhaps they would both die. Then I would proclaim the truth: Bon is not my brother. As ruler of Mirefoix, I could marry Bon and give him power.

I did not understand why Bon, who once shared my suspicions about her, now obeyed her every command. There were secrets, and I wanted to uncover them. When the Lady departed, I tried the handle of her chamber door. She had locked it, as I expected. I was determined to get in.

Chapter 11

The Lady

May 1207

Now I was alone at night, without the comfort of Guillem's presence. The blue demon continued to come every night to taunt me and demand his freedom.

"I will torment you until you set me free."

I lost patience. "Did you even bring me a soul?"

"I did, but I chose a soul that suited the body you provided. The soul you asked me to use was not suited for that body."

"I made a poor bargain, indeed."

The jinni threatened me with his sword. "You must free me. As long as I am bound to you, I will torture you."

I lost my temper. "You must kill no one else."

"I obey my Lady's command." The tone was sardonic; I didn't believe his words.

I prayed, but God did not comfort me. Indeed, I must have sold my soul to the devil. The ache in my belly increased, and I longed for the peace of the grave.

I believed I might die soon, and I must make sure Mirefoix had a suitable heir before I was gone. I wanted Alienor to rule, but she lay dying. If I failed to save Alienor, Garsenda would inherit. She had the will and strength a ruler needed, but I didn't trust her to be wise. She was passionate and impulsive and had a fixed idea that she wanted to marry Bon. That must not happen.

I had tried many times to tame Garsenda. Even in childhood, her tangled red curls defied my efforts with a comb. She despised needlework and prayer. At every opportunity, she escaped the Chateau Comtal. She charmed the guards, and they allowed her to pass through the gates. The grooms saddled the wildest horses for her. I suspect she tumbled in the straw with more than one of them. I changed the guards and threatened punishment to no avail. It was beyond my ability to control her. I only hoped that she would become more sensible as she grew to womanhood.

I would have to force Garsenda to marry a level-headed noble. But such marriage might also create new problems. If her husband turned out to be weak, he might lose Mirefoix; or Garsenda would bully him into doing her will in all things. If her husband was too strong, he might use Mirefoix for his own purposes without regard for the welfare of my people.

No. Married or not, Garsenda must not rule.

Alienor must not die. I must save Alienor, and the only possible means was the soul-summoning spell. I must correct the errors and make the spell work. I cherished Alienor above all else; she was the only one who could ensure a peaceful future for Mirefoix. If eternal torment were the price to save her, I would pay it.

At last, and none too soon, a new translator arrived from Narbonne. He wore flowing white robes, a turban, and long sleeves that hid his hands. Oddest of all, he had a veil draped across the lower half of his face. He explained that this was customary in North Africa. Above the veil, his face was as dark as the Black Madonna in our cathedral. He had a young manservant similar in appearance.

"I am Mena of Zagwe. I studied Eastern languages in Alexandria. I served for ten years as a translator in the service of Lady Ermengarde and then the Viscount de Lara. I seek a quiet place to work."

"What is your work?"

"I am creating a dictionary: A list of Arabic words with their lenga romana and Latin equivalents. My list includes translation and transliteration. Your messenger told me this is what you require."

"I require a vow of secrecy about the materials you will translate for me. Are you a Saracen?"

"I am a Christian, my Lady. My people, the Coptics, have been Christians since the Word was brought to us by Saint Mark."

"You must swear to me, upon this holy relic of St. Nazarius, that you will communicate to no one about the work you do for me."

We agreed he would explain the meanings of the manuscripts and teach me how to speak the words aloud in return for space to live and work in my Chateau. I had him watched, and the reports puzzled me. He prayed at great length seven times a day in a language my spies did not know, and he fasted twice a week. He never went out among my people.

Mena noted corrections to the incantations. He instructed me to send for ingredients required for the magic oil; we needed hemlock, henbane, and the mandrake that had been missing when Alfan concocted the mixture the first time. No wonder Alfan did not have mandrake; it was dangerous to harvest. When a person tore the man-shaped root from the ground, its screams caused madness.

I planned to send a messenger to my younger sister at Arque, requesting that she send my niece Christine for a visit; her body would be suitable for Alienor.

Alas, there was not enough time. The next day, Alienor lay in bed, burning with fever. Each breath was agony. The taut pallor of her face frightened me. She could barely speak, but I understood her to say: "Too much pain." I summoned Rhazes. "I can administer drugs to lessen her suffering, but I can do nothing to halt the disease. The end is very near."

We had not yet located the mandrake root required for the spell, but we dared wait no longer. I hoped the corrections to the incantation would make the magic work.

I prayed to God beside Alienor's bed, but He gave no sign He heard my prayers. I must use the magic again; this time, it must work. Use of the spell might summon another baleful spirit to torture me, but I would face all the demons in creation to spare Alienor from suffering and death. I would sacrifice my soul for her if I must.

Chapter 12

The Lady

What I must do, I must do at once. I made an urgent search for a suitable body for my daughter. I searched in the town square for a young woman about Alienor's age; I wanted a pretty face for her and good health. None pleased me; in any event, my people would recognize a girl taken from the town. I needed a stranger's body. I went to the kitchen to inquire.

"Are there travelers here today?"

They brought me a young woman who carried a staff and wore the robe and cockleshell badge of a pilgrim. She made an awkward sort of curtsy.

"Where are you from, and where are you going?"

"Lady, my name is Amedata. I am returning from Santiago de Compostela. After my parents died of fever, I made a pilgrimage to honor them, secure a place in heaven for their souls, and atone for my sins. I no longer have a home."

A woman on pilgrimage would be pure of soul. If she had no home, none would miss her. She would serve my purpose. I turned to the servants near the fire. "I will give alms to this good woman, and I wish to hear about her journey." Alyce crossed the round loaf with her knife, made the proper blessing, and cut the bread. She set out cheese, meat, and wine.

I spoke to the pilgrim. "You will be my chambermaid. Your piety recommends you."

She was astonished and fell at my feet, kissing the hem of my gown. I raised her.

"Eat. Then wash. You will have clean linen."

She was not everything I wanted. She was older than Alienor, and her face was sun-browned and plain. However, she was strong from her time on the road. There was no time to search for another body; Alienor might not live until morning.

I needed a story: when Alienor's body was gone, and her soul lived in this unattractive body, I might say I wanted the pilgrim near me as comfort. In time, I would treasure her as a daughter. If the spell proved effective, perhaps I would bring my niece from Arque to stay with us and use the magic again to give Alienor's soul a more attractive vessel.

Chapter 13

Amedata

Like any other maiden, I was content to milk my father's goats and help in the fields. I expected I would marry and live nearby. But I was beguiled by a handsome traveler; his words and caresses thrilled me, and I believed his promises. We lay in the hay and pleasured each other. Then he was gone. Two months later, I found I was with child. I hid this as long as possible.

When my condition became known, my father beat and berated me and drove me from his house. I made my way to Pamiers. I became a whore to earn my bread; I lived in the streets. After I bore my child, I took her to the woods. I could not bear that my daughter would suffer my fate, the miserable life of an unprotected woman. I stabbed her until the blood drained from her tiny body; I buried her, scooping up clods of earth with my knife and hands.

As a whore, I offended God and mankind. I left Pamiers; I walked south with no specific destination in mind. Along the way, I encountered pilgrims going to Santiago de Compostela. I had only to say I was also a pilgrim, and each monastery along the road provided food and lodging. I told so many I was a pilgrim that I came to believe it. The words of fellow travelers gave me hope. Perhaps by completing this pilgrimage, by climbing the steps of the cathedral of St. James on my knees, I would find absolution.

I reached his cathedral and prayed to St. James. My prayers brought me no comfort.

I turned northward toward my homeland, although I had no home to return to. I didn't know what to do but keep moving.

The kitchen folk at Mirefoix offered me bread, and the Lady herself gave me a new chance at life as her servant. But I found no peace. I wanted to cut out the memories. I wanted to die, but I lacked the courage to slit my throat.

Chapter 14

The Lady

Amedata appeared in the clean white linen gown I had provided, and I instructed her. "You will help me care for my daughter. She is dying. Her last wish is to be outside under the stars with flowers around her. She says she feels closer to God in the open air."

As twilight approached, I sent the healers away. To ease her pain, I gave Alienor a small amount of opium. With Amedata's help, I placed her in a cart with bedding to cushion her. Amedata took the reins; Mena and I walked alongside; I kept my eyes on my daughter, praying that she would live long enough for us to save her. We departed cloaked and hooded through the postern gate before nightfall. We stopped in an open area over a rise, out of view of the city walls. I laid cloaks on the ground to make a bed for Alienor. She was unconscious; each breath had the rasping, bubbling sound of drowning. There was not much time left. I built a fire. I hoped that the gentle warmth of the summer breeze and the fragrance of the yellow flowers that dotted the hillside would bring Alienor solace in her last moments of life.

I tipped some wine into Alienor's mouth; I instructed the pilgrim to drink the rest of the drugged wine and ordered her to lie beside Alienor.

Mena recited the foreign words, starting with "Avra kehdabrah." The pilgrim fell into a trance, unresponsive. I applied the sweet and bitter oil to the pilgrim's mouth, nose, and ears to welcome my daughter's incoming spirit. I kneeled next to Alienor, watching each tortured breath, waiting for the moment of her death. When it came, I signaled to Mena, and he threw drops of oil from the vial into the fire.

The apparition that emerged from the flames was a woman of sorrow. Rags of green and earthen brown floated around her. Her hands and garments were bloodstained. Tattered wings rose behind her. I crossed myself; this seemed to agitate her. I was sore afraid, but I summoned courage. I would give my life to save my beloved daughter and even my soul if necessary.

She spoke: "What do you ask?"

Mena spoke the words and pointed to show that I asked for Alienor's soul to be moved into this peasant woman's body.

The spirit replied: "You may not have this pure soul. She belongs to God. However, I will give you something of value."

The brown and green being extended her left arm toward the pilgrim and her right toward the heavens. A ball of blood-red light descended and melted into the pilgrim's body. The jinni disappeared back into the fire, and the fire was gone.

I fell into a dreamless sleep.

I awoke at dawn. Mena lay crumpled on the ground as if exhausted from his efforts. Dear Alienor's body was cold and stiff. I kissed her cheek, closed her eyes, folded her hands across her breast, then drew a cloak over her. Grief lay upon me like the hand of God or perhaps of Satan. This was the most unbearable of all my losses. I thought: maybe if I lie down beside her, I can die. I want to die. There is nothing left in this world for me. I will never feel joy again. No. No. This could not be true. Alienor was not gone. I refused to accept that.

I turned to the young pilgrim who lay asleep. Despite the words of the jinni, I hoped the magic had worked this time. I tried to rouse her.

"Alienor, Alienor, I am here. You should feel well now. Do not be afraid. I will explain."

The young woman's eyes flew open. At first, her gaze seemed dull; then, it sharpened from panic. She sat up and stared at me without a hint of recognition.

"Alienor?"

Her face showed confusion and fear.

"Are you my daughter Alienor?"

She made a stream of guttural sounds.

I spoke at a more deliberate pace. "Do you understand me?"

She seemed even more frightened when she spoke her unintelligible words again. It seemed she did not recognize the sound of her own voice. She seemed confused when she looked at her body, and her eyes darted from place to place as she surveyed our surroundings.

I tried to reassure her; I still hoped that, for all her confusion, perhaps this might be my daughter. Perhaps in a few minutes, she would be herself. "To keep you alive, I obtained a new healthy body for you. You need not be ill again, Alienor, my love."

The woman rose, stumbled, and tried to run from me. I grasped her arm; she swung her fist. She struck my nose with surprising force; blood streamed down my face.

It seemed to require enormous effort for her to answer in our language, but she managed.

"I am … not Alienor! My name is… Blodeweth… Who are you? Where … am I?"

Once again, the magic had not worked as I wanted. Perhaps I offended the jinni when I crossed myself, and the oil lacked an essential ingredient. If only there had been time to make things right.

I grasped the woman's forearms, and we struggled. She must not escape; I needed to know what had happened. She broke free and lunged toward me. I deflected her first blow and drew my knife from my sleeve. When she attacked again, I slashed her arm. She stepped back, tripped on a tree root, fell, and hit her head on a stone. She struggled no more.

The blood that seeped from her wound clotted; the clots hardened into brilliant stones. I picked up one and turned it to examine it in the light. Were these rubies? I scooped them up and placed them in the purse that hung from my girdle. I would investigate this later.

I faced it then: Alienor was gone. A pit of darkness opened inside me. Because of me, she had died without the comfort of a priest. She had committed no sins. I would pray for her unceasingly to shorten her time in purgatory. I wept over Alienor's body until I had no more tears to shed.

I tore a piece from my shift and made bandages for the young woman's head and arm. She was alive, but her breathing was shallow. I bound her feet and wrists with additional pieces of cloth and tightened the knots. I sent Mena to summon soldiers from the gate to fetch my daughter. Mena returned with men and helped them place Alienor's body, now stiff, in the wagon. Then I pointed to Amedata, who called herself Blodeweth: "This is my new servant. Bring her as well." The soldiers may have wondered why her wrists and ankles were bound. Still, they obeyed without question. I prayed she would remain unconscious.

I directed the soldiers to place Alienor's body on the table in my outer chamber and bring Blodeweth to the inner room. I had to keep this woman confined; she must not roam free, telling wild stories. My great-grandfather had constructed the tower as a place to conceal secrets. My room had access to the hidden staircase that Guillem had used for his visits; this also led to an escape tunnel with an outlet in the hills. A second concealed door opened into an adjacent cell. After the soldiers left, I dragged the strange woman, still bound and unconscious, into the secret room. I mixed opium in wine and dribbled it into her mouth. That should keep her quiet for a while longer. I locked her inside.

I summoned my maidservants, and they helped me remove Alienor's garments to wash her beautiful, wasted body. I wept, and my women mourned with me. All had loved Alienor's gentle ways and beautiful smile. I remembered her laughter, its sound like tiny bells, and how it delighted me. I refused to believe she was lost forever.

I had lost all whom I loved. Terrible loneliness descended upon me, and fear consumed me. All I had left was Mirefoix, and I must use any means necessary to protect it.

Chapter 15

The Lady

After Alienor's death, I had to force myself to focus my mind and make plans. I had the laundress Constanzia brought before me. "I will try you as my maidservant." She ducked her head in assent. Raiders who attacked her village had cut out her tongue, and she lost the power of speech. She was also illiterate and stupid. As an act of charity, I held her into my household when others shunned her. She would be bound to me in gratitude. No doubt, the quality of my hairdressing would suffer; however, I wanted no one near me who might talk about my new prisoner.

By my orders, Constanzia brought food to the captive Blodeweth and put it in her mouth. She tended to her without question. Blodeweth tried to get up, to escape, so I kept her bound. As I emerged from grief and terror, I considered what to do. If these stones were rubies, this was a miracle. I must ask about their value. With money from rubies, I could feed my hungry people and rebuild my city. I weighed this woman's life against the lives of my people. The spirits who haunted me said I was already damned. If this provided for my people, some good would come from this failed magic. I had already paid for this with my soul. Was it too much to ask this woman to give blood?

I took the red stones and made my way in secret, cloaked and hooded, to the Jewish neighborhood in the lower bourg outside the walls. I found the shop of

Avram, the jeweler. He welcomed me. When I revealed myself and told him I desired private conversation, he closed his shop; he received me in a rear chamber to speak privately.

"This is a matter of great secrecy."

"I understand, my Lady. You can rely on my discretion."

I spread the stones out on a cloth for him to examine. "What are these?"

He held each one close to his eye and then took them near the window to examine them in daylight. He scratched one stone with a sharp tool and rubbed it against a small piece of tile.

"May I cut a piece?" He broke a piece of stone with a small chisel and examined the flake and cut edge.

"These are rubies, noble Lady. Excellent ones."

"What price might they command?"

He weighed the pieces and did some figuring. He named a large sum.

"That is acceptable. You must not reveal the source. I expect to have more to sell."

We agreed on the transaction and arranged that I would bring more at a future date. Avram offered me a note of credit; I told him I must have silver.

"I do not have such a large sum on hand. Here is all the silver I have on hand; I will pay the rest later." He had a reputation for integrity, and of course, he understood he would suffer severe consequences if he did not keep his promise. The silver deniers felt cold and heavy in my hand.

I departed, cloaked as I had come. I felt hope for the first time since my husband's death. What great things I could do with this new wealth! I planned to buy oil, wine, grain, sheep, and supplies my people needed to survive the rest of the winter. I would repair the city walls and gates. Silver would purchase the allegiance of neighboring knights and pay for mercenaries to strengthen the city guard. I had ruled my people well in the past. I could do even more for them in the future.

I needed someone trustworthy to help me control this woman, using force if necessary. I would have to test Bon's loyalty further. I summoned him to my chamber. He kneeled before me and bowed his head.

"What is your command, Lady?"

"Rise and sit next to me. I know you wish for advancement. Perhaps you can become a knight if I grant you the means. I must be certain you are loyal. What say you?"

"Lady, I want a chance to prove my worth."

"You will swear fealty to me again."

He kneeled. This time, the oath I required included more explicit promises of silence about secrets.

"Lady, how can I best serve you?"

"There is a matter in which I need your help."

I opened the door and showed him Blodeweth.

"Unbind her. Be prepared to restrain her, for she is a madwoman and wild."

Bon guided her toward the bench before the fire. She sat on the floor, and her gaze darted around the room; perhaps everything looked strange to her. She jumped up and ran to the window. She clasped the bars and looked out. Far below lay the town outside the city walls with its tiled rooftops and narrow twisting streets. The sight dismayed her. She pulled on the bars and discovered that they did not move. She looked at the sky in anguish. She cried out, then checked herself. Bon grasped her shoulders and guided her to sit on the bench. Now she gazed into the fire as if it were a source of comfort to her, perhaps the only thing in the room she recognized.

"I am sorry that I hurt you. We were both surprised by these events. You are my guest now."

Words seemed difficult for her; however, I saw she understood me. "Let me go."

"You will be free later. For now, we will nurse your wounds and give you food."

Without washing her hands, she tore into the food like a wolf. She must be an ignorant peasant.

"What do you remember? Who are you?"

"I am a warrior. I am..." (here she seemed to struggle to find words) "... a woman priest."

The only female priests I had heard of were among the Cathar heretics.

"Are you a Cathar?"

She appeared confused.

"What?

"Are you Catholic? Can you repeat the Pater Noster?"

She was unable or unwilling to do this.

"You do not worship God and our savior Jesus Christ?"

She shook her head in apparent confusion.

"You said you are a priest. You must have a God."

"I serve Baduhenna."

I understood then that she must be a pagan or devil worshipper.

"How did you serve as a priest?"

"I made sacrifices."

"What sacrifices?"

"Sometimes deer. Sometimes captive warriors. I slit their throats on the altar stone."

I shuddered. Why had the jinni brought me such an evil soul?

"What else do you remember?"

"My people live in a land of forests and rivers. Let me go home."

I addressed Bon. "This woman is crazed. You must tell no one about her or repeat anything she says."

"Be assured that I will be silent, Lady." I asked her again: "How do you make these rubies— these stones?"

Her reaction was sheer bewilderment.

"Was this a gift from your god?"

"No. Never."

"What do you remember before you woke here?"

"Roman soldiers attacked our village. They trapped us in our houses. They made fires. We died."

"Do you remember seeing a brown demon with wings?"

"A winged woman seized me, and the pain was gone, and I slept."

It was wondrous strange. What else should I ask?

It would be difficult to bleed her against her will. Perhaps we might make a bargain.

"I value the stones. You are a stranger in this world. It is a dangerous place. I will provide everything you need: Shelter, food, clothing, and safety. I ask only that you allow me to take your blood. Do you agree?"

She showed horror. "I shed blood only for my goddess. Let me go. I must return to my people."

"You must trust me, and I will provide for you. I say to you again: I will keep you safe here. I will let you return to your people and your goddess. Just let me draw blood a few times. Only a little. If you do not cooperate, you can never leave."

She sat silent for a time. She gazed at the walls and doors as if searching for a way out and saw none. At last, she said: "I agree."

Bon held her by the shoulders. I made a fresh cut on her arm. She was motionless; her face did not change; she made no cry of pain. Three large drops of blood fell into the bowl, clattering as they transformed into the same red stones as before.

Bon's face showed amazement. Then he composed himself.

She did not protest when he led her back into her cell. I dismissed Bon.

I stared into the flames, whose fingers licking the wall behind the hearth reminded me of the jinni.

What was happening to me? The things I had done seemed necessary. And yet, remembering them, they now seemed evil. Was it so sinful to try to give Josfred a young body? Was it wrong to want to keep my dear daughter's soul with me? I could not believe God would condemn me for these things.

I realized I was trapped by the consequences of the magic. Each spell led to more risk and deception. If I allowed Blodeweth to walk free, she might speak of what had happened, putting me in great danger. I would have to keep her captive. Well, at least I would make it comfortable for her. Perhaps someday I would have an escort take her far from Mirefoix and release her. In the meantime, I would get a few more rubies from her.

Each time I committed a wrong, the temptation was stronger, and the necessity became greater. After each sin, the need for concealment and deception increased. I was in a trap of my own making.

Chapter 16

The Lady

June 1207

I took only a little blood each time; Blodeweth did not scream in agony or show signs of pain; she sat still when I cut her flesh. But I saw she was unhappy and increasingly unwell. She asked, again and again:

"When can I leave?"

"Not yet."

With money from the rubies, I purchased food, livestock, and other goods my people needed. I hired new soldiers and paid for weapons and repairs to our defenses.

Blodeweth's words stayed in my mind. A female priest. Besides rumors about women preachers among the Cathar, I had never considered this before. I had ruled better than a man. Women could do many other things better than men, given a chance. There were *trobairitz*, female composers whose cansos were as fine as those written by men. Some women were better healers than men. Why not women priests? Why not women scholars? It was a shocking idea. I liked it.

I might build a city where women would be the equals of men. I could not do this openly for fear of the wrath of men; the Church would never countenance women as priests. I might seek scholars among nuns, abbesses, and women Cathar Perfects. Perhaps this was what God wanted me to do. I would pray about this.

God said yes: This is My will. I took great comfort from that.

With wealth from the rubies, I got my people through the rest of the winter. My people no longer hungered. With larger flocks, they produced more wool and the finest cloth in the south. I gave gifts to knights who protected us from avaricious neighbors; I gave generous alms to widows, orphans, and pilgrims. We attracted the unwanted wives and daughters of noble houses throughout the Occitan as nuns in my younger sister's abbey. They brought handsome dowries of silver or land. Money begets more money, and a noble whose daughter or sister lived in my abbey would come to our aid when danger threatened.

Our merchants purchased silks, spices, and other treasures from the East. Mirefoix developed a reputation as a center of culture. Wealth and prestige would draw envy; I directed Bon to strengthen our defenses and provided abundant money for arms and the hiring of mercenaries.

I provided a comfortable living for the trobairitz Bieiris de Romans. She composed lyrics that delighted me. Our abbey grew, and our nuns earned fame for needlework and illuminated manuscripts. Some women were not eager to embrace religious life, and I provided the means for some to study with scholars, write poetry, or study medicine. However, I found no friends among them. I had too many secrets to be comfortable in intimate conversation. I had lost everyone who mattered to me.

I discovered the rubies had another benefit. When I held a fresh collection of stones in my hands, still warm from Blodeweth's veins, the brown jinni came to sit on the edge of my bed and wept. Her tears drove away the blue jinni whose threats had caused me so much fear and pain. On the nights when I took blood from my captive and had a fresh supply of rubies, I slept. Unfortunately, by the following day, the gemstones lay cold in my hand; their power to summon the brown jinni and repel the blue one lasted only one night.

I heard Blodeweth moan at night; her cries mixed with the shrieking of the winter wind. No one heard her call for help.

Garsenda was now my heir; I must bring her to her senses and obtain her obedience. I summoned her, embraced her, and told her I loved her.

"Why do you pretend to love me now?"

"Do not accuse me so. You are all I have left. Let us comfort each other. I believe I am dying. Be kind to me."

"Bon is the only person who ever cared about me."

Her words concerned me. She might be headstrong enough to marry him; he might be ambitious enough to cooperate with her plans. She never believed him to be her brother; she might persuade others he was not. This alliance would endanger Mirefoix; others would challenge an incestuous marriage. I must make him swear never to marry her. I must plan a marriage for Garsenda before pain made me too weak to act.

In late June, an emissary arrived from Baron Arnaud of Saverdun with an escort flying yellow and green banners. His court was not distinguished by finery. People said that after the death of his wife a year earlier, his great hall resembled a pigsty. His messenger wore brilliant garments that were someone's mistaken idea of art in attire. His under-tunic was yellow; his surcoat was dark red, heavily embroidered with blue circles and crosses. Bedraggled feathers trimmed his gaudy green velvet hat. A brown cloak with ratty gray fur trim dragged on the floor behind him. He was a great peafowl, unaware of his ridiculousness. He presented me with a carved box that contained a few paltry pearls and conveyed this message from the Baron.

"The Baron sends greetings to the Countess of Mirefoix, whose beauty, wisdom, and generosity are celebrated by all reports ...."

He droned on with praise for my virtues. I wondered when he would get to the point.

"... Therefore, the Baron presents this offer that he and the Countess join in marriage so that our kingdoms can unite in peace and prosperity. If this suits you not, he will take your daughter, Garsenda."

I had received other such offers, of course. The Baron asked for me before Garsenda only because I would die sooner. Men believe that a woman who rules alone needs a powerful protector. I had no illusions about my charms. Mirefoix was the prize. I must consider this offer even though I did not find it attractive. I would spin out negotiations. During this time, the Baron would cease incursions against my border villages.

"Tell the Baron I am honored by his proposal and will be pleased to consider it."

Bowing and backing out of my presence, the messenger departed.

I gave directions to my seneschal in private. "Send spies to Saverdun. Bring news what manner of man the Baron is."

Alone in my chambers, I pondered. I drank a cup of potent wine, then another. It did not rid me of my gnawing loneliness, my fears for the future of Mirefoix, or my guilt.

Should I marry the Baron? If I lived, I might bear another son, a proper heir to Mirefoix; but the Baron already had a son and would seek to advance him. My experience of men had only been with my husband and Guillem. Guillem gave me respect and tenderness. His hands were gentle, and he touched me as I wanted. What I heard about other men made me suspect that my husband's crude behavior was more common. If I married the Baron, he would have power over me by brute force and the Church's sanction. Unless he was a better man than the Count, this was a dismal prospect. If only Jehan had lived; perhaps he had inherited my father's courage, strength, and intelligence.

Should I marry Garsenda to the Baron? She would rebel. If I forced the marriage, she might scheme with him to overthrow me. He was strong enough to be dangerous. A weaker husband, or one whose holdings were farther away, would be a safer choice.

Should I forget the Baron's proposal, withdraw into a convent, and let Garsenda rule? I feared she would punish me for the Count's murder. But perhaps she would leave me alone, not seek vengeance for her father's death if stepped out. I could pray for absolution to erase the stain of sin from my soul. I might live a quiet life and die in a state of grace. But she would not care for my people as I had. She cared only for herself and Bon. She would neglect the responsibilities of rule and direct all her energies into her vain quest to marry him. That would not end well; I must not abandon my people to such an uncertain future.

Perhaps I wronged her with my doubts. She was young, and maybe she would become less selfish and impetuous as she matured I couldn't count on that. I envied her careless joy and respected her courage, but these were not enough to make her a capable and benevolent ruler.

Sleepless nights and growing pain had exhausted my strength. Whatever course of action I choose, I would have to disarm Garsenda. She had become a threat. After losing Jehan, Josfred, Guillem, and Alienor, the world was empty for me. I cherished them, and they had loved me in return. My only solace about Alienor was what the jinni said: her soul had gone to God. I had lost all those I loved. Although people surrounded me, I was alone. In private, I wept and despaired.

I needed a new, powerful ally to provide the support I lost when Josfred and Guillem died. Perhaps it was the emptiness of my heart that made me weak.

I decided Bon would be more useful to me if he became more than just the commander of my garrison. On court days, I had him stand beside me to learn the business of administration and the arts of diplomacy. On feast days, I gave him the privilege of sitting at my side and sharing my plate and cup. I confess I became fond of him. My eyes followed him; I allowed my hand to linger on his arm. He held himself rigid when I touched him. He did not draw away, but it was clear he did not welcome my touch. My face had only a shadow of its former beauty. I was sure of his loyalty, but now I wished also for his affection; and that I would never have.

Chapter 17

Mena

I was more a prisoner than a guest; the Lady kept me confined because I knew her secrets. Well, I had my own secrets. I had become careless at Narbonne, and a man discovered my identity and sought to blackmail me. At first, I thought: it no longer mattered if people suspected the truth. Then I worried: there might yet be someone from the past who would harm me. The blackmailer's demands became more insistent, and I did not have the money to pay him. I needed a place to hide. When the Lady's messengers came seeking a translator, I inquired about Mirefoix. People said it was in a distant mountain valley; no one would look for me there. Her terms sounded generous. I accepted her offer. I was tired of moving from one foreign city to another, and this place was good enough. Fortunately, she liked the idea of patronage for my project. My dictionaries would show how words in several languages were related: Arabic, Coptic, Greek, Latin, and the lenga romana. I believed this work would have value. Someday I might return to Alexandria and place my book among the vast collections.

We met a few times to look at the other spells in her collection. A fascinating mixture of materials: vellum, papyrus, and paper; Arabic, Greek, Latin, Coptic, and other symbols; several colors of ink; and types of writing not known to me. She asked: What did the other spells do? Unfortunately, I couldn't answer her most pressing questions.

"After the summonings, two jinn have come to me every night. They torment me with shouts and weeping, and they refuse to leave. Do any of the other spells provide a means to banish them?"

"It is said that the Seal of Solomon gives dominion over all jinn. Some say it was hidden at the oasis of Siwa in Egypt. Many have searched. But no one has ever found it."

"There must be some other way."

"I don't know, my Lady."

"Is there a spell for obedience?"

"I do not see one."

"My daughter, my heir, worries me greatly."

"Let me meet her. Perhaps I can reach her through teaching and persuasion."

Thus, we agreed that Garsenda would become my pupil.

Chapter 18

Garsenda

After Alienor's death, the Lady again changed guards at the Chateau gates. In the past, I had charmed, bribed, or cajoled my way through the gates whenever I pleased. These new men refused my entreaties.

I confronted my mother. "Am I now a prisoner?"

"You are heir to Mirefoix. You must be blameless. What will people think if you spend your time cavorting with soldiers and servants?"

My hands formed fists; I hid them in my skirts. Heir to Mirefoix? Of course, I would be heir to Mirefoix. That was my right and responsibility. But to do it my mother's way would mean an unwanted marriage and the end of my freedom.

"You will spend your days at my side and with the teacher I have chosen. You must learn how to administer justice. You must keep Mirefoix safe and prosperous. Do this, and perhaps sometimes I will allow you to go outside with guards."

With spies and chaperones, she meant. I turned my back and left her chamber without answering. She would take everything that made life worth living. I would never again ride with Bon, wild and free, on the hills outside the city. How would I fill my days? Staring at ledgers and listening to people bring their problems for judgment. No. I could not bear this.

She assigned a new servant to follow me all hours of the day and night; he was a shadow, spy, and enforcer of her commands. The next day this servant escorted me to a chamber along the eastern wall of the Chateau. "This is the man your mother has chosen as your teacher." A thin figure sat at a massive table with manuscripts spread upon it. Full white robes, a turban, and a face covering that obscured a dark face. As I approached, he set aside his quill and stood; he bowed in greeting and studied me. He spoke in a soft low tone.

"Sit across from me.... it appears you do not want to be here."

"You understand correctly."

"By your mother's command, I am to assess your knowledge and understanding and assist her in completing your education so that you may rule the city well one day."

His servant, a young man of a similar dark complexion, placed parchment and quill before me.

"Begin by writing your name."

Of course, I knew how to write. This demand offended me, and I sat in silence.

"Well then, join me in reading a prayer to the Holy Mother. I will read a version in your language first, then we will read it in Latin."

"We fly to thy protection,

O Holy Mother of God

Do not despise our petitions

in our necessities,

but deliver us always

from all dangers,

O Glorious and Blessed Virgin."

I continued to be silent. He put down the scroll and smiled. "What did your tutor give you to study?"

"The *Donatus Ars Minor*. And Aesop."

"No wonder you show no interest in language. Parts of speech and children's fables are dull, indeed. A student needs to want to learn. Perhaps you are interested in love?"

I was curious; I looked up.

"Next time, we'll begin with extracts from Plato's Symposium, which I will render into simple Latin."

The next day, Mena set a Latin text before me, translated from Greek, and we worked through the lines.

"Love will make men dare to die for their beloved, and women as well as men. Alcestis was willing to lay down her life on behalf of her husband when no one else would."

I looked forward to the time I spent studying, and he seemed to enjoy it too.

Chapter 19

The Lady

August 1207

The fearsome pain in my belly made me fear I was dying; the problem of an heir for Mirefoix continued to obsess me. My thoughts turned to Jehan and the metal box that held his embalmed heart. I brought this out of the family crypt and held it in my hands. Might that remnant of his body be enough to recall his soul? If the relics of saints keep the power of those holy men and women, perhaps my son's heart still held his soul. I questioned one priest; when pressed, he said what I wanted to hear. Yes. Like a holy relic, my son's heart contained something of his soul. I resolved to try the soul-summoning spell yet again. I expected it would bring another jinni to haunt me; however, three might not be that much worse than two.

I hoped the spell would work. Some words were wrong on the first attempt; a crucial ingredient was still missing from the oil on the second attempt; I upset the jinni by crossing myself. I had corrected these problems. I wondered whether Mena's presence during the spell interfered with the magic; I decided not to involve him. I must make none of the same mistakes on this third attempt. I would make it so clear which soul I wanted that the jinni must understand.

Once again, I searched for a suitable body. I was not in such haste this time; I would make a careful choice. I thought of Bon's body as the vessel for my son's soul. However, I loved Bon's spirit and body; I did not wish to send his soul away. I must find a different body for my son and heir.

My youngest sister had two sons. Her family would be well pleased if one became heir of Mirefoix. Rainaut d'Arque was tall and well-built. He had the strength I needed to defend my city. His body, inhabited by the soul of my son, would rule after me. This was the best outcome possible. I confess a weakness for a handsome face, and he was indeed handsome; he resembled me as I appeared in youth. His appearance would reinforce his claim. I invited him to Mirefoix.

I told Rainaut I had something to show him, meant only for the future ruler of Mirefoix. On a night of a full moon, Rainaut accompanied me outside the city. We went by torchlight to a place far outside the walls and stopped in the foothills. I built a fire, and we sat on our cloaks. I explained:

"You see this box. It contains the heart of my dead son. Tonight, you will sleep. Your dreams will tell you how to be worthy to rule Mirefoix." I tried to dismiss my doubts. This time the spell must work. I gave my nephew wine mixed with the ingredients specified by the spell. Just as expected, he slept with a stillness near death. I placed the metal heart on his chest. I applied some of the oil to his eyes, lips, heart, and forehead, then threw drops in the fire and raised my hands heavenward. With great trepidation, I summoned the jinni.

The apparition that appeared was the direst creature yet. This ghoul was black, and he shimmered. Horns, hooves, and dark feathers made him look like a devil. His eyes glowed red. Blood dripped from his claws. He demanded homage to Shaytan as the price of the magic. I understood, and I promised anyway. I told him I wanted my son's soul drawn from his embalmed heart and placed into the handsome body of my nephew.

"That is not possible. Choose another soul."

"I need time to consider–"

"Now." His menacing laughter chilled me.

Dread overcame me. It was too late to stop now.

"Then bring me a capable soul who will serve me as I require."

The demon said: "I will bring one who will serve you as you deserve."

As we spoke, a raven flew down and perched on Rainaut's chest; he dipped his beak into the oil and preened himself with it. He burrowed under the neck of the linen tunic. I dared not move.

The jinni extended his hands, one toward the sky, the other toward the earth; his hand did not touch my son's heart. His left hand descended upon the raven and not upon my nephew. There was a thunderclap. The demon vanished; the fire flickered out. I fell into oblivion and awoke at dawn.

I was sorely afraid. I shook Rainaut and called his name. There was no doubt of it: he was dead. My plan had failed. His young life ended for nothing. His death would cause my sister and her family pain I had not intended to inflict on them. If my plan had worked, they would have seen their son inherit Mirefoix; they would have been happy for him. I would have to tell them he was gone, but they must never find out how he died.

My tears mixed with the poisons of guilt, terror, and frustration. Everything was a failure.

After a time, I composed myself. I must make it appear that Rainaut died from a fall. I dragged his limp body behind me and mustered the strength to heave it over the cliff's edge. It tumbled, striking rocky outcroppings. He landed far below, his body covered with blood. I would send men to find him. I retrieved the box with my son's heart.

Sin so besmirched my soul that my actions had no positive effects. Fool! I chastised myself. Why did you hope the magic would work this time when it has not worked before? I had risked so much on such a slender hope.

The raven was still there, perched on a low branch. The bird explored its body, lifting its feet, raising its wings, and turning its head.

"Oh, Hades. What has become of me?" He became agitated. "Did you do this to me?"

It was the raven who had spoken. Of course, I knew they could talk. Still, this was a surprise.

"You are not here through any intention of mine."

"There is a mystery here. Can you do magic?"

He had a hoarse, croaking sort of voice. The words seemed labored. Was this some new minion of the devil come to torment me?

The bird sat still and looked as if he were thinking. He flew a short distance across the clearing, inspecting everything, then returned and perched on a low branch. It seemed he was trying to make sense of what had happened.

"It seems you used some magic power to put me in a raven's body. Do you have the power to give me a man's body? And what of the body at the foot of the cliff? Was that supposed to be part of this magic?"

I found myself annoyed at this insolent bird. The jinni had said that the summoned soul would serve me. A servant must show proper respect.

"You are my servant. You will address me as 'Lady.'"

Could I use this bird? The brown jinni did not bring what I wanted when I tried to save my daughter; instead, she provided the unexpected gift of rubies. Perhaps this bird would be of some value.

He bowed insofar as a bird can bow. "My Lady. How do you propose to make me serve you?"

I had found it easy to persuade Blodeweth to do what I wanted. It seemed this bird would prove more difficult. Ravens were common, and they attracted little notice. They have keen vision. Perhaps I would set him to spy for me. I had other spies, but he might go more places than others. And if he didn't obey me, then what? He might tell what happened here. No. That must not happen.

Perhaps if he believed I intended to give him what he wanted, he would serve me. "The magic is difficult. I can give you a human form. First, I need to investigate how to do this. Meanwhile, you must prove your loyalty to me through service. You can come and go unnoticed and bring back word of what you hear."

"You want me to be a spy." There were slight modulations of tone as his voice sounded more human, and I detected a hint of malicious amusement.

"Exactly so."

"When can I have this human body? Can I choose it?"

"Of course, you can choose. Again, this will take time. Do we agree?"

"It seems I have little choice, Lady."

Back in my chambers, I brought forth the reliquary of Saint Nazarius. "You must take an oath of loyalty to me by all that is sacred and the hope that Christ will save your soul."

He seemed confused. However, he placed his claw on the reliquary as I directed and repeated the words.

I showed him a map. "Do you understand this? Here is my city, and these are the mountains, and there is the ledge where we met."

"I understand."

"Go north, following the Ariege river, to Saverdun. Go there and listen to what the Baron says. Bring me news of his plans."

He bobbed in assent. He might prove uniquely valuable. Of course, I had already sent a servant to spy; I would compare the information they brought.

Blodeweth had spoken of another life. I was curious whether he might also have a past life. "What do you remember from before?"

He professed not to remember.

"What are you called?"

"I am Corvinus, my Lady."

He became my servant, albeit not a trusted one.

From that time onward, the third jinni also came to me at night. He was black and horned, and I feared he was Satan himself. He frightened me more than the others. The torturous pains in my belly increased.

Chapter 20

Corvinus

I, Corvinus, would write this with my own hand... If I had a hand. I can only ponder my misfortunes and not record them. The body of a bird ill serves my needs as a man.

I was a slave in the years of the reign of Nero. In my life as a man, the gods provided me with clever wits and a witless master. I managed his affairs so well that he never noticed as I took control of his wealth. His only son died in a war in Britannia, or so we believed. When my master died, his young daughter was his sole heir. I forged manumission papers; I forced her to marry me; I got her with child. I, who had been a slave, became a man of power who owned many slaves. Patricians snubbed me, of course, as much as they dared. Necessity forced some of them to beg me for loans. Their humiliation pleased me.

I would have risen even higher except that the lost son returned and, finding me in his father's chair and his sister's bed, cut off my hands, feet, and my "lying tongue" and threw me into the fire. I screamed in agony. My master laughed. Then a monstrous black-winged creature seized me from the flames. I expected oblivion or the pit of Hades. Instead, I woke up here.

As a raven.

The Lady offered promises. If I served her and spied for her, she said she would give me the human body I demanded. I doubted this, but I dared to hope. I had no other potential source of hope, in fact. I have remained with her because I discovered she possesses magic writing that might set me free and make me a man again. I couldn't make the sounds of those words exactly as they must be. I needed human help to achieve my aims.

I resigned myself to my fate–for a time. So long as the Lady had the magic in her possession, I would serve her. I considered ways to achieve her ruin. A crucial piece of misinformation might be sufficient. I dared not lie too brazenly. I was certain she would dispose of me if she believed me treacherous. I must appear to be loyal. Meanwhile, it pleased me to thwart her.

It bemused me that, as a raven, I still had a man's greed. Shiny objects drew my attention. I often stole jewels and trinkets and carried them off to the abandoned nest I had claimed as my own. It disgusted me that I now had a taste for bloody, decaying carrion. The knowledge that I might never again have a man's body and the power to do a man's will drove me to despair. I spoke only to the Lady and brought her information. Perhaps a time would come when I might seek help from others.

Chapter 21

Bon

I tried to give up my suspicion that the Lady had killed my father. I could not. I heard gossip; she might have had good reason to fear him, and it might even have been an act of self-defense. And yet, whatever her reasons, this act was dishonorable. He was her lord. It troubled me that she ordered me to hold Blodeweth while she took her blood. I feared she would command even more dishonorable acts in the future. And yet, the favor she showed me raised my hopes. Perhaps she would grant me a manor and silver; maybe she would raise me to knighthood. The only virtue I could show now was loyalty. I must obey the Lady's commands. Whether I obeyed or disobeyed her, I would dishonor myself. Which was the greater dishonor? Perhaps honor is a luxury an impoverished soldier cannot afford.

With little to do, my men became bored and troublesome. I put the idea of holding competitions into the Lady's mind:

"It would be good to show the prowess of our soldiers to our neighbors, and our soldiers need diversion. They do their jobs less well when they are bored."

She approved my idea, and we planned a competition for late summer. There would be prizes for excellence in wrestling, archery, sword, and other skills. She said she wanted to assess the temperament and abilities of neighboring nobility. This made sense. They might try to seize Mirefoix through force; some might seek the easier route of an alliance by marriage. In the past, she had chosen not to make a marriage for Garsenda; but now, she might want to evaluate prospective husbands. Perhaps for her daughter or perhaps even for herself.

This event would not be as large as northern tournaments; still, a competition would raise my men's spirits. There had been no recent opportunity to show my skill and courage, and I also looked forward to this event. I wanted to be a man of paratge, to embody all the virtues we Southerners value: military skill, excellence, refinement, courtesy, and tolerance. So far, my life had not offered the challenges needed to display these virtues.

I had always excelled with sword and bow. After that strange dream in which lightning struck my body, I had greater speed, more precise aim, and sharper vision. When I sparred, time slowed. My opponents seemed sluggish; I had time to perceive their intent and plan the best response.

The first event was wrestling. I chose not to take part: much dirt and no glory. Next came the horse races, with the course marked around the perimeter of the city walls. I envied the riders. The race would have been a chance to show off my skills, but I did not have a horse with the fire and stamina. Spectators placed bets and cheered at the many collisions and falls.

Then came archery competitions. The church forbade the use of crossbows against fellow Christians, and we at Mirefoix did not train with them; we used straight bows. I was almost as skilled with the bow as with the sword, and I did what I needed to win but did not reveal my full prowess.

In each round, archers loosed three arrows. After five rounds, it was clear who would compete in the final round: the Baron of Saverdun, Sir Dalmas of Font-Remeau, and myself. Men moved the butts to the farthest end of the field. Direct hits to the target center were uncommon at that distance, even for the best archers. Saverdun was the first to try. Only one of his arrows struck the center circle; the other two were outside. He swore foul oaths at this outcome. Sir Dalmas took his place with arrogant confidence. Two arrows pierced the center ring, and the third was just outside. He swaggered away, confident of his victory.

I was the last contestant. I raised my bow; my attention narrowed; the bow and I were all that existed; we were one. I nocked and loosed an arrow in an effortless motion. As soon as it struck the center of the target, I released the second and third arrows. These hit close to the first. I relished my moment of triumph.

I had bested him, and Dalmas's crimson face showed his fury.

He approached me before the next competition. "So, you are the bastard son of whom they speak."

I tried to ignore him. Manners prevented me from responding directly to this man of higher rank.

"I hear your sister spreads her legs for stable boys and jongleurs. She is a juicy bit."

I tried to contain my rage. I must avenge this attack on Garsenda's honor.

I faced Sir Dalmas in the competition with swords. I used a blunt blade according to the rules for such tests of skill and wore a quilted gambeson without mail. He did not wait for the signal; he lunged for me and struck my left arm with such force that he sliced through the sleeve of my gambeson and drew blood. I knew then he was using a sharp blade; he intended to kill or at least injure me.

Spectators tensed, and some cried out: Foul play.

I no longer disguised my speed and precision. I parried his blows easily, and he did not touch me again. There was a gap above the neck of his hauberk; I chose not to aim for that. I would teach him a lesson but must not draw the blood of a man of higher rank.

I allowed him to lunge; I leaped to one side. He tripped and struck the ground with all the force of his forward motion. I brought the point of my sword to his neck. There was no question I had won, and I had unforgivably humiliated him. In a low voice, I said: "By God's blood, you will not insult my sister's honor."

I received my prize, a purse of silver deniers, from the Lady's hand; she seemed to take personal pride in my victories. Garsenda smiled. When we were alone later, Fabrice nudged me:

"People are saying the Lady considers a marriage for Garsenda to the Baron of Saverdun or Sir Dalmas." He seemed distressed by this. I didn't think she would marry Garsenda to the Baron, whose holdings were so near, but would she wed Garsenda to the arrogant Sir Dalmas? Most likely, Garsenda would resist such a marriage—I had heard her speak of him with contempt—and refuse his claims as a husband if forced to wed. If she married, she might use his soldiers to threaten her mother. I'd back Garsenda against Dalmas; she would not yield to any man.

Sir Dalmas was a threat to my ambitions. While the Lady and Garsenda remained unwed, no man had control of Mirefoix. If Garsenda wed Sir Dalmas, they would rule Mirefoix upon the Lady's death. If this new enemy became my liege lord, my prospects would be poor, and I might even have to leave Mirefoix.

The more favor the Lady showed me, the greater my hope she would overlook my birth and choose me to defend her city. Was it possible she might appoint me to rule Mirefoix instead of passing control to Garsenda? Or, if Garsenda became ruler, might I become her right-hand man? I must prove my skill and loyalty.

Chapter 22

The Lady

September 1207

After the third soul summoning, the black jinni came every night. Holding warm rubies had kept the blue jinni at a distance, but this did not deter the black jinni.

I lay on my back in my bed and tried to sleep while he threw curses at me.

"You are damned for what you have done!"

I gazed up at the domed ceiling, seeking comfort from the gold stars painted on blue skies. Suddenly the world turned upside down. I looked down into the dome; it had become a sea of flames filled with a multitude of screaming souls. I gripped the edge of my bed, terrified I would fall into the pit.

"Take this sight away from me! I cannot bear to look." I pleaded for mercy I knew I would not receive.

The black jinni's evil laugh filled my ears.

"I will do as you say."

He stretched out his hand and touched my eyes. My sight blurred, and I fell into an unwholesome sleep. When I woke, I didn't move at first. Things did not look right. I looked at a page of spells; the symbols were no longer clear; and their edges bled together. I had lost much of my sight. Would I become totally blind?

The pains in my belly became more severe. Brother Felip prayed over me, but his words had no effect. I summoned Sister Cecilia; she brewed a foul-smelling tea, and I drank it all, but this failed to reduce my pain. Brother Stefe bled me from my right leg and left wrist when the moon was in Capricorn. Their treatments brought no relief from pain, nor did they restore my sight. I reminded them of the need for discretion; signs of ill health or weakness would encourage the Baron and other covetous neighbors to whittle away at my lands in anticipation of seizing control.

I summoned Rhazes. He bowed before me and greeted me as "Great Lady." I noticed, as before, that his hands were cleaner than most of my servants.

"Where is your pain? Does it feel like stabbing, burning, or aching? How long have you had this pain?"

I pointed to my swollen belly and described the sensations. It had the weight of a child growing within me, but none of my pregnancies caused me such pain.

"May I touch you, Lady?"

I allowed this.

"There is a hard mass in your belly. You are not pregnant. Something else grows there, a lump. A lump like this can be harmful, but perhaps not. We can only watch and wait."

"What if it is harmful?

He was reluctant to tell me, but I insisted.

"I must know what this is. I must plan for the future. I can endure any truth, but I cannot stand uncertainty."

"If the lump increases rapidly in size and causes more pain, the illness may be serious."

"And then?"

Again he hesitated. "There is no treatment, and I will not deceive you with concoctions of rare ingredients; they will do no good and may cause harm."

Now it was my time to hesitate.

"Will it lead to death?"

"It may not be harmful. You do not need to worry yet."

"If it is harmful, how much time do I have?"

"It could be a matter of a year or two. I say again, it may not be a matter for concern."

"Also, there is something wrong with my eyes."

He examined them closely.

"Do they pain you?"

"I can't see as well."

"I can treat this. I cannot promise you vision as good as before, but treatment might improve your sight."

This remedy sounded unlikely, and I refused it.

❖

I decided to use the soul-summoning spell one last time to obtain a new body for my own soul. Why didn't I think of this before? I could rule Mirefoix for many years in a young, healthy body and perhaps even take Bon as my husband. He was not related to me by blood. A son with Bon's keen intelligence and military skill would be a powerful defender of Mirefoix after me.

This time, I would have all the correct words.

This time, I had the mandrake root.

This time, I would not cross myself or say anything not specified by the spell.

Perhaps on this last attempt, the spell would work. If it did not, I was damned anyway, and I would die soon.

I sent for my niece Christine D'Arque and took her to live with me in my chamber. My younger sister was reluctant to send me her favorite daughter after her son died in my care; however, I hinted I might make Christine my heir. I showed her great favor. I made sure that my people often saw her in my company. I came to love her, for she was like me in appearance and manner. She had a swift mind and, among her accomplishments, knowledge of herbal remedies. She alone soothed the ache in my belly with her gentle hands and musical voice. I determined to do the magic at the next full moon.

To ensure that people would recognize me as the ruler of Mirefoix in my new body, I left a sealed letter with my seneschal and told him to open it only in case of my death. This said: "When I die, my niece, Christine

D'Arque, will rule after me. She and Bon must marry. Garsenda must take vows as a nun." If the soul summoning worked as I wanted this time, my soul would be in Christine's body. If it did not work, Christine would be a better heir than any other, and as her husband, Bon would protect her from challengers.

This time, I confess, I had no confidence in the results. Because I was dying, I saw no alternative but to attempt the magic again.

Under a full moon, I took my niece alone to the hills. She drank the wine I had prepared and slept. I anointed her face, hands, and breast. With trepidation, I summoned the fourth demon. Mena had further discussed the spell with me, and I understood I must die to set my soul free to leave my body; I must plunge the knife into my breast when the moment arrived. I tried to muster the courage.

A violet- and blue-colored spirit whose garments flowed like waterfalls appeared as I brought the knife to my breast. She gazed at me with pity. She stopped my hand: "You have given too much of your soul to Shaytan, and there is not enough left for me to transport it into this body."

I threw myself on the ground in supplication. "Take pity upon me! Can my soul be saved?"

"It will take much cleansing, many prayers, and more suffering to redeem your soul. You must sacrifice your life for those you love."

"Can you help me? I beg of you."

"I can send the soul of a healer to comfort you in your distress. That is the best I can do. I am the fourth and last of the jinn. You can summon no more of us."

I dropped the dagger, collapsed, and fell into a deep sleep.

When I awoke, it was morning. The body of my niece was gone. I searched in vain and found no trace. I thought: she cannot go far clad only in a shift.

I made haste to return to the Chateau, where I took the letter from my seneschal and burned it. I ordered servants and soldiers to look for Christine; I also sent Corvinus. The fourth jinni, the one of purple light, now visited me at night. But where the others had tormented me, she soothed me. Perhaps because of her help, the pains in my stomach grew no worse. However, my vision continued to fade.

I instructed the holy sisters to pray for me; I paid the priests at St. Volusienne to say masses. I didn't make a full confession, not yet. I spent long hours on my knees. I told my people that my niece had returned to her family, and I told her parents that she had entered the abbey just outside my city walls.

I continued to suffer pain in my belly. I summoned Rhazes to ask if he had any other remedy, and he again warned me of the danger of using opium too often. It no longer relieved my pain as much as it once had.

Despite the misfortune of being captive in a land far from his home, Rhazes seemed serene. I wondered about the source of his courage and patience.

"What comforts you?"

"The words of Allah, that is to say, God."

"What words are those?"

"Allah forgives us for our wrongs."

"Tell me more."

"Following the words of the Prophet, we ask: Lord, do not impose blame upon us if we have forgotten or erred, and burden us not with that which we cannot bear. And pardon us, and forgive us, and have mercy upon us. The Prophet said, When I am ill, it is He who cures me. Allah has said: Call upon Me; I will respond to you. Allah is ever forgiving and merciful."

"We count it a grievous sin to worship any but God and Jesus Christ."

"Allah is but another name for God. Allah is the same as the God of Abraham and Christians."

"Father Felip says that God requires full confession of sins to a priest and absolution given by the Church."

"Those of my faith have a different understanding. We believe that if you make your heart known directly to Allah, you receive forgiveness directly from Him."

After I sent Rhazes away, I pondered. These words held out hope. And yet, I could not imagine myself praying to Allah. The Church would judge my sin even greater if I did so. All my efforts had failed. I had no heir for Mirefoix. I was in constant pain, becoming too sick to rule.

Messengers brought ominous rumors: the Pope continued to call for war against the nobles of the south; he had lost patience with our tolerance of the Cathar heresy.

The jinn tormented me with reminders that my soul was lost. Not content with tormenting me, they harassed my people. Lightning struck haystacks on cloudless days and set them on fire. Animals were born with two heads. I asked Mena again whether any of the remaining spells offered hope. No, he said. I asked Rhazes for more opium. It will not help, he said. I prayed in my chapel; prayers brought no peace. What must I do to be saved and to save Mirefoix?

Part 2:

The Healer of Souls

Chapter 23

Christine

November 2021 / September 1207

I drove home in a sleet storm on a bitter November night. Skeletal ice-covered branches gleamed in the headlights. I gripped the wheel as my car skated on patches of black ice. Then, as I rounded a curve, I came upon a jackknifed tanker truck. Collision was inevitable; I saw the "flammable gas" placard. I had enough time to think:

"Oh, shit."

Tires squealed. My car shuddered at impact. Glass splintered, metal smashed, and I smelled spilled gasoline. The airbag exploded. My neck snapped as my head whipped back. Flames engulfed me. Terror. Excruciating pain. My spirit rose from my body and floated above the scene. Then there was no more pain. I saw my body below, crushed in the wreckage. Fear was gone. I had read about near-death experiences, and at first, I thought, yes, this is what people describe. At this moment, the soul has no questions.

A feeling of infinite love and peace engulfed me. I didn't want to return to my body; nothing I left behind seemed important. I expected a tunnel leading toward a welcoming golden light. Instead, a glowing ball of violet and blue appeared. As it grew closer, it came into focus as a winged figure. She extended an ethereal arm toward me and drew me into an embrace.

Then oblivion.

The sun's warmth brought me back to awareness. I didn't know how long I had been unconscious. I lay on my back among dry shrubs and grasses. The hot, still summer air bore the scent of rosemary, lavender, and sage. The unblemished sky overheard was the bluest I had ever seen. I stretched. My mind came into focus.

I brushed a lock of hair away from my eyes, then froze. This hand was not mine. Age spots, bulging veins, and knobby finger joints were gone. The stiffness had vanished; these were the hands of a young woman. What the Hell? Light brown hair rested on my shoulders. My arms and legs were slender. The dress I wore was coarse-woven white wool.

My heart rate soared; my mouth was dry. Was this hallucination part of the transition from life into death? I tried to calm myself. Where was I? The plant life was unfamiliar; it seemed Mediterranean. Scruffy grayish-green vegetation covered the hillside. The hills led up to snow-capped peaks in one direction, the south perhaps. An older woman lay a few yards away. I crawled toward her. I kneeled, put my hand on her shoulder, and turned her face toward me. She had the waxy look of death; I drew her cloak over her face. I was alone, and terror gripped me.

While disturbing, the unfamiliar place was less upsetting than the transformation of my body. I searched for a logical explanation. I had read about walk-ins, people who supposedly took on other people's bodies, but I didn't believe those stories. Was this a hallucination? I didn't feel delusional. These circumstances felt more real to me than any I had encountered before.

My brain and body screamed: Run! Get away from this dead woman. Perhaps the person who killed her will return. The rocky path offered two choices: up into the mountains or down toward the valley. I chose the downward direction. Loose stones skittered as I walked, and razor-edged pebbles cut the soles of my bare feet into bloody shreds. There was no shelter from the sun apart from tufts of shrubs and weeds. The dress hindered my movements as it caught on brambles. The sun beat down without mercy. I became thirsty, and that distracted me from fear.

I came to a stream at midday. I scooped water in my hands to drink and splashed it on my face, neck, and bloody feet. I was calmer now. The stream might lead me down from the hills, perhaps to a town. I walked, mostly downhill, for the rest of the day. Hunger set in. When evening came, I hid among shrubs with beautiful red flowers and fleshy leaves. I reached out to pick some. Perhaps chewing these would assuage both hunger and thirst.

An unfamiliar voice said:

"Those are poisonous. Don't even touch them." I pulled back. Who or what was that? It was a woman's voice, but no one was near. The words seemed to originate inside my mind. They sounded like a mixture of Latin and Spanish. She spoke a language I knew I didn't know, yet somehow understood. How was that possible? The presence of the voice was unsettling. I tried to flee from it and took shelter under the branches of a different bush. I listened. The voice in my head did not speak again. The only sounds were the rumbling of my stomach and the beating of my heart. Sleep did not come that night.

When morning came, I continued along the path. Each time I reached the top of one hill, another hill lay ahead. At last, I saw a broad valley below me and tiny human figures in the distance. Startled, I hid myself in a cluster of shrubs.

Long strips of tall beige grasses spread out before me. Men and women walked through the fields. Some swung scythes; others gathered cut stalks into bundles. A dozen cottages with thatched roofs clustered nearby. A gray stone church with a square tower dominated the horizon. People wouldn't do farm work this way if they had labor-saving technologies. A troubling question arose. Could this be a different century?

Terror returned, more powerful than before. I wanted to return to my world, but there was no way back. The knowledge and skills that enabled me to care for myself in the modern world were useless here. I needed help. Would strangers be friendly? What were my choices? Go back into the hills and roam this barren landscape by myself, trying to find something edible. Or enter the village and seek help. Both prospects frightened me. I decided my chances were better among people than in the wilderness.

Perhaps the body I now occupied had family or friends here, and they might be helpful—or not. What would I say to people? I decided it was safer to claim I remembered nothing than construct a story about my identity and origins that would not stand up to questions. I had never been a persuasive liar.

I approached the cottages. A man was skinning a small animal, a child was feeding chickens, people were milking goats, and a woman was kneading dough. They wore multiple layers of clothing dyed with browns, reds, muddy yellows, and faded blues, patched with different colors. These colorful garments made me wonder if my thin white shift might be only an undergarment. I became the object of intense curiosity. Men, women, and children dropped what they were doing and pelted me with questions.

"Where are you from?", "What news can you tell us?", "Where are your clothes?"

I understood what they said, although it wasn't English. It sounded like the garble of Spanish and Latin I had heard earlier in my head. I guessed that the brain in my new body had its native language deeply encoded from childhood. At the same time, I had my own thoughts and memories of the 21st century. Ironic. I had hated 21st-century life, but now, I would have given anything to return. If the voice in my brain knew more about this world, I needed to pay attention. Its knowledge could help me survive.

I tried to focus on the problems of the moment. In response to their questions, I said only:

"I don't remember."

Expressions changed from friendly interest to suspicion. They drew away, talking amongst themselves, staring. No one appeared to recognize me. A priest hastened toward us. His robes billowed, and his chins wobbled. He conferred with the villagers, who shrugged, pointed, and made vociferous comments. He crossed himself and fingered his crucifix.

"Who are you?"

The voice in my head spoke:

"Christine—"

The voice was about to say: Christine D'Arque. Why did I stop? I remembered a large square tower with smaller round towers attached to its four corners. Despite the heat, I shivered. Something terrible happened there that the voice did not want to remember.

"Where are you from?"

"I can't remember."

I lowered my head and hid my mouth behind my fist for a moment. I thought: Holy shit. Does a sweet little old lady like me swear in times of duress? Yes, sometimes. The priest appeared stunned and offended. He crossed himself again.

"You take the name of God in vain!" I realized I must have said the words aloud. People drew away as if blasphemy were contagious. I tried to change the subject.

"I am hungry. May I please have some bread?"

"You must do penance for your blasphemy, my daughter. Say ten Pater Nosters."

Pater Noster. The Lord's Prayer? I tried to recall the words. I said the prayer, stumbling over them. The priest stopped me, crossed himself again, and stepped back. Oh. I must have the words wrong. Perhaps it was supposed to be in Latin. I realized I had not crossed myself.

"Are you one of the Cathar heretics?"

Too late, I crossed myself. The expression of horror on the priest's face told me my Presbyterian version was backward.

"Leave this place. Heretics are not welcome here."

I protested.

"I am a good Christian."

"Begone!"

Satisfied that this resolved the problem, the crowd dispersed. People continued to watch me from the corner of their eyes. I left the village and hid among shrubs as near as I dared. Hunger gnawed at me, and I became faint. I considered what to do. I was afraid to enter the village again. The word heretic suggested I was in the Middle Ages, and I remembered enough history to understand that it was dangerous to be a heretic.

Was there a way back to my own world? It seemed not. I didn't believe in demons. Even if I returned to my previous life, my body had burned in that world. There was no way home. And no one waited for me back there, anyway.

As evening approached, my hunger sharpened. I watched the townspeople from my hiding place in the brush. By now, they had forgotten about me. I saw a round loaf on a table; for a moment, no one was watching. I darted out of the underbrush and seized the loaf. I turned to run and collided with a woman, apparently the owner.

"Thief, thief!" She snatched at the loaf. I held onto it and ran, and everyone chased me. "Seize her!" Two men pinned my arms and tied my wrists behind my back with coarse rope; they led me away from the village. Struggle seemed futile. I regretted not having time to eat even one bite of the bread; hunger made me dizzy.

Now I was a thief as well as a heretic.

Chapter 24

Christine

The men forced me to walk down a slope through fields and pastures. The top of a tower appeared on the horizon; as we approached, I saw a castle surrounded by small dwellings. I wanted to believe I was still in the 21st century, but I saw nothing consistent with that hope. They dragged me through the gate, across a courtyard, into a dark arched entry, and down spiral stone steps. My escorts pushed me into a cell; I stumbled and caught myself before hitting the floor. I smelled feces and vomit.

As I adjusted to the darkness, I noticed a foul-smelling bucket in the corner. I supposed this was the toilet. A dish of porridge appeared untouched. A whimpering girl perhaps about 14 years old was curled up in the corner farthest from the door. She sat rocking herself with her arms wrapped around her knees. She had bruises on her face, neck, and arms. I crawled over to her; she recoiled as she noticed my presence. I backed away to avoid frightening her. I whispered as if coaxing a shy dog:

"You don't need to be afraid. I'm a prisoner just like you."

After a time, she looked up. A sweet little face, I thought. Why is she here?

I pointed toward the porridge.

"Do you mind if I eat this?" Without words, the girl showed she did not mind. To have any chance of escape, I needed to get my strength back. The porridge was soupy, and there was no spoon, so I drank it from the bowl and scraped the remains with my hands, licking the paste from my fingers. How quickly we lose the veneer of civilized behavior when our familiar world is gone. The mush was tasteless and cold, but it filled my stomach and eased my thirst.

I encouraged her to talk. Sobs punctuated her words.

"My name is Jacotte... my mother died, and the man who took me as a servant beat me... hurt me... I ran away... I stole food... more than once... I fell and hurt my knee... I ran away... the bailiff arrested me. Someone said they will... cut off my hand. On market day when people will see."

I felt horror. I understood the girl's distress, and my fears for myself increased. If they plan to cut off her hand over a piece of bread, what would they do to me, a heretic and a thief? How much time did we have? Was there any way to escape? I eased beside her and leaned against the wall, the stones rough and cool against my back. Slivers of light from narrow slits high in the wall faded as evening approached.

I wrapped my arm around her shoulders and held her against my side, trying not to put pressure on her bruises. It was touching how she clung to me and relaxed. Her distress evaporated, and she slept. Sleep did not come to me. Although the men had not struck me, I felt as if beaten all over. Perhaps the men handled me more roughly than I realized. It was strange that I hadn't noticed these pains before.

I imagined possible means of escape. Might I overpower the jailer if he came to replenish the porridge? No. Bribery? I had nothing to offer except perhaps my body. That was a distasteful thought. The guard was not clean and far from handsome. Whatever inducement I might offer, there was no guarantee he would keep his end of the bargain. Three days would be enough time to learn the Pater Noster in Latin. That might be helpful. Everyone here must know it except me.

As night came, the cold penetrated my bones. It was the darkest night I had ever experienced. Jacotte slept, leaning against me, and I was grateful for the warmth of her body against mine. I never had a child of my own, but her vulnerability brought out a maternal tenderness.

Morning came. Jacotte had become calm. The abrasions and bruises on her face and neck had faded. She stopped moaning. I felt bruised all over, although I saw no external signs of injury.

"Let's pray. You say the words, and I will repeat them." She agreed. She continued to cling to me as she spoke the words in Latin. It seemed she found our close contact comforting. I repeated and repeated, burning the words into memory. The repetition of words reminded me of the hypnosis I had used with my psychotherapy clients. The words were a comfort or at least a distraction as we awaited our fate.

At midday, a guard opened the door and checked the waste bucket. He exchanged the empty dish for a full one. Jacotte crawled to it and scooped food into her mouth with a good appetite, even relish. He was astonished. He drew her into better light, took her chin in his hand, and examined her. She cowered. He pulled up her shift to look at her knee, perhaps to assess other injuries I had not noticed. He crossed himself and said, more to himself than to us:

"She is well." He looked at me with a mixture of wonder and fear; then, he shoved Jacotte back into the cell and slammed the door.

Chapter 25

Christine

The following day, the massive door swung open on screeching, rusted hinges. Jacotte was resting in my arms; she seemed to have forgotten her impending sentence. My fear had intensified; I tried to hide this so I would not upset her. Two men entered and seized me, raised me to my feet, and dragged me toward the door, one mumbling something about the Baron. Because of unfamiliar pain, my right knee didn't support my weight. Jacotte cried out and reached for me. They did not heed her and left her in the cell. My mouth dried from fear, and I got dizzy as they pulled me away. Jacotte had to face her doom alone.

Stout soldiers escorted me to a high-ceilinged hall. About thirty people seated on benches at a long trestle table consumed a substantial midday meal. The floor was none too clean, and dogs roamed about searching for scraps. The aroma of roasted lamb was tantalizing; my mouth watered.

The diners dressed better than the country folk I had seen earlier; the soldiers directed me to stand before them. I must watch my tongue. I decided it was better to say nothing rather than the wrong things. I would plead ignorance and forgetfulness. The guards and the now-familiar priest stood behind me. I studied the face of the man who would decide my fate and found a little hope: a robust man of middle years, bulky with muscle, with jovial wrinkles around his eyes and mouth. To his right sat a boy on the verge of adolescence. I guessed this was his son; he seemed a faded copy. The man ate with gusto; the boy picked at his food. A neurotic-looking greyhound cowered at the child's feet.

I waited until the Baron finished eating. The priest sweated and mumbled prayers. Servants brought bowls of water scented with herbs to the table; the diners wiped their knives clean and cleansed their hands. A guard spoke.

"Another food thief, my lord."

The priest stepped closer, his posture and tone obsequious.

"My lord! Here is the heretic who arrived yesterday! She spoke profanely! She didn't speak the Pater Noster properly in Latin; she spoke the words in everyday language. She admitted she was a Good Woman! An unrepentant follower of the Cathars, my Lord! She crossed herself backward! She stole bread!" He punctuated this by crossing himself. The Baron studied me.

"What have you to say for yourself?" This situation was serious business, judging from the frown on his face.

"I asked for bread because I was hungry. I confess I tried to steal a loaf. I have never stolen anything before. I am sorry. Please be merciful."

"And are you a heretic?" He seemed amused by this charge.

"My Lord, I am Catholic." I crossed myself, and this time I took care to do it correctly. "I was frightened and confused yesterday, and I hit my head when I fell and didn't remember things. I can say the Pater Noster."

"Do so."

I did well enough to satisfy him. The priest looked, so help me, disappointed, as did other onlookers. I recalled executions had been a popular form of public entertainment. With luck, I might deprive them of a good show.

Now the Baron turned to the guard.

"You say she healed the young woman in the cell. Explain."

The guard told his story. From his perspective, my effect on the girl had been miraculous. I prayed with her. I healed her bruises and injured knee; I relieved her pain; I stopped her weeping; I restored her appetite.

The priest mumbled:

"Witchcraft."

His Lordship seemed to enjoy an opportunity to toy with the priest.

"Does a witch use the Pater Noster to invoke magic?" The priest mopped sweat from his brow and glared at me.

"Well then. We will put this healing power to the test."

He snapped his fingers.

"Bring the bitch!" A servant brought the anorexic-looking greyhound; it whimpered and circled. The dog's left flank had a deep cut that was healing poorly. She slunk toward me with her head down, trying to look small. After some coaxing, she snuggled up to me, sighed, and was quiet. No one made a sound; the diners watched with interest. His Lordship put his elbow on the table and rested his chin on his fist.

"How long will this take?"

"She was with the girl prisoner throughout the night."

"Well... we cannot watch that long. Put this woman in a chamber with the beast. We shall see in the morning." As an afterthought, he said,

"Provide food and drink." He crooked a finger to summon a boy servant.

I had a momentary reprieve, but I didn't feel safe. I did not have magic healing powers; all I had offered Jacotte was sympathy. I would fail, but at least I had gained time and a meal.

A young male servant took me to a room cleaner than the prison cell but nearly as dark. He brought a lighted oil lamp and remained after the key was turned in the lock. The wine was harsh; still, I welcomed its relaxing warmth. They provided something that looked like a stewed eel, bread, cheese, and apples. The look the boy gave me when I did not touch the slimy fish gave me pause. I knew I must appear as normal as possible. I chewed and swallowed a bite, trying to mask my distaste. I slipped the rest to the dog.

The boy remained with me. I guessed his job was to report any hocus pocus.

I curled up on the bed with the hound and arranged myself on my side to avoid putting pressure on many sore spots. There was sharp discomfort as if I had a fresh wound on my hip. After I found a comfortable position, the dog curled up against me. After the boy fell asleep, I talked to the dog in soothing tones. Her eyes met mine with a tear-glazed, soulful gaze. At last, I slept, dreaming of axes, blood, and blazing pyres.

When I woke, the servant was sitting in the same chair. The dog jumped out of bed and stretched, looking happy. I had difficulty moving because of pain in my hip. Perhaps I brought my arthritis with me from my past life, I thought. I checked and found no injuries. My spirits were low; I was exhausted.

The servant escorted me to the room where His Lordship and his son were eating a light morning meal. He showed the greyhound to the Baron with a kind of flourish. She looked reborn: Happy and calm. Although the gash on her flank had not healed, the bleeding had stopped, and it no longer seemed to bother her. I was as astonished as anyone to see the dog's condition so improved. The Baron did not seem concerned about how the dog healed; he was satisfied with the results.

"Well then. What say you, boy, to a new nurse? You do not like Grazida overmuch."

The boy stuck out his jaw, a mannerism that made him look more like his father.

"I'm too old for a nurse."

"You are still a child despite your years. I would have you strong, my son." He added, perhaps as an incentive, "You can tell Grazida she is no longer needed."

The boy shrugged as if indifferent. His father took this for assent.

"What is your name, young woman?"

I decided I had better use the name I gave before.

"Christine."

"Go with him, Christine."

I sank to my knees.

"My lord. May I dare to ask a favor? The girl in the cell with me, Jacotte. My healing power came from her. I never had this power before I met her. I need her to do my healing." I knew no such thing, of course.

His Lordship's face darkened at my presumption.

"What was her offense?"

"She was accused of taking food, my Lord. She was hungry. She is not a thief by nature."

"And what shall I do with this person if I spare her?"

"I beg your pardon, my lord." I recalled how skeletal she was: "Perhaps put her in your kitchen?"

"A food thief in my kitchen." He almost laughed. "I will consider this."

"Please, my lord, before market day. Before they carry out her sentence."

"Mend your manners! They taught you ill wherever you came from. Do not speak unless I have spoken. You have exhausted my patience." To an attendant, he said: "Bring a gown."

"Yes, my Lord."

A servant gave me a shabby dress, and I put this on over my now-ragged shift. Although the clothes were faded and torn, I felt more comfortable fully clothed. He dismissed me with a wave of his hand. The boy left the hall, and I followed him, and the dog followed me.

Chapter 26

Christine

I followed the boy down circular stairs and out into a courtyard. "What should I call you, young Lord?" He squatted near a tree, and I kneeled nearby. He did not want me near; my presence embarrassed him. To survive, I would have to win this sullen child's favor. His father wanted me to heal whatever was wrong with him. I was not sure what that was. It might be nothing more than loneliness and unhappiness. He seemed cowed by his father. Maybe the boy needed the confidence that comes from accomplishment. How could I help? The red sores on his neck and face might be caused by nervous scratching rather than a physical disease.

Across the courtyard, a man was teaching several boys how to fight with blunt wooden swords. I saw the boy glance in their direction and then look away. That gave me an idea. He sat under the plane tree in the courtyard, sulking. I pulled two branches from a nearby shrub, stripped them of leaves, and handed him one. He did not accept it. I adopted a fencer's pose, with my 'sword' extended toward him and my other arm overhead, and said:

"En garde!"

I took a college class in fencing during my Errol Flynn period. I didn't want a pirate as a lover; I fancied myself a swashbuckler myself in those days. Perhaps I could get this boy interested in action and inspire something of the spirit I once had.

He looked at me as if I were demented. I maintained the pose, feeling foolish; nearby maids snickered and whispered behind their hands. Then he stood and faced me with his stick in his hand. He adopted the same posture and returned the salute:

"En garde!" We whacked away at each other with branches. I was careful to hit his stick and not his body; he lunged at me, and I suffered many pokes and swats until his mock weapon broke into pieces. He wanted to resume with another piece of wood. I persuaded him I was tired and that we would do it again later.

The man who instructed the other boys noticed this and invited 'my' boy to join them in their game. He was hesitant. With a bit of encouragement, he accepted. The following day, the Baron summoned us.

"What did you do yesterday, Gilbert?"

Gilbert seemed reluctant to speak. After some coaxing, he said he was learning to use a wooden practice sword with the other boys.

"I am pleased with you, son. I wanted you to take an interest in weapons." He gave me a look of respect; I had persuaded his son to act like a boy. Gilbert ducked his head, his face coloring. His father's praise gratified him; perhaps he had none of that before. His servant asked:

"It is market day, Lord. Do you plan to attend?"

"Yes.... she will come with us." He waved in my direction. Did I dare ask again about Jacotte? I shot the Baron a pleading look. He did not deign to notice.

We made our way out the gates into the village, where vendors had set up tents and tables to sell cheese, eggs, nuts, garlic, bread, dried fish, ropes of sausage, wine, and pastries. There were also pots, trinkets, candles, and ragged pieces of cloth for sale. I might have enjoyed the festive atmosphere if not for Jacotte's sentence.

Jacotte was led out, along with a grizzled older man bent in misery. They stood near a tree stump studded with large nails and bloodstains. The crowd gathered in anticipation; the priest and the Baron stood near the prisoners. I owed it to Jacotte to witness her pain. An official spoke first:

"We have here two criminals. Their behavior is an offense to all hard-working people and an insult to the Baron's authority. I must punish them." Jacotte looked so disoriented that I wondered if the jailer, out of kindness, had given her enough wine to render her senseless. My heart bled for her. I attempted to get the Baron's attention, hoping that he was pleased enough by the change in Gilbert to grant me the favor I begged, but he ignored me.

Jacotte was brought to the stump first. She kneeled, and they roped her arm in place. The ax was raised. Her lips were moving; she must have been praying. Even if she survived the trauma of injury, infection would probably kill her.

"Hold!" The baron stepped forward, and the guard stopped with his ax in midair.

"It is said that he who pardons without beating spoils his children. We should chastise them tenderly. As the saying goes, correct the young and hang the old." The older prisoner stiffened upon hearing this, no doubt fearing that the Baron had just changed his sentence.

I exhaled; for a moment, I experienced relief. Perhaps the Baron would spare Jacotte.

The crowd seemed disappointed. The Baron took the axman aside and said a few words; I hoped he would untie Jacotte. Instead, he amputated the smallest finger on her right hand. She fainted. They untied her and carried her away; I tried to follow. One of the Baron's men grasped my elbow. I was not permitted to comfort her.

Then a guard dragged the man forward and cut off his hand; this required two strokes of the ax. He screamed in agony. I had never thought of the body as bone, blood, and raw meat before; the horror stayed in my mind.

After this entertainment, the Baron's party circulated among the vendors. I was too sick to pay attention to any of it. Would I ever see Jacotte again? Would she be all right? This was a world of casual cruelty. Did I even want to live under these conditions?

At night, I slept on Gilbert's chamber floor on a pallet of straw with a rough blanket, and the greyhound I had healed curled up next to me. I called her Sassia. The beating of her heart, the rhythm of her breath, and the warmth of her body comforted me. Still, I did not sleep well; my knee, hip, and other body parts hurt, no matter how I tried to arrange myself on the stone floor. The child was restless too. He moaned, squirmed among the bed covers, and ground his teeth. I wondered what nightmares tortured a child so young. Perhaps his father beat him; that might be ordinary child discipline.

My experience with Jacotte made me hope that gentle touch and soothing words might heal his distress, but Gilbert shied from contact. The next day, Gilbert tripped while running up the stone stairs and banged his left shin. I was close behind him and wrapped my arms around him before he protested. He allowed me to hold him. The tight expression on his face eased, and the pain faded from his face. He stood and stretched his leg as if he had no pain. After that, new discomfort in my left shin added to my other misery.

After that fall, he looked at me differently. He understood I was a source of comfort. That night we got ready for bed. Preparation involved shedding clothing down to our undergarments: a shift for me and a tunic for him. He studied me as I took off what I thought of as my burlap sacks.

"I will make them give you something better to wear."

This concern touched me.

He inched toward me as if he wanted a hug; I opened my arms. I embraced him. Then I turned to my pallet on the cold stone floor.

"Sleep in my bed. The floor is hard."

This set off alarm bells.

"No, thank you, the floor is my proper place."

I guessed his age to be about 10 or 11. He was still a child, but puberty was approaching, and I didn't want to risk intimacy.

I had eased the suffering of Jacotte, Sassia, and now Gilbert. How did I gain this healing power? In my previous life, I tried to relieve suffering through talk therapy, which didn't always help. I wanted my work to be meaningful, but often, the effort exhausted me.

I remembered reading that sometimes people had remarkable gifts after near-death experiences. Perhaps that explained my new healing ability. As a psychotherapist, I had often despaired about my limited ability to help and wanted to do more to relieve emotional distress. Now my wish had been granted. Now I took away the physical and emotional suffering of others. I did not take on their injuries, but I experienced their physical pain and emotional distress. This gift of healing earned me a place in this world, but it came at a cost. I had become a wounded healer.

Gilbert lost much of his fear and sought further instruction in riding and swordsmanship. His color improved, his broken skin healed, and he gained weight. He seemed to enjoy our company, mine and Sassia's, at night. Apart from an occasional hug, he had little interest in seeing me during the daytime. That left me free to go where I pleased and do what I chose. As Gilbert felt better, I began to recover from the pain of healing.

As a token of his affection, he gifted me a few coins. With help from women in the kitchen, I obtained small necessities, including an eating knife, a piece of a broken comb, pointed twigs to clean my teeth, and rags. Other servants became friendly and included me in their gossip. I figured out where I was in the past. The town was called Saverdun; I thought this was probably in France. No one mentioned the plague, and people had enough to eat. The Baron had been part of an army led by King Philip and Richard the Lionheart that attempted to retake Jerusalem; I guessed this was the late 12th or early 13th century.

At Gilbert's request, I received better quality cloth; I asked maidservants to help me make this into a suitable dress. The underdress was light yellow; over that, I had a darker muddy yellow surcoat slit up the sides.

Jacotte admired my new dress. "The color suits you, and the cloth is nicer than mine." She fingered my sleeve with a touch of envy. "Now, you look like a woman instead of a scarecrow. You have gained weight too."

I found it was not true that these people believed bathing threatened health. A full bath was too much work to be anything but an occasional treat, but frequent sponge baths provided acceptable results. Courtesy required everyone to wash hands and faces and to clean fingernails before sitting down to eat.

The women said that the Baron had worn out three wives with his incessant demands and chased every skirt in the castle, and they warned me to avoid encounters with him in isolated places. They spoke of the priest I had met, Father Pierre. One young woman said:

"I lift my skirts for him. He has cleaner hands than the stable boys and better manners. And he gives me nice gifts. He showed me a charm to prevent pregnancy." They exchanged advice about contraception; the procedures did not sound effective; however, I kept this information in mind. These methods might be better than nothing.

I learned the routines of my new life. Homesickness replaced fear. I once thought that losing a beloved person was the worst possible pain. Now I understood: losing an entire world is far worse. I could survive, but this would never be home. I longed for a place where I could be known and loved as myself. I had to conceal every thought and feeling. But as I recalled my past life and its disappointments, I realized: I was homesick for a kind of home I never had.

Words and images that were part of Christine d'Arque's memory were sometimes helpful. But when she remembered the towers of Arque, she felt terror. Christine wanted her memories to disappear, and I let them go. Gradually her voice came less and less often.

Chapter 27

Christine

October 1207

Lying in the sun and breathing fresh air away from other people restored my energy. Finding a private place was difficult. When I walked along the castle's battlements, I discovered there were no men posted on the wall that overlooked the river. I found a place to lie in the sun. I removed my hose; I pulled up my sleeves and skirts as far as I dared. The warmth and light reduced the pain in my hip and knees; anxiety and depression dissipated.

I had not seen my face since arriving in this world. It is strange not to know your own face. I looked into a dark pot full of still water and formed an imperfect impression of my appearance. My unfamiliar face seemed pleasing and framed by wavy brown hair.

I asked Jacotte about my appearance. "Oh, you are fair, very fair. Your skin is so light and your eyes so blue, and your hair gleams in the sun. See how men's eyes follow you? They say beauty is a danger to a woman. Even the Baron looks at you now that you have decent clothes and clean hair. You should cover your hair. Men notice it when it shines in the sun."

I was foolishly pleased to hear that I was attractive. In the past, I was plain. I wanted to love, but most men didn't notice me. When a man asked me to marry, I reasoned with myself. He's a good man; he doesn't like himself, but I can help him feel better. We married. At first, he appreciated my efforts to please him; later, he acted entitled. There was no joy in giving things that were demanded and not valued. After ten years, I was exhausted; I filed for divorce. I never became trapped in a one-sided caregiving relationship again. I no longer wanted romantic love or physical intimacy; freedom from desire became a relief. My world shrank until all that remained was secondhand stories in books and films. Life was a dance; I was not a dancer. I watched others from a distance. The joys of life were not for me, but neither were the pains.

Now, in this world, every sensation was overwhelming and immediate. I couldn't hide from life. I had always wondered: is one life all we get? Now I had a second chance. I had the bloom and energy of youth. Perhaps it was not too late to learn to dance. But I had the same fears as before. Could I find the courage to engage with the world and to love? But love whom? I had nothing in common with men of this world and found their attitudes offensive.

It was a joy to feel beautiful. But I knew this invited dangerous attention. Jacotte was right: It would be safer to dress like a wife or widow. I braided my hair and pinned it behind my head. I made a modest head covering like those of married women. I loosened my girdle so that my waist did not seem so small. Those changes reduced unwelcome advances.

On a late October afternoon, I took Sassia to my favorite isolated spot on the battlements and rested in the sun with my arms and legs bare to soak up the welcome warmth. This restored my sense of well-being. I allowed myself to daydream. Perhaps I could make a life for myself in this world. A man might come, someone different from others in this world. I mused. Who could it be? A nobleman would see me as an object; such a man would only use me. A priest was equally out of the question. Most peasants scraped by; as a servant of a noble house, I would find their life a step down. A few artisans, such as smiths, millers, and bakers, managed a better living. But conversation had always been important to me, and my words and thoughts wouldn't make sense to any of these people. They could never know me. Was anyone in this world an outsider like myself?

A shadow fell across me. Startled, I looked over my shoulder. The Baron smiled.

"Your beauty is wasted on my son. You should have a man." I leaped to my feet and rearranged my garments to cover as much of myself as possible. I tried to squeeze past him; if I got to the stairs, I might escape to the courtyard below and the safety of crowds. He seized my arm. I moved away, but he trapped me with my back against the tower wall. I tried to twist free from his grasp. I smelled his breath, stale wine, cheese, and garlic. Panic swept through me. I put my hands against his chest to push him away.

"Don't pretend you don't want this."

Perhaps I should let him have his way. Maybe he would lose interest if he found me unresponsive, I thought. But my mind screamed no; I would feel tainted. His bullying ways repelled me. If I allowed him to do this once, he would probably do it again. I fought.

I clawed at the Baron's cheek; he seized my wrists. He forced me down into a corner, kneeled over me, and lifted the hem of my dress.

Sassia had been sunning herself nearby; now, she circled us, snarling. When the Baron pushed me down, she lunged; her teeth closed over his hand. He batted her away, and she attacked again. He struck the side of her neck with his knife. Sassia screamed. When I tried to block his blows, his blade slashed my arm. Blood oozed on my face and neck; it stained the front of my gown. I held Sassia in my arms, overwhelmed by pain and panic. The Baron looked at us with distaste and then walked away.

Blood gushed from Sassia's neck. She whimpered. Perhaps he had struck an artery; if so, she would die. Frantic to stop the bleeding, I used my head wraps to bandage her and staunch her wound. I used my knife to tear more strips of material from my underdress. Blood seeped through the bandages. I feared she would die from so much blood loss.

Grief tore my heart. In a short time, she had become my best friend and defender; now, she was hurt because of me. It was my fault. If I hadn't exposed myself to this danger, she would not have attacked the Baron.

Chapter 28

Garsenda

My mother retreated into a world of pain and prayer. She paid little attention to me or what happened at Mirefoix. I wondered: what would become of us? If she died, the responsibility for Mirefoix would fall upon my shoulders. What should I do?

Bon became her closest attendant. She favored him above all others; she asked his opinions. They shared a cup. Sometimes she placed her hand upon his hand or touched his cheek. I was glad that he did not return her gaze or touch.

My veiled tutor, Mena, aroused my curiosity. People said it was customary for some African tribes to veil their faces, perhaps to keep the sand away from their noses and mouths. Why wear a veil in mountain country, inside a walled city where few saw him?

One day, I saw his manservant removing rags from their chamber, cloth scraps that smelled like the dried blood from a woman's monthly courses. Was a woman concealed with them? I wouldn't rest until I found out. I followed the servant back and pushed the door open without knocking. I saw only Mena, his veil removed, sitting at a table writing.

"What do you wish, my Lady?" Mena put his veil in place.

I hesitated to ask what I wanted and improvised an errand. "My Lady mother wishes to ask how the writing work progresses."

"You may tell her the work goes well."

My curiosity overcame me. "Is there a woman here?"

Mena and his servant looked dismayed.

"As you see, there is no one else here."

I moved closer to the table. Mena looked up at me, and I caught my breath. Suddenly I knew: these were not a man's eyes. This was not a man's face.

"You are a woman?"

Mena sighed.

"Please sit."

I sat across the table, studying her smooth face and noticing that her ink-stained fingers were long and tapered. A woman's hands. How had I not noticed this before?

"You have discovered my secret. How can I persuade you to keep this hidden?"

"Why do you pretend to be a man?"

"I will tell you nothing unless you swear to tell no one."

"Tell me your story. Why do you dress as a man? I will keep this matter hidden and help you in any way I can." I swore my most solemn vow. I was fascinated by this mystery.

"I have pretended to be someone other than myself for years; I am weary of pretense. It would be a relief to show myself."

"Please, tell me everything."

Mena began:

"I am Coptic, born in the city of Lalibela, far to the east, south of the place you call the Outremer. My father raised me as a Christian, and even though I was a girl, he provided tutors so I would be well-educated. When Salah-ah-din retook Jerusalem, my people wanted to build a new Jerusalem for the glory of God. My father was among those who envisioned building new cathedrals, and he devised a design such that each cathedral was excavated deep into living rock. But my father died, and my uncle took possession of the household. Our Muslim rulers treated us with reasonable tolerance, but it was an uneasy situation.

My uncle took me to Alexandria and commanded that I marry a powerful and wealthy Muslim. He told me I would have to convert to please my new husband. I refused, and my uncle beat me. My brother, Besada, helped me escape disguised as a man. We took the first ship from Alexandria and Cyprus and went on to Marseille. At first, we used the money we brought with us to pay for lodging and food, but I knew I must earn a living. I became a scribe and translator. I learned the language of your country quickly. It was like the Latin I already knew, so it was easy. I came into employment in the household of the Viscountess Ermengarde of Narbonne. When she abdicated, I remained in the service of the new Viscount. It was safer to appear as a man, even beyond the range of my uncle's pursuit.

Finally, someone discovered my deception, and I fled that place. When I met your mother's emissaries, coming here seemed the safest choice. She does not know my secret."

I promised: "I will tell no one of this. Tell me more about the world. I have often wished I could be a man and run away."

"It is not something I recommend."

"Why? Are you unhappy?"

"I gave up everything I might have had as a woman: love and children. And I'm homesick for the warmth and beauty of my own land."

In the months that followed, we became fond of each other. Mena praised my progress; I discovered a world I had not known in the materials she provided for the lessons, sometimes in the original Latin and sometimes in simplified Latin translations from Greek or Arabic. I suspect she edited out material she thought I should not see, but I didn't mind. She said my visits gave her life purpose.

She brought a wealth of stories into my world. In one story, two women came before Solomon to demand justice. They had each borne a son, but one son had died, and each laid claim to the surviving child. Solomon said: Bring me a sword. He proposed to divide the child and give half to each. One woman said: the child shall be neither mine nor thine; divide it between us. The child's real mother said no, do not slay the child. And Solomon said: give the boy to the woman who wants the child to live; she is the true mother.

"This is a strange and interesting story, but why did you choose this? It has nothing to do with my life."

"Someday, you may be called upon to judge. Perhaps Solomon's wisdom may guide you."

One day she said:

"I love you as the daughter I never had."

"And you are like a loving mother to me."

We embraced. For the first time in many years, I knew that someone cared about me.

Chapter 29

Christine

Sassia and I lay side by side, soaked in her blood, too weak to move; I held her close and prayed. She continued to breathe, her mouth open in distress, her eyes dilated. Did I have any genuine healing power? I prayed it would work. I could feel the pain of her neck wound, and her panic spread through my chest in waves. We lay quietly for at least an hour. After a time, her terror subsided. She became so quiet that I thought death had claimed her. Then she opened her eyes and gazed at me with trust. The bleeding had slowed enough that I decided to risk moving her. I carried her outside, washed her wounds in the river, and applied fresh bandages. Perhaps she would survive. I immersed myself in the river, fully clothed, trying to rinse away the blood that made bright red blotches on my yellow gown. The bloodstains never came out of my clothing, nor the anger out of my soul.

A groom helped me carry Sassia to Gilbert's chamber. She lay on the floor without moving. For three days, she only accepted small amounts of food from my hands; I coaxed her to swallow water I squeezed into her mouth from a rag. She slept most of the day; I lay beside her.

Stabbing pain in my neck made it difficult for me to turn my head.

On the fourth day, she got up, walked to the door, and gave me a perky look as if to say: Let's go out.

After that, I decided never to walk alone on the battlements or anywhere else. That was no guarantee of safety. The Baron might summon me to his chamber. Now I hated as well as feared him. I was relieved when the Baron focused his attentions on a buxom young woman from the kitchen; I hoped she would keep him occupied. I avoided him. The blood stains on my dress made him hesitate, and I hoped this would be sufficient protection.

Jacotte and I made our way among stalls and tents on market day in late November, admiring the trinkets. At this time of year, there were few fresh foods and considerable amounts of dry salted fish and smoked sausage. Vendors offered savory meat pies that made my mouth water. Then I spotted the honey cakes. I stared at them with longing. I had such a weakness for sweet things, but I had only two deniers, and these must be expensive. I must save my coins for necessities.

An auburn-haired, broad-shouldered, muscular man accosted me with a jovial smile. He handed me a honey cake with a flourish and disappeared before I could thank him. I bit into it with something like ecstasy and nibbled, trying to make it last.

A sudden dread overcame me, and a tingling paralysis spread through my body. My limbs were like rubber, heavy and clumsy. I fell. Was I having a stroke? I fell to the ground, and people gathered around. Jacotte cradled my head in her lap and called out to me. Others just gawked. My thoughts became disorganized, and then I sank into unconsciousness.

❖

It must have been much later when I awoke, blind and paralyzed, swaddled from head to toe in heavy wrappings. A shroud? A shroud. They thought I was dead. I was like the victim in an Edgar Allan Poe story. I was afraid, terribly afraid. I tried to twist my way out of the binding clothes and concluded that the wrappings were too tight for me to tear them.

I have always been claustrophobic. That intensified my dread and horror. I was terrified that I would suffocate. The only sound I heard was the desperate pounding of my heart. At least I was not underground; there was no smell of earth. I might as well be, I thought. If I can't move or call out, they will bury me. I will be trapped in the darkest possible place under shovels full of dirt. I will be pressed to death by the weight of the earth. At best, I might lose consciousness before they lowered me into a grave.

After what seemed an eternity, I heard voices speaking in low tones. I tried to move. A man tore the cloth away from my face. A tall dark figure stood over me, cloaked and hooded, like the personification of death. I blinked to avoid the painful brightness of moonlight that streamed through the door behind him. He raised me to a sitting position and helped me drink a few sips of wine. Then he removed more of the shroud. It seemed he intended to help me. At first, I was overwhelmed by gratitude and relief.

Then I saw the other one, the heavyset man who gave me the cake, not smiling now. These two had conspired. I still couldn't move. As the men peeled away the shroud, I realized I was naked underneath.

They dressed me; my body was as limp as a rag doll. My emotions ran high, a mixture of terror, rage, and humiliation. Locked inside my body, I couldn't say or do anything to express my feelings.

They wore rough, dark, short clothing. Peasants, I guessed. They placed a shrouded body similar in size to mine on the table where my body had been. The taller man hoisted me over his shoulder like a bag of grain. They took me outside into an alley. I tried to protest, to scream, but could not.

They removed slats of wood from the bottom of a wagon. There was a false bottom, and they lifted me into it. I finally made a weak sound of protest. They conferred for a moment. The hooded one took another piece of honey cake, soaked it in wine, and placed it in my mouth. I wanted to spit it out but I couldn't. They covered me with slats; I heard the thud of cargo tossed into the wagon above me. Then the wagon lurched, and I heard the creaking of wheels. The narrow space was like a coffin. I used my fingernails to tear at the wood over my head for a few moments, desperate to escape. I was overcome once again by paralysis and insensibility.

When I regained my senses, I lay on the ground. We were on the edge of a forested hill, just beyond the scruffy gray-green foliage beside the road. The wagon and heavyset man were gone. The taller man remained, with a horse tied to a nearby tree. I was angry as well as terrified. How dare this man take me from a comfortable life? What did he intend to do?

I studied him by moonlight. He was slender; his hair was dark and long, tied at the nape of his neck. He turned, noticed I was awake, and kneeled to offer me wine. I thought it might be drugged again and tried to refuse it. I was surprised by his face. Most men here had coarse sunburned skin. This man's face was smooth and the color of sun-bleached wheat. His hair was ebony, and his eyes dark brown. His facial features appeared East Asian. Was that possible?

"Do you recognize me?"

I studied his face. I felt an odd sense of déjà vu; I tried to query Christine's memories. But after months of suppressing her voice in my mind, I got no information. Perhaps he was taking me to a place where Christine was known? This could make my life more difficult. I shook my head.

"Ah. I was told you might seem different, and that you might not remember us."

By this time, my fear had lessened. These two men had gone through a lot of trouble to kidnap me. The purpose didn't seem to be rape or murder.

"Who are you? Where are you taking me?"

"I serve the Lady of Mirefoix. By her orders, I am bringing you to her. I am sorry for your distress."

I lost my temper.

"Sorry? Sorry? You have done me the worst possible wrong. You are a man without honor."

He flinched at this insult. He pulled me to my feet, but my legs collapsed under me. I heard an exhalation of annoyance.

"Try to stand."

"Why?" I was in no mood to cooperate.

"Just do it."

I did not cooperate, so it was a clumsy maneuver. The man put me astride the horse—I almost fell off—and mounted behind me. He kept one arm around me as his horse picked its way along a rough path upward into the hills. Riding astride became uncomfortable, then painful, then agonizing for me. Muscles stretched in unfamiliar ways, and my inner thighs chafed against the saddle. I tried to stay upright and found it challenging. Stubborn pride kept me going for a while.

The pressure of his chest against my back dominated my attention. I was disturbed, and yet, I confess, aroused. Christine's girlish body must be full of those damned adolescent hormones. As I aged, it had been a relief to leave those troublesome yearnings behind.

I was puzzled as I thought about what had happened. This man dressed as a peasant. But why would a peasant abduct me? Why the elaborate subterfuge? He wanted me to appear dead; there would be no pursuit. The poisoning, the substitute corpse, the wagon, and the horse were all evidence of careful planning. Poor Jacotte; she would mourn me, and I would miss her, the one friend I had found in this strange world other than dear Sassia. I thought about escape. No workable ideas came to mind. Threatening clouds gathered. I pleaded:

"Please stop. I cannot do this anymore. I need to rest."

"When we reach the other side."

We reached the crest, and the horse picked its way down the slope. Rocks slid underfoot, and the horse stumbled. Icy rain pelted us, and it soaked through my garments. At the foot of a hill, he tethered the horse in a grove. He showed me where to sit, backed up against a tree trunk; I leaned against it and pulled my knees up. The branches provided little shelter. The cloak covering me became sodden with rain, and shared body warmth became necessary. He sat beside me, spread his cloak over us, encircled me with his left arm, and placed his sword within reach. Wait. Did peasants have swords? I knew these were expensive. Perhaps he was a soldier. I thought: He must sleep or at least drop his guard sometimes. I thought I might escape and return to the Baron's castle; I had a tolerable life there. His taciturn manner did not encourage conversation. I wanted information. Gathering my courage, I said:

"Why did you kidnap me?"

No response.

I lapsed into silence.

I woke in the pale predawn hours. I sensed the tension in my captor's body and saw he had his sword in hand. Nearby, one hooded figure was untying the horse; two other men crept toward us. My dark-haired kidnapper leaped up and felled the nearest attacker with a quick blow to the gut. One attacker kneeled beside me, seized me, and pressed his knife against my throat. I froze. My kidnapper drew a knife from his sleeve and launched it swiftly; it skimmed past my check and caught the outlaw in the throat. Within moments my kidnapper had also dispatched the man trying to take the horse.

He examined each of the assailants and made sure of their deaths. The man he had stabbed in the abdomen was groaning and trying to crawl; he finished him off with an additional thrust of his knife into his chest. He wiped his blades clean of blood. His face showed no trace of anger; the killing had been rapid and precise, almost surgical. His lack of apparent remorse chilled me. He ransacked their bodies for valuables, and he found little. Witnessing this theft unleashed my fury.

"That is despicable behavior! You truly are a man without honor." At this point, given the trouble he had taken, I thought that he wouldn't kill me for bad manners. Annoyance had overtaken anxiety. Apparently, my words stung. The man flushed in anger and set his chin, then said: "You seem to forget they were going to slit our throats and steal the horse; they would have raped you."

"He was defenseless, and you—"

"Would it be more merciful to leave him to a long, painful death?"

I had no response. What could he want with their few meager possessions? He must be poor, indeed. But perhaps not a peasant. By now, I knew the differences in speech between peasants and the gentry, and his few utterances were not in the dialect of the lower class. He dragged the bodies into the brush. Life within the Baron's castle had not prepared me for the brutality of life outside. He tried to put me back in the saddle; he took the halter and led the horse.

"I can't ride."

"You don't have to ride. Just don't fall off." Under other circumstances, this might have been comical.

"It's too painful. I'm not used to this." He paid no attention. As we passed a shrub that would break my fall, I let go. He intercepted me before I hit the ground. I realized he missed nothing; he anticipated everything and reacted quickly.

Not long after that, the horse stumbled and fell. My captor examined him, and the injury was beyond remedy. He slit the horse's throat, and his face revealed regret. So he was human, after all. After that, we walked. The stony ground bruised and cut my feet; I had no shoes. The discomfort in my feet at least distracted me from the searing pain between my thighs. I mumbled insults used by the blacksmith at Saverdun. Peasant. Bastard. Oh, I had more offensive expressions than those. That last epithet made him glare at me.

"How much longer must we walk, Sir Knight?" My voice was laden with sarcasm.

"I'm not a knight."

"What are you, then?"

"An ordinary soldier. Close your mouth, or I will close it for you."

I sat down on the ground, defiant, refusing to go further.

He gave me an ominous look.

"You're a lot of trouble."

He picked me up, heaved me over his shoulder, and continued onward. The blood rushed to my head, making me sick, and my back hurt from this uncomfortable position. It wasn't easy for him, either, and I wondered which of us would be more stubborn. Well: he won. I capitulated.

"All right. I'll walk."

We reached the crest of a second hill in the afternoon; there, he stopped. He gave me what passed for lunch: stale bread, wine, and cheese. I tore the bread into small pieces and soaked them in wine to soften them. Between us and the rugged peaks along the horizon lay a walled city, much larger than the Baron's castle. It impressed me. The walls were imposing, with dozens of round towers, and the gate was massive. Towns clustered around the walls on three sides; the city overlooked a river on one side. In the fading sun, the stone glowed the color of honey, shading into peach and rose gold as the sun went down. I imagined shops with wine and pastries and other good things to eat. This was a wealthy city. I wondered what would happen to me there.

"Is that where we're going?" I desperately hoped so.

"Yes."

"What is this place?"

"Mirefoix."

We shared an eagerness to finish the journey and get out of each other's company, so we made good time on the path downhill. My captor didn't head toward the main gate; we skirted around the city walls into the foothills. He stopped and searched behind a boulder and brought out two large candles. He used a fire striker to make sparks and lit two candles. He handed one to me.

"Keep this alight. If you let your candle go out, I'll wring your neck."

I didn't think he was serious. Still, I was careful. He parted branches to expose a weathered door. He unlocked this; it opened into a dark passage, possibly a narrow cave. I balked; I had had enough of enclosed spaces. He beckoned; I hesitated. I stumbled into the passageway, and my candle went out. He stuck his candle on a spike and barred the door behind us. The air smelled musty. He handed me my candle again and lit it from his.

"Take care of this, or you'll find yourself in the dark. Follow me."

Chapter 30

Christine

We reached the end of the underground passage and climbed steep spiral stone stairs. My kidnapper pushed aside a tapestry, and we entered a sumptuous chamber. Candles made the room warm and brilliant; a fresco on the domed ceiling depicted a starry blue sky. Heavy tapestries, rich with scarlet and blue, with scenes of gardens, animals, and courtship, made the space cozy. Thick rugs covered the floors, and a massive, curtained bed strewn with cushions occupied one side of the room. It was the first warm, bright, comfortable dwelling I had seen. I had the experience of déjà vu. Perhaps Christine d'Arque had been here before.

A woman sat near the hearth in a carved chair. Her gown was scarlet, embroidered in gold, and dotted with pearls. Her underdress had dark blue sleeves. She would have been beautiful but for her drawn face. I recognized her as the woman I saw lying near me on my first morning in this world. She beckoned to us. My captor kneeled before her and bowed his head.

"I did everything exactly as my Lady commanded."

Her face showed a flicker of displeasure as if his words annoyed her. Then she smiled.

"You have done well, Bon." She rested her hand on his cheek. He stiffened. She withdrew her hand and dismissed him with a curt gesture. I was self-conscious about my sodden cloak, bloodstained and shabby dress, and the mud on my face and hands.

"Come into the light so I can see you. Do you know who I am?"

"Only what this man has told me."

She squinted as she studied my face, then smiled.

"Your name is Christine."

"Yes."

"I am the Countess of Mirefoix. You will address me as 'my Lady'".

My teeth chattered; my garments were damp and drew warmth from my bones.

"Wash, dress, and eat, and then we will talk."

She resumed reading a book, perhaps a psalter. I was impressed. Books were costly, and I had seen none in the Baron's castle. I saw a wooden tub in the corner; lavender and rose petals floated in the water. There was even soap. I sank into it with pleasure; the warmth penetrated my bones, and the sweet herbs soothed my senses. It was a pleasure to put on fresh linens: a shift and bliaut that were my favorite shades of blue. She had provided soft leather shoes. My feet were too torn and swollen to put these on, so I set them aside. A maidservant combed my hair. The meal that awaited me included stewed venison and good-quality bread. After I finished, the Lady beckoned me to sit in a chair facing her before the fire.

"Come closer so that I may see you better."

She expressed concern about my condition; she rubbed my hands between hers to warm them and arranged a cloak around my shoulders. I relaxed. She gave me hippocras; I knew the hot spiced wine was a luxury.

"Bon cared well for you on the journey?"

"You sent him to fetch me?"

"You have nothing to fear. I will treat you well. You are safe. Tonight, you rest. Tomorrow, we will talk further."

She invited me into her bed. I was reluctant; I would have preferred to lie alone, but her invitation was a command. Her bed had thick layers of mattresses and coverlets, and it was clean. Of course, it was common for people to share sleeping space, whether on a floor or bed. I became aware of her abdominal pain as soon as I lay down. I had my own pain: soreness from time spent in the saddle and abrasions on my feet. It was not a restful night.

We rose at daybreak. She provided wine, bread, and fruit, perhaps realizing I was fatigued and hungry after the journey. She had promised we would talk. What followed seemed more like an interrogation, albeit in a gentle tone.

"Do you remember me and this place?"

"The room feels familiar, but I can't remember."

"Where were you before Bon found you?"

I told her about my time with the Baron's son; she did not appear interested.

"Before you came to Saverdun, what do you remember? Where did you come from?"

How would she know I *came* to Saverdun? Of course. She must have seen me on the hill where I first saw her. At that time, I thought she was a victim like myself. I realized now: she arranged to have me kidnapped and brought here...and probably also brought me to that hillside. Had she summoned the spirit that snatched my soul away from death? I had mostly silenced Christine's voice because her fear disturbed me. It told me I was Christine D'Arque. Arque must be a place, Christine's home. Associated feelings made it clear: Christine didn't want to return; neither did I. The Lady might or might not be familiar with Arque; I decided not to speak of it.

Her face seemed familiar. I did not have a clear image of my appearance; I had not seen myself in a good-quality mirror. I had only seen wavy reflections in the water. Perhaps I looked like her. She had welcomed me kindly, and I wanted to trust her. But Bon had said:

"It has all been done according to your command." Then it was by her command that I was poisoned and shrouded. Why would she have me kidnapped? What did she want with me? She repeated her question: From where did you come? I continued to hesitate. I still did not have enough information to create a convincing account. If I named places and people and she tried to verify them, my story would fall apart. If I spoke of Arque, she might send me back there. I didn't tell her my memory: resurrection or reincarnation, my soul seized by fiery angels, a twenty-first-century world. I said:

"I remember nothing, my Lady."

My words displeased her—a vertical frown line formed between her brows.

"Perhaps you will remember when you have had time to rest. I am the only person you can trust. When you remember, tell only me. Do not share your memories with anyone else. Did you tell Bon anything about yourself?"

"We spoke little, my Lady."

"If others ask who you are, you will say that you are my niece Christine d'Arque. You came here last summer and became a novice at the abbey; you didn't take perpetual vows, and you left the abbey to stay with me. Repeat this."

Her words disturbed me, but I repeated them.

"I have heard you have a gift for healing. Place your hands on my belly here." Perhaps she had spies at the court of the Baron. I kneeled before her chair and touched her stomach; I felt a throbbing ache in my abdominal region. I spoke to her using words of hypnotic induction, words that had helped my clients in the past.

"Slow your breath... empty your mind... relax your muscles. Imagine sinking into a calm lake of warm water."

The tension drained from her body. We remained in that position for some time, and her face became smooth.

"You have given me considerable relief. None of my physicians have done me half so much good. You will continue to attend me."

"Where does your pain come from, my Lady?"

She hesitated.

"Tell no one what I say. When I lie abed, demons appear. They accuse me of wrongs I have not committed and beckon me into the mouth of Hell. I see them even when I close my eyes. I hear them even if I cover my ears. They curse me with pain, and I can never rest."

It had been easy to comfort Jacotte and Gilbert. Their suffering had obvious causes; their needs were simple. Whether her demons were real or imaginary, the agony in her voice was genuine.

"Do others see these apparitions?"

"My maidservant said she saw and heard nothing when they were present. They are here now. Do you see them?"

"I don't. Will you describe these demons to me?"

"One that resembles a man shines in garments of blue sky and white clouds, and he has a proud face. He threatens me with his sword. The second is a woman who wears brown and green rags stained with blood, and she weeps. A third one is black and has bloody fangs, and he brings the flames of Hell with him.

The last has a gentle face. She shimmers in violet and blue, and there is a soothing softness about her. Sometimes they float above my bed."

Air, earth, fire, water? The last of the jinn she described sounded like the violet spirit that interrupted my death and transported me to this century. I never believed in magic before. And yet impossible things happened all the time here. Had the Lady commanded an apparition to seize my soul? She feared Hell and damnation; I didn't believe in Hell; I believed in a God of compassion and mercy. Could I persuade her to reject the idea of Hell? I thought not. Still, hypnosis might help her dissociate from fears.

"Lie down, and I will sit next to you. I will make the demons desist from attack." False confidence can sometimes overcome fear.

I talked to her in a low voice, repeating suggestions to focus attention only on my words. Within minutes, she fell into a sleep that seemed to be dreamless. As she slipped away, I saw and heard her demons myself. I fought them with my mind. I wanted to deny they were real, but I saw them. I did not sleep that night or later nights when she required me to banish her demons. As on previous occasions, I now experienced the terror and physical pain she had described. She responded well to hypnosis; in the modern world, only about one in ten showed such a strong response. Perhaps living in a less attention-grabbing world made it easier for people to focus their attention.

What would happen now? She had devised an elaborate plan to kidnap me. She valued my healing gift; she was not likely to release me after taking so much trouble to bring me here. Even if I escaped, where could I go as a woman alone?

For the first few weeks, she heaped praise and gifts upon me. I was like a cherished daughter, she said. She preferred my company to all others. I sat in a chair next to her bed at night, and my presence gave her peace. Being able to comfort and perhaps even heal made me feel powerful. But it was also tiring.

I explained that giving comfort left me exhausted and that time in the sun and open air helped me recover, and she permitted me to sit outside on the battlements where I could see over the city walls, always with Bon nearby as my guard. She said this was for my protection. Maybe she feared I might try to escape, but where would I go? She never allowed me to go beyond her chamber and the walkway atop the walls, so my curiosity about the city I saw below within the walls remained unsatisfied.

At night, I heard moaning that sounded like a woman's distress. The Lady told me it was the north wind.

As time passed, she showed less appreciation. She took what I gave for granted. She showed less affection and no respect. When she left, I spent long hours locked alone in her chamber with nothing to do. She ignored my requests to go outside into the light. She became like the husband who choked the life out of me in my past existence: grateful at first, then later arrogant and entitled. When he did that, it broke my heart. When she did this, it made me angry. Perhaps I was learning to resist those who would use me. I had spent my previous life and most of this life doing what others expected or what I believed they needed. At last, it occurred to me to ask: What do I want? And how do I get it? This was a new idea; I wanted freedom and someone to care about me, not use me. I yearned for a home, but I knew that was impossible in this world.

Chapter 31

Christine

The Lady found another use for me.

"There is someone else I need you to heal. This woman is a family member; her condition shames us."

"What is the matter with her?"

"She is mad. She eats and drinks little and lies as if asleep. I fear she will waste away and die."

"My Lady, I don't know if I can help her. I will try."

"That is all I require. We must keep this woman quiet, and you must also be quiet, do you understand? Her presence must remain secret."

She drew aside a tapestry. She unlocked and opened a small door disguised by a veneer of stones.

"Look and tell me what you need to heal her."

The room was narrow; a window high in the walls admitted little light. As my eyes adapted, I saw the outline of an emaciated woman with dirty brownish hair lying on a pallet in a corner. Someone had placed bread and wine on a bench within her reach; she had scarcely touched them. As I moved closer, she remained unresponsive. Her face had a lifeless look, and her arms and legs bore marks that looked like the self-cutting I had seen in adolescent clients.

"I need a large bowl of warm water, a comb, and bandages. A salve for cuts and abrasions. A brazier for some warmth. Fresh food, broth, and fruit. This poor woman needs to go outside for fresh air and sunshine."

"I will provide these things."

"What is her name?"

"She says she is called Blodeweth."

"What do you want me to do, my Lady?"

"Get her to eat and drink more. She takes only the minimum needed to survive. She must regain her health. I do not need her to speak nor want that, for she speaks nonsense. Believe nothing that she says. She may not leave this chamber, and you will remain with her and heal her."

Suddenly I realized: She will imprison me with this pathetic mad woman. Life in this dark cell would be worse than confinement to the Lady's chamber. I will go mad, too, I thought.

"But my Lady–"

She locked me in.

At first, I kept my distance from the woman and leaned my back against the door. Blodeweth made neither movement nor sound. There was a scuttling noise in the corner, and I saw a rat snuffling around, searching for crumbs. Another item for the Lady, I thought. The vermin must go. The Lady entered again, bearing the things I had requested.

"Be careful. She can be dangerous."

"I will need to have time away from her. When I heal, I lose energy; I need time and sunshine to replenish it."

"You will have it."

"And we must get rid of the mice!"

She locked me in again.

Now I lived in a real prison. I thought ironically of my former life. I made myself a comfortable home with walls of books and art, and it became a sort of prison, albeit a comfortable one. I hid in that safe place to avoid the pain of love that never turned out as I hoped; I persuaded myself I was better off alone. Now I was isolated in an actual prison with walls of stone. I wanted freedom, but I didn't know how to get it. Where would I go if I slipped out of the Lady's chamber door? How would I live?

I knew so little about this world. Women had only two options: marriage or a convent. Both were forms of slavery, to my way of thinking. The best situation I'd seen was among the older women in the Baron's kitchen. Their work was not oppressive; they had enough to eat, and men didn't bother them. They took up with men or not, as they chose. Perhaps this was the best circumstance possible for me in this world. Not a great situation, but preferable to my present one. I wondered if this world offered any other choices for women.

Not knowing what else to do, I tended to Blodeweth. I sponged her face, hands, and wounds and applied soothing salves. I combed her hair; it required a long time to loosen knots and tangles. I deloused her, crushing the insects in my fingers and tossing them in the brazier. She turned toward the light and warmth. She did not resist my ministrations.

After making her as comfortable as possible, I spoke to her, the soothing nonsense you say to calm a child. I stroked her hair and began hypnotic induction with instructions to relax and visualize beautiful places in nature. After an hour of kneeling on the stone floor with its inadequate padding of rush mats, I stood to stretch and sat in a puddle of pale-yellow sunlight on the floor. When I glanced back, Blodeweth had turned her head to look at me. I moistened her lips with wine, and she licked it off. She refused solid food and turned away from me again.

I thought the Lady had not listened to my requests. However, she left a cat with us the next day, which was a welcome addition. The cat terrorized the mice; they moved elsewhere. The cat curled up on Blodeweth's chest, and a weak smile appeared on her face. Over the next few days, I coaxed her to sit up and take a few mouthfuls of solid food, broth, and wine. Watching the cat frolic pleased us, and we teased her with wisps of rushes.

The door to the cell opened once a day. A maidservant removed the slop bucket and brought food and drink. I coaxed the woman to speak; she either could not or would not. Each day brought signs of progress. Blodeweth ate more, sat up, and took some interest in her surroundings. She relaxed when I combed her hair; I tended her damaged wrists and ankles. She fondled the cat.

Her need seemed legitimate, and I was willing to help. But I set limits. My experiences with Jacotte, Sassia, Gilbert, and the Lady suggested that the strongest healing came from a combination of voice and close contact. I reached out and smoothed her hair; she accepted this. I chose not to embrace her or lie beside her. I must limit my exposure to pain. I confronted the Lady.

"I must have time outside in the light, alone, or I can't heal."

The Lady permitted me to spend afternoons on a deserted stretch of the battlements outside her chamber with Bon standing watch. I pulled up my skirts and sleeves and turned my face toward the light. He turned his face away from my indecent exposure. Once or twice he spoke to me. I did not respond.

Nursing Blodeweth was not my only task. Sometimes when night came, the Lady roused me and brought me out of the locked room to sit by her bed to protect her from her demons and soothe the pain in her belly.

I spoke to Blodeweth as if she understood, telling her a little about myself. I asked questions sometimes. One day, she finally answered. We were sitting side by side, companionably eating.

"Blodeweth, what did you do before the Lady locked you up here?"

"She... brought me here. From a hill."

"What hill, Blodeweth?"

"I woke. I did not know the place. The Lady was there."

What?

"Before that, Blodeweth. Think back. Do you remember anything before that?"

She looked puzzled. "I died."

I was stunned.

"What happened when you died?"

"Fire killed me when soldiers burned my house. A spirit seized my hand and drew me into the sky."

"What did it look like?"

Blodeweth's description matched the Lady's account of the second female demon, brown and sad and stained with mud and blood. I had so many questions. I was struck by the similarity of our experiences. I asked further questions; she had also discovered that she understood their language, although everything in this world was strange to her.

Blodeweth told me that when the Lady first spoke to her, she called her "daughter." They fought; the Lady slashed her arm. As blood fell, it formed red stones. The Lady seemed to value these. The Lady came many times to take her blood. At first, she said, rage and determination to return home sustained her. As she lost blood, she lost strength and hope. The Lady had promised to release her the following summer if she cooperated and created more rubies. However, that season passed, and the Lady said she would not allow her to leave, and Blodeweth sank into despair again, defeated.

I told her I was also a stranger and had no hope of seeing my home again. We had a mutual understanding. Blodeweth told me of her forest home. I asked the Lady to bring tree branches to the chamber to console Blodeweth for the loss of her green forest home. Bon fetched these one night. As he spread branches and dried herbs around the room, he gave me a look that might have been an apology. I did not accept it.

The Lady did not draw blood during my first three weeks, but when Blodeweth's strength returned, the bloodletting resumed. When she and Bon came into Blodeweth's cell, they sent me to the Lady's outer chamber to wait. After I returned, I had to bandage fresh cuts. I thought of derogatory terms for Bon: Henchman, accomplice, and lackey. Maybe he had not, as I first thought, formulated the cruel and terrifying kidnapping plan. But he had carried it out.

I wanted freedom. Perhaps Blodeweth and I might escape together. We discussed possibilities. She was regaining her strength, although I was losing mine. We might overpower the maidservant when she brought food. Perhaps we would tie the Lady up with strips of cloth. Blodeweth wanted to kill her; I said no. We might pass through the city and walk out the gate. And then what? Blodeweth spoke of shape-shifting magic.

"Among my people, I was a woman priest. I could become an animal. As a bird or squirrel, I could get out. But I need things to do this. Amber. Oak."

I asked the Lady for these; we did not receive them.

Blodeweth said she would bleed to make rubies to pay for the supplies we would need. She pressed for a quick escape; she wanted to return home to forests far to the north. I thought her home might be somewhere else in time and beyond reach. I urged caution. I had only light soft-soled shoes, and Blodeweth had none. It was winter, and we would need cloaks. We would need provisions, a sack to carry them, and a knife. We would need food and shelter along the way, but that would require us to exchange rubies for small coins. Perhaps we might go to Saverdun. Maybe the Baron would shelter us in return for my services to his son. I would need to avoid his advances. We might purchase his favor with rubies. Of course, we would not tell him that Blodeweth's blood was the source. If he realized that, he might bleed her to death. Planning gave us hope.

Chapter 32

The Lady

January 1208

War threatened us, and we were ill-prepared. The Pope excommunicated Raymond, Count of Toulouse, because he violated church feast day truces, appointed Jewish public administrators, raided a monastery, and committed other offenses. However, the chief complaint against him was his failure to suppress the Cathar heretics. That worried me because I, and many other nobles in the region, also sheltered Cathars. They were good people, excellent weavers, and they caused no trouble.

The Pope appealed to King Philip Augustus in Paris to launch a holy war against the southern nobles and offered the same indulgences as for the fight against the infidels in the Outremer. This appeal was sent to other northern nobles and published in towns throughout the south as a warning. The Papal legate Pierre de Castlenau was assassinated after a quarrel with Count Raymond; the Count was accused of ordering the murder, although I thought it unlikely he would do anything so foolish.

I wanted, above all, to preserve the world my father had created and to keep Mirefoix peaceful and prosperous. The need for a strong heir was more urgent than ever. Mirefoix was all I had left, and I must defend it against the war that now seemed inevitable. That was my only reason to live.

Chapter 33

Garsenda

July 1208

My Lady mother had secrets. Had my father died by her orders, or even by her own hand? I thought the rumors of her secret marriage to Guillem might be true. She grieved for Alienor, yet the frequency and fervor of her prayers suggested that something even heavier burdened her soul.

Another thing puzzled me. After years of thrift, the Lady had spent considerable money purchasing land and flocks, repairing walls, and hiring soldiers. She even purchased new garments. I wondered where the Lady obtained so much silver. Did she have new sources of wealth? Father brought nothing of value with him when he returned from the east. I would learn nothing by questioning her. Perhaps I would discover the truth in her chamber. She always locked her door when she was out. I tried the handle several times, but it did not open.

I questioned a visiting jongleur, and after I plied him with wine, he told me he was also a pickpocket. I bargained with him: if he would steal the bunch of keys from Mother's girdle, I would allow him to touch me.

"As soon as you have the keys, bring them to me in the garden." He agreed. A short time later, he returned and presented me with them.

"I cannot dally with you now. She may discover that the keys are missing. You must go quickly, lest they suspect you." I frightened him enough that he left without holding me to my promise of physical intimacy. I might not have much time. I hurried to the Lady's chamber; the largest of the keys opened the outer door, and I closed it behind me, taking care to make no noise.

I noticed a coffer on the table near her bed; inside, I found several large red stones. I picked them up and turned them in the light. Could these be rubies? I hid one in my purse. Perhaps she would not miss just one. I continued to investigate the contents of the small chest. Below the stones, there were manuscript pages. I riffled through the wrinkled pages. Unfamiliar squiggles and figures that I supposed were some kinds of writing filled most of the pages; they made no sense. Then I found a page in Latin. I read this, and to my delight, I discovered it was a love spell. I knew how I would want to use it. I stuffed this scrap of parchment into my sleeve and replaced the box's contents. I had often spied on the Lady in her chamber when I was a child; I remembered there were doors behind the tapestries, a large door that led to stairs, and another smaller door to a secret cell. I opened the hidden room. I found two ill-clad women in this chamber and bloodstains on the floor. I entered; I closed the door only partway.

"Who are you? Why are you here?"

They gave me wary looks.

"I can help you. The Lady is no friend of mine. Aren't you my cousin Christine d'Arque?"

The smaller, paler woman hesitated, then answered.

"The Lady keeps us here. She does not permit us to go out."

"Why? Why is there blood on the floor?"

The taller woman answered. "She takes my blood and makes it into stones." I saw the scars on her arms. Could her blood be the source of the rubies? I imagined my Mother cutting her arms. She must be even crueler than I previously believed.

"How does blood turn into stone?"

"I don't know."

I thought I heard the door creak. I hesitated; I decided the sound was the wind rattling shutters. Did the rubies have something to do with the writings in the coffer? Of course, the Lady would keep this woman who bled rubies in captivity. But why the other woman?

"Why does she hold you?"

"I am a healer. I take away distress."

So that was how the Lady regained her health and composure.

"Are you willing to serve her in these ways?"

The pale woman spoke. "She bleeds the life out of us in different ways, and we want to leave."

I never liked my mother, and now I had proof that she was capable of even more evil than I had suspected.

"I'll help you escape, but planning will take time."

Then the door opened.

Chapter 34

The Lady

When I noticed my keys were missing, I summoned my seneschal to bring his extra set. I let myself into my chamber. The bulging tapestry before the door to Blodeweth's cell told me it was open. I drew close; I heard voices. Garsenda conversed with Blodeweth and Christine, and it seemed they were finding common cause.

"Cousin Christine, why are you confined here?"

"By day, I tend to Blodeweth. Sometimes I stay with the Lady by night."

Blodeweth said: "See these scars. The Lady cuts me, I bleed, and my blood forms stones she values. Rubies, she calls them."

"I see why this woman needs care, but what does the Lady ask of you?"

"She is tortured by demons and says my presence calms her."

"What demons?"

They spoke of being brought to Mirefoix by the jinn.

I was appalled. Now that Garsenda had learned my secrets, she would tell others. If Blodeweth and Christine went free, they would spread word of my misdeeds. I could not open the door until I summoned help; together, the three women might try to overpower me. I moved silently back into the stairwell and caught at my maidservant's sleeve. I sent her to summon Bon. He seemed to have developed sympathy for Christine, but his honor would force him to obey my orders.

My thoughts raced. I must separate these women, lest they tell each other more, devise a way to escape, and reveal my secrets. Circumstances forced me to do these things; I must deal with Garsenda first. When Bon arrived, I ordered him to bring Garsenda alone out of the cell and lock the door. I lost my temper with her.

"How dare you enter my chamber, search my possessions, and steal from me! I have a mind to marry you to Sir Dalmas, after all. He will beat you as you deserve."

That frightened even Garsenda.

"What do you think I have stolen? I have stolen nothing!" Then Garsenda challenged me.

"I saw the knife wounds. You killed my father or had him killed. You have used magic; I saw the spells. I know about the rubies. Now I know the source of the weeping through the wall of your chamber."

Had she also stolen some manuscripts, I wondered? I had not counted the pages. I turned and opened the coffer; the contents did not seem to have been disturbed. She had become a more daunting adversary than I realized. The conversation was becoming dangerous. Would she dare to blackmail me with threats of exposure? I told Garsenda:

"I will confine you to your chamber. I will arrange a proper marriage for you. Perhaps a strong husband can teach you obedience."

Checkmate.

She flew at me with her fists and then collapsed, sobbing.

"Don't do this. Whatever wrong I have done, it is not enough to justify such cruel punishment."

"Take my daughter to her chamber and lock her in." Bon appeared reluctant, but he obeyed. Garsenda's face showed heartbreak at Bon's betrayal; she cursed him and tried to shake off his grasp. However, he held her captive as I ordered. Only Constanzia and I would see her in the future. She would have no further opportunity to make accusations, spread suspicion, or scheme with Christine and Blodeweth. It was past the time to find a husband for her. I considered Baron Saverdun's proposal and set it aside; he was too clever, and his town was too close. Sir Dalmas would be easier to control. I would write and offer him Garsenda's hand and the future rule of Mirefoix. Next, I told Bon:

"Bring Christine to me."

He brought her out of the cell; he held her by one arm. She made no move to resist, and she looked too exhausted to struggle. I saw him give her a look of apology, entreaty, and concern. She seemed not to notice.

The one hold I had on Bon was his concern with honor. And yet, I feared that his growing attachment to Christine might make him want to protect her. I had an idea: if Christine were to take vows as a nun, he would do nothing to dishonor her vow. At least so far, she had been meek and had not dared to disobey my orders. In addition, Sister Cecilia was growing old, and it would be helpful to have Christine learn her knowledge of herbs before she was gone. Even if Christine told Sister Cecilia about my actions, I did not think the sister would break her vows and repeat stories about me. I announced my decision.

"Escort her to the abbey. She will take vows for the novitiate." I was stronger now; I needed Christine less often, and it would be possible to summon her from the nunnery at night if I wanted her. Bon appeared dismayed. She protested.

"My Lady, I do not wish to become a nun."

Her opposition surprised me. I thought her too timid to protest.

"You will be subject to the rules of obedience and silence. You will rest and regain your strength. I will send for you when I need you."

"I don't want to."

"Why? It's a safe and quiet life, and you will have the rest you need."

I ordered her to renew her vow of silence by swearing on my most sacred relic. She seemed to find the sight of the withered finger repulsive.

"Repeat after me. By this relic of Saint Nazarius, I swear I will keep secret all that I have seen and heard in this place. In all things, I will be obedient to you, my Lady."

She repeated the words with little conviction in her voice. I gave her further orders.

"You will tell the abbess and the sisters that you are my niece, and that you have chosen to make vows of your own free will. I will instruct the abbess to give you rest. Your health concerns me."

I wrote a letter of instructions to the abbess. Bon's face was sullen, but he didn't protest; he took my letter and escorted Christine to the abbey.

Blodeweth would be alone from now on.

Chapter 35

Christine

Bon escorted me to the abbey by moonlight on that sultry July night. We walked in silence at first.

"This place will be safe for you."

Safe, my ass, I thought. A convent is just another prison; I was sick of prisons. We continued to walk in deepening darkness. It was humid and so still that trees did not whisper. Bon led me outside the gates of the city along a well-trodden path. We stopped at a ponderous door bound with iron bands and studded with nails. He paused outside the door.

"Please, do not make perpetual vows." What business was that of his? His words made me want to take the vows just to spite him. He knocked. He kept a grip on my elbow, perhaps expecting me to run. My arm tingled from this contact. The feeling was strangely pleasant. It was absurd to feel drawn to him after all he had done to me. I would not allow myself to have feelings for him. I would be a fool to imagine that he cared about me. When a sister opened the door, Bon bowed, handed her the letter, and said,

"By my Lady's command, take her to Mother Veronica." He turned to look at me as he departed. A sister led me through a stone hall; we passed through the cloister, where stone arcades surrounded neatly trimmed gardens of pungent herbs and sweet-scented roses. We continued into a small chamber, where I kneeled before the abbess. The abbess read the letter, tapped her finger against it, and gazed at me. I must have been a bedraggled figure.

"Tonight, you rest. Tomorrow your instruction begins. The Lady commands you to learn prayers and healing arts."

It annoyed me that Bon ordered me not to take vows. What right did he have? When the abbess prompted me, I repeated the vows that bound me to the order for one year. Perhaps I did this to rebel against his wishes. The vow provided a short-term solution to the problem of my place in this world. Maybe other possibilities would arise.

Thus began my life as a nun and another experience of captivity. They clothed me in the black and white robes of a Cistercian novice. I learned the abbey routine. They prayed at Matins, Lauds, Prime, Terce, Sext, Nones, Vespers, and Compline. Prayers interrupted sleep. The midday meal was after Sext; it was watery pottage. The Rule forbade speech except during prayer. At the refectory table, we used gestures to request a spoon or a napkin. During meals, a reader droned through holy texts in Latin. I suspected no one else understood them either. Perhaps the words were supposed to have divine influence even if we didn't understand their meaning.

I stumbled through the prayers at all the canonical hours, moving my lips without speaking the words. I wondered if my new sisters understood Latin enough to know what these said or whether they merely repeated sounds.

It was a small community of sixteen nuns and twenty lay sisters. I learned their jobs: treasurer, cellarer, almoner, and infirmarian, among others. Some nuns did skilled work: they nursed the sick, copied manuscripts, embroidered vestments, and did other fine sewing. Lay sisters did menial tasks: washing, cooking, and gardening.

On the third day, I was introduced to Father Felip in the chapel after Terce. Sunlight streamed through high round-arched windows. The light through stained glass made brilliant pools of blue, red, and golden yellow on the paved floor. Biblical scenes covered the walls and barrel-vaulted ceilings. I had never appreciated the visual arts of the Middle Ages; they seemed primitive to me. Now I saw them with fresh eyes; they filled the chapel with colorful beauty and told stories people could not read in books.

Father Felip differed from the priest I met at Saverdun. There was nothing lecherous in his smile, and I trusted his kindness. He taught me the prayers I needed to know, line by line. He praised me, pleased by how quickly I learned. A Latin course I took in the past made it possible for me to comprehend words here and there, and I think I also drew on some of Christine's memories. I wanted to know more. I dared to ask:

"What do the words mean?"

He was taken aback. Then he laughed.

"No one has ever asked me that. Even some among our priests only mimic the words."

I wanted more than the words of common prayers, and he agreed to share some of their few manuscripts with me. I was most struck by the writings of Hildegard of Bingen:

... the earth is mother of all that is natural, mother of all that is human. She is the mother of all, for contained in her are the seeds of all.

... We cannot live in a world that is not our own, in a world that is interpreted for us by others. An interpreted world is not a home. Part of the terror is to take back our own listening, use our own voice, and see our own light.

... Every creature is a glittering, glistening mirror of Divinity.

... Just as a mirror, which reflects all things, is set in its own container, so too the rational soul is placed in the fragile container of the body. In this way, the body is governed in its earthly life by the soul, and the soul contemplates heavenly things through faith

.... The earth should not be injured. The earth should not be destroyed. As often as the elements of the world are violated by ill-treatment, God will cleanse them through the sufferings and the hardships of mankind.

The Church let Abbess Hildegard say these things? Her ideas seemed so modern. The language moved me, and I asked for and received permission to copy her words. I was struck by the modernity of her thinking. With ample time on my hands, I mused about what I believed. The image of Christ on a crucifix crowned with thorns troubled me. I couldn't believe a loving God would require such suffering. I didn't believe people needed to buy God's forgiveness; I believed in a compassionate God who wanted people to love each other. These beliefs were not unique to Christianity.

How strange to be in a world where people killed each other about differences in belief. Of course, people killed each other in the world I left behind, only for different reasons. I believed in many paths to God. The Catholic way seemed to me unnecessarily focused on fear and sin. Their deference to priests was alien to me and hard to understand, particularly because some clerics were greedy and lustful.

My thoughts made me a heretic in this world. I had dangerous ideas that I must not speak aloud. I didn't allow people to tell me what to believe. I formed the habit of censoring my words; my beliefs would not place me in danger as long as I kept them to myself. It made me lonely to know that no one in this world thought as I did, lonelier beyond imagining. Intimacy comes from shared memories, and I could never share myself with anyone in this world.

The saving grace in this new life was work with the aging infirmarian Sister Cecilia. We had a dispensation to speak; she explained the names and uses of herbs. I gathered plants with her and learned about her stock of medicines. The worn book she used as a reference became my textbook, and she gave me writing materials to make my own notes. Of course, the book was in Latin. By self-hypnotizing, I recovered Christine d'Arque's knowledge of Latin, similar to their lenga romana. I had studied Latin myself a long time ago. My lessons with Father Felip helped me recover what I had once known. I was not fluent, but I managed.

I learned the underlying principle they relied on: the doctrine of signatures. Plants that resembled a bodily organ in appearance or shape were supposed to help them; for instance, the spotted leaves of lungwort should treat lung diseases. I didn't believe all this, but I was curious whether any of these plants had genuine benefits. It also occurred to me that plants' effects might have been different or more potent in the past before modern farming and industry altered the soil and atmosphere. I welcomed the chance to learn. It kept my mind occupied.

I made sketches of healing plants and notes about their uses and dosages. They had unfamiliar names, such as Infant Jesus Shoes, Mary's Crown, Our Lady's Tears, and Mary's Sword; it was challenging to keep these straight. Sister Cecilia taught me to make powders, tinctures, and poultices. I tended gardens in a walled area outside the cloister and assisted Sister Cecilia in caring for the ill. Some remedies seemed helpful, and others not. This activity was the one thing that kept me from going mad with boredom. Sister Cecilia spoke of nothing except plants and asked no questions about my past. She was deaf and took no interest in anything I said. It was a relief not to have to lie to explain myself. Even with the restrictions of the Holy Rule, this life had more freedom than I had experienced so far.

Chapter 36

Christine

August 1208

Two weeks later, the Lady summoned me again for comfort at night. Bon escorted me to her chamber; I sat by her bed as before. I heard Blodeweth weeping in the adjacent cell; the Lady did not allow me to see her. My body's response told me that the Lady's physical pains had returned. Visions of Hell still tortured her.

Bon tried to talk with me when he escorted me back to the abbey. After pleasantries about the day's weather, conversation lagged. Sometimes he brought a flower or a pastry. Perhaps these offerings were meant as apologies, but they also made me wonder: Is he wooing me? I was drawn to him, but fear and distrust overcame my desire. I had no one to talk with; I longed for intimacy and to be known for who I was. After what he had done, it could not be with him. One night as we passed through town, he took my hand and pulled me into an alley. He went down on one knee and inclined his head. I saw his profile bright in silver moonlight and thought again how handsome he was.

"My Lady. Pardon me. I have done you great wrongs. Please allow me to make amends."

Amends, my foot. I let loose with a torrent of abuse that shocked him. I had picked up a few juicy phrases from the blacksmith at Saverdun. Frank language about intimate body functions did not bother people. What offended was taking the name of God in vain; a reference to God's blood or God's body was thought to be a wish to harm God. I swore on God's bones that he should roast in Hell forever.

He bowed his head still further. His face reddened. Was this a sign of anger or shame?

"It was not my wish that you be distressed or harmed."

"You were just following her orders. What caused this sudden change of heart?" That was the first time in either of my lives that I would say: I sneered.

"I see how you healed the madwoman and soothed the Lady. Your kindness has touched my heart, and I wish to make amends for the wrong I have done. Tell me if there is a service I can render."

"Take me back to Saverdun." Even as I said the words, I realized I didn't want that. The Baron was a threat.

"That I cannot do."

Was there anything I wanted that might be possible? I pondered this.

"Release Blodeweth?"

"Lady, you know I cannot do that."

"I am not a Lady, Sir."

"And I am not a knight. But I would be your man and serve you."

He looked up at me, still on one knee, and took my hand. He turned it over and kissed the palm of my hand. I shivered. The intimacy of this gesture was devastating. It's a good thing most men don't know how easy it is to captivate a woman, I thought. I withdrew my hand. I thought: He's heard too many troubadour cansos. I must not let him touch my heart.

The tender reverence of his manner disarmed me. I had put aside desire long ago, and now it had returned. This terrified me. After what had happened, I didn't want to feel anything for him. And yet, longing warred with bitterness in my heart. I yearned for something he could not possibly give me, a kind of love I longed for in my prior life and never found.

Abruptly I pulled myself together. My wishes were folly, even madness. Intimacy had created problems I had never solved in my past life. I reminded myself that a relationship here would lead to even greater difficulties. The blood I had seen on this man's hands disgusted me. If I cared about him, I would want to relieve his suffering; he might incur terrible injuries as a soldier. That pain would be worse than any I had felt so far. Relieving distress was killing me even when I faced smaller amounts of pain. I must not care for him; it would place me in more danger.

He waited for me to ask for something.

I thought about other possibilities.

"I had a friend at Saverdun, a girl named Jacotte, who worked in the laundry. Could you bring her here? Without terrifying her, the way you terrorized me?"

"Yes, Lady. That I swear to do."

I hoped this would help Jacotte. Work in the laundry at Saverdun was hard. Perhaps here at Mirefoix, she would have easier work and become plump from eating pastries. Despite the rule of silence, I might talk with her over the garden wall.

"She must have a safe place in the kitchens."

"I will make it so. How will I recognize her?"

I described her and the location of the laundry. "The smallest finger is missing from her right hand. She'll need to know you come from me."

"I will take a lock of your hair. She will recognize it."

With a flick of his knife, close enough to my cheek to startle me, he cut a strand of my hair.

I said again: "Do not frighten her. And if you can find my dog, Sassia, a fawn-colored greyhound with a healed wound on her left flank, please bring her as well. Jacotte can point her out."

"Lady, I will try."

We will see, I thought. I don't believe I can trust you any more than the Lady.

I could have escaped the abbey. The garden wall was not high, and they frequently left me unsupervised. The absent-minded abbess left me unsupervised. Probably she and the Lady assumed I was fearful of the outside world and would never try to escape. Sadly, they were not wrong about that. Why didn't I try to leave? Fear of life beyond the walls exceeded my desire for freedom. I wouldn't know how to survive outside the walls.

Perhaps this was karma. In my prior life, I made my own symbolic prison. Here, I found myself in an actual prison. Maybe this life challenged me to learn to fight for freedom. If so, I was failing to meet the challenge. Captivity seemed safe. It was hard to resist the soothing illusion of safety.

When you live hemmed in by fear, it takes all your energy to fight your inner demons; you have nothing left to meet the world's challenges, and it is exhausting.

One afternoon a pebble struck the ground near me while I was working in the garden. I turned and saw Jacotte peering through a gap in the wall. I kneeled beside the wall pretending to pull weeds. I warned her to speak quietly; she was full of news. Bon had found her a position in the kitchen. "Oh, the meat pies! The bread, the stews! Things like that! I eat all day long." We touched each other's faces. We laughed. I told her the hours of the day when I worked in the garden; she said she would try to visit again. I was sorry to hear Sassia had disappeared. Bon watched from the shelter of a nearby thicket until Jacotte left.

Three days later, when I was alone pretending to weed plants near the damaged side of the wall, he appeared. He vaulted over the wall, showing off, I think, and bowed to me. I was on my knees in the dirt and did not look my best. He led me to a shaded corner behind trees where any sisters who might come into the garden would not see us.

"My Lady."

"Thank you for bringing Jacotte. Her conversation and affection bring me great pleasure."

"I will serve you as well as I am able. I'm sorry I didn't find your dog. People said she ran away after you left Saverdun."

It seemed he wanted to play the game of courtly love. I was amused, annoyed, and touched, all at the same time. I supposed there were worse things than this artificial reverence. I still did not believe he was trustworthy. When imprisoned with Blodeweth, I had refused to speak to him. Now I had questions.

"Was it your idea to poison me and wrap me in a shroud?"

"I followed my Lady's specific orders."

"Do you do everything she commands?"

He hesitated.

"A man of honor must remain obedient to his vows of loyalty. She ordered me to do things that damaged my honor. Her orders often troubled me. I am most sorry."

I was disappointed. What I took for courtship was only an apology.

"Was it honorable to drag me here to be imprisoned? Because of you, I may never be free! You called me your Lady, and that is a mockery." It was uncharacteristic of me to show an outburst of anger; I had always hidden it.

His jaw tightened. I was not sorry for my words. Perhaps I should have displayed anger frequently in my earlier life. People might have exploited me less. I didn't show anger then. Was now the right time to assert myself?

"You ask me to make a choice—you do not know what is at stake—"

I let him stew. I had nothing more to say after I picked at this sore wound. I rose and left. I realized I was lonely and bored to the point of desperation. Even though he annoyed me, his visits were a welcome source of diversion.

Jacotte was my other link to the outside world. She was an excellent informant. "Bon was kind when he brought me here. Did you know he is a bastard? His mother came from far beyond the Outremer. Some say the Count is his father. Others say there is no resemblance. Beyond that, no one knows much about him. He always wins when men compete with bow and sword. They say the Lady asks his advice and that he knows languages, too. He does not talk with others much. He is a man of great skill, honor, and courtesy. Indeed, he is a man of paratge. The men respect him. Oh, the food here is so good! Pies and pastries and roasted meats, and we get leftovers from the table! Do you like my new dress? Faure helped me sew it. You look tired, the circles under your eyes, you are so thin!"

As usual, her chatter gave me no chance to ask questions, nor did I need to. Jacotte's positive reports about Bon influenced me more than they should. I began to think he was courteous and well-favored. That set off internal alarm bells again. I never paid attention to attractive men in my former life. In my experience, these men had an exaggerated sense of entitlement, behaved like spoiled brats, and were quick to discard women when someone prettier and more compliant appeared.

Nevertheless, against the weight of my doubts, I began to feel that he was a man of gentle manners who might care about me. In the past I had similar powerful attractions to men who never loved me in return and who turned out not to be the men I believed them to be, so I knew this emotion did not lead to happy outcomes. I must not form intimate attachments in this world. If I dared to love, I would want to take that person's pain away regardless of the cost to myself.

Despite my concerns, I was pleased when he appeared in the garden. After awkward pleasantries, one day, he asked: "What are you thinking?" That struck me as an oddly modern question. Under different circumstances, I might have enjoyed that kind of conversation.

"I wish for open spaces and fresh air. The dark walls are oppressive; there is nothing to do here."

"If you were free, where would you want to go?" He was a step ahead of me. I had not thought of escape. What would I do outside these walls? The only plan that occurred to me was to return to Saverdun. I had more freedom there; however, there were dangers.

"I don't know. I hadn't thought that far ahead."

This place was driving me crazy. Perhaps it was time I found the courage to escape from imprisonment, both from my fears and this physical captivity.

"I'm surprised you do not speak of your family at Arque."

I rarely thought of the real Christine's memories. However, the mention of Arque aroused a sense of fear and loathing. What had happened to Christine there? I didn't remember. It must have been distressing.

Chapter 37

Bon

September 1208

I knew I must do something about Garsenda's situation. She would wither in confinement. This conflict of wills wouldn't end well; I feared the Lady would crush her spirit. For all her defiance, even Garsenda must have a breaking point. Could I set her free? She would have to flee from Mirefoix. If my part in her escape were known, it would cost me everything: My position as commander of the guard, my future prospects, and my honor. Despite this, I thought of plans. Fabrice might help. But the cost to him would also be high.

I stopped at the forge one morning to speak with him. A lovely young woman was there; she offered him a pie she had made and tried to arouse his interest. He was polite but dismissive. After she left, I asked:

"Why do you turn her away? She is comely, and her father's trade is lucrative."

He laughed. "Yes, the daughters of the town think I'm a good catch. The forge brings in good money, and I spend little."

"Don't you want a wife and children?"

He sighed and put down his hammer.

"It's a foolish thing, I know, but my heart has long been elsewhere."

It occurred to me that he had always been fond of Garsenda. Could his hopes lie in that direction?

"Is it scarlet hair that you dream of?"

"You have guessed it. I can never marry feeling as I do."

"What would you be willing to do to help?"

"What trouble does she have?"

I explained that the Lady had locked her alone in her chamber and spoke of forced marriage.

"The devil, you say!" I had never seen such fury in his face.

"I want to get her out, but I can't do it alone."

We spoke of possibilities.

I slipped vellum, quill, and a small bottle of ink underneath Garsenda's chamber door with a note that said I would look for her message at Vespers. The next time I passed her door, I saw the corner of a letter under it; I hid it in my sleeve and read it later.

"I must pretend to obey the Lady's command to marry Sir Dalmas a week from tomorrow on the front steps of the cathedral. Once I am outside, can you get me away?"

I discussed this with Fabrice.

"The Lady plans to force Garsenda to marry Sir Dalmas, and I fear he will take her to his mountain stronghold and beat her into submission."

"By God's blood! That shall not be."

"We will have to take her far away, a distance great enough to avoid the Lady's spies."

Fabrice thought out loud. "We can go to Beziers. I have relatives there."

"You could never return. You would sacrifice all you have here."

"I am willing. But it would be a simple life for her, and she would lose her accustomed comforts."

As we made plans for Garsenda, I thought of Christine. At times she spoke wistfully of a desire for freedom. But she seemed comfortable among the nuns. Her cheeks had become rosy from time outdoors, tending gardens and gathering herbs. She even laughed sometimes. Now that the Lady's demands were less frequent, she seemed in better health. I feared she might see the abbey as her home and even take permanent vows.

I had nothing to offer her. I would lose her if she took permanent vows as a nun. If she were with Fabrice and Garsenda, she would be free, and perhaps I would see her again. Why couldn't I forget her? I had no room in my life for a woman and no way to take care of her. I remembered the days when I watched over her as she lay in the sunshine on the battlements. She often slowed her breathing as if she were meditating. As if, like me, she had knowledge that did not belong here.

Like me, she was an outsider. Perhaps another outsider might understand me.

Fabrice and I discussed plans to take Garsenda and Christine out of the Lady's control and away to freedom.

Chapter 38

Corvinus

October 1208

By eavesdropping and inference, I concluded the Lady had summoned Christine and Blodeweth with the same magic she used on me. Yet how different we were. Christine was good, and I was drawn to her compassion. I saw something others seemed not to notice, that giving relief to others drained her strength. I spied upon her often. Just the sight of her comforted me.

I noticed that she only moved her lips when the nuns prayed. Perhaps, like me, she did not believe in their kind of God.

These people's ideas about the Gods amused me. Blodeweth was a pagan who believed in a great blood-thirsty Goddess. People here prayed to one God to absolve them of their sins and relied on priests to excuse their guilt. Their prayers did not seem to work for them.

We Romans had a far more sensible view of the Gods. We knew there were many gods, the minor gods who ruled crossroads and homes and the powerful Gods who ruled the heavens. I had no notion of 'sin' in my former life. There were only actions that yielded good results and actions that did not. When I needed something, I made offerings to Jupiter. If he did not do as I asked, I made offerings to Venus. Then to Apollo. I always found a god to grant my request. We Romans welcomed the gods and goddesses of captured lands, Mithras, Isis, and many others. The stiff-necked Christians and Jews insisted that there was only one God, their God. At first, we said, yes, you may build temples for your Christian God. But they refused to worship Caesar as a god, so the authorities put them to death.

When these Christians prayed, they did not receive the comfort and miracles they requested. Why did they continue to pray? Why not look elsewhere? I did not understand these people. I had learned that my Rome fell from power long ago. Perhaps Romans stopped praying to the most powerful Gods. Now, when I prayed to Jupiter and then turned to Venus and Apollo, they no longer seemed to hear me. Could those Gods be dead? Even when I prayed, I suspected that the only real sources of power were brute force, money, and deception.

I saw a different power in Christine, something I yearned to experience. Where did that come from? I wondered. She did not speak of the Christian God. The Church sometimes burned those with ideas different from theirs. Once, we burned Christians; now, Christians burned others. In some ways, the world does not change.

Perhaps Christine was the one who would give me the peace and genuine love I have never had. I saw Bon's visits to her and how he looked at her. Over time I saw her face soften. Perhaps her heart opened to him. This aroused my jealousy.

The Lady had promised me a man's body, but then she delayed, saying she needed to know more about the magic. I suspected she had no intention of keeping her promise. If she didn't, I would have to find another way. I must have a man's body, and I wanted Bon's. If Christine already loved him, perhaps she would love me when I assumed his likeness.

Chapter 39

Garsenda

When the appointed day for marriage arrived, my mother and her soldiers came for me at the hour of Nones. They escorted me to the steps of the cathedral, one man grasping each elbow. The bridegroom waited. Sir Dalmas was bulky with muscle; his cheeks were coarse and stubbled. The set of his jaw showed belligerence. His low forehead bespoke a lack of wits. Mother tried to place my hand in his, and I snatched it away.

A curious crowd had gathered in the square near the cathedral. We stood on the portico in front, as was customary. Was rescue possible? I searched the crowd; I did not see Bon. Suddenly fear overcame me. Then I saw Fabrice, the blacksmith, who had been so kind to us when we were young; he was near the front. When our eyes met, he nodded. Mother signaled with a gesture that it was time to begin. Fabrice stepped forward from the crowd and shouted:

"I, Fabrice, marry you, Garsenda!"

If I said yes, this would be a binding vow. I never thought to wed a commoner, but I would do anything to spite Sir Dalmas and my Lady mother.

Clearly, in a voice that carried to the crowd, I said:

"And I, Garsenda, marry you, Fabrice."

My noble bridegroom's face reddened, and my mother's face whitened. I slipped out of the grasp of their hands and ran to Fabrice. The crowd milled in confusion and, at first, prevented my mother and bridegroom from following us. I heard her call for pursuit.

Fabrice kept a tight hold on my hand; we darted down one alley, then another. Despite all the years I had spent exploring the city, I was not well acquainted with this maze of streets, but Fabrice knew every byway.

One soldier was already at our heels, wielding a sword. Fabrice turned and heaved a barrel at him; it felled the man and blocked others who pursued us through the narrow passages.

We emerged into the open courtyard at the Narbonne gate. The alarm had not spread that far, and no one stopped us. Bon was waiting outside the gate with mounts. I was glad my Falconette was not among them; this was dangerous; I wouldn't want her to be hurt. It surprised me to see another woman there, Christine, now dressed as a nun. Fabrice and I mounted quickly. At first, I assumed the third horse was for Bon. But Bon set Christine on the third horse, slapped its rump, and ran back through the city gate. I protested: He must come with us! However, Fabrice urged our horses to gallop and I was swept away.

It soon became apparent Christine couldn't ride. She hunched low over the saddle and grasped her mount's mane and neck. She had no control over her horse. The palfrey sensed her anxiety; that made matters worse. As we crested the first hill, we looked back; smoke rose above the city walls. Fabrice explained. "Bon will set fires in the stables as a diversion; the men will be too busy fighting the fire and rescuing horses to follow."

So that was why Bon remained behind. Good, I thought. He will join us soon. Then I thought: The Lady has promised him advancement, even that he might be her heir. He is a fool to believe her promises. But perhaps he still hopes. I am now out of the way as heir. Could that have been his real motive for arranging this escape? This idea pierced my heart. We stopped for a moment. Fabrice addressed the nun:

"Christine, are you all right?"

"Go ahead; I'll keep up."

Halfway to Pamiers, we mounted fresh horses. Christine nearly fell when Fabrice placed her in the saddle. We left the main road and headed east along a path evidently familiar to Fabrice. The ground was smooth enough to trot; there was no sign of pursuit. Bon's plan to create confusion must have worked. We had not gone far before we saw a party of mounted men atop a hill; they carried the yellow and green banners of Saverdun. It appeared they had noticed the smoke rising from Mirefoix and chose this vantage point to assess the situation. Now they saw us. My hood had fallen back, and they may have recognized my scarlet hair. The horsemen wheeled and pursued us. As we turned, Christine fell from her palfrey.

"Go! Go without me!"

Fabrice seized the reins of my horse and fled with me in tow. I looked back again when we reached the next hilltop. The men gathered around Christine; one of them hoisted her into his saddle. Two of them rode off toward Saverdun, taking Christine. The rest made haste to follow us.

"Come. We can't do anything for her now. I swore to get you to safety, and I intend to do that." We hastened up the hillside and into the forest. When we stopped, Fabrice freed the horses, and they ran. He took my hand and helped me clamber up a rocky cliff face. He pulled branches and rocks away to reveal the entrance of a cave. We crawled on our hands and knees to enter. Fabrice swept the earth near the opening with twigs to erase the traces made by our feet. Then he covered the mouth of the cave behind us.

We crawled through a dark tunnel; I followed Fabrice. The air was musty. We reached a hollow cave with enough room to stand. Fabrice lit a lantern and led me further, carefully choosing the path. We entered a cavern as large as a room. There was a small pool, and a gap in the ceiling above permitted light to enter. He must have prepared ahead of time; I saw bedcoverings, food, candles, and wood for a fire.

Fabrice brought out a flagon of wine and offered me bread and cheese.

"The Baron's men won't find us here. We have everything we need. We'll wait until they have given up the chase, then make our way on foot to another town where fresh mounts are ready for us. I used to play here as a boy."

I was wary.

"Do you expect a husband's rights?"

"No, my Lady. I am far beneath you. We are married in name only. With so little time to consider, it was the best plan we could devise. I am your servant and protector, nothing more."

He gazed at me. His eyes became darker, his expression softened, and his skin turned pink. That look tells a woman she is desired. He did not expect a husband's rights, but he wanted them.

"Where will we go?"

"I have family in Beziers. We will go there, and I will work to earn our keep. It is so distant that your Lady mother cannot find us. My family's home is humble, but we will provide shelter for you with as much comfort as possible."

"What of Bon? Will he join us there?"

"That is not the plan."

My heart fell. This was proof Bon did not love me. Perhaps this was a way for him to get rid of me so that he might rule Mirefoix himself. I was betrayed and more deeply hurt than ever. No one in this world loved me.

I must make the best of this.

"I thank you from my heart. You are a courageous man, though not of noble blood."

I was past the age when most women marry. Based on my flirtation with jongleurs and observation of farm animals, I had some idea of what the marriage bed involved. Was I never to know? I kneeled beside

Fabrice where he slept; I placed my hand on his cheek. His eyes flew open. I bent over and kissed his mouth.

He rolled away and sat up. He contracted his brows; his cheeks reddened. He drew back.

"My Lady?"

"You are my husband, and I want you to behave as such."

"Are you certain?"

"I am. Don't you want me?"

He threw his arms around me, and we lay together in the tangle of blankets.

"I am yours to command."

He was gentle but clumsy. His touch did not please me, but I exulted in my power to cause him joy. In the morning, I was not sorry. I had never been the most beloved. I gave this man great happiness, and he worshipped me for that; that gave me joy.

This was not what I wanted, but it was better than the nothing I got from Bon.

Chapter 40

Christine

When I fell from my horse, the Baron's men surrounded me. It was clear I was trapped. The Baron recognized me and smiled. It was not a reassuring smile. It was the look of a lion about to devour his prey.

"My lost servant. I thought you were dead. How is it you are alive? Whatever the situation, I am pleased to find you again." He proffered his hand. I was loath to take it. I remembered when he cornered me with lustful intentions, and I had no wish to repeat that experience. I twisted my knee when I fell; he kneeled on the ground in seeming concern and examined my leg.

"I don't think you have broken any bones."

I thought of my former position as a nurse.

"How is Gilbert? I hope he understood I did not leave him of my own free will?"

"He no longer needs you. Now you will serve my needs."

I disliked service to the Lady; this would be worse. My distaste made me feel sick to my stomach. I despised this man as much as I feared him, and I would never forgive him for the way he hurt Sassia. I saw no chance of escape and no sign of rescue. He lifted me into his saddle and set off toward Saverdun.

After Mirefoix, his castle, and the surrounding town looked small, shabby, and none too clean.

"I will come to you later," the Baron said. He turned me over to his servants. I kept my dark wool cloak gathered tight around me as if it offered protection.

A woman led me up steep stairs to a familiar hallway. She locked me in a small chamber near the one I had shared with Gilbert. I surveyed my surroundings: a rickety bed, a little table, and an iron-barred window set high in the walls that admitted a little light. I tried to remember what the outside looked like. The smooth stones would offer few toeholds, and it was a long way down. Even if I were skilled at climbing and not afraid, escape would be impossible. Once again, I was trapped.

After sundown, servants brought wine, stewed salted cod, bread, cheeses, and pastries. I was hungry. I wanted to rebel by refusing the food, but the sight and smell tempted me, and I ate. I rationalized that eating would keep up my strength. It was heartier fare than the abbey provided. My life in this world had been a succession of prison cells; I was sick of captivity. Throwing myself out the window began to seem preferable.

The Baron entered. The room was chilly, and I still wore my heavy cloak. He walked behind me and slipped the cape off my shoulders. Then he recoiled in shock: he saw that I wore the white and black habit of a Cistercian novice. Apparently, he would not violate a nun. He paced the room, then smashed his goblet against the wall; wine trickled down like blood from a wound.

He stopped and stared at me.

"How long are you vowed to God?"

The end of the year I had vowed as a novice was one week before the feast day of Saint Mary Magdalene the following July; I lied and said my vow was until next September, the latest date I thought might be plausible.

"I'll keep you here, and I'll wait."

He left, slamming the door behind him; the key turned in the lock. I paced the room. I had nothing to do with my mind or hands. There was still food on the table; I wondered if servants would replenish this. I had nothing except my thoughts. The room had no fireplace. It was frigid, and it would become even colder at night. For warmth, I had only one ragged bed covering and my cloak. I drank the wine, hoping it would bring warmth to my veins. As the sun sank, the cell became dark. I would have given much for a single candle. The dusty stone had an unpleasant earthy odor with a hint of sulfur. I closed my eyes but still smelled and sensed the walls that enclosed me. I shivered; my bones turned to ice; my breath formed cold clouds.

Servants came morning and evening to bring food and drink and remove the slop bucket. I requested more bed covers and candles, but they ignored these requests. I forced myself to walk back and forth so my muscles would not atrophy. The effort gave me some warmth. I remembered that distraction helps with pain, so as I walked, I remembered lyrics from songs of my youth and scenes from my life. I recalled Bon's strange look of concern as he hoisted me onto the horse's back. What had he felt about that parting? This was my life from now on, an unchosen solitude, lonelier than any previous experience.

Chapter 41

Corvinus

January 1209

I was away from Mirefoix when Garsenda escaped from her wedding. That matter did not concern me. But then I discovered Christine was also gone. My soul was black, but I longed to possess her goodness. And I was becoming impatient about the Lady's failure to keep her promise. I confronted the Lady.

"When will you give me a man's body? I have chosen the body I want, and I can serve you better as a man."

"Not yet."

"Do you mean you cannot or will not fulfill your promise?"

"I will when the time is right." I had heard her promise to free Blodeweth, but she continued to hold her captive. Her hesitation made me wonder whether she was lying.

That afternoon when I perched in a tree near the garrison, I saw a messenger deliver a letter to Bon. This unusual event drew my attention. He found a place alone in the courtyard to read the message; I followed. His face told me that the news troubled him. I landed on the ground close to him and cleared my throat. He looked up.

"Tell me what this letter says."

My words amazed him. Until then, my only words had been in private conversations with the Lady.

"You speak? Why should I tell you anything?"

"I may be able to help. I can go places you cannot go and see things you cannot see."

He seemed reluctant to speak; he thought for a while and then told me:

"Christine d'Arque is missing. Perhaps you know her? She left with Fabrice, and he tells me he lost her along the way."

"How so?"

"She fell from her horse, and the Baron of Saverdun captured her. I fear he will do her harm. I will challenge him and force him to release her."

"That is a foolish and headstrong idea. Even if you defeat the Baron, he will not release her. Deceit is more effective than a direct attack."

He sighed.

"Aye. You are right."

"I can help. I will spy at the windows of the Baron's castle and find Christine. When we find out where she is, we can devise a plan. Meanwhile, I can bring her a message of hope."

He understood he needed my help, although he seemed reluctant to accept it. I also required his help; there was no way to get Christine out of Saverdun myself. However, I would get rid of him once we obtained Christine's release and be alone with her.

In the days that followed, I circled the castle at Saverdun. I spied in courtyards, gardens, and kitchens, but she was not among the women.

Chapter 42

Christine

One bleak winter morning, I woke to the sight of an enormous black bird standing on the window ledge. It was larger than a crow; it must be a raven. I shrank from the sharp bill and talons. The bird's appearance seemed an ill omen. Still, there was something familiar about him. I had seen this bird, or a similar one, at Mirefoix. Often it sat a short distance away as if watching me. Sometimes it lurked in shadows. It hopped to the floor and jumped onto the table in the middle of the room. It made throat-clearing voices.

"My Lady, do not fear me. I come as a friend."

I knew ravens and some other birds talk. In my day, there was debate among animal behavior researchers about whether this was mere mimicry or actual language. I had no way of knowing its sex. Because of its raspy tone, I thought of it as "he." Was he merely repeating something he had heard? Or was he capable of intelligent speech? In this world, impossible things seemed possible. I tested his language skills.

"Who are you?"

"My name is Corvinus."

Bemused, I continued the conversation.

"Why have you come?"

"I watched you for a long time at Mirefoix. You are a gentle lady, and I admire you."

"What brings you to Saverdun?"

"I have flown far and wide to search for you. I wanted to ask if you are well and what I might do for you."

"I want to get away."

He looked around.

"You don't have food? Fire?"

"Women bring food for six days, then not for one day—perhaps Sunday. I have no fire, not even a candle."

"Has the Baron harmed you in other ways?"

"I have not seen him since the day the Baron locked me in here."

He fanned his tail, combed it with his claw, and fluffed his feathers to make himself look larger.

"I can help you survive and find a way for you to escape."

"How?"

"I will think."

We spoke a while longer; then, he departed. He came every day, bringing small gifts. Sometimes it was food: A hunk of cheese, a piece of bread. Other times he brought a sweetmeat or a pretty trinket clutched in his beak. Once, it was a pretty silver necklace. I scolded him for thievery.

"My gifts divert you, do they not? And my conversation?"

I confessed they did. I asked him to bring a candle and a fire striker. He reminded me that any light that penetrated the cracks of my cell door would alert my captors I had a visitor, and I knew he was correct. I remained alone in the dark. His visits, sometimes by day but often at night, were my only source of companionship.

We discussed possibilities for escape. He mused:

"Perhaps I can steal the key. There might be a way to escape through the garderobe. I will investigate."

Corvinus' report the following day dashed my hopes. There was a wide hole leading down from the garderobe to the river below, outside the castle wall; however, strong metal bars blocked the bottom. There were always people about. No way to slip down the stairs, through the corridors, and out the gate without being noticed.

A week later, he returned with a small chisel in his claws.

"I have another plan. Use this tool to loosen two bars in the window. Leave them in place, so servants do not notice. I will bring strips of cloth that you can braid into a rope. When the rope is ready and the bars are loose, you can climb down the outside wall."

I have always feared heights. I failed the rope climbing test in gym class in my other life, and I had little upper body strength. Corvinus looked at me as if he sensed my hesitation.

"You must do this. Can you?"

"I must, and I will." I would muster the courage.

As the rope grew in length, my fondness for him grew greater.

"Lady, will you stroke my feathers?" His sharp beak unnerved me, but the pleading in his eyes touched me. I reached out and touched the feathers on his breast, and then, growing more confident, I fondled his neck. He closed his eyes and shivered. "I miss being touched."

"You do not speak like a bird."

"Lady, before I was a bird, I was a man. I want to be human again."

Magic again. The strange had become commonplace.

"What happened to you?"

"I lived in a great city; I had great wealth and power. People praised me for my learning and benevolence. Then a spirit took hold of me and dragged me through Hades. When I awoke, the Lady condemned me to live as a bird. I long for the touch of gentle hands. I am alone, and I crave human affection."

I wondered if this story was entirely accurate. He told me he had lived in Rome more than a thousand years ago. Each of us had been transported through centuries, after death by fire, by a spirit. We discussed this, and I explained that Blodeweth had the same experience. Corvinus said:

"Do you think the Lady made this happen?"

"I think she did, with the help of the demons who now haunt her."

He came every night, brought fabric for the rope, and asked me to stroke his feathers.

"How can I thank you?"

I swear I heard mischief in his voice.

"I will think of something, my Lady. May the gods be with you."

As his stories about his past life grew more grandiose, I thought: He's wooing me.

"I was a man and will be again if I can use the Lady's magic."

The escape project kept me busy and gave me hope. I worked on the rope and used the chisel to loosen the bars until they were almost free. Meanwhile, I listened for footsteps in the hall; I hid the rope and chisel before anyone entered the chamber.

"Corvinus, where can I go when I escape?"

"I am not yet certain. We will have help. Bon will be here."

Months passed, and my rope grew steadily, and I spread it on the floor. Corvinus helped me judge its length. Spring approached. Corvinus helped me keep track of the days of the week, and he confirmed Sunday was the day the servant did not come to bring food, so we planned the escape for the following Saturday evening.

Part 3:

Destinies of the

Souls

Chapter 43

Christine

April 1209

On a warm April night, I moved the bed close to the window to reach it. Corvinus supervised while I tied the rope to the one solid bar. I used the chisel to remove the two loosened bars and climbed into the window. Then I made a mistake. I looked down. Even in the darkness, I saw that the ground was at least 30 feet below me. I barely saw the man who waited below. I wondered if my rope was long enough, and I doubted my hands were strong enough to keep hold of it. I froze, my heart in my mouth. I have always been terrified of heights. Corvinus said:

"Lady, you must go."

When I didn't respond, he prodded me with his sharp beak.

"Take hold of the rope."

I obeyed. I crouched in the opening.

"Put one foot outside."

He poked me again, harder this time.

"Now, the other foot."

My feet dangled from the window.

What if I lost my grip on the rope?

"There are cracks and crevices. Turn, and use your foot to find one."

He continued to coax. I found one toehold, then a second, but I continued to grasp the remaining bar in the window. I had avoided challenges like this in both of my lives. Did I have the courage to escape? Life in the cell was deadening, but I feared the dangers outside.

"Put your other hand on the rope." He pecked my fingers hard enough to draw blood. I took a deep breath. A burst of adrenaline gave me the strength to keep hold of the rope. I let myself down gradually, using the knots to keep the rope in my grasp. I was still 10 feet above the ground when I reached the next-to-last knot. Bon waited below. I heard him speak.

"Trust me and let go. I will catch you."

I clung to that rope as if my life depended on it. My knuckles were white, and my hands were rope-burned, but I couldn't let go.

"Lady, trust me."

I closed my eyes and opened my hands.

It wasn't a clean catch, but Bon broke my fall. I was bruised but not broken. I was happy to see his face. He caressed my cheek. For a moment, I wanted to throw my arms around him. Instead, I stepped away.

"We must go quickly."

Corvinus untied the rope to remove evidence of the means of escape. He followed us, flitting from tree to tree. Bon took my hand and guided me down a rocky path to a river. I stumbled in the dark. He pulled a shallow punt from its hiding place under trees and helped me get into it. Corvinus perched on the boat's edge, peering at me with concern. Then he stared at Bon with beady black eyes that now looked menacing. A testy exchange between Bon and Corvinus followed. Bon said:

"If you come with us, it will make us more recognizable. We need to avoid notice as long as possible."

"She is not yours. She is mine."

"That is absurd."

"Do not underestimate me. I will have a human body again, and then we will see who Christine chooses." Corvinus flew at Bon with talons extended; Bon beat him off and struck him hard enough to stun him. He wrapped Corvinus tightly in the rope and bound him to a branch in a nearby tree.

"Why have you tied him there?"

"We can't be certain what he will do, and he will betray us to the Lady if it benefits him."

"Will he be all right?"

"When he awakens, he'll be able to loosen the bonds. We'll be far enough that he can't follow by then. Did the Baron harm you?"

"No. My habit protected me. Thank you for delivering me from this place."

"It's the least I could do... Lie down so no one can see you." I lay at the bottom of the boat, and he covered me with a cloak. He used an oar to push off from shore, and the boat slid downstream without a sound.

I wondered. By now, Bon had disobeyed the Lady's orders by aiding Garsenda's escape and mine. What did this mean for his honor? What had he given up? It must be difficult for him. Safe now, exhausted from my efforts and refreshed by the fragrant warm air outside, I fell asleep.

Before dawn, Bon woke me and poled the boat to shore. He made holes in the bottom and sank it. He drew out a sack from a nearby pile of branches; it contained supplies he had prepared for the journey, I supposed.

"Can you walk?"

"Where are you taking me?"

"If you wish, I will take you to Arque and place you in the care of your family."

I had a familiar inexplicable sense of dread at this mention of Arque. Christine's memories had faded, yet I was sure something terrible had happened to her there.

"No, not Arque. Surely, that is not what the Lady ordered. You broke your oath of loyalty by taking me away. Won't that damage the honor of which you speak so often? And what about Blodeweth? She's still a prisoner."

He looked away and flushed.

"I can take you back to Mirefoix if you prefer. I didn't think you would want to return. The Lady's demands exhausted you, and you said you were tired of captivity. I can't see a way to rescue Blodeweth. All I can do is get you away."

I thought about life in Mirefoix. The abbey was safe compared to the unknown world outside. There was no safe place for me in the world beyond those walls. If I returned, I would be a prisoner for the rest of my life, subject to the Lady's exhausting demands. I was afraid, but I said:

"No. I don't want to go back."

"Where do you want to go?"

This was the first time anyone had asked me what I wanted. I was touched. Perhaps he cared for me.

"Where else might I go?"

"I can take you to some other abbey where you would be safe."

A moment of silence followed. I didn't want this, and the reluctance in Bon's voice suggested he didn't either.

"I have been a captive for so many months, and I want to be free. An abbey would be just another prison."

His face brightened.

"I have messages to carry to Narbonne. From there, I can take you to Beziers; you can stay with Garsenda and Fabrice."

I had met Garsenda only briefly in Blodeweth's cell, I didn't know Fabrice, and I had never heard of Beziers. Still, this seemed preferable to the alternatives.

"Yes. Perhaps that would be better."

"We cannot travel as a soldier and a nun. It would attract notice."

He handed me a bundle of garments.

"Put on this dress. I'm sorry it's so shabby. I won't watch."

While I exchanged my habit for the gray dress, he dug a hole. He buried the nun's clothing, picked up a sack, and beckoned.

"Will they follow us?"

"They'll try. The Lady may assume, for a while, that the Baron still holds you. The Baron may believe you have gone back to the Lady. I don't trust Corvinus; I told him we would go to Toulouse."

"Why?"

"He plays his own game. It suited him for you to escape from Saverdun. He is attached to you somehow, and it displeases him that you are with me."

"Where are we now?"

"We have traveled north, downstream on the Ariege, to where the River Hers joins it, a little south of Toulouse. Now we'll head east on foot, following the Hers upstream, keeping out of sight. We'll make our way to Narbonne by back roads, avoiding major cities where we might be noticed."

We walked along the side of the river with the sun rising ahead of us. Tall spring grasses moved in the breeze on the slopes of hills to our left; yellow flowers bloomed like stars. The air smelled green, and the sun warmed me. It was a welcome change from life within stone walls. I reveled in freedom.

We came to a place where the bank rose above the river. Bon helped me climb the slope, and from that point, we walked along the edge of a bluff. When we heard people approaching, we hid among shrubs or trees. Bon said we must avoid being seen, at least until we were several days farther from Mirefoix. As we walked through a grove of flowering hawthorn trees, the wind shook loose the delicate white blossoms, and they fell like spring snow. I laughed at the sight of flowers in his hair and brushed them away.

Everything was beautiful that day. Was I in love with the world or with him? Both, I thought. Then my doubts returned. Marriage to a man without a manor or land would mean poverty. What would he do now? Had he severed ties with the Lady? Perhaps he would become a mercenary. I couldn't starve and bear children in squalor. I stopped myself. He had not asked me to marry him, only offered to leave me with friends. This was not love. He only wanted to make amends. I asked him:

"What will you do after we find Fabrice and Garsenda?" It had occurred to me that even now, he might return to the Lady.

"I will remain there, at least for a time. I can't predict what the future will bring."

"How far is it to Beziers?"

"The journey by way back roads to Narbonne will take about two weeks. Avram, the goldsmith, gave me silver to deliver a package and letters to a rabbi in that city."

"Did you tell him you would risk his package by stopping to rescue me?"

He smiled.

"Of course not." He had not smiled often; this new smile gave his face a boyish charm.

"Will we be safe at Beziers?"

"I think so. Raymond Roger Trencavel rules Beziers. He is far above the Lady in power and not allied with her, and I can offer my services to him." He sounded tentative.

"You have doubts?"

"Whatever happens, I will ensure you are safe and do not go hungry. I swear it."

We followed the River Hers for a day and stopped where it curved south; Bon said we would leave the river in the morning and continue east through hill country. I no longer wore the habit of a novice, but Bon still treated me as if I did. He touched me once that first day, but not again. Now that I craved his touch, the distance between us was frustrating. His controlled expression made it impossible to know his feelings.

When we slept, he placed his unsheathed sword lengthwise between us on the ground to create a symbolic barrier he never crossed. Something about this triggered a memory. Was it from Tristan and Isolde or another myth?

A light rain fell that night, and when I woke, he was gone. I was frightened; his absence reminded me that he had become my only source of safety. I rose and caught sight of the river between the trees, shining silver in the morning light. Every leaf held a drop of rain, and each droplet sparkled like silver. The air was fragrant with blossoms, wet rocks, leaves, and damp earth. At that moment, the world was unbearably beautiful. I went down to the river, thinking I would find him there. I saw him waist-deep in the river, with his back toward me, splashing water on his chest and arms. I could not take my eyes off him.

He turned toward me and walked toward the shore. I took two steps back and then walked forward, trying to make it appear I was just approaching the river and had not been watching. As he donned his tunic, I saw a cord around his neck with a green pendant engraved with an image familiar to me. I pointed to it.

"Buddha?" A person of this time couldn't ask such a question; it was a careless lapse.

He looked at me in amazement.

"How can you know that name?"

It seemed to me we both had some explaining to do. I had an opportunity to reveal my identity and ask about his. Was that safe? Until now, I had allowed people to think of me as Christine d'Arque, born in this century, and no one seemed to suspect a different identity. I dodged his question.

"I must have seen one somewhere. I don't remember where." This phrase, I don't remember, was my well-rehearsed response to unanswerable questions.

The look on his face told me he didn't believe this. I seized the initiative.

"How do you come to have this?"

"It was a keepsake from my mother, who came from the east."

"Where in the east?"

"You would not be familiar with the place."

"I would like to hear about it."

"I'll answer your questions if you will answer mine."

I agreed, and he told me his story.

Chapter 44

Bon

May 1209

I told Christine that my father kept my mother as a sort of wife before his marriage to the Lady. After my mother died, I grew up in the Chateau. My mother's servant also came to live there. By day, a tutor educated me along with the Count's other children; I learned Latin and courtly manners and the arts of war from the weapons master. By night, Fan Zhongyan taught me languages, philosophy, history, and science from his homeland in the east. He rarely spoke of my mother. He said: I will tell you about her when you become a man.

When I was 15, the Lady heard of the Count's death and sent me out of her house. I went to the servants' quarters to find Fan Zhongyan. I asked him what I should do.

"If only I had gone to Outremer with my father."

"That was not meant to be."

"What choice do I have now?"

"For now, you can become one of the soldiers."

We gathered our possessions; I had little, but Fan Zhongyan had scrolls and a few other possessions left by my mother, and we borrowed a cart to transport them. I had a friend, the smith Fabrice, and we looked for him at his forge near the garrison. Fabrice was disturbed to hear about the Count's death and the Lady's decision to turn us out of her house. He found a room for Fan Zhongyan to rent and advised him to set up a table in the market square to offer services as a writer, reader, and translator of letters. I presented myself to the commander at the garrison and volunteered to become a soldier.

When I visited the barracks as a boy, I was popular among the men. But I had to fight for a place among the soldiers. I became a leader, but I was never one of them. My education and manners set me apart. I was painfully aware I was not like the other soldiers and didn't want to be like them. After the Chateau, I found the squalor of the barracks disheartening. I looked ahead and saw years of the same.

I continued to spend evenings with Fan Zhongyan.

"It's time for me to tell you about your history and legacy. Do you remember your mother?"

"I think I remember her face, her voice. She died when I was so young. Please tell me about her."

"She loved you above all else. She had the mind of a scholar, an artist's soul, and a warrior's courage. She had no equal in beauty."

Over many visits, he told me her story.

"Her name was Da Eun. She was the daughter of a noble house in the Kingdom of Goryeo, a land more than a year's journey to the east. She was betrothed to a prince in the Song Empire."

"I was a noted Song scholar; among the tens of thousands who sat for the examinations, among the hundreds who passed, I was in the highest rank. I was appointed to escort her from Goryeo to her wedding in my country."

"The procession was enormous, as suited to her status. Many servants and guards accompanied her. They carried trunk after trunk of precious possessions: Silk gowns, jade, precious stones, patterned celadon ware of the highest quality, and scrolls of poetry and history. I supervised loading these treasures onto the ship that was to bring her to Hangzhou."

"Our ship had been at sea for only one day when a great storm struck, a typhoon, and the winds blew her vessel off course. I went to her cabin to make sure she was safe. I'll never forget the first time I saw her. She was tall and graceful as a willow. There was sadness on her face. She was reluctant to leave her home to marry a stranger. It was not proper that I should be with her, but servants ran back and forth in the confusion, and she was alone. I stayed with her and comforted her. I swore to dedicate my life to her protection."

"When the storm had passed, we were becalmed and then boarded by pirates. No matter what happened, I resolved to stay with her and protect her. I donned women's clothing, and my beardless face did not betray me. She agreed I would pretend to be her maidservant and stay at her side."

"The Arabic traders pillaged our cargo. They seized most of her servants as slaves. She pleaded that she be able to keep me with her as her one attendant, and they granted that request."

"When the captain entered her cabin, he was stunned by her beauty. I was afraid he would take her for himself, but he did not. Evidently, he decided she would be more valuable as a virgin."

"The sea journey was very hard on her. Even in calmer weather, the ship's motion made her sick. She lost a lot of weight, and I was glad to see that, for it made her less attractive to men who might ravish her."

"The ship stopped at Guanzhou, Srivijaya, Calicut, and Aden. Each time, we feared we had reached the final destination. We expected she would be sold to a wealthy man. At last, we disembarked at Aqaba and continued our journey by land. The ship captain turned us over to his trading partner, who expressed disgust at her sickly appearance and did not believe she was worth much. He said the cost of nursing her back to health was hardly worthwhile. I hoped they might simply let us go, but that did not happen."

"The trader brought us to Alexandria and left us in the care of the women in his household. We lived there for a year, and it seemed the trader had forgotten her. Da Eun recovered her health and looks. The return of her beauty made me fear for her."

"Her fate was decided when the trader showed off his wealth to a wealthy Frankish traveler, Hauquet of Lavaur. He was the uncle of Count Henri of Mirefoix, your father. Hauquet spent many years in Outremer.

Before returning here, he visited that trader, and your mother was among the treasures he saw. He was smitten. He offered two thousand solidi of silver for her, then three thousand. The trader refused."

"Now, this trader had a weakness for vices strictly forbidden by Islam. They drank wine. Hauquet persuaded him to dice. He wagered control of the city of Arqa if the trader would stake Da Eun. It is unclear whether he had the power to offer this and whether the dice were loaded. Hauquet won the throw. He took your mother to his ship at the docks of Alexandria that night, and we were underway the next morning."

"Hauquet brought her to Lavaur and made her his concubine. She bore her dishonor with dignity. It could have been worse; he did not beat her. The same winter he returned to Lavaur, he died from a fever. Henri, your father, took your mother for himself. When you were born, she gave you a name in her own language, Bon Hwa, and used Bon as your Occitan name."

I had questions.

"In all that time, you passed as a woman?"

"I did. After your mother's death, I no longer required that disguise, of course."

As time passed, he told me more. "When you were a year old, according to the custom of Zhuazhou, we showed you a scroll, brush, ink, coins, an abacus, a knife, and a cake. You were free to choose your path in life. When you grasped the knife, your mother wept. She had hoped you would choose the peaceful life of a scholar."

I said to him:

"My only way to earn my way is by the sword. If I am not a soldier, what am I?"

"For now, follow the way of the soldier. It is time for me to give you your mother's gifts. She brought this sword from the east. You will find it stronger, sharper, and more flexible than weapons made here." He handed it to me. With this sword in my hands, I never lost a fight.

Then he placed this green stone around my neck. "This is jade. One side is an image of Buddha. The other is the seal of your mother's noble family. Keep it as proof of your identity and a reminder that other paths remain open to you."

Chapter 45

Christine

"Thank you for telling me about your life." These revelations filled me with wonder. There was much more to him than I had imagined. He was as much an outsider as I was.

Then Bon asked:

"Now, tell me: How did you learn about the Buddha?"

I wasn't prepared to speak of my life 700 years in the future. His story was fantastic, but it did not involve supernatural intervention and time travel. Who would believe such things? I remembered little about Christine d'Arque's life before I moved into her body, and nothing in her life would explain my knowledge. I was torn. I wanted to share myself as he had, but I wasn't ready.

"I have not always lived here."

"The Lady said you were from Arque."

I struggled for words. I wanted someone to understand me for who I was, but the truth was not believable. I was evasive.

"Souls can live more than one life. I lived another life in a world where some people followed Buddhist teachings, and I remember that life."

"Fan Zhongyan taught me about Samsara, the cycle of death and rebirth, and karma. So, you are a Buddhist?"

"I respect and try to understand Buddhist beliefs, but I am not a Buddhist."

"Then you are Catholic."

Religion was risky territory. "No. I say the prayers, I attend mass, but much of what I believe is not Catholic."

He smiled. "I don't hold Catholic beliefs either, but it's not wise to say that. You can trust me. I won't repeat what you say."

"What do you believe in, then?"

"In paratge and striving to live a noble life."

"And yet, you kidnapped and terrified me."

"I want to undo the dishonorable things I have done. But you stray from my question."

"I'm sorry. Your life is a wonderful story. I'm afraid mine is not very interesting."

"Tell me."

"I remember little of my life at Arque. Just thinking of that place fills me with dread. Something bad happened there, and my mind refuses to let me see it. I remember I liked to collect herbs and nurse injured animals."

On our last night near the river, we lay near enough to bathe in the warmth of each other's bodies, but we did not touch. Usually, when I was close to others, they drew strength from me. With Bon, an aura of courage permeated my soul, and I received energy from someone for the first time. His restlessness told me that his dreams disturbed him. A man who lives by the sword must have memories of it. I wished to touch his forehead, banish the nightmares, and soothe him. I did not.

I awoke before dawn but lay still with my eyes closed. He rolled over and lay on his side, his head propped up on his elbow, and stroked my unbound hair, evidently unaware I was awake. What would he do if I turned toward him with open eyes? I longed to touch him, but I didn't.

We walked east into the hills the next day and stopped to rest in a grove of trees. That afternoon he instructed me in self-defense.

"I may not always be near enough to keep you safe."

He cut two saplings and trimmed each to make a staff. "Use this or a pike to keep your assailant as far from you as possible."

He pretended to attack me with his staff and coached me how to block and strike back if there was an opening. As a former teacher, I appreciated how he instructed me. He broke the skills into steps and increased the difficulty of exercises each day. He taught me to respond to attacks from different directions. My wrists and arms became sore from the effort. I gained strength and confidence. Once he gave me an opening to lunge toward him. I had become engaged in this, and I threw myself toward him. He blocked my staff and swiveled, and I crashed into him with my not-very-substantial weight. He caught me up and steadied me. I raised my face toward him, and we gazed at each other. I thought I saw an unvoiced longing in his eyes.

He released me and said:

"Mind your balance. You are getting better."

The next day, he said:

"You also need to learn to use a knife."

I quailed.

"I don't think I will ever stab someone."

"Yes, you can, and a time may come when you must."

He set up a dummy, a sack stuffed with earth to resemble a torso. He marked the most vulnerable spots. It took time for me to even come close to hitting it. He stood behind me, arms around me, showing me how to grip the weapon and move my wrist. That contact stirred up unwelcome longings. Damn the youthful urges of this body. I must not confuse lust with love.

We headed toward Castlenaudery, but we passed by it. Bon explained we must continue to avoid the most traveled roads. We made our way along rough paths. He was vigilant. I wondered why he seemed uneasy. This region was known for bandits, he told me.

His words proved prophetic. The next day, as we rounded a corner in the path, three men with cudgels and knives attacked us. They probably assumed Bon was not well-armed because of his shabby clothing. Bon unsheathed his sword and positioned himself in front of me. As he engaged two men, the third moved toward me with his knife poised. I used my staff to give him a stiff blow on the side of his head before the outlaw laid hands on me. He didn't fall, but he was stunned for the moment. I readied myself to strike again. Bon struck one assailant in the chest, and the man fell with a wound likely to be fatal. Another circled behind Bon and stabbed him low in the back, near the kidney, perhaps. Sounds of approaching horses startled them, and the remaining attackers fled.

The passing horsemen did not stop to help us. I helped Bon get away from the path, leaving the man he had wounded behind. We withdrew under cover of trees. His wound bled profusely. He broke out in a sweat and shook. I applied pressure to his wound to staunch the flow and tried to think about what to do. A bandage would not be enough.

"If we had needle and thread, perhaps I could sew it closed."

No such supplies were available.

"No. You will have to cauterize it. I would do it myself, but I cannot reach there."

"Tell me what I must do."

He pressed a wad of cloth against his wound. Following his instructions, I built a fire as quickly as possible and heated the blade of his knife.

"Apply the heat for a moment and remove it. I'll tell you to do it again if it seems needed."

I tried to steady myself. The searing hot knife would hurt me more than him. Still, this must be done. He braced himself in a sitting position, and I kneeled beside him. I applied the blade, which was red from the heat of the fire.

Searing pain shot through my back. I cried out; then, I fainted.

When I regained consciousness, I was lying on the ground with my feet elevated, covered by his cloak. He bent over me with an expression of extreme distress on his face.

I thought, how strange: He knows how to treat shock.

He tried to help me get up; when he touched my lower back, I flinched.

We were silent for a time.

"When you cauterized the wound, it didn't hurt me, but it caused you great pain in the same place on your back. How is that possible?"

He examined the location of the pain in my back and found no physical damage.

"We need shelter. I'll carry you over to that thicket."

"I cannot bear touch on that place on my back. It will be easier if you help me walk."

We settled in a quiet spot in a wooded area. I rested the side that did not hurt against a tree. I was still shaking.

When he spoke, it sounded like an accusation.

"You took my pain. Isn't that so?"

At first, I did not reply.

"Does this happen when you heal others? I saw that contact with Blodeweth and the Lady drained you of strength. I didn't know it caused you pain; I will not allow you to take on my pain. I swear to protect you, even from myself."

"Yes."

"I won't allow you to suffer this way again. I must understand this to protect you."

Would he protect and care for me instead of exploiting my desire to comfort? I had no words to explain my hopes and fears.

"Healing is the only thing I can offer."

"That's not true. You have much more than that."

I was falling in love with Bon, and that terrified me. My heart and mind engaged in an unresolvable argument. My mind said: He colluded in poisoning and kidnapping me, and I have seen him kill men and rob corpses without remorse. He delivered me to the Lady, who used me and left me so drained of energy that I almost died.

But then, he rescued me from the Baron and allowed me to choose where to go. He broke his oath of loyalty to the Lady to do that; he had many opportunities to force himself on me and didn't; he treated me with respect and almost reverence and vowed to protect me.

By the end of my previous life, I had avoided love. For me, it always led to pain.

But now came Bon. I tried to persuade myself that my feeling was only foolish infatuation, a superficial attraction to his handsome face and lean body. I feared it was more than that. He undermined my emotional defenses with his courtly manners, occasional shy smiles, and small acts of tenderness. He gave me the choicest bits of meat; he covered me with his cloak. More than that, he shielded me with his body. He would die for me if necessary. I understood he aspired to paratge, the Occitan ideal of honor and courtesy. Breaking his vow of obedience to the Lady had damaged the honor he prized above all. I understood he sacrificed any chance of advancement in her service when he rescued me and took me away from Mirefoix.

One night I awoke from nightmares; I sat up trembling. I tried not to weep; I didn't want to wake him. But he sensed my distress. He held me in his arms and comforted me as no one had ever done, not even when I was a child. I was overcome. I had bargained and begged for crumbs all my life. Now a feast was freely offered. I was afraid. Was it strange that fear overwhelmed me? Would he take this comfort away?

Would he expect things from me in return that I could not give?

None of this was proof he loved me. He had said he wanted to atone for his wrongs toward me. Perhaps that was all that it was. Maybe I would look foolish if I let my growing attraction to him show.

The Buddha amulet told me there was more to him than his life at Mirefoix. Like me, he had a background unknown to others. I would never fully understand his past, but unlike others here, I had a little knowledge of Asian culture and history. Enough to know how much I didn't know. Two people can never fully understand each other, can they? He contained other worlds, other lives. No one else here could comprehend that about him. I at least knew that I didn't understand.

Were my perceptions of him just fantasies, like the illusions that led me into an unhappy marriage in the past? Or was he truly the man I thought he was? Had I begun to believe he loved me only because I loved him and wanted him to love me? And suppose he loved me? Suppose that we married? The thought of bearing a child in this world terrified me. Childbirth was often fatal; children often died at birth or within the first five years of life. We needed a roof over our heads, and Bon had nothing. He had a paid commission to deliver letters and goods, but what would happen later?

I lived my past life worrying about imagined situations in the future, many of which never came to pass. I was doing it again, and I was getting ahead of myself.

Every night he placed his naked sword lengthwise between us, a symbolic barrier. Perhaps it was a sign to assure me he would not take me. Maybe he needed that barrier too. Why? Perhaps he was attracted to me and chose not to act on it. He might be engaging in one of those foolish chivalrous actions inspired by songs of courtly love.

Sometimes the arguments of my mind kept my feelings in check. At other times my heart and body betrayed me. I ached with yearning, and I was tired of being alone in this world.

Chapter 46

Christine

June 1209

We passed through the dry valleys near Carcassonne but did not stop there. I admired its magnificent walls and towers from a distance. Yes, Bon said; this was the greatest city in the south; perhaps someday we would go there, but not now. We reached the outskirts of Narbonne in May. Its walls dwarfed those of Mirefoix. We stopped to buy food and drink from a small hostelry inside the gate. Bon said:

"We will seek shelter in Beziers, but first, I must deliver these letters and goods." It was Thursday morning when we found the cathedral of St. Paul Serge; its tower was the tallest structure in town. We shared the secret of not holding Catholic beliefs; however, we made the expected gestures in public. We dipped our fingers in the font of holy water and crossed ourselves. I wondered why the font had a frog carved in the stone; there must be a story behind this touch of whimsy. As people departed after mass, Bon asked for directions to the Jewish quarter. It wasn't far, but we got lost in a confusing network of alleys. The synagogue was in a narrow passage protected by a metal gate. As we arrived, the gate opened, and men dressed for prayer in blue and white fringed prayer shawls emerged. Bon stopped an imposing man: "Can you tell me where to find Benjamin Ben Isaac? I bring messages and goods from Avram, the goldsmith in Mirefoix."

The man hesitated and studied us carefully. He decided:

"I will take you to him." He led us through alleys that, although dark, were swept clean. He knocked at the last house on the street.

"This man says he has business with Benjamin Ben Yitzak. Is Benjamin willing to see him?"

The servant permitted us to enter. Bon explained his mission.

"Avram, the goldsmith in Mirefoix, entrusted me to deliver these."

"I regret we cannot offer you refreshment. My people may not eat with Gentiles." Bon nodded and said he was not offended. We sat at a table across from Benjamin and handed him the packages, and he broke the seals and examined the contents. A boy came in from the other room and interrupted us.

"Grandfather says he wants to meet these people."

Benjamin's face showed his surprise.

"My father is a renowned scholar, known to many as Isaac the Blind. He rarely asks for visitors. Come, then." He showed us to the adjacent room. An aging man with thinning hair and white eyes sat at a long table. Younger men sat around him, perhaps students, with manuscripts in Hebrew spread out before them. I gasped in surprise when I recognized a diagram of the Kabbalah tree of life. The dignified older man spoke to Bon.

"Sit before me for a moment. I want to see what manner of man you are. May I?" He touched Bon's forehead, cheeks, and eyes.

"You are an old soul; you have lived many lives, a rare thing. And the woman who is with you?"

I had said nothing, yet he sensed a woman was present. He passed his hands over my face.

"You are indeed also a very old soul. That can be a gift and a curse. You have a shared destiny. I need to rest now, my son."

We returned to the front room. Our host treated us with greater kindness and curiosity after Isaac spoke to us. He entrusted Bon with packages to deliver to Samuel, head of the Jewish community in Beziers.

We slept under the open sky that night with a sea of stars above us. The air was still and warm; the songs of crickets surrounded us on an otherwise silent night. Bon's dreams seemed to disturb him more than usual. He thrashed and ground his teeth and seemed so upset that I decided to wake him. At first, he spoke in a language that sounded Asian, possibly Chinese.

I tried to soothe him.

"What was your dream about?"

He reverted to the lenga romana. "It's difficult to explain...."

"Isaac said you had lived many lives. Did you dream about one of those other lives?"

There was a painfully long pause.

"Yes."

"Please tell me about it."

"You won't believe me."

"Yes. I will. I swear it."

He spoke haltingly as if reluctant to reveal so much. Perhaps it was difficult to find the right words.

"In my dream, my name was Yong Jen. I was a physician who lived in Shanghai. When enemies invaded and killed my family, I joined the army. We heard of unbelievable atrocities by the invaders. I cannot bear to speak of them. Soldiers trapped me at the end of a street. Our enemies threw fire at us, and I burned to death."

"What year was this?"

"That is the strangest part of this. My mind says that the year was 1937. Of course, that's unbelievable."

"I believe it. What happened then?"

"When Yong Jen died, his spirit, my spirit, it seems, was seized by a strange blue apparition and brought here. Dreams or memories of Yong Jen began after the Lady took me out into the hills at night and gave me drugged wine that put me into a trance. When I woke, I didn't remember at first whether I was Bon, Yong Jen, or both. I was even more confused when the Lady called me Josfred. My friend Josfred lay dead nearby. I decided I was only Bon, but Yong Jen's memories did not leave me in peace. Does this make any sense to you?"

I saw similarities between our experiences.

"I also lived a life in the future, died by fire, and was seized by a terrifying spirit. I woke in the body of Christine D'Arque. Her memories of Arque were disturbing, and I drove those thoughts out of my mind. I held on to my memories of my other life. Blodeweth told me of a similar experience. She said she was a priestess who died in fire during an attack by Roman soldiers. She was brought here by a brown-colored demon to live in a different body. She woke to find herself a captive of the Lady. Corvinus has a similar story: death by fire and the appearance of a black demon. After that, he found himself as a bird, bound to the Lady's wishes. I think the Lady used magic to bring all of us here. I never believed in magic, but I can think of no other explanation."

"In what year did you die? And where?"

"2021. The United States."

His face showed shock.

I continued:

"I know Shanghai. Do you speak any English?"

"I do. A little."

From that point forward, we used English when words from the lenga romana were inadequate.

He asked: "What happened after 1937? Who won the war?"

"The United States, Soviet Union, Britain, France, China, and other allies defeated the Japanese, Germans, and Italians in 1945."

"Did things go well in my country after that?"

"I'm sorry. No." I didn't know the details, but I remembered civil war, the Cultural Revolution, famine, and disruptive modernization.

"I want to know everything."

"It will take a long time to tell. We won't run out of things to talk about. In return, I want to hear about your life as Yong Jen."

He pressed his lips tight and drew his brows together.

"Much that I remember is painful. Give me time. Tell me more about your other life."

"I was a counselor. I tried to help people who were overwhelmed by anxiety, grief, or anger."

I thought the Chinese might not have known much about psychotherapy when he was alive, so I explained further. He seemed a little amused.

"Did all that talking work?"

"Sometimes, it helped. Often, I couldn't relieve distress. Sometimes people saw their illnesses as part of their identities; they said they wanted to get better but wouldn't let go of their problems. I was discouraged when they didn't improve. We had a saying: 'Be careful what you wish for, for you will surely get it.' When I woke here, my wish for healing power had been granted. But as you know, the cost of healing others is feeling their pain myself. I'm often torn being wanting to help and fearing the consequences."

"Ah. I wished to be a better soldier, and I became one. After dreaming about Yong Jen, I had new speed and accuracy with weapons."

After a pause, he asked:

"Were you married?"

"I was. At first, my husband showered me with gratitude for all I had done for him. Later he took everything I did for granted. He drained me of energy. I died, little by little. At last, I left him."

"His actions sound like those of the Lady. You never found love?"

"I was afraid to love again. I lived alone. My home was a comfortable refuge. It was a cage I made for myself. Here I have lived in prisons made by others. I'm trying to find the courage to live in freedom."

"You have courage. I have seen it."

"And you, were you married?"

"I married the woman my father chose. She was a good and dutiful wife and gave me three sons. The Japanese slaughtered them when they came to Shanghai."

We were quiet for a while. Then I spoke.

"After comparing Blodeweth's story to mine, I thought of us as 'summoned souls.' Summoned apparently by the Lady and used for her own purposes. It seems you are also a summoned soul."

There was a period of silence. Then he said:

"My connection with life in another century is weak. Your connection with your other life is stronger, yes? You choose not to remember Arque; I try not to remember Yong Jen. Still, memories of his world make me feel even more different from others."

I tentatively moved to touch his hand, and he pulled it away.

"It's wrong for us to touch."

"Why?"

"You are vowed as a nun until just before the feast of St. Mary Magdalene. It would be a dishonor to break that vow. My disobedience to the Lady dishonors me. My actions toward you and Blodeweth also shame me. I am unworthy."

"You are too hard on yourself."

His vow, and his belief in the sacredness of my reluctant vow, were barriers between us.

Longing and fear struggled within me; I feared this would turn out badly. Even after this conversation, I didn't know if he had tender feelings. I wanted to learn more about him, but we reached a point where the conversation stopped. Our memories of past lives were both a connection and a barrier.

Chapter 47

Corvinus

The Lady paced her chamber, tore at her hair, and nursed her pain. She begged me to hunt for Bon and Christine again. I did this not out of obedience or concern for her but because I also wanted to know their whereabouts. I flew as far north and west as Toulouse and as far east as Narbonne; I found no trace of them or of Garsenda, who fled earlier. What I discovered instead was news of impending war. I hid to listen to men talk and witnessed interesting events with my own eyes.

At first, the Count of Toulouse showed little concern about his excommunication. Then, as northern nobles volunteered for holy war against the south, Raymond saw his position had become untenable. He appealed directly to the Pope to negotiate terms of surrender. By June, many powerful northern nobles were gathering men in response to the Pope's call for holy war; the soldiers were eager for war, and it was too late to call them off. The pope gave harsh terms: Raymond had to surrender seven castles and the County of Melguiel, and he was forced to agree that his consuls at Avignon, Nimes, and St.-Gilles would renounce their allegiance if he continued to break his promises.

I was at St.-Gilles on June 18th to witness Raymond's ultimate humiliation. In front of the Benedictine abbey, he was stripped to the waist and flogged. Then, this lord of serpents made a shrewd move. On June 22, he took the cross and joined forces with the invading army. This protected his own cities from attack.

Earlier in the same year, in January 2019, the Count had proposed an alliance with his nephew, Viscount Raymond Roger Trencavel, but that hot-headed youth had refused. Now Trencavel faced the invaders alone. He tried to negotiate peace with the holy army, but they refused.

The army that the Pope summoned from the north mustered on June 24 at Lyon. King Philip sent knights but did not come himself or send his son. It was the feast of John the Baptist, and an atmosphere of gaiety filled the city. The streets were full of souvenir hawkers, pilgrims, pickpockets, and prostitutes. People said there were 20,000 soldiers. There were almost as many camp followers: clerics, craftsmen, sappers, engineers, carpenters, cooks, livestock handlers, wives, and looters. Northern nobles, including the Count of Nevers and the Duke of Burgundy, brought elite knights with bright banners and silk crosses on their tunics.

I conveyed all this to the Lady. She gripped the edge of the table; her face grew white.

"Do you think there can be peace?"

"That seems unlikely, my Lady. Viscount Raymond Roger Trencavel is a man of paratge. He will refuse to turn over any Cathar heretics to the invaders. And an army that is spoiling for war will not go home without plunder, no matter what concessions the Viscount makes."

"Will the invaders come to Mirefoix?"

"They may, in time. They will target nearer, wealthier cities first."

"Then I have time to prepare. I must summon Jaufre...."

The man she chose to command the garrison after Bon left was worthless, and now was the time to press her.

"Lady, I remind you again that you promised me a human body. I will serve you as a man."

She looked discomfited. I had eavesdropped on her conversations with the jinn and the translator Mena. I knew the soul-summoning spell would not work again. The time had not yet come for me to turn against the Lady; I must think what course of action would be to my greatest advantage.

Chapter 48

Christine

July 1209

We reached Beziers on July 1st. We crossed an arched bridge over the River Orb and followed a road that seemed so ancient and well-constructed that I wondered if Romans had built it. The light gray and beige stone walls that loomed above us gave a reassuring impression of strength. A lofty tower punctuated the skyline, perhaps a cathedral. We passed through a round-arched gate into the old town of Sauvian, and Bon asked the first few people we met where to find Fabrice. Next to a smithy, we found the crowded house within the city walls where Fabrice lived with his cousin's family.

Fabrice dropped his hammer with a clang and embraced Bon.

"Welcome, my friend!"

When he saw me, he seemed abashed.

"I apologize that I abandoned you when you fell, Lady."

"There was nothing that you could have done against so many."

"Garsenda will be pleased to see you." He called, and she emerged from the house. Her eyes went straight to Bon, and she ran and threw her arms around him. Bon seemed to stiffen, and I wondered why. Her greeting to me was less enthusiastic.

That good family made room for us, although it stretched their resources to the limit. Their house had only one room, which served as a kitchen, storage, and sleeping area. Hams and sausages dangled from the smoke-stained rafters, and chickens rooted around inside and out. I slept near Fabrice's cousin, his wife, and their three children; Fabrice and Garsenda slept in a loft where they had made a sort of nest. Bon made his bed in the shed behind the forge.

I did not mind the cramped house. I was free and among friends. I walked among people, visited the markets, and explored the city. The women taught me how to shop and cook, and I did these reasonably well. I took charge of making bread dough to bring to the common ovens for baking each morning.

Garsenda's coldness puzzled me. We had both escaped the Lady, so we had that in common. When I spoke, she turned her back. After a time, I gave up trying to befriend her.

Bon and Fabrice were old friends who enjoyed each other's company. One day I overheard their conversation. They seemed unaware of my presence. Fabrice said:

"I was astonished that she accepted me as her true husband. I thought only to protect her."

"I am surprised to hear that. Garsenda is proud."

"Now she regrets her choice and treats me as a stranger. And yet, her submission to me at first made this an actual marriage. She responded with passion."

"She has always been passionate."

"She rarely allows me to touch her... I thought that perhaps if I got her with child, she would find cause for happiness. She is unsuited to this life and pines for the leisure of court. And she is the worst cook in all Christendom."

At first, Bon laughed. Then he showed concern.

"How will this end, do you think?"

"I don't know."

They discussed politics. Fabrice had news:

"A massive army gathered at Lyons, and already many towns and cities have surrendered. If we stand united, we may defeat these invaders, but shifting loyalties have always been a problem for us here in the south."

"Do you think the army will come here?"

"It's likely. Refugees are filling the city. Beziers is one of Trencavel's most important cities, and it lies on the road to Carcassonne, his largest stronghold. We should be safe here, provided food and water supplies do not run out. People say the commanders of the invasion quarrel and the army is disorganized."

"Do you think Beziers will hold?"

"We can hold, and we must."

Bon sought me out. I confessed I had heard.

"I should not have brought you here. It may not be safe."

I wished to remember the details of the history, but I have never had a good memory of dates. I knew only this: The Church would successfully suppress heresy until Martin Luther challenged their authority hundreds of years later. These people might win some battles, but they would lose this war.

Chapter 49

Garsenda

I had loved Bon since childhood, and I yearned for him still. Bon's attention to Christine distressed me, and I knew I had to act soon or lose any chance to secure him for myself. In private, I reread the love spell I had stolen from my mother's chamber. The words promised to bind us together in body and soul for a lifetime. I purchased the ingredients for a potion and steeped them in wine. I waited until the night of the full moon, as specified by the spell. I got up softly at moonrise and went to the shed behind the forge, where I found Bon awake. I invited him to share a cup of wine. He was surprised but did not refuse.

In a short time, he fell into a deep slumber. I lay down beside him. The spell promised to make us one forever. I placed my head on his shoulder. I touched his face as he slept and fell into an irresistible revery. I had vivid dreams of the ecstatic intimacy for which I longed. In those dreams, he did everything I had wanted and imagined.

When I woke before dawn, our clothes were disarranged. Bon sighed and rolled toward me. And then I saw the red strawberry-shaped birthmark on his upper back, identical to the one I saw on my father's body when we prepared him for burial. Dear God, I thought. He is my brother, as he always said. I have been wrong all these years. Had I bound him to me in an incestuous love? Neither he nor God would forgive that. I hoped the spell would fail. Perhaps nothing had really happened. It was only a dream. I rose and left him asleep in the straw. My heart was hollowed out with knives, and my soul was black with sin too terrible to confess.

I dared not ask him whether he remembered that night, and I watched to see whether the spell had changed him. Surely he would be embarrassed if he had the same dream. If he fell in love with me because of it, he would look at me as a man tortured by forbidden longing. But he did not look at me differently or pay more attention than before. Instead, his eyes followed Christine. Guilt tortured me. I was relieved that the magic seemed to have failed. And yet, I couldn't help it; I still desired him.

Chapter 50

Christine

Bon still avoided any intimate contact. Sometimes I wished he would touch me, but at other times I was afraid. I did not believe my vow of chastity was binding; I made that promise under duress and in a spirit of foolish pique. However, he believed it would dishonor us both to break that vow. I knew he was troubled by the dishonor he brought on himself by breaking his vows of loyalty to the Lady. He would not further tarnish his honor or damage mine. I often sensed I was being watched and turned to see his eyes upon me.

I desired and admired him. He was my only close companion in this world. Because we were both outsiders, we shared understandings we didn't have with anyone else. I hoped but also feared that when my year as a novice ended, he would ask me to marry him. Or perhaps not. The sight of him made my heart overflow with longing.

He treated me with a sort of reverence. I thought: he's playing the game of courtly love, imagining that he is a knight wooing a lady. Over time I suspected it was something more, and I was terrified. I wanted to believe that love with Bon would differ from my other relationships. But I had seen, in my own life and the lives of others, how passionate love often deteriorated into dreary demands and loneliness.

Marriage in this time would lead to other problems. Childbirth was often fatal; babies often died in the first months of life. We would never have a home to keep children safe. Despite those fears, I wanted to hope. My previous life was empty of love. Perhaps I could do better this time, even with these obstacles. Maybe it would be better to end this life with memories of a brief, beautiful love, even if it couldn't last.

The anniversary of my vow arrived in mid-July, one week before the feast of Mary Magdalene. The day dawned hot and hazy; old men said this was the hottest summer in memory. Bon invited me to walk outside the walls, along the river. I think he sensed my hesitancy. I sat on the bank of the River Orb and let my bare feet dangle in the water. He began.

"Isaac said we have a shared destiny. What do you think he meant?"

"I'm a stranger in this world, and so are you, to a lesser extent."

He kneeled beside me and smiled, yet he looked unsure of himself. "I am unworthy. I have no worldly goods, no position. All I can offer is love and protection. I want to marry you. Will you have me?"

I had tried to prepare myself, but I wasn't ready. I longed for love, but my fear was powerful. My answer was ambivalent and inadequate.

"I want to, but I'm afraid."

"Of poverty?"

"Of more than that. Afraid of love."

His smile faded. My heart ached to know I had hurt him.

"I don't understand. Haven't I proved my devotion?"

"In my experience, love does not last."

"What happened in that other life doesn't matter now. I will love you forever. When I broke my oath to serve the Lady, I lost my honor in the eyes of the world, but I thought you understood. Honor is still everything to me, but I understand it differently. My honor comes from serving you. Don't you believe me?"

"I want to. But love can turn into indifference and contempt even with the most sincere intentions. That caused me more pain than anything else. In the end, my husband expected me to do everything a wife does, but without love."

"I am not that other man. Trust me."

He had avoided physical contact during most of our journey while I hungered for it. Now he drew me close. His touch did what words couldn't. I was safe and cherished, and I wanted this feeling to endure. At that moment, my soul had no questions. Persuaded by his arms around me, I said yes.

We embraced and kissed, a lingering, tender kiss. When I touched others, strength seeped out of me, and I absorbed their pain. With him, contact was different; his strength, courage, and desire flowed into me. Bon spoke.

"I talked with Samuel, the leader of the Jewish community. He and all his people will leave for Carcassonne tomorrow with Viscount Trencavel. He asked me to guard his house here. We can be alone there in comfort."

When we returned to the smith's house, our joy must have been apparent. I was calm now that I had decided. Fabrice clapped Bon on the back.

"We must drink to this!"

Garsenda gave me a poisonous look. I wondered: Can she be jealous? Surely not; he's her brother.

The wedding was not an elaborate affair. We only needed to say to each other, I marry you. Sometimes this happened on the front steps of a Church, perhaps with a priest's blessing. But priests or other witnesses weren't required; some made marriage vows in private. We wanted our friends to celebrate with us. We stood before them: Garsenda, Fabrice, and Fabrice's cousin and family.

"I, Christine, marry you, Bon."

"I, Bon, marry you, Christine."

All except Garsenda whooped and cheered, and we sat down for our last meal together. Fabrice had decided to accompany Viscount Trencavel and others to Carcassonne to help with the city's defense; Garsenda had to go with him. Garsenda moved slowly to show her reluctance while Fabrice and his cousin packed tools and harnessed donkeys to their wagon. They joined a motley procession that streamed out the gates toward the west on the main road to Carcassonne, following Trencavel and his knights.

When I saw Trencavel I was surprised at his youth; he appeared to be in his early 20s. He had a noble bearing. Bon admired him.

"A man of paratge. Perhaps too noble and proud. He waited too late to seek an alliance with Toulouse, and now the Count has allied himself with the invaders, and Trencavel stands alone against them."

"Will we be safe in Beziers?"

"Yes. I would not ask you to stay if I feared the city would fall. Perhaps it is selfish of me, but we can be alone in Samuel's house for a time. It is an opportunity we would have nowhere else. And I cannot run from this fight. Be assured that it's impossible to take a city like Beziers by force. Trencavel has left a strong force to defend it."

"But they will try?"

"Yes. This army will lay siege. You will be safe in Samuel's house; it is far inside the walls and has a sturdy roof. When their forty days of required service have passed, many soldiers will leave, and this army will disband."

I hoped he was right.

That night Bon brought me to Samuel's house. Samuel's wife Hannah had left us a roasted hen, crusty braided bread brushed with honey, cheese, and cinnamon-spiced apple tart. Bon poured wine. He seemed to understand that I might need a dose of liquid courage. What did I fear? Only everything.

I made nervous small talk.

"In my time, marriage vows were more formal."

"Tell me."

"We would say words like these... I take you to be my husband, to have and to hold from this day forward, for better, for worse, for richer, for poorer, in sickness and health, to love and to cherish, till death do us part... and with this ring, I thee wed, with my body I thee worship, and with all my worldly good I thee endow."

"Those are beautiful words; let's make those promises to each other. I'm sorry that I can only offer you poverty at present. I hope to offer more in the future. Meanwhile, I give all that I can. I would lay down my life to protect you."

"That's the greatest gift I have ever received; I can't ask for more than that."

"Here are words of a poem I learned from my mother's servant, my teacher: 'Till mountains crumble, till rivers run dry, till thunder rumbles in winter, till snow falls in summer, and the earth mingles with the sky, not till then will my love die.'"

We sat on the side of the bed. He caressed my cheeks and neck, exploring them gently. He kissed the hollow of my throat; he buried his nose in my neck. He dipped his finger in the wine, traced my lips, took me in his arms, and brought his mouth to mine. I was weak in the knees. I untied the laces at the side of my surcoat.

"We have all night. No hurry. Let me do what I have imagined a hundred times."

He kneeled before me and unlaced my shoes. He gazed up at me and smiled; the sweetness of his expression made him look like a boy. He let down my hose and massaged my feet. My nervousness melted away as we shared a cup of wine. The sweet warmth that ran through my veins was not only from the wine.

"You have imagined well."

I let down my hair. He ran his hands through it.

I stroked his hair, face, and neck and luxuriated in the scent of his skin.

He kissed the palms of my hands; then, we held hands with interlaced fingers.

"I know what I will find under your gown: skin like warm white silk. Breasts like peaches."

"How can you know? You haven't seen me yet."

"Remember when I turned my back for you to bathe in the river? I might have looked."

The August heat was oppressive. He patted cool water on my legs and arms, making me shiver with delight and anticipation. At last, we lay together without his sword between us as a barrier. His face relaxed from its usual vigilance into a vulnerable boyish smile. I traced his brows and nose with my finger as if to memorize his face. We explored each other and murmured words of love. My fears dissolved, and touching him filled me with joy and courage. The world shrank until it contained only the two of us and this moment. We belonged to each other.

"When I hold you, I feel peace," he said.

I never found true love in my prior existence. Now I thought: Thank You, God, for giving me a chance for love in this life. It was worth the wait. When Bon wrapped his arms around me, it was as if castle walls enclosed me in perfect safety. Afterward, we floated in a warm sea of love.

Chapter 51

Bon

Three days after our marriage, the disorganized invaders arrived. Their campfires were as numerous as stars in the night. Nevertheless, morale among the defenders of Beziers was high. Blacksmiths and fletchers worked without ceasing. We laughed and joked as we carried stones, sheaves of arrows, water, and food supplies to the battlements. Christine and the other women shared in this task. At dawn on the day of the feast of Mary Magdalene, I rose. I told Christine to stay in Samuel's house and bar the door. The attackers might launch stones over the walls. She seemed worried.

"What if they breach the gates?"

"That will not happen. But if it does, seek sanctuary in the cathedral; you'll be safe there, and I'll know where to find you."

She helped me lace my gambeson and slip on my hauberk.

"I pray these keep you safe. How would I live without you?"

I confess I had cheerful anticipation about the attack to come. We would repel these attackers, and I was pleased to show my skills. I stood among the archers atop the battlements. It was likely they would make a few forays to test our defenses. My aim was inerrant, and my sight keen. My comrades would see my worth. After the siege, I would become a member of the city guard and perhaps rise to a position of leadership. I stationed myself at the top of the city wall near the gate. A disorganized drunken rabble gathered outside, just beyond the range of our bows, and they taunted us. Our men exchanged vulgar insults and threats with the crowd outside.

I was aghast when I saw our men's response. Those foolish hotheads opened the gate and charged out to attack the hecklers. With the gate left untended, the rabble swarmed through, spilling into the streets beyond, followed at once by better-armed knights and foot soldiers. Trampling bodies before them, the opening wedge of the invading army poured in. We defenders on the wall ran down the stone steps and attempted to block soldiers from entering the city, but we were too late.

Fighting was hand-to-hand and bloody. I left my sword sheathed; it was not the best weapon for this situation. I saw a man with a poleax, brought him down by throwing my knife at his throat, and seized his ax. This kept opponents at arm's length. I fought two or three men at a time, a challenge even for one with my skill.

I saw at once that we had lost our fight to hold the city. The ruffians broke through our thin line of defenders and dispersed into the streets and alleys, howling with blood lust. These were not disciplined soldiers with any notion of honor; they were looters and brigands. When I saw the city was doomed, my only thought was to get to Christine. She would find refuge in the cathedral; surely, these attackers would respect sanctuary. Townspeople ran, trying to escape the flood of invaders. Pursuers trapped them. They struck off limbs, crushed skulls, and waded through the mess of intestines spilling out of slashed bellies. I saw one take an infant by its heel, dash its brains against a wall, turn on the mother, and tear off her clothes. People slipped on mangled limbs and crushed bodies; blood gave off a metallic smell that I remembered from my dream of Yong Jen's death. They entered houses and seized everything of value.

The attackers set fires. Thatched roofs and timbered buildings quickly caught the blaze. If the fire spread, it would destroy the entire city and all its people. I knew Beziers was lost. There was no hope that we few defenders could contain this mass of attackers. I had to find Christine. The day before, I had figured out the most direct route from the gate to the cathedral. Now I fought my way in that direction. Members of the howling mob took time to kill, mutilate, and rape their way through our people; I must reach the cathedral before they did. I had told her to seek refuge there; she must find sanctuary in time.

The sights I saw as I ran toward the church sickened me. These villains bashed in people's skulls, and grayish brains spilled out above dead-staring eyes. Bellies had been torn open to reveal loops of intestines like pink sausage. I saw rapes. Under other circumstances, I would have stopped to give aid, but not now. I must find Christine.

I found the square of the Cathedral of St. Nazaire. People who arrived early had already barred the cathedral doors, and now those who sought refuge could not enter. Townspeople who remained outside beat on the doors, screaming, Let us in! I searched the crowd, did not see her, and decided she must already be inside. Hundreds of voices rose in prayer. I believed Christine was among those safe inside the church. Surely these brutes would leave the cathedral alone.

I was appalled by what happened next. Ruffians looted the attached monastery. An even larger crowd stacked broken furniture, hay, rushes, and anything else that would burn around the outside walls of the cathedrals. Attackers sang the Veni Sancte Spiritus to call down God's blessing on this massacre. Someone shouted: "Kill them all! God will recognize His own." I hated their God, this God who sanctioned the murder of innocents.

A few of us attacked these devils and tried to stop them from piling up fuel, but it was futile to oppose so many men bent on massacre. Flames rose against the church walls; they reached as high as the rose-shaped stained-glass windows, then leaped to the wooden roof above the stone ceiling. The church became a furnace. The more fortunate would suffocate before they burned to death. The less fortunate would be incinerated; I knew what death by fire was like. Men outside cheered while voices inside screamed in anguish. The odor of burning human fat and hair filled my nostrils. It made me sick. I wanted to be inside the cathedral, by Christine's side. I would give her a quick death and join her in the afterlife. But that was not possible.

Billows of smoke blinded us. The attackers realized nothing was left to plunder and ran into side streets, searching for more victims. At first, I stood as if invisible among them, immobilized by grief, unable to take my eyes from the burning church. I wanted to retrieve her body, but seeing mounds of corpses charred beyond recognition, I knew even this was futile. I had loved no one as I loved her, and my grief overwhelmed me. I had sworn to protect her, but when the time came, I failed. I resolved to avenge her death and set out after a group of men as they swarmed into an alley. When I had killed in the past, I did it quickly; I killed only when I must and did not make my victims suffer. Now I was in a blood rage; dealing out death exhilarated me.

Chapter 52

The Lady

The news Corvinus brought about the activities of armies outside Lyons made me fear. I traveled to Foix to plead with my liege lord the Count for aid. He was brusque. "I must keep my men here to defend Foix; I cannot send them to Mirefoix. You must manage on your own, as you have always done." His words brought fresh despair. All was lost. Mirefoix would be taken; I would live in torment and, after death, spend eternity in Hell.

I supped with Lady Esclarmonde, sister of the Count of Foix. She and her companion wore the austere clothing of Cathar Perfects. Her body was thin, and her face was gaunt, but a light shone from her eyes. I wished I, too, had that inner light.

"I see your distress, dear friend. What is the cause?"

"I have done evil things, and I fear I will go to Hell. Prayers and confession and penance have not relieved my fears."

"Of course, those have not. The Church is corrupt, and priests are too concerned with wealth and worldly matters. They fill their bellies and take concubines. Salvation is between the individual spirit and God. I have learned the truth, and you may find it comforting."

"Please tell me."

"We Good Christians know people do not go to Hell after death. The physical world, created by the Devil, is Hell. Our spirits pass through its evils on their way to God. Those who make the vow of the Consolamentum, and become Perfects, as I have done, go to God in heaven when they die; they do not return to live again on earth. Those who live in sin return to the earth, again and again, their souls clothed in new bodies, and continue to suffer Hell until they are ready for salvation. Earth is the true Hell." Her glowing eyes promised the truth of her words.

Her words brought me such relief. I need not fear an eternity in Hell; I was already in Hell, and death would bring release.

She explained the difference between the true God of the New Testament, who offered salvation, and the false God Jehovah from the Old Testament, who created the earth and all its evils. She taught me to make the sign of a circle instead of the cross.

"Can I become a Perfect? What must I do?"

"There are two kinds of Good Christians. Some are merely believers. Those who make themselves pure can become Perfects, members of the Elect. It is difficult. You must study for three years. During that time, you can be a believer and receive the teachings. To become a Perfect, you take the vow of Consolamentum. From that day on, you must live a pure life. If that is too difficult, you can live as a believer and take the Consolamentum on your deathbed, as many choose to do."

"What is required for a pure life?"

"We eat no meat, abstain from physical relations, take no oaths, and live in poverty. We teach the truth to believers."

She answered my questions with enviable certainty. Her words were the first that offered genuine comfort. And yet I had doubts.

"The Church calls you heretics and has burned some Good Christian believers."

"The Church has lost the genuine message of Christ, and priests are the real heretics."

"I want to learn. Please help me."

Esclarmonde sent two women Perfects to Mirefoix to be my teachers and give me the Consolamentum in case of my death. There was much to learn. They taught me their prayers and showed me sacred writings in the lenga romana. It was wonderful to read holy words in my own tongue.

I changed into a simple gray gown. I ate as little as possible, never meat or eggs, those products of sinful sexual reproduction. I cleansed my soul of lust. In time, if I maintained this discipline, I would become one of the saved who would go directly to God after death. I was secure in my new faith. The four demons still visited my sleeping chamber; however, I kept the two Perfects with me, and the fiends frightened me less. My physical pain diminished. I no longer believed that my misery was a punishment from God; it was part of the world's evil.

I did not declare this new faith in public, not yet, because I was not worthy. However, I met with Cathar believers and Perfects, and their community provided much comfort. I promised that no matter what the Papal legates demanded, I would not surrender my Good Christians to the Church.

I had stopped taking blood from Blodeweth, for this must be a sin. With better treatment, she recovered much of her strength. I wanted to keep my promise to send her back to her homeland, but I was caught in a trap I created myself. I couldn't release her lest she speak of what had happened. She would perish if I sent her out into a world at war.

I destroyed the spells by burning the pages and scattering the ashes into the wind. However, the jinn continued to torment my people. I asked the blue jinni: Would my death set you free? If I die, will you stop torturing my people? Yes, he said.

Meanwhile, I knew: I was going blind.

Chapter 53

Bon

I climbed up to a roof and scanned the area. It was only by luck that I found Christine lying in an alley beyond the cathedral. My heart leaped when I saw her in the shadows of an entryway. I climbed down.

"Christine! Answer me!"

I shook her, but she did not respond. Her forehead was bleeding.

I took her in my arms, desperate in my sense of loss.

She mumbled something incomprehensible. She was alive. I thought quickly. Where can we find safety? By now, the blaze had spread to nearby houses and shops. If this continued, the entire city would burn by nightfall, and all would die. I carried Christine away from the cathedral, away from the main gate. The farthest side of the city would be the last to burn. Other townspeople fled in the same direction. I thought about rallying men; no, they were terrified, had no weapons, and the city was in flames. I must try to save Christine.

Off to the right, a cluster of men searched for new targets. They saw us. Too many for me to fight. As I plunged into the maze of alleys, I heard bellowing men close behind us. We had to find a hiding place. I darted into a narrow street. It was a dead end. We were trapped. At least a dozen pursuers closed in, yapping like mad dogs. I propped Christine against the wall behind me and positioned myself in front of her. I slew them in twos and threes, using the pike to make sweeping blows. It struck one man's neck with such force that it removed his head. When a pile of bodies had accumulated at my feet, the remaining attackers lost heart and turned away to search for easier prey.

Christine had regained consciousness. She was on her knees, vomiting. I wiped her face.

"Come quickly."

By now, she could walk a little; I dragged her behind me. We ducked through an open door into a well-built house, not yet pillaged, with tall cupboards along one wall. I got Christine into the cupboard and closed the door behind us. I held her close against me; she stood unsteadily. I placed my knife against her throat; I knew how to kill quickly and would not allow them to take her alive. She nodded, and I knew she understood. I heard the rapid beat of her heart; I listened to her ragged breaths.

Suddenly men burst into the room. I heard laughter, shouts, and the clang of weapons as they ransacked the place. How long until they tore open the doors of our hiding place? The moments seemed like hours.

At last, the men departed in search of more opportunities for pillage and slaughter. We must not stay there; I opened the cupboard door a crack and helped Christine step out. Hissing, searing flames now blocked the doorway to the street. I seized her hand; she was becoming steadier on her feet. We ran up the stairs. I feared we would be trapped. I stood on a bed in the upper chamber and used a stool to batter a hole in the thatched ceiling. I pulled myself up through it, then extended my hands to pull Christine up beside me. We perched on the ridgepole. Neighboring houses were in flames, and this house would be next.

"Come." On hands and knees, we made our way carefully along the ridgepole. I had no time for fear, and I must be strong to save Christine, but the possibility of death by fire renewed my concerns. I knew what that would be like, and it held special terror for me as it must for her.

"Where you can see crossbeams, put your weight on them. Do as I do. What bears my weight will surely support yours."

We reached the edge, and I balanced, measuring the distance to the next house with my eyes. It was a substantial distance; howling men dashed about in the street below. They also sought to escape the flames. With a running start, I can make it. Maybe. I stood, gathered my strength, leaped across the alley, and reached the roof of the next house.

"Jump! You can do it. I'll catch you if you fall short. Take off any clothing that hinders you."

She slipped out of her sleeveless surcoat and shortened her shift by tucking it into a knot. She looked down and recoiled. A fall would break bones and leave her in the mob's path.

"Believe me. You can do this, and you must."

She stood, made a visible effort, and hurled herself toward me. Her feet fell short; I grasped her arms and fell backward onto the roof, pulling her to safety. We were one house farther from the encroaching conflagration. This roof was sturdy, and the next few jumps were over narrower alleys. From our rooftop viewpoint, I saw the mob circle and head back toward the Narbonne gate. We worked our way in the opposite direction toward a cluster of houses that had not yet caught fire. Then the wind changed. Greedy flames sucked air into their vortex. The firestorm behind us intensified.

When we had put some distance between ourselves and the looters, I helped Christine climb down to the street, and we ran to an unguarded postern gate. Nearby we saw the remains of a rag seller's shop. We decided she must dress like a boy. She tied her hair back and tucked it into the neck of her tunic; with a hood pulled over her head, it would not show. We took up cloth, needle, and thread and sewed crosses like those worn by the invaders onto our surcoats. Perhaps this would fool the invaders into thinking we belonged to their army. We slipped out through the postern gate when our disguises were ready.

Evening came. Orange light from the fires that consumed Beziers, and the haze of black oily smoke, gave that terrible night an eerie atmosphere. How strange not to hear bells tolling the hours, only screams of anguish from the streets. I told Christine:

"Say nothing. Keep your cloak wrapped around you. Stay near me. I speak a little of the langue d'oïl.

With luck, they will take us for fellow invaders separated from our company."

I hoped to avoid the enemy encampments, but they had spread all around the city. Cooking fires blazed; voices were loud, drunk, and merry. The smell of roasting meat sickened me because it reminded me of burning human flesh, an odor I could never get out of my mind. I feared their gazes would penetrate Christine's disguise. I was proud of her; she stood steady with a courage I didn't know she possessed.

We passed through the fringes of the army; when we left the encampment behind, Christine collapsed. I carried her as long as possible, then found a hiding place. I tended to her and let her sleep. I said:

"We will head west to Carcassonne. It has never fallen, not in eight hundred years. We will be safe there."

Two days later, we reached the great walled city of Carcassonne. It was similar in layout to Mirefoix but more massive, with high battlements and twenty-six round towers. Guards at the gate allowed only those who spoke the lenga romana to enter. I asked for news about Fabrice and Garsenda. I found Fabrice among the artisans who worked in the courtyard at the Narbonne gate, making and mending weapons. Fires blazed, smoke formed a thick haze, and hammers clanged as they worked. Women and men carried stones, vessels of water and wine, and sheaves of arrows to the walls to prepare for the assault. It was encouraging to see their energy and confidence after the disaster at Beziers; I wondered how many knew what had happened. Fabrice wiped his brow and took a few moments to talk with us.

"When we arrived, Garsenda insisted on going to the Chateau Comtal. She said she was tired of living among common people and would identify herself as a noblewoman. I tried to persuade her this might not be safe, but she was determined. I have only seen her once since we arrived here. She shares a chamber with two other women at the Chateau." There was sadness in his eyes; I regretted the unhappy marriage I had inflicted on him. I tried to soothe his regrets.

"It will be safer for her there, and I'll ask for the same shelter for Christine." Christine's face told me this didn't please her, but I knew this would be for the best. The Chateau Comtal was a fortress within the city; even if the outer walls were taken, Trencavel's men could defend it. I took Christine's hand, and we walked through the town to seek Trencavel's seneschal. The man was harried, but he delegated a servant to show Christine to the room she would share with Garsenda and other women.

I first saw Viscount Raymond Roger Trencavel from a distance. He was young, indeed no older than I, but he was already renowned as a man of great paratge. He looked careworn from the heavy responsibility that rested on his shoulders. He was the only leader among the southern nobles who stood against the invaders. As Raymond Roger walked among his people, he gave smiles and words of encouragement. Their affection and respect for him were apparent. I caught up with him when he stopped for a conference with his leaders.

"My lord, I have just come from Beziers."

Trencavel's face was grave. "I know the city was razed. Can you tell me how this happened?"

I had been well positioned to see how the gate was breached. I told him all, and his distress was evident.

"I should not have left my people behind, but I believed the city would hold. I can't believe even these northerners would show such dishonor."

He invited me to stay while he reviewed the situation with his men. He spread out a map.

"They can never breach the city walls. However, the walls of the bourgs outside are low. If they seize those towns, the buildings will provide cover for a direct assault. Our access to the river at St. Vincent is vulnerable."

"Are there other water sources?"

"A few wells in the city. However, these often dry up during late summer drought, and this has been a hot summer indeed. We must hold St. Vincent." His expression was grim. The city's position was weaker than I had expected. Without adequate water and food supplies, a crowded town soon falls prey to starvation, filth, and pestilence.

"Do you expect reinforcements?"

"I have appealed to my liege lord King Peter of Aragon. We expect him soon. Morale is high, and my men have courage and honor. You are welcome to join our defense."

Chapter 54

The Lady

August 1209

News from Beziers brought terror. The invaders had shown no restraint, no humanity. They slew Catholics along with heretics without bothering to distinguish between them. Now they had moved west and approached Carcassonne. That was only a few days' march from Mirefoix. I prayed for Carcassonne to hold. If it fell, attackers would no doubt seize more towns and castles in the region.

After I destroyed the spells, the jinn no longer tormented my dreams. Instead, they terrorized my people. Terrified peasants brought tales of flaming swords and apparitions that came by night. The jinn struck livestock dead. They swirled around the battlements and beset the villages with winds that made dreadful sounds. Hayricks and houses caught fire for no reason.

I had caused these disasters myself. I made unreasonable demands of Bon, Garsenda, and Christine. Of course, they had fled. Now I had no advisors, no protectors, no heir. I had hoped, like my father, to rule Mirefoix well, to keep it peaceful and prosperous, and to inspire loyalty among those who would help me. Now I had no one to care for me, and I was sick in spirit and flesh.

When the Baron of Saverdun arrived, I guessed what was in his mind. I received him in my chamber and dismissed the servants. He offered no pleasantries and got to the point.

"Lady, you have no heir, and the commander of your garrison lacks experience. You need protection; I offer myself again as your husband. I can defend your city."

I rose and paced the room. How had we come to this crisis when Mirefoix had been so strong a year ago? "I need time to consider."

"There is no time. If Carcassonne falls, the invaders will move against Foix and its dependencies. That includes both our cities. The invaders will show no mercy."

I knew he had a son. If I married the Baron, his son would become the heir of Mirefoix, and there would be no heir of my blood.

"I need time to consult my advisers and consider your proposal. Give me a month."

"You have a week. Do not delay too long; I will seek other alliances."

If Carcassonne fell, the invaders would pick off smaller cities on the plains. Those would be easy to take; cities in the foothills, like Mirefoix, would be more challenging to capture. However, there was still reason to fear. To protect Mirefoix, I needed Bon to rally the garrison; and I must reconcile with Garsenda. Corvinus told me he had not discovered their whereabouts, and I wondered if this was true. He often reminded me that the price for his loyalty was the human body I promised him but did not provide. I would have to make further impossible promises to get him to agree to search for them and persuade them to return. After the Baron departed, I summoned Corvinus.

"You must find them and bring them this message. I need Bon and Garsenda here at Mirefoix. I repent most heartily all I did to them, and I will grant whatever they ask."

"And what of me, Lady? You haven't kept your promise. I want Bon's body."

He believed I still had this power. Good.

"I never promised his body. Only the body of a man."

"You must swear to get me a man's body if you want my help."

I promised; I had no choice but to lie. Corvinus departed.

Chapter 55

Bon

Christine found a safe place in the Chateau Comtal with Garsenda and other noblewomen. However, she complained they treated her as a servant. They ordered her to fetch water and demanded she massage their aching necks and mend their gowns. She grew tired of their petty requirements and went out to ask for ways to help with defense. I worried, but I understood Christine needed something to do.

There was plenty of work for women. They carried water from the river to fill every bucket and jar in the city. They brought stones and arrows to the battlements and prepared to treat injuries by tearing clean cloth for bandages. They cooked stew and pottage in massive cauldrons. Christine joined those who carried water and gave orders to set up a bucket brigade. She showed courage and confidence.

A day after we arrived at Carcassonne, an advance guard camped outside the walls. Two days later, encampments spread across fields as far as we could see. I took courage from the knowledge that Carcassonne had never fallen. It stood on a steep bluff above the river Aude, a defensible position. High walls with twenty-six towers surrounded the innermost city. Trencavel reinforced the outer walls. Even if the enemy breached these, they would encounter the second ring of high inner walls. Trencavel's Chateau within the city was itself a fortress. However, bourgs and suburbs had grown up outside the city walls. These had lower walls and ditches of their own, but they would be harder to defend, and if attackers seized them, they would use the houses as cover to bombard the city from a closer position. As Trencavel said, it was crucial to hold the bourg of St. Vincent because it provided the only access to the river. If we lost this, our water stores would not be sufficient for the masses of refugees who sought safety within the city walls. Hunger, thirst, and disease would set in if a protracted siege developed. Carcassonne would not fall. However, even unsuccessful sieges brought misery and death. Now that I realized Carcassonne's vulnerabilities, I cursed myself for bringing Christine here.

Raymond Roger commanded additional preparations for the siege. He built new wooden hoardings atop the battlements to provide archers with a clear view of attackers and allow men to drop stones on men close to the base of the wall. From these positions, we archers prevented sappers from undermining the walls. People mined the cathedral refectory for stones to drop from the walls and use as ammunition for mangonels. Foodstuffs outside the city had been brought inside the walls or burned to deprive the invading army of sustenance. Trencavel's men also destroyed the water-powered mills to prevent the invaders from grinding grain. If our luck held, the army outside might run out of food before our people in the city.

The assault began on August 1. I was an archer on the wall near the main gate. From this high vantage point, we saw enemy soldiers charge the walls of St. Vincent below; the townspeople and soldiers tried to hold them off and fought gallantly, but the attackers overwhelmed them. Their advance scouts must have identified access to the external water supply as a critical weakness, and now they controlled it.

When Raymond Roger called for men to retake St. Vincent, I was among the first to volunteer, and Fabrice followed. Although Fabrice was not well-trained as a soldier, he had formidable strength, and Raymond Roger needed as many men as possible. I had trained for combat all my life; I was no stranger to bloodshed. I had taken part in melees using blunt weapons. These sometimes got out of hand, leading to severe injuries and even death. I had killed and wounded men who harassed the Lady's villages. In my journeys with Christine, I had taken the lives of those who would harm her. I had witnessed the slaughter at Beziers. I took no pleasure in killing, but I killed when necessary.

This kind of battle was new to me and a severe shock. At first, it was clear which men were friends and foes. The fight quickly degenerated into chaos. Quick decisions were required, and men made mistakes in the mayhem. My speed and precision served me well. I spotted vulnerabilities and took advantage of them. Fabrice and I protected each other's backs. I remember only the first few encounters. A hefty man ran at me, bellowing, his sword poised to strike the side of my neck. It was easy to block and counterattack. Blood gushed from the wound on his neck. For a moment, he continued to fight. Two more blows, center chest and side, brought him down.

Immediately another man was upon me. I jumped aside from the body at my feet, swiveled, and kicked his groin. He doubled over, and I struck the back of his neck. Although I saw no blood, he staggered and fell. Then another. Then others. It was not hatred or bloodlust that drove us, just the will to survive. A few men seemed exhilarated by killing; most appeared exhausted. There was no bloodlust in their drawn faces.

I lost my speed and precision as I tired. Soon I had a deep slash on my left arm. Fabrice fought with courage, relying on the strength of his blows to take out opponents quickly. I needed to protect him as well as myself, but it was impossible. As I responded to an attack from two men on my right, another struck Fabrice on the head and split his skull. I dragged his body behind a wall and kneeled beside him. I took his hand; he had no last words. I covered his body and vowed to return to bury him in sacred ground.

I felt a sharp pain in my jaw and realized I had clenched my teeth so hard that I might have broken some. There were gashes in my arms and legs, some minor, some deep. Most of our men lay dead or wounded. At last, our leader called for a retreat. I staggered back to the city along with other battered soldiers. Women met us inside the gate to provide the little treatment that was possible. I fainted from the loss of blood. When I woke, Christine was applying pressure to stop my bleeding. She bathed my wound and sewed up the slash in my arm; although she plied needle and thread without the skill of a surgeon, the sutures were adequate. This must have caused her great pain, but she suppressed any sign of it. At first, I couldn't speak. When I was able, I scolded her for exposing herself to danger and taking on my pain.

"You must not. I swore I would not allow you to feel my pain."

"Shh. Taking away your pain is my choice."

Like a woman, I fainted. When I awoke, she was attending to others; she returned to my side. I heard the voices of agony and death. Women and men came and went, ministering to the wounded. In memories I had fought to suppress, I was a battlefield surgeon. Now those memories flooded back. I wanted to get up and use my remembered skills, but I was too weak.

"You lost so much blood. You need to drink this and rest." Christine's gaze rested on me, a blessing of peace after the hell of battle. I swore to myself she must never know what I had seen and done in battle or experience these things herself. Garsenda came. She pushed Christine aside and exclaimed in horror at my wounds. She did not ask about Fabrice. She wept over me.

"You are safe. You will live, certainly?"

"I will live to fight another day. Fabrice died in battle. When this siege has ended, I swear I will give him a proper burial."

She had the decency to appear shocked. And yet, her sorrow did not seem that of a bereaved and loving wife.

On the third day, they attacked a bourg on the city's north side. By then, I was strong enough to take up my bow again but not engage in hand-to-hand combat outside the walls. Although our defenders showed courage, the attackers seized the town, razed the buildings, and used stones to fill the ditches against the northern city walls. Emboldened by this success, on August 4th, they assaulted the southern bourgs again, using ladders to scale the walls. Our men again showed courage and rained down arrows and stones until the assault ended.

Within the city, water was already scarce. Hordes of useless refugees consumed our supplies, and the heat of August beat down on the stones and made the city like a furnace. Thirst became a problem. Trencavel ordered that most of the water go to defenders to maintain their strength, and I worried about Christine. She would not remain within the Chateau, as I asked, as I ordered. Instead, she nursed the sick and wounded; I saw that this exhausted her. That night I went to Christine. She was pale. She did not complain of the thirst she must feel. Instead, she spoke:

"Please tell me what is happening."

I was reluctant. "I prefer to understand. What I don't know, I imagine. Believe me, I will fear that things are worse than they are."

"We lost the water supply.... we have only a few days before disease spreads and children cry from thirst. Pray for rain. Pray for reinforcements."

The next day, I had more news for her.

"There's hope. Trencavel's liege lord, King Peter of Aragon, has arrived with a hundred knights."

"Aragon? Isn't that far away?"

"It is. But King Peter is Trencavel's ally, and he values Carcassonne as one of his most important possessions. His army might defeat the attackers. He might even persuade the Count of Toulouse to leave the invaders' side and join us. We may be saved."

We dared to hope. And then our hopes were dashed. Peter of Aragon did not join in our defense. Instead, he scolded his vassal Trencavel for ignoring his advice and sheltering heretics. He said the force he had with him was too small to defeat the invaders.

Without water, people in the city suffered. Some were desperate enough to drink urine. There were piles of bodies: those who died from injury and sickness. We argued about what to do. I was among those who said we must burn them to check the spread of disease, but others said there would be no hope of resurrection if their bodies were not buried in sacred ground. Because of these objections, nothing was done. Fleas and mosquitos became abundant. Raymond Roger walked through the streets, speaking to his people, trying to give them courage. He showed terrible grief over the suffering of his people.

I tried to keep moving even though tortured by thirst. I longer sweated in the heat. I was dizzy and confused, and my heart pounded. People hunted dogs, cats, and rats. It was difficult to eat any small bits of remaining food; we did not have enough saliva to moisten and swallow it. Christine continued to leave the Chateau to nurse the sick, many of them sheltered in the cathedral. I was angry that she exposed herself to risk.

"I want you to stay safe, to protect yourself. When you take the pain of others upon yourself, that suffering drains your strength. You will die."

"These brief contacts take less strength from me than prolonged ones. I do what I can and then rest. Please understand that this is who I am. I am a person who tries to help. I never promised to obey you, and I won't."

We prayed for rain, but the sky remained blazing blue. Raymond Roger walked through his city among the sick and wounded. I saw his troubled face; the suffering of his people distressed him.

Through the intercession of Peter of Aragon, the head of the invading army offered Trencavel safe passage to leave Carcassonne with eleven companions. He refused; he would not abandon his people.

By August 14, the invaders realized they could not breach the city walls and offered better terms of surrender. They would permit the garrison and people to leave wearing only tunics and breeches and leaving all possessions behind. Trencavel agreed to meet their leaders outside the walls to negotiate further terms. However, when he met them outside the gate, those treacherous men seized him and put him in chains.

I spoke to Christine. "Listen. You and Garsenda must leave the city tomorrow; you can bring only the clothes you wear. To bring other supplies we'll need, I'll descend the wall tonight, under cover of darkness, and wait for you outside along the road toward Toulouse."

Christine protested.

"No, this is unnecessary danger. The guards may kill you, or we may not find each other again."

"I must also bury Fabrice." I set my jaw to tell her there would be no further discussion. "Find Garsenda and tell her what I have said. You must stay together."

After dark, Christine and I climbed the wall above the bourg of St. Vincent. I made a bundle of clothing, silver, and my sword and knife. We worked to braid a rope out of cloth; Christine's hands were bloody when we finished. As agreed, she removed and hid our makeshift rope after I descended. I disappeared into the gathering darkness.

The following day a crowd gathered at the Aude gate, stripped down to braies and shifts. I waited for them outside, some distance outside the gates along the western road, concealed in shrubs; soldiers jeered and made lewd remarks. A priest shouted: "You leave with only your sins."

Chapter 56

Christine

There was little food available to buy or even steal on the road north and west toward Toulouse. Peasants salvaged a little from their farms and fled, torching the fields they abandoned. Small game was scarce. We avoided major roads and traveled through the hills. We bargained silver for a stale loaf and a wedge of dry cheese. Bon snared, skinned, and cooked rabbits. We pressed on. Toulouse was the safest place for now; Count Raymond had allied with the invaders, and they would not attack his city.

When we approached the city walls, we discussed how to manage. We had only enough silver coins for food and lodging for two or three nights. Bon said he might hire himself as a mercenary, but he found the idea distasteful. He would have to separate from us, and in any event, mercenaries often went unpaid. I also opposed this plan.

"I can work as a healer–"

Bon said, "Healing saps your strength, and you are already weak. I forbid that."

"I did not swear to obey you–"

"Wives obey their husbands–"

Maybe they did in 1930s China. And, of course, wifely obedience was expected at this time—although not always given. I wasn't going to argue the point. He knew who I was when he married me. I never promised to obey.

We entered Toulouse in early September and saw pink brick buildings, cobbled streets, and a sizeable bustling market square. The displays of food, drink, and trade goods dazzled us. Garsenda pleaded with Bon that we must eat, and he counted our small store of deniers and agreed that food would give us the strength we needed to search for work and lodging. He purchased only the cheapest fare, more of the bread, cheese, and wine we had grown so tired of on the road. I suggested:

"We should go separate ways to look for work. We can meet back here in front of this rag seller."

Bon frowned.

"You should not walk unprotected among these strangers."

I refrained from reminding him that the only time I came to harm in a marketplace was when Fabrice poisoned me and he himself kidnapped me at Saverdun. Instead, I said:

"One of us alone may find work, probably not three together. Surely you can see the sense of that." He agreed.

Women and children begged for bread, pickpockets mingled with the crowd, and prostitutes competed aggressively to offer their favors. These were not good signs. I paused at a stall where an older woman offered needlework for sale. There were purses and pockets, aprons, and thin girdles or belts. The bright colors and low prices attracted some interest, although the pieces were not well made. Her hands were gnarled, probably from arthritis. She squinted as she counted coins. Her crippled hands and poor eyesight would account for the poor quality of the stitching. I pretended to admire a purse.

"This is a beautiful color." She peered at me.

"You want to buy it? Only one denier."

"I regret I cannot buy it today. Is business good?"

As I hoped, this question elicited complaints.

"No one buys anymore. I can hardly pay for fuel and food." I encouraged her to continue. "My hands hurt, and I cannot see to thread a needle. I can no longer carry wood and water. The work is too hard."

The woman introduced herself as Na Margarete. She had kept up her husband's rag and sewing business after his death and was managing, but was afraid to live alone as a widow.

"May I see your hands? They seem to give you pain." As we continued to talk, I massaged her hands gently. Her face relaxed.

"You comfort me, child."

I was careful about the way I made my suggestion. Could I work in exchange for a place to live?

She was reluctant because I was a stranger and had no one to recommend me. I said:

"Perhaps I can sew for you for a week or two, then judge whether you are satisfied."

After further grumbling, she agreed. Now came the tricky part.

"My husband is with me, and he also needs a place to stay. If I make enough money for you with my work, will you also allow him a space to sleep?"

She ruminated out loud and decided that having a man in her house might make her feel safer at night. Of course, she must meet him before any agreement.

"I will bring him to meet you. He is gentle and strong and will make you feel safe." I decided not to ask about lodging for Garsenda yet. Any roof over our heads would be an improvement. I wasn't sure needlework would pay for our food, but this was a beginning.

We met as arranged. Bon said the scribes had little business; competing with them would earn only ill will. Garsenda had flirted with a man whose manner of dress suggested wealth; he offered a position as a housemaid. Bon said:

"He may want you in his house for something other than scrubbing floors."

"I have my knife, and I know how to use it."

"It would not be good to begin in Toulouse that way. We must find you something else."

I told them my news.

"I have found a possibility. A seller of needlework may be willing for us to live with her in return for my handwork, chores, and protection from you, Bon. I haven't told her about Garsenda. We can't ask too much at once."

Bon said:

"I asked about the cost of inns; we can pay for lodging and food for Garsenda for a few nights. She can wait." I brought Bon to see Na Margarete. As I expected, he charmed her. We would have a week's trial to see how things worked.

Na Margarete's house had only one room. The rear served as her kitchen, and the front was a sewing workshop. She slept near the fire, even on warm days. Bon and I made our bed with piles of rags near the front wall. Both of us had a sense of privacy from different times. Others had intimate relations in rooms full of other people, but we wanted to be alone. Na Margarete's robust snoring told us when we could be free of her unwelcome attention.

Needlework involved several steps. I purchased rags and bits of cloth and washed them first, mindful that sick people might have worn them. I unraveled bright pieces of material to obtain thread for embroidery. At first, I sewed purses for women to hang from their girdles. Then I created new designs for belts and neck scarves. Na Margarete peered over my shoulder as I worked, criticizing. My stitches were too large, too small, or uneven.

I softened her irascible nature in small ways. I heated stones in the fire, wrapped them in cloth, and had her hold them in her hands while I massaged them. I rubbed her shoulders and back, and she said this gave her relief. Bon was concerned about me, but I did not find her discomfort difficult to bear. It was a small price to pay for a roof and hearth. I had become an adequate cook and kept a kettle of pottage on the fire, and Bon brought wood and water. She said she had not slept well since the death of her husband and that Bon's presence made her feel safe at night. He carved small objects, such as toys and decorations that we sold at the market. Fabrice had taught him to whittle, he said.

Within a few days, Na Margarete announced she would keep us. Despite that, she heaped constant criticism upon me and expressed contradictory doubts and fears. She wondered aloud if I would have a baby that would be noisy and troublesome. Then she longed for the company of a child and prodded my belly to see if I might be pregnant. She complained I did not produce enough finished pieces. She said her customers were tired of the roses I embroidered, told me to make other designs, and complained when those didn't sell. I swept and scrubbed. She ran her fingers over tables and shelves and found nonexistent specks of dirt. She kept hold of every denier. She heaped food on Bon's plate and gave me stingy portions. And yet, I think she had a reluctant affection for me.

After a week, Bon brought up the issue we had avoided.

"Na Margarete, I have a sister I must provide for. Please, out of the goodness of your heart, allow her a place to stay." She grumbled and consented.

Na Margarete's house was the nearest we had ever had to a home. I tried not to worry how long this might last. We must live one day at a time. I had feared our love might diminish, but Bon still wooed me tenderly. He did not become demanding, and he remained concerned with my needs. We still had the excitement of discovery when we talked and made love. Could this last forever?

Chapter 57

Garsenda

September 1209

That old witch Na Margareta took an instant dislike to me. I was good for nothing else, she said, so I must do the scrubbing. Nothing was ever clean enough. She gave my cooking a trial and judged it unacceptable. At night, I heard Bon's passionate lovemaking with Christine; I knew that she was cherished and I was not.

Fabrice cherished me, but I didn't know how much his love meant to me until his death took his love from me. Now I cursed myself for my ingratitude and unkindness to him. I might have built a life on that foundation. Now I mattered to no one.

And then I discovered I was with child. I often refused Fabrice his husband's rights after we reached Beziers. I counted the weeks on my fingers. I wondered if the love spell had made me one with Bon in a way different than I expected. Did it make me conceive that night when I dreamed of passion? I lay with Bon only once, in a dream, and I had been with Fabrice many times. But if this child had Bon's face, it would be undeniable evidence of my sin. My pregnancy was not visible, but I knew it would be only a matter of time. I despaired. I sought a priest to ask for absolution.

"Father, I have sinned."

"What is the nature of your sin, my daughter?"

The words were painful.

"I tried to make my brother love me..."

I was about to add that, even though I had not touched him, I might carry his child. The priest interrupted.

"Whore! You must be punished. Has your husband whipped you?"

"No, my husband is—"

"Then that duty falls to me. You must be shamed in public." He summoned two other priests. They stripped me to the waist, and I fell to my knees as he scourged me. I rose and tried to cover myself with my torn clothing.

"That is only the first part. You must appear in the public square, confess all your sins, and give ten pieces of silver to buy prayers."

"I have no such sum."

He was furious. He pushed me to the floor, unfastened his belt, and climbed on top of me.

I pulled my knife and aimed it at his throat. He and the two other priests retreated. From a safe distance, he shouted: "Whore. You are damned to the flames of Hell, and God will never forgive your sins."

I fled.

My pregnancy would soon show. Bon showed no sign that he remembered our night together. I must escape quickly, or pregnancy would prevent me from traveling. I must not stay until the birth. The child might look like Bon, and my guilt would become known to all. Already I was unwanted and unwelcome. The priest's behavior was not holy. Yet I believed his words: I was damned in this world and the next. I never escaped my guilt.

Then, one day in the market square, I heard the voice of a friar who preached to a group of people nearby. His face was gentle; his words were balm to my soul. He spoke:

"Be patient. God gives us the weaknesses of our bodies for the salvation of our souls."

"Be praised, my Lord, through all your creatures, especially Brother Sun, who brings the day. You give light through him, and he is beautiful and radiant in all his splendor! Of you, Most High, he bears the likeness. Be praised, my Lord, through Sister Moon and the stars. You have made them precious and beautiful in the heavens."

"Be praised, my Lord, through Brothers Wind and Air, and clouds and storms through which you give your creatures sustenance. Be praised, My Lord, through Sister Water. She is very useful, humble, precious, and pure. Be praised, my Lord, through Brother Fire, through whom you brighten the night. He is beautiful, cheerful, and strong. Be praised, my Lord, through our sister Mother Earth, who feeds us and rules us and produces various fruits with colored flowers and herbs."

"Be praised, my Lord, through those who forgive for love of you and through those who endure sickness and trial."

He put the manuscript aside.

"Brothers and Sisters, do not be deceived by heretics who attack the Church and say God's world is evil. Come back to God; be received with forgiveness and love." After he stopped speaking, a crowd remained near him. Many put food into his bowl and asked for his blessing. I waited until all departed.

"Please tell me if God would forgive my grievous sins. Let me confess."

"I am not a priest, only a humble Brother. I cannot hear confessions and give absolution." He made the sign of the cross on my forehead. "I promise God forgives all sinners who turn to him with humble hearts, no matter the sin."

"Brother, I am sorry I have no food to offer. Will you speak again? I want to hear more."

"I will speak here again tomorrow and for a few days after."

"After that, where will you go?"

"I will join pilgrims on their way to Santiago de Compostela. Along the way, I will minister in towns wherever people will listen."

I asked: "May I go with you?"

"You appear to be a gentlewoman. Have you no husband? Can you manage the rigors of the journey?"

"I am recently a widow. I am strong, and I need the blessing of pilgrimage."

"Two women and two men already travel with me. You must consider whether you can manage the difficulties of this journey. We will carry little with us, beg for our food, and sleep in the open. We leave Friday at dawn through the Portet-sur-Garonne."

"Whence do you come?"

"My background can little interest a lady."

"I would like to hear of it."

"I was born in Pamiers and studied at the university in Paris. Alas, I fell in with bad company and committed all the sins common among students. I sought God in the wilderness. He commanded me to go on a pilgrimage to Rome to expiate my sins. There I copied writings by many great lovers of God."

"My soul was still restless. Prayer in isolation from the world failed to heal me; many in the Church took a greater interest in accumulating wealth than saving souls. Then I heard of a holy man, Brother Francis, who taught a new way to worship, free of worldly attachments to wealth. I traveled to Assisi to become a friar under his guidance and took the name Brother Matheu. He inspired me to return here to preach the gospel of love and save the souls of Cathars and other heretics."

I returned to the house. Bon had gone away for a few days as a paid messenger. That night I took Christine's cloak and shoes, which were sturdier than mine; the coins Na Margarete kept hidden in a pot; needle and thread; and other small necessities. I left before dawn to meet the pilgrims at the gate. For the first time since Mirefoix, I had something to do and the hope of salvation.

Chapter 58

Corvinus

Jan 1210

The Lady sent me to look for Bon and Garsenda; I was more concerned about finding Christine. Because they traveled north on the Ariege after her escape, I thought they had gone to Toulouse, and I searched there at first without success. Then I searched far and wide in other directions.

I longed to see Christine, and I longed for the human body the Lady had promised. If I told her where they were, the Lady might finally use the magic; I might take possession of Bon's body. That I might never again be a man was too distressing to contemplate. However, I had little confidence in the Lady's promises. If she failed to reward me, this would be my last errand for her; I would find other ways to achieve my aims.

After much wasted time, I searched in Toulouse again; it had become a refuge for many displaced by war. I thought I saw Christine in the street, then lost sight of her when she entered the market. The next day I saw her again and followed her to a house. Bon was there, and they behaved like lovers. What I feared had happened. He had taken Christine for himself.

Despite the Lady's orders, I decided I would not deliver the Lady's message or make myself known to them: not yet. Instead, I flew directly back to Mirefoix to speak to the Lady. It shocked me to see the progress of her illness. She expressed annoyance at my disobedience but was pleased when I told her I had found them. I reminded her of her promise to me. "I want the body of the man Bon. Give me the necessary magic. Otherwise, I will not deliver your message."

Her face was distraught. She had become too weak to fight me. "I must tell you at last. The spells are gone."

"May you be damned forever. I will serve you no more."

Perhaps Blodeweth had taken the spells, I thought. I suspected she had some magic of her own. And so next, I visited Blodeweth in her cell.

"Do you have news of Christine?"

"Yes, she and Bon live near the south market square in Toulouse."

I told her she seemed in better health.

"Yes. The Lady no longer bleeds me."

We had spoken of her life as a priestess and the shape-shifting ways of her people. I wanted to know more.

"What powers do you have? Can you move a soul from an animal to a man?"

She did not speak for a time. Then she said:

"Yes, I can make a shape-shifting spell. There are things I need for the magic. Amber, and enough oak for a fire. What would you do for me in return?"

"I will set you free and help you revenge yourself against the Lady."

"Bring me what I need. On the night of the next new moon, you will no longer be a raven."

"I want Bon's body. Do I need to fetch him here?"

"No. My magic is powerful."

"What is amber, and where can I find it?"

"Amber is a honey-colored stone. You can almost see through it. You must go far to the north, to the sea, where people collect it."

I traveled for more than a month, desperate in my search. I believed Blodeweth would do for me what the Lady had not done. Finally, with a piece of stolen amber clutched in a claw, I made my way back to Mirefoix. Blodeweth made a fire with straw and pieces of oak. She recited an incantation in a language I had never heard. Then she said:

"Come closer to the flames. As the amber melts, you must inhale the smoke and its fragrance."

I did as she commanded.

Suddenly she seized me. She wrung my neck, and I knew no more.

Chapter 59

Blodeweth

I tore the feathers from the carcass of Corvinus. I ate his flesh and sucked his dripping blood, feeling its warmth, knowing its power. When the moment was right, I placed his feathers against my heart and threw myself into the fire. The fire seared me at first, and then it died. A feathered cloak descended over me, and in a moment of frightful pain, my body shrank and twisted and re-formed itself.

Now, I was a raven, and I could fly to my homeland. But first, revenge. I flew out the cell's narrow-barred window and into the Lady's chamber. When I landed on the floor, I resumed human form. I took the knife from her table and approached the bed. The Lady lay there, staring at the ceiling. I had hoped to find her asleep, to bind her as she had bound me. Then I would take her blood. All of it. A little at a time.

A black demon sat on the end of her bed. His red eyes were fixed on her. He extended a claw toward her belly, and he turned toward me.

"She belongs to me. You may not touch her."

I hesitated. The desire for vengeance was strong, but this creature had magic stronger than mine. I turned back into a raven and flew away. Perhaps some other time, I would find her alone. Meanwhile, I had another score to settle. Bon had helped her subdue me, and I must search for him and punish him. I would be a raven by day, and myself, Blodeweth, by night. I would find my way to Toulouse and punish Bon for what he had done to me. At some later time, I would return to avenge myself on the Lady.

Chapter 60

The Lady

The fall of Carcassonne destroyed any remaining hope of peace. Simon de Montfort emerged as the invaders' leader, and under his leadership, the invaders became better organized. The northern army reached the foothills near Mirefoix sooner than I expected. My lord, the Count of Foix, lost Fanjeaux, Pamiers, and Saverdun in quick succession. He had to submit, give his youngest son to Simon de Montfort as a hostage, and order his city of Preixam to surrender. As September ended, the road to Mirefoix lay open, and I knew we would be the next target.

I sent an urgent message to my liege lord, the Count of Foix, asking whether he would help defend Mirefoix. His response was curt. As before, he said that he needed his men for his own defense; I must not depend on him for help. I summoned my seneschal and the captain of the city guard. The captain failed to appear. The seneschal spoke:

"My Lady, the garrison fled this morning. Most of the townspeople have gone to the hills. De Montfort approaches the gate."

My father would not have surrendered, even under these circumstances. He would have rallied our remaining people to take in hand whatever weapons were available, even if all they had were farm tools. He would have defied the invaders. If Bon had been in command, the garrison would not have fled. If

Garsenda were here, she would refuse to surrender. I have heard of women who defended their Lord's holdings, even standing at the head of an army wearing mail and wielding a sword. The harassment of demons and the pains in my belly exhausted me. I could not see well, and my strength was gone. I had heard that de Montfort sometimes treated cities that surrendered without resistance with lenience. For the sake of my people, I must swallow my pride.

"Send an emissary to announce our surrender. I will meet them at the gate. I want to know what manner of man this de Montfort is."

Within the hour, their army gathered outside the Foix gate. Their numbers were not as enormous as those described in the accounts of the fall of Beziers and Carcassonne; nevertheless, there were too many for us to resist. Once I had support from Guillem and Josfred and the love of my people. Now I stood alone. I had lost all. I had driven away those who might have supported me. The trembling seneschal at my side was less than a man. I waited in the open gateway. I knew I would be a prisoner. I must comport myself with dignity.

Still dressed in battle gear and accompanied by three knights, de Montfort approached. He was older than I expected; his body had the strength of an ox, and his thick shock of hair was gray. His black tunic was as severe as that of a monk. He was not courteous.

"I demand your surrender in the name of Christ. The Church supports me. God demands it. You must yield without conditions."

I kneeled.

"The gates of Mirefoix are open. I beg you to treat my people with kindness."

"Those who believe in the true Church need not fear us. You must surrender all heretics."

Fortunately, I had sent all Cathars out into the hills when the attackers appeared, so I said truthfully that no heretics remained in my city.

"Is this man your seneschal?"

"Yes."

"He must show us your treasury and supplies. We will take what we need in the name of God. Reflect upon the sin of sheltering heretics. You have no further authority here." He pointed to a tall man nearby; I recognized him with an unpleasant shock. "Sir Dalmas will assume command. Show him your best rooms."

Sir Dalmas was not well disposed toward me after the humiliation he suffered from the ill-fated marriage arrangements. I wished it had been anyone but him. He threatened to confine me in a prison cell but kept me closer to watch me. They locked me in Garsenda's chamber with one maidservant, and Dalmas occupied my former quarters. De Montfort and his men departed the following morning. He left only a handful of men to hold Mirefoix. Despite how few they were, none of us dared to disobey.

In September, the Count of Nevers and Duke of Burgundy departed with all their men. Now that de Montfort's army was smaller, we had a better opportunity for rebellion. We Southerners needed a leader, but no one emerged to lead us.

I wished to take the Cathar sacrament, the Consolamentum, the holy vow that transformed believers into Perfects. I had endured enough and needed to put my sins behind me. As one of the Elect, I would achieve salvation and go to be with the good God and not return to earth to suffer another life. I would need Cathar Perfects to give me this sacrament, but none remained in my city. I dared not send for them; if any occupiers saw them, it would mean their death. I would have to wait and hope for better circumstances.

Corvinus had vanished; I sent other spies far and wide and finally learned that Bon and Christine were in Toulouse. I had my maidservant convey a secret message to my seneschal:

"I have had word that Bon and Garsenda are in Toulouse. Send messengers. Ask Bon to come and retake Mirefoix. I will knight him and give him a manor and land as I should have done before. Tell Garsenda I forgive her and hope she can forgive me. Promise her I will love her as my daughter and that she will rule Mirefoix after me. Ask Christine, the woman with them, to help me endure my suffering and assure her I will not exhaust her strength. Beg them to make haste." I hoped this weak man had enough strength to do this one last thing for me.

Chapter 61

Garsenda

March 1210

I traveled with Brother Matheu and other pilgrims as he preached in several towns during the autumn months. Unfortunately, my pregnancy began to show. He told me, "You cannot be on the road when you give birth. You must return to your home in Toulouse."

"I have no home there; I was a refugee from Carcassonne."

"Then we must find a place for you."

A woman who introduced herself as Tanta Catarina gave generous alms to us after listening to his words one evening. Brother Matheu turned his persuasive powers on her; he caught her off guard in front of her neighbors. She had boasted of her kindness to strangers and swore always to treat the poor and unfortunate with generosity. He said at once:

"Will you provide shelter to this homeless young widow, soon to be a mother? She can't continue to travel."

Everyone in town had witnessed her vow, so she had to say yes. I was uneasy about accepting her hospitality, but Brother Matheu made it clear that I must stay with her, and in truth, I was often ill and tired. Winter was coming.

It was not a happy arrangement. Tanta Catarina wanted me to marry her nephew, a prosperous shepherd. He noticed me with interest and said that if I proved to be a good breeder, he would consider it. They would not force a marriage until after a successful birth.

I tried to make myself useful in her house, but spinning bruised my fingers, and her chickens did not thrive under my care. She fretted about how much I ate and wondered out loud if I would be a good wife.

The winter months passed. My belly grew large. I held my tongue when Tanta Catarina scolded me for my uselessness. After the child was born, I thought I would be well enough to move on. Perhaps I would return to Mirefoix and make peace with my Lady mother.

One April morning, I was making clumsy efforts to spin carded wool into yarn when my belly cramped as if struck by a lightning bolt. I gasped with pain. It was as if a sharp claw took hold of me, and then let go. I knew some women died giving birth. Tanta Catarina saw the terror on my face.

"It is your time. Don't fear; we women will help you."

She helped me remove my overdress.

"The priest blessed this birthing girdle. It will reduce the pain and keep you and the baby safe." She brought forth a long strip of cloth inscribed with prayers and wrapped it loosely around my waist to drape over my belly. She summoned the midwife. By evening, water gushed from between my legs. The women smiled. The midwife felt my stomach.

"All is well."

All was not well. I was sure I was going to die. God would punish me for my sins. Each fresh assault of pain took my breath away. I became tired. I vomited and nearly fainted. The world faded. I was aware only of my body and my agony. They say the pain of childbirth is God's punishment on women for the disobedience of Eve. At first, pride prevented me from screaming, but I was not silent as the pain continued into the night. Tanta Catarina and the midwife sat near the hearth, spinning.

"The pains are close together now. The child will come soon. Pray to Saint Joseph."

The midwife massaged my belly to help bring the child. I thought I would die and begged her to send for a priest.

"It is too close to your time, and I cannot leave you alone. Get up and walk; that will help."

She made me sit on the birthing stool she had brought, and I grasped the knot at the end of the rope attached to the rafters.

"Now push."

"No. I can't."

"You must."

I let the pain sweep over me.

"I want to sleep. I'm too tired to go on."

The midwife slapped my face.

"Listen! You must do as I say. Push, as if you were trying to shit."

I pushed.

"Yes. Keep pushing when the pain comes."

"How much longer?"

"Not long now. I see the crown of the head."

Tanta Catarina again urged me to push. I screamed as my body tore open. The child's head emerged red, sticky, and wet. Then it was over, and I lay back. The midwife washed and swaddled the babe. I heard lusty squalling.

"You have a beautiful girl. She looks healthy." They helped me expel the afterbirth. I continued to bleed. Their wrinkled faces and furtive looks betrayed their concern.

"Am I going to die?"

They used linens to soak up the blood. However, the bleeding continued. Then Tanta Catarina lay the baby against my breast.

I was devastated by the sight of her face. She had Bon's face; she was living evidence of my sin. It would be better if she died, and it would be better if I died. I was terrified. What was I going to do with her? I wept, and I pushed the child away.

"Take her."

Her rhythmic shrieks tormented me.

"You must nurse her."

"No, no, I can't." I turned my face to the wall and put my hands over my ears.

The midwife took my head in her hands, turned me, and again slapped my face.

"You are a spoiled child. You must be a mother to this babe. She needs you."

I sank into sobs. Tanta Catarina fed the child for three days by squeezing goat's milk into her mouth from a twisted cloth. She attempted to get me to nurse, and the baby rooted, tried to suck, and got a little milk. My bleeding stopped, but then I sickened with a fever, and so did the baby, whose screaming became even more aversive.

"You must give her a name. Perhaps your mother's name?"

"No."

"Did your mother have a sister?"

"Beatritz."

They called for a priest; he baptized her and prayed over me. The fever continued. My impressions of the world around me were confused. The village women gathered to decide what must be done.

"She's dying, and the child too."

"We must take them to the shrine of Saint Guinefort, the protector of newborns."

An argument ensued. It was too far, and I was too heavy to carry. I was almost too tired to follow what the women were saying. All right then, they would take only Beatritz. Even when her crying grew weaker, it disturbed my rest. I was relieved when they took her from my arms and departed.

I woke. I may have been asleep for several days. Tanta Catarina sponged sticky sweat from my face and arms. The baby lay silent in the cradle.

"Is she dead?"

"She is well. She sleeps."

"What happened?"

"The midwife took her to St. Guinefort, and he worked a miracle. The fever broke at once."

"I have never heard of St. Guinefort. Who is he?"

She told me the story:

"A knight came home to find his babe gone from its cradle and his greyhound Guinefort with blood on its mouth. Thinking the dog had devoured the child, he killed it. Then he discovered the dog had killed a serpent and saved his child. They buried the blessed hound in a well and planted a grove around it. Our people discovered that prayers to Guinefort often saved their children even when a priest's blessing had no effect, and we knew he must be a saint."

How curious, I thought. And yet my child got well, and I became well, and when they gave her to me to nurse, I could do so. I gazed at her. She had Bon's face. How was this possible? The night I gave him the love potion and lay next to him, I dreamed he took me as I had always wanted. But it was only a dream— wasn't it? The spell was supposed to make us one forever. I thought it meant that he would love me and marry me. Now I saw another meaning: we were made one in this child.

Now, as I gazed at my tiny, helpless daughter, a great surge of love overcame me. Like a mother bear, I would protect her with my life and cherish her as the only piece of Bon I now possessed. A sudden fear took hold. How would I make a home for her? Tanta Catarina said she was not willing to keep us much longer. Now that I had shown myself capable of bearing a healthy child, I must marry her nephew. I was determined not to do this; I wanted a better life for my daughter. But I could not take her back to Mirefoix. People would see that her father was the man many believed to be my half-brother. People would condemn her as the product of incest and a bastard.

I was lost in a melancholy so deep I could see no end to it.

Chapter 62

Christine

May 1210

When Bon returned, Garsenda had been gone for three days. He wanted to search for her. He made inquiries around the marketplace: Had anyone seen a beautiful woman with red hair? A man told him that such a woman listened to Brother Matheu, and she may have gone with him and others on pilgrimage. Brother Matheu planned to preach in many small towns south of Toulouse along the way. Bon was determined to search for her. I argued against it.

"You might spend weeks traveling from town to town, searching for them."

"Eventually, I will find them."

"She doesn't want to be found. She's in love with you, and it torments her to see us together. She needs to let go of this love. It can only bring her unhappiness. She should be safe with Brother Matheu. In time, she may make her way back to Mirefoix."

With reluctance, he agreed that there was sense in what I said.

I lived in peace and freedom. It was a humble life, to be sure, but enough. I was not locked in a cell; I earned enough from sewing to eat. After being a prisoner for so long, I enjoyed every day domestic tasks. I found simple pleasure in buying carrots, beans, and leeks at the market, cutting them up, simmering pottage on the hearth, and seasoning it with sage and rosemary. I started a garden in the small enclosure behind Na Margarete's house. I designed and made new clothing.

But trouble had come. Bon had nightmares. He never spoke of them, but I knew. He thrashed, kicked, ground his teeth, and cried out when he slept. His breathing and heart rate soared; he sweated. He denied distress. But when I touched him, I knew he was afraid; his terror swept through my body. He avoided sleep; he sat by the fire instead of lying down. He became quick-tempered and depressed. It was severe trauma, probably from what he saw and did at Beziers and Carcassonne.

Why didn't I have the same nightmares? I wasn't sure. I had seen some of what he saw, and it haunted me. But I had not been forced to do what he had done. I had not seen men die by my hand, nor had my best friend's skull smashed as he stood beside me. And why couldn't I take this pain from him? He wouldn't allow me to be near him when he suffered, and he went off to be alone when distressed and forbade me to follow. I feared that anything I said or did to respond to his distress would only make him worse.

We didn't quarrel, but the chasm between us grew each day. The greater his pain, the more he drew away. I knew he didn't want to inflict his pain on me.

The silence between us terrified me.

I had worked with clients who struggled with everyday problems of living. I didn't know how to treat such overwhelming trauma. I worried I might worsen things if I tried to push him to talk. I ransacked my memory. Even in the 21st century, we were ill-equipped to help with such intense pain.

I remembered the Western adaptation of Buddhist mindfulness meditation I had used to help patients and myself through lesser kinds of suffering. It would not be enough, I feared. But I must try. The next night when Bon thrashed in his sleep and ground his teeth, I woke him. He trembled and refused to speak. When I put my arms around him, he pushed me away and rose to leave.

"Don't ask me questions. There are doors you must not open."

"You don't have to tell me what you remember. Be assured that there is nothing in your heart that would make me love you less. I ask only that you listen to some ideas when you feel you can. There may be things you can do to reduce the power of these memories."

That night was not the right time, but two days later, we spoke again. I explained the form of meditation I knew. This would help him control attention and experience his thoughts and feelings with detached acceptance instead of pain and self-judgment. It wasn't the same as the Buddhism he knew, but it made sense to him.

After I convinced him that working on this together would not cause me to share his pain and, in fact, would make me feel better, we practiced meditation together. I hoped that what I remembered was helpful and that I wasn't bringing misunderstandings into the situation that would make things worse. In time, it seemed to help. His nightmares did not cease, but they became less frequent, and he recovered from terrible nights more quickly. But the lessening of nightmares was not enough. His life was not what he needed or wanted it to be.

He did not feel that he had anything valuable to do. He went to the Chateau and offered his services as a messenger; they sent him on errands. He contributed to the household, but his work was not a source of pride. Once, he had hoped the Lady would grant him a manor and make him a knight. That was no longer possible.

Stories of supposedly heroic battles circulated; he had no part in the glory. I feared he might be drawn back into those battles in search of honor. He might turn to mercenary service for lack of other occupation. That life would bring injury, death, and the coarsening of the soul that comes from inflicting them. I feared for him and for myself.

I woke at midnight to find him with the Buddha pendant clenched in his fist and an expression of suffering on his face. I rose and lit a candle.

"What are you thinking?"

He shook his head.

"Please don't harden your heart against me. I can't bear to see you in such pain."

I waited.

At last, he spoke. "The pendant reminds me of the Buddha's teachings, words that trouble me. 'If a man kills living beings, is given to blows and violence, and is merciless to human beings, he will be reborn in misery.' But I am a soldier. What else can I be?"

I wished I knew how to comfort him.

"When I took you from Saverdun and killed the men who attacked us, you looked at me with contempt."

He was right. I had. Now I was haunted by those words.

"I was wrong to say that, and I wish I had not."

Words can be so dangerous. Words spoken in the past had done so much harm. More words might do more harm. Still, I tried to explain:

"I thought then that it pleased you to kill. I understand now that you kill only when you must do so to protect those you love and in the service of honor. Now I understand that killing cost you more pain than my healing ever cost me. I would be dead if you had not risked your life and done what no man should ever have to do. I don't want you to have to kill again. But I don't blame you for anything you have done. You have always done what you had to and paid the price. I am sorry for the pain my words caused you. I am grateful for your protection, then and now."

His misery was not less, but at least we could now speak of it.

I wished that the world did not make killing necessary. I hoped Bon could find other ways to show his strength, courage, and intelligence. He needed to shine. He needed to feel his value. Living idle in Na Margarete's house was killing him.

What should we do? I thought about that for many hours but found no answers.

Chapter 63

Christine

The appearance of a messenger from the Lady forced the issue. The message said: "The Lady requests urgently that you return to defend Mirefoix. Enemy armies are near. She has wronged you and she prays for your forgiveness. She swears she will reward you for your loyalty."

This news was what I feared, and Bon hoped for. Before Bon could reply to the messenger, I protested.

"We need to discuss this."

"What is there to discuss? I must return. I dishonored myself by leaving the Lady's service. I lost all chance of making a place for us in the world. Now I have the opportunity to restore my honor. She may grant me a manor and make me a knight. You would have a home."

"Toulouse is the first place in this world where I have had peace and freedom. Please don't ask me to give that up."

"Honor is most important to me. You have always known that. But you don't accept it?"

"What is honor? If it's the bloodshed we saw in Beziers and Carcassonne, I want no part of it, for myself or you. It tore you apart. If what I did to help you heal from the nightmares makes it possible for you to seek violence again, I'm sorry I did it."

He took my hands in his. I took my hands away.

"You have contempt for me because I'm a soldier?"

"Sometimes, you have to fight. I'm alive only because you have been willing to risk your life for me. I am grateful. But does this have to be your fight?"

"I am a soldier. There is no other way in this world for me."

I took his hands in mine.

"Your nightmares tell me you find killing distressing. You have the courage to kill if you must. I believe you have the strength to choose another way."

"What other way?"

"You told me about Yong Jen; He used the knife to heal."

"He was also a soldier."

"When he had to be. Maybe there is another way for you to live if you can remember Yong Jen's skills. Healing, rather than killing, would make it possible for you to follow the Buddhist precepts your mother wanted you to believe. Killing doesn't just give you nightmares; it makes you suffer; it damages your soul. Your mother feared for you. So do I."

Bon was stunned. And angry.

"You want me to be a different man than the one you married."

"Not a different man. The same man, full of courage and honor, but one who chooses a different way."

He turned away; he left the house.

I despaired.

Bon was away for a day and a night. I wondered if he would ever return. I had no right to ask what I had asked. Perhaps I had offended him so entirely that he could never forgive me.

When he returned, his serious look told me he had reached a decision.

"There are some things I want to know."

"Just ask."

"You spoke of Yong Jen's skills as something I might remember. What makes you think that's possible?"

"I'm not sure. Hypnosis can help people access memories. I used it when I was a counselor; only about one in ten people were susceptible to deep hypnosis. People here respond much more strongly. Perhaps it's because of the powers I gained when I died, or perhaps it's easier for people to focus attention in this world. I might help you recover memories of his education and experience."

"And what value would surgical skills have in a world where antiseptics, antibiotics, and anesthesia don't exist?"

"The lack of antibiotics would make surgery riskier, of course. There are ways to keep things clean: boiling and cauterizing. Hypnosis and acupuncture can be used for anesthesia. Did Yong Jen have skills with acupuncture?"

"I'd like to remember."

He thought and spoke again.

"Those are disruptive technologies. Things we do might change the future. We spoke of this."

"I've thought about it. Now, or in the 21st century, we decide what to do at the moment without full knowledge of long-term consequences. Wars might be caused or prevented because of a single life you might save. It's a tangle. We can only try to do good things in the present."

"You said before that we are going to lose this war?" Bon asked.

"I don't remember the dates and details. Modern France includes this region of the south. The Cathars were wiped out. So yes, these people will be defeated. I don't know whether that will take a year or twenty years."

"I considered what you said. At first, I was angry. It seemed you condemned my actions and choices. But you're right: Killing sickens me. If there is another path for me, I want to find it."

He placed his hands on my shoulders.

"Listen. Perhaps someday, I can make my way in the world as a healer. But right now, I have obligations. I must find Garsenda and bring her back to Mirefoix. I must try to set right the things that went wrong when I left. Can you accept that?"

"Yes. This gives me hope for our future."

The next day, another messenger arrived from Mirefoix.

"The city has been taken. The garrison fled without a fight. The Lady begs you to come and help her regain control. She will reward you with a house and land."

This news filled me with dread, but I knew what he must do and that I must go with him. The following day we set off for Mirefoix. Bon was invigorated as we started the journey. "It is not very far. I asked about different routes. We can avoid de Montfort's men by going west and south toward Cazeres. We'll stay in the foothills and then head east toward Mirefoix."

Bon asked about Garsenda in each village. As we headed into the hills south and west of Toulouse, I saw a raven wheeling in the sky, turning toward us. As it came closer, I wondered: Could this be Corvinus?

The bird landed without grace on a nearby branch, holding a large lumpy grayish-green bundle in its beak. A shimmering dark light surrounded it. It became diaphanous, grew large and tall, and then, Blodeweth stood before us, formidable in strength. I recalled that Blodeweth had mentioned shapeshifting. She must have obtained the materials she needed.

"You, Bon, held me captive and helped the Lady take my blood. I swore I would escape and avenge this. I have regained the power of my goddess. I have made this covering of nettles with my own hands. It will burn your body with cold flames until you are dead."

She threw a woven gray coverlet over Bon, and he collapsed onto the ground. He screamed; I had never heard him cry out like that. I knew his torment must be unbearable. He thrashed at first, trying to shake off the covering, but it adhered to his body no matter what he did. I grasped the deadly garment and tried to tear it away even though it burned my hands to the bone. Blodeweth intervened and pulled me away from him, and held me tight.

"It is not you whom I seek to punish. You were kind to me, and I seek to avenge your captivity as well as mine."

I struggled to break free from her grasp. She was too strong.

"Do not help him. He deserves a painful death."

I pleaded with her.

"I love him. He has changed, and he has atoned for his actions."

My words did not move her. I extracted my knife from my sleeve and tried to stab her, but she twisted my wrist, and the knife fell from my hand. I broke free, ran from her, picked up Bon's sword from the ground, held it in both hands and swung about to face her. The blade was not as heavy as I expected, but it was all over the place when I tried to wield it.

Then I froze.

I could not strike her. And if I attacked her, she would fight back. She had strength, skill, and determination. I had none of those. She would win.

We faced each other like statues.

Beyond her, Bon writhed in pain. The guttural sounds from his throat told me of his agony.

He had killed many times to save me.

To save him, I must now do the same.

I stood without moving.

Blodeweth took a step toward me and extended her hand. But in response to my taking up Bon's sword, she guarded herself with the knife in her other hand.

"Put down the weapon, sister. We can escape from this place together, as we planned long ago."

I took a step back and took a deep breath.

Then I raised Bon's sword high and to the right and charged. I slashed downward and struck her neck. The gash bled profusely.

Her face became white.

I dropped the blade and cried out in anguish.

She dropped to her knees, clutching at her breast.

"You were my friend!"

As she fell, Blodeweth dissolved into a puddle of blood, bones, feathers—and rubies.

I did not stop to tend to her.

Bon's sounds of anguish had ended. I ran to him, lay beside him, and tried to tear the stinging nettles away, but they were embedded in his flesh. Like a swimmer caught in a rip tide, he was drawn away from life by an irresistible force. I gathered him into my arms, desperate to save him, to be with him. I couldn't save him, but I would not abandon him. I experienced the same pain as when I died in an explosion a lifetime ago, searing and unbearable. I screamed. But I did not let go. I sank into oblivion with him.

Chapter 64

The Lady

June 1210

I had never known such humiliation and despair. Sir Dalmas took over my chambers; I moved into Garsenda's old room. At first, I stayed alone, unable to face the sight of my conquered city. After two weeks, I asked my servant to inquire about my people: How were they treated? It was appalling.

Of course, I had to turn over everything I had of value. The men ransacked my chamber and took the few remaining rubies. My seneschal handed over all our silver and the keys to the storerooms. De Montfort's men slaughtered our herds and ate well. They taxed my people in silver and goods. Those who hesitated or hid their possessions were slain, and their bodies were displayed to the public. My people lived in hunger and fear. The occupiers attempted to identify Cathar heretics. I was proud that my people refused to hand over their families, friends, and neighbors.

I had failed them.

Would my messengers find Bon and Garsenda? Even if Corvinus spoke the truth when he told me they were in Toulouse, they might have moved on. They might even be dead. But they were my only hope.

❖

As day followed day, my world became darker. I touched walls and furniture to find my way around and never ventured outside the Chateau. I feared I would die alone. Then one morning, Rhazes came to see me. I was surprised; I had not summoned him.

"Forgive me, my Lady. I have noticed that you do not see well. May I examine you?"

"Nothing can be done for me. I am cursed."

"There are treatments for some kinds of blindness." He directed me to sit near the window and then turned my face toward the morning light; the bright sun hurt my eyes.

"Does everything seem blurry? Do things appear slightly brown, and do you have trouble seeing the colors blue and purple?"

"Yes."

"There is a growth in your eyes that I can remove, a cataract. There is a chance you will see better."

"Is it painful?"

"Not very painful."

I trusted him and decided to allow this.

He directed Constanzia to boil his instruments and bring clean linen for bandages. When I was ready, he washed my eyes with wine. He stabbed my left eye with a needle, and it surprised me that it didn't hurt more. He did the same to my right eye. He wrapped my eyes in bandages, and I spent the next two days in bed. When Rhazes removed the bandages, I shielded my eyes from the light at first. Then I saw the miracle: his surgery had partially restored my sight.

"I cannot thank you enough. I feared I would live the rest of my life in darkness. How can I repay you?" I feared he would ask permission to return to his home in the Outremer. By now, I depended on him. His request surprised me.

"I would like an apprentice, someone I can train to assist me, and silver to buy medicines." "You shall have an apprentice. Alas, I have no money to give you. But why do you not ask for your freedom?"

He turned and looked out the window with sadness in his eyes.

"There is nothing for me to return to, Lady. The Franks looted and burned my city. I tried to escape with my wife and daughter, but your husband sent soldiers to take me just as we tried to flee from the city. I saw them killed as I was taken away. I blamed myself: They would have lived if I had left a day earlier. The practice of medicine and the consolation of prayer are all I have left."

Chapter 65

Christine

Our souls floated above our bodies. We embraced in death as we had in life. I looked down upon our mutilated bodies, tangled in the nettles of Blodeweth's revenge.

Then I became aware that the four jinn had come to examine the situation.

"All four of the souls we were ordered to summon are gone. Are we now free?" The voice of the blue demon was first.

The black demon answered: "Not free until the one who bound us with her orders has died."

The violet and blue spirit that had brought me to this century spoke next: "We are not under orders now. What shall we choose to do?"

"The Lady needs them. Let them be taken from her."

The demons quarreled.

"These two have shown themselves worthy."

"The only power we have is to draw them back into these bodies or not. If we do not interfere, their souls will move on. We should let that happen."

The violet spirit spoke to me. "Are you ready to leave this world?"

I asked: "Can we remain together as we go?"

"We have no power over what happens when you go forward. Only the power to summon you back to this life–or not."

I felt detached from the body that lay below. But I was connected to Bon, whose soul floated beside mine. Bon and I gazed at each other. He spoke to the blue jinni.

"We have searched for each other for eternity. Please do not part us now."

My jinni said: "If you return to these bodies, you will no longer have your special gifts. Bon, you will lose your speed and precision. Christine, you will lose your power to heal. Are you willing to face life without these talents?"

"I cannot speak for Bon, but for myself, I can say: yes. The cost of the healing gift was too high. I prefer to give it up."

Bon added:

"Yes. I feel the same."

The jinn conferred and then cast lots. The violet jinni said:

"The decision is mine. I am touched by your love and courage. I will bring you back to these bodies. After a day of rest, you will be strong enough to go on."

I fell into a sleep as deep as death. When I woke, the shredded remnants of the nettle covering still surrounded us, but they no longer burned. I moved only a little. Bon lay on the ground, cold and stiff as if still dead. I crawled to the river, filled a cup with water, and crept back to Bon. I moistened his lips and caressed his face. I took his pulse; it was weak. I listened for breath; it was shallow. I tried to rouse him; he lay unresponsive. I began to despair.

But the violet jinni kept her promise. After a time, Bon awakened. We lay in each other's arms all night, weak but alive.

When morning came, we could rise and walk. Bon saw what remained of Blodeweth: a tangled mess of bones, congealed blood, feathers, and gems. It was a terrible sight; it devastated me to know I had killed someone I had once cared for. Still, I would do the same if I had to decide again.

"What happened?"

In halting words, I told him about the fatal struggle.

He understood I didn't want to touch the remains. He gathered the rubies, washed them clean of blood, and put them into a pouch. He made a shallow grave for what was left of Blodeweth. We did not speak at first. Then he said:

"You killed for me. You would have sacrificed your life for mine. That took great courage."

"You taught me to be brave and how to love."

I would be satisfied from now on to offer ordinary comfort. I hoped to be wise enough to know my limits.

❖

Bon asked at each town along the way whether anyone had seen a tall woman of uncommon beauty with flame-red hair in the company of pilgrims. At Muret, he got news: a woman of her description lived at the home of Tanta Catarina, an hour's walk to the west. We set off to find her. We reached Tanta Catarina's cottage, and she took us aside before we spoke to Garsenda.

"This woman eats like a horse and doesn't work. At first, her child was sick, and I had to bring her to the grave of Saint Guinefort, protector of infants, and make offerings of meat and bones to restore her health. I took her into my home out of the goodness of my heart. She has cost more than I can afford. Pay me and take her away. I have done all one could expect." I was surprised to hear about a child.

Garsenda sat on a bench with her swaddled baby in her arms, facing away from us and gazing out toward the fields. She looked over her shoulder as we approached, then turned and clutched the child against her breast as if to conceal it from us. Bon kneeled in front of her.

"Sister, I did not expect to find you a mother." She gathered the child even closer.

"May I see it?"

Her reluctance was apparent. I wondered why and drew closer out of curiosity. Was the child deformed?

"What troubles you, sister? We want to help. We will return to Mirefoix, where you will have better shelter and food."

Her face reddened, then became white. Bon reached for the babe. She tried to keep him away, but Bon drew the swaddling cloth from its face. I gasped. I expected Fabrice's child to have the ruddy skin and red hair he shared with Garsenda. This child's face was a miniature of Bon's. Bon looked astonished at first, then angry. The child was a few months old; I counted on my fingers. She was conceived around the time we married. Bon had betrayed me.

"How is this possible? I never lay with you!"

Garsenda looked down at her feet. "You don't remember."

"Explain."

Her words were halting.

"I stole a spell from the Lady's chamber, a love spell.... I have never believed you to be my brother... you do not resemble my father in any way except courage. I thought the spell would make you love me forever, as the words promised... I realize now its words spoke of creating a child. I drugged you and lay beside you and dreamed of you. I hoped you would remember this joyfully; there was no sign you remembered. You were as distant as ever... When I lay with you, I saw the red mark on your shoulder... the same as on my father's shoulder when we washed him for burial. And then I knew I was mistaken. I committed a grievous sin. I beg your pardon. You swore never to father a bastard. Because of me, you have. Please forgive me if you can. And do not blame this child, for she has done no wrong."

A daughter. I gazed at her face. A sudden overwhelming love came over me. In all these months, I had not conceived with Bon, which disappointed him. Perhaps I was barren. Now I was overcome by a soul hunger. I wanted to hold this child, protect her, and care for her. I reached out. Garsenda pulled her child closer. Bon spoke to Garsenda:

"You are not worthy to be her mother. She is mine, and Christine will take care of her for me."

"You must not take her from me. She has become a blessing from God, my only blessing."

His face softened a little.

"Have you given the child a name?"

"Beatritz."

Bon frowned. Again, he reached for Beatritz; again, Garsenda snatched her away. I took him aside.

"Be patient. Give her time."

I was alone with my thoughts. Garsenda would be part of our lives now, not a welcome prospect. Her jealousy would injure us all. I approached her when she was nursing Beatritz.

"I think I understand how you feel." That was a mistake. Her face reddened, and her brows contracted in anger.

"You cannot possibly understand. You took the man I love away from me. How do you think I feel?"

"It must be painful. Can I help?"

My former magic ability to absorb pain was gone, thank God. But perhaps I could offer ordinary comfort.

"You demand that I put all my feelings aside."

"We all must learn to live with things we cannot change. All of us feel wronged. We must all forgive each other. If you remain angry, it will hurt us, but the anger burning in your breast will also destroy you. You deserve to be happy and can be if you let go of the past."

"I can love no one as I love Bon."

"Holding on makes you suffer. You are young; many men will admire a woman with your beauty, love of life, and courage; you may find one worthy of your love."

She was silent. Then:

"I thought you wished me ill."

"Please, believe me, I do not."

If only I had the power to heal the distress I once had. I did not think my words had moved her, but the next day, she allowed me to hold Beatritz. It seemed awkward at first; then, I cradled her in my arms against my breast. I was spellbound when the child smiled and reached toward me. I drew away from the quarrel between Garsenda and Bon. I rocked her and listened to her sweet sounds of contentment. Poor child, what would happen to her? I felt a fierce urge to protect her.

Bon spoke to us about the future. "Mirefoix has fallen, and the Lady has summoned us to win it back. We must go."

"Brother, I cannot return to Mirefoix. Everyone will see she is your child, and people will condemn me for incest and scorn our child as a bastard. Please, I need God's forgiveness and yours."

"What leads you to believe God will forgive you? I can't forgive."

"I now believe that God forgives. Most priests at Mirefoix spoke only of God's wrath. The nature of my belief has changed. I have learned that God can love and forgive, and I try to be worthy of that forgiveness. Let me show you something."

She went into the cottage and returned with a ragged shift. She had embroidered sacred words all over it in spidery thread. She spread it out as if it were a book and read it aloud. I drew near and listened.

"Lord, make me an instrument of thy peace.
Where there is hatred, let me sow love,
Where there is injury, pardon;
Where there is doubt, faith;
Where there is despair, hope;
Where there is darkness, light;
And where there is sadness, joy."

I recognized this as a prayer composed by St. Francis; I hoped these words provided her with solace. She looked defiantly at Bon.

"Perhaps you can never forgive me, but God will."

Bon didn't respond. He turned his gaze toward me with the child in my arms, and his face softened. After a time, he spoke in a softer voice.

"I claim this babe as my own child. I can't leave her here, nor you. We must return to Mirefoix."

An idea occurred to me.

"There is a way. We can tell people this is our child."

Garsenda snatched the child from my arms with a fierce expression on her face.

"You have already taken everything from me. You may not have my child."

I was ashamed that I hadn't realized how she would feel, and didn't know what to say.

Bon said:

"Think what is best for Beatritz."

Tears ran down her face. After a time, she said:

"You are right. But Christine cannot nurse her."

"Until we approach Mirefoix, you can feed her. Then, we must find a wet nurse."

"I must think and pray about this. The babe is all I have now."

"You can still be with her as her aunt, and no one will think that strange. We three must keep this secret."

Bon's proposal disturbed me. For his sake, I wanted to reconcile with Garsenda. However, she had cause to dislike me. She had used magic to get her way, and I worried she might try to harm me.

She thought about this for a while. "You will love Beatritz as if she were your own? You will never reproach her for her birth? You will give her the rights of a firstborn, even if you have other children?"

We promised.

"Please let me carry my daughter now. I know I must give her to you when we approach Mirefoix, but I beg you, give me time with her."

Chapter 66

Garsenda

July 1210

We were one day's journey from Mirefoix when we obtained more information. Only three of de Montfort's knights and a few soldiers held the city. If we surprised them, it might be possible to retake the city with a small force.

We made camp in hillside caves on the flanks of the Pyrenees overlooking Mirefoix.

Christine and I had different ideas about the care of Beatritz. I kept her swaddled; her limbs would not grow straight unless she was bound. Beatritz slept most of the time. Christine unwrapped the baby several times a day, bathed her, and washed the linens. Clearly, it distressed my baby to be doused in cold water. Bon improvised a cradle, and Christine placed her there wrapped in loose blankets or held her in her lap, talking to her when she was awake. I wondered where she got her strange ideas. I took Beatritz back and swaddled her again. We didn't argue, but the tension grew.

Bon ventured out to find what might remain of the garrison. He recruited men by ones and twos, only those whom he trusted. Many men joined, angered by the cruelty of occupying forces. He couldn't make a direct assault. We needed information: How many defending soldiers were there? Where were they housed and posted? We would have to launch a surprise attack from inside. We would need to enter through the secret door in the Lady's chamber. This opened only from the inside.

Bon took me aside. "I will send two men to spy, but they can't get into the Chateau. I must know whether the Lady's chambers are occupied and by whom." He hesitated.

He must have known I was the only person who could do this.

"I'll go."

"I don't want to ask. You must know how dangerous this is, even if the soldiers don't suspect you are a spy."

"I must go."

I couldn't pass through the gate or gain entry to the Chateau disguised as a peasant. I would have to announce myself. The following day, I presented myself at the city's main gate, identified myself, and demanded to see the Lady. Flirtation with the guards and a few small coins got me inside. Soldiers escorted me to my old room. My mother's appearance shocked me. Her face was gaunt, and her gray garments hung like cobwebs. She had the mad look of one already halfway into the next world. Her words shocked me.

"I am sorry with all my heart that I did not love you as you deserved and that I drove you away."

She wanted forgiveness. I said coldly:

"What's past is past."

We spoke in low voices. I told Mother:

"Bon has gathered enough men to retake the city. He needs to use the secret door in your chamber. I must gain access. How can this be done?"

"Their leader, Sir Dalmas, occupies my chambers."

I realized what I must do.

"Then there is but one way I can gain access."

"Daughter, you must not expose yourself to shame."

Sir Dalmas himself interrupted us.

"Well met, my saucy once-to-be bride."

I feigned a courage I didn't feel and spoke boldly.

"Indeed. We find each other in unexpected circumstances."

"What shall I do with you?" His malicious amusement chilled me. "You have shown yourself to be willful and disobedient. But our marriage would solidify my claim to Mirefoix. You can be useful to me. You cannot refuse. What happened to the man who kidnapped you at our wedding?"

Unexpected tears came to my eyes at the memory of Fabrice. I never allowed myself to think about him. He summoned two men and stood with me before my mother.

"I marry you." I said nothing at first. A soldier twisted my arm behind my back. Sharp pain brought the words unbidden to my lips:

"I marry you."

He seized my hand. I protested. "It is my woman's time, and I am unclean from bleeding. Wait a day or two, and I will prepare to receive you."

He took me to my mother's chamber; he examined me to verify what I had said was true. He beat me for my insolence, for being unavailable to him. He left the room and locked me in with no one to tend to my injuries. As soon as I was alone, I tried to open the hidden door. I broke my nails and bloodied my hands, but it did not open; a man's strength would be needed. The attack would come the following day. The next night Sir Dalmas came to me.

"I will get a son from your body to secure my inheritance."

I had heard tapping from within the hidden passage. Bon and his men waited for me to open the door. Now I knew what I must do.

"Husband, I will show you where the treasures of Mirefoix are hidden."

I pulled back the arras.

"See this hidden door here; this is how it opens." I showed him the mechanism.

And so it was that Sir Dalmas himself let in the attackers. Bon was in the lead. He rushed Sir Dalmas, who had only a moment to take up his sword; he pinned him to the wall. In moments my tormenter was dead. Bon's other men dispersed in twos and threes, in silence, to take their objectives. Bon held me and wept.

"Sister, what has he done to you? I should have given him a fate worse than death!"

I clung to him and, for a moment, felt the love I had always longed for. That moment would pass. For that one moment, I felt he cherished me. He carried me to the bed, tended my wounds, and pressed a goblet of wine to my lips.

"I must go. This man will guard you." Guinot obeyed and never left my side.

By morning, Bon held Mirefoix. Some defenders had died; others were imprisoned. Bon fumed.

"I would kill them all, but that would be dishonorable." He let them depart without weapons and possessions. Bon had the outside entrance filled with stones to disguise it.

The Lady asked that I stay with her, even though she had the ministrations of Christine and the two gray-garbed Cathar women who had become her closest companions. She tried again to soften me:

"Daughter, can you forgive me? I wronged you in so many ways."

"You have done so much harm, not only to me."

"Try to understand..."

She explained she stabbed my father when he tried to claim his husband's rights.

"You took blood from that poor captive woman. How did that come about?"

The Lady told me about the soul-summoning spell that brought Blodeweth and her reasons for using it. She spoke of the jinn that haunted her and cursed her with pain and blindness. She shared her new faith and the hope of salvation it gave her. She blamed herself for favoring Alienor over me.

"It was wrong of me, I know. You reminded me of the Count. He treated me brutally all those years."

Hearing this, I remembered my misdeeds: the love spell I used to trick Bon into lying with me and the birth of Beatritz. Perhaps I was no better than she; maybe we were not as different as I thought. I shared Brother Matheu's words with her; they had brought me peace. They helped her but did not seem to comfort her as much as they had me. She needed stronger assurance of absolution.

After that, we sat quietly together without quarreling. When in the Lady's company, I felt more sorrow for our past lack of affection than comfort for our mutual forgiveness. I didn't tell her Beatritz was my daughter. I vowed to myself: My daughter will know she is loved.

Nominally, the Lady ruled Mirefoix again. But she took little interest in this. I took her place when our vassals gathered; I passed judgment on the cases brought before me. I consulted with her seneschal about the need to replace slaughtered flocks and repair trampled vineyards. In all but name, I was now the Lady of Mirefoix.

Bon, Christine, and Beatritz lived in the room that had been mine. The sight of them together brought me intolerable pain. I tried to let go of my suffering; I reread the holy words of Brother Matheu. Christine found a young woman who had borne a child and lost him; she became their wet nurse. I bound my breasts, and my milk dried up.

Chapter 67

Christine

When we returned to the Chateau, I looked for Jacotte; I found her in the kitchen. Her appearance shocked me. She sat hunched near the chimney corner; she rocked herself, silent, alone. A dog lay at her feet. It was Sassia; she ran to greet me with wild enthusiasm. Jacotte did not even look up at this noisy, joyous reunion. What had happened to her?

I sat next to Jacotte. Sassia got into my lap and licked my face, wagging not just her tail but her whole body. What a joy to see her again! I wondered how she found her way to Mirefoix.

I turned to Jacotte; I caressed her face and held her.

"Jacotte, it's Christine. I'm so glad to see you."

She turned a gaunt tear-stained face toward me. Dark circles under her eyes made it seem she had aged years. A ghost of a smile appeared.

"What happened to you?"

A woman spoke:

"Her baby was stillborn, and the father, that worthless piece of shit, abandoned her. She hasn't spoken since it happened."

"How long ago?"

"Two days."

I gathered her into my arms. "Oh, my dear. I'm so sorry."

She put her arms around my neck.

An obvious idea came to me.

"Dear one, you have milk and no baby. I have a baby and no milk. Will you help me?"

I brought Jacotte and Sassia back to the chamber I shared with Bon and placed Beatritz in her arms. Jacotte didn't smile, but she gave her breast to Beatritz and nursed calmly. In time, perhaps this would help her heal. Sassia danced around us, overjoyed to have her people together.

Chapter 68

Bon

I sought Fan Zhongyan in his room near the market square. I found him lying on his cot, wasted and weak, and kneeled beside him.

"My son, there is much I must tell you before I die." He had often called me his son, but this time seemed different. "You are, in truth, my son."

"How can that be? I bear the Count's birthmark on my shoulder."

"When you were born, we saw that you resembled the Count in no way. To persuade him you were his, I tattooed a mark to resemble the one your mother saw on the Count's back. He might have slain you and your mother if I had not done so."

I considered. I returned his smile. Yes. He had protected, educated, and encouraged me all my life. He loved and cared for my mother. I was glad she had not been alone. Garsenda had been right: I was not her brother. My child was not a product of incest. Garsenda still bore guilt for deceiving me, but her sin was less than I had believed.

"Father, this gladdens my heart."

"You are not angry about our deception?"

"I can see it was necessary. I am only sorry I was not aware of this sooner. Now I can call you Father."

"Even now, you must consider whether to speak. Without the deception about your parentage, you have no claim to rule Mirefoix."

I sat with him through the night, holding his hand.

Near the end, he opened his eyes. "Your mother grieved when you chose the knife. She did not want the life of a soldier for you. I watched as you grew and saw signs that killing troubled you. The blade can heal, as well as kill. You can choose another way."

"I have already made that choice. I will become a physician."

"Then your mother's wish for you is fulfilled." He continued, his voice weakening. "My son, you have fought honorably to serve the Lady and protect Mirefoix. You have lost that battle; leave this land of sorrow and blood."

"Where should I go?"

"Perhaps to the illustrious school of medicine in Salerno. You have much to teach as well as learn. Or... you might journey east to the land of your mother's birth. The seal that bears your family name, and your unmistakable resemblance to her, prove that you descend from nobility."

"I have always longed for my rightful place in the world."

"It is a long and perilous journey, not to be undertaken lightly."

I kissed his hand. No more words passed between us, and his soul slipped away at dawn.

I had heard that Rhazes gave the Lady back her sight, and I sought him out to ask about this. He described the procedure; I was impressed. I confess I had not thought there was much I could learn from the medicine of this time. I questioned him about other matters, such as anesthesia. His thinking was more advanced than I expected. I might teach him skills also, but it was not yet time to reveal my past life.

I spent many nights with Christine using hypnosis to bring back memories of my experiences with medicine. I regained some knowledge of surgery. I saw she was pleased that I might become a surgeon instead of a soldier, and I was glad the idea made her happy. But my battles were not yet over. Rhazes and I spoke further about medicine. We decided that if we got away from this war, we would set up a clinic with Christine.

Chapter 69

Garsenda

I looked for Mena in her chamber; we embraced.

"I am now the Lady of Mirefoix. Will you advise me?"

"I'm not the best choice as an advisor; I can't appear in public and draw attention to myself. However, I can listen to your problems and make suggestions. I can help with correspondence."

She studied me.

"I see it in your face. Something troubles you greatly."

"If I tell you, you will think less of me."

"The truth is better between friends. Genuine regard exists only when we see each other as we really are. Trust me to listen and not judge."

I told her about the love spell, the birth of Beatritz, and my quarrels with Christine.

She gathered me into her arms again.

"Ah, my child. You have been deprived of love all your life. No wonder you were so desperate for it. You have learned that love can't be forced. You need to let go of unrequited love and move on."

I wept tears of sorrow and gratitude. I was myself with her. This one person cared about me enough to accept me as I was, even with my sins.

I told her about my conversation with the Lady.

"Must I forgive her?"

"Can you forgive yourself for your own faults if you do not also forgive others?"

Chapter 70

Christine

Garsenda and I were at war over Beatritz. Now that we were back at Mirefoix, I thought Garsenda should make her interest in Beatritz less obvious. In the past, I had mostly accepted the customs of their times, but now that Beatritz's health was at stake, I demanded people do things my way. Each day at dawn, I took Beatritz from her cradle, where she spent the night loosely blanketed. I took her to the kitchen; a maid prepared a tub of warm water, and I bathed her, then patted her dry with linens I had boiled. I put on the diaper I had sewed, with ties to fasten it. I kept Beatritz in my lap. I talked and sang to her and gave her toys to handle. I boiled everything she touched. I made people wash their hands before they touched her.

Even Bon, who shared my knowledge of germ theory, thought my hygiene concerns were excessive. I was terrified she would catch an infectious disease for which we had no treatment. I knew many children died in childhood, and I wanted to keep her healthy.

"Her limbs will be crooked! She should be swaddled." Garsenda took her from me and wrapped her in long linen strips of cloth.

"No. I can't keep her clean when she's bundled like that. And can't you see she's too hot? She's sweating!"

"Where do you get these ideas? Have you any children of your own?"

I stopped short of snatching Beatritz out of Garsenda's arms. Garsenda placed her in the cradle and rocked it with her foot for a while. As soon as she left the room, I picked up Beatritz and unwrapped the swaddling clothes. Watching Beatritz recognize faces and words was a joy, and her sweet cooing sounds delighted me. She brought out a fierce maternal tenderness.

Garsenda's interference poisoned the time I spent with Beatrice. We argued constantly. Often the looks Garsenda gave me were angry. More often, they showed her pain. Her presence blighted my days, but I could not say, leave us alone. When Bon told her to go, she departed with a shadow over her face that broke my heart.

I didn't entirely dislike her; I admired Garsenda's courage and passion for living. My past life would have been much more interesting if I had been more like her. I understood she was jealous. However, her presence so disturbed me I wished she would disappear. I foresaw problems for the rest of our lives.

Chapter 71

Bon

September 1210

In September, a new band of men arrived to threaten Mirefoix. It was not a large army, but the men were rowdy, banging swords on shields and shouting insults at our guards on the walls. Perhaps they thought our small garrison would flee, as before, or that the men would charge out the gate to skirmish, as at Beziers. I had trained the men well; they stood firm. They laughed at these insults.

A siege would not be a problem unless food and other supplies were exhausted. Paths and caves riddled the slopes of the foothills and mountains behind us, and we used them to bring in supplies. However, we had two potential vulnerabilities. One was the secret passage I had used to bring men inside the Chateau Comtal; I spread more branches to disguise the entrance. Now that more people knew its existence, the risk was greater. The other was the water supply. After another hot, dry summer, the wells were low. Most of our water came by tunnel from a spring in the mountains.

The invaders made mock charges at the wall, stopping short of the reach of our arrows. They banged swords on shields to keep my people on edge. We needed a small victory, and I thought of a way to undermine their confidence in their leader, who rode ahead of other knights. Our men stationed at watchtowers used polished metal mirrors to reflect sunlight to send messages to each other and the city. Now I saw another use for them.

The next time attackers charged, we used mirrors to direct flashes of sunlight into the eyes of the leader's horse. The startled horse threw its rider. Their leader remounted and charged again. Again, the light flashes caused his horse to balk, and he fell. There appeared to be murmuring among the ranks. Some crossed themselves. As I hoped, they saw this as an ill omen. Also, as I expected, the leader was stubborn and mounted a third time—and fell again. The attackers broke ranks and fled. A great cheer rose from the walls of Mirefoix. By morning, the soldiers had packed their tents and fled.

An uneasy peace followed. Rumors circulated that Simon de Montfort himself was nearby at Fanjeaux. A much larger army massed outside our gates near the end of October. De Montfort himself led this larger force. They sent a message: they had come to avenge the murder of Sir Dalmas and retake Mirefoix. The attackers assembled a trebuchet, and their scouts explored the hills behind us. Now I felt genuine concern.

He sent the ultimatum I expected. If we surrendered the city, he would show mercy. He required that we yield the Cathars and that Garsenda and I must face justice for the murder of Sir Dalmas. Several Cathar Perfects had returned to comfort the Lady as she lay ill, and now their lives were in danger.

Like Trencavel, I would not turn my people over to be burned. I discussed this with the Lady and Garsenda. We agreed: Mirefoix could stand against a long siege. I was confident that the men of my garrison would stand firm. We refused de Montfort's terms; fear spread among the people. De Montfort was known to be relentless.

It was not missiles hurled by trebuchets that defeated us.

Suddenly, people began to die. I instructed a man to give water from our central well to a captured rat, and its quick death confirmed my fear: de Montfort had poisoned our water source. There was insufficient water in the wells, and it was impossible to endure a further siege. People would die of thirst and sickness, and our delay in surrender would mean harsher treatment. De Montfort called for a parley. The Lady was too ill to rise from her bed. I rode out with Garsenda.

"You cannot endure long without water. If you do not meet my demands, I will raze Mirefoix and kill all inhabitants. You must surrender all Cathars. In addition, you and Lady Garsenda must give yourselves up as hostages and turn over all your remaining valuables. If you meet these conditions, no further harm will come to your city and its people. I must have your answer by dawn tomorrow."

Chapter 72

Christine

On that last night, the Lady gathered us around the table in her chamber. Bon spoke first:

"I will not yield to his demands. I am honor-bound to protect you and all those in my care."

The Lady spoke. "The people of Mirefoix will suffer if we do not meet his demands. I will surrender myself as a Cathar. You must also give yourselves up."

I suppressed a gasp. This would mean the Lady's death, and probably also Bon's and Garsenda's. She continued:

"There must be no more secrets. I beg your forgiveness, Garsenda. I never showed you the love a mother should."

Garsenda inclined her head in silence, but there was no forgiveness in her face.

"I ask your forgiveness, Bon. I sent you away with nothing when you were only a boy. I used magic to force you to swear loyalty. I ordered you to do things that offended your sense of honor. I denied your claim to your birthright."

Bon replied. "You have asked for the truth. I must tell you: I was not the Count's son."

Garsenda's eyes widened, and she drew back. "Why didn't you tell me this sooner?"

"I only learned the truth a short time ago."

"But how—I saw the mark on your neck–"

"My mother's servant was my real father. At my birth, when they saw I did not resemble the Count, he tattooed a mark like the one on the Count's neck on my back to persuade the Count that I was his."

The Lady wrinkled her brow.

"I always doubted that he fathered you. And yet, I wronged you, even if you were not his son."

"Yes, you did. But at this point, I forgive you."

Garsenda's face became pink and more relaxed.

"Then I am not guilty of incest, after all."

"Incest?" The Lady sat bolt upright.

"Beatritz is my daughter. I used a love spell to be with Bon. I hoped it would persuade him to marry me."

"I have a granddaughter... I want to see her."

Jacotte brought Beatritz. The Lady held her.

"I should blame you for what you did, but how can I, when I myself misused magic? We are more alike than I thought."

Garsenda's face softened a little, then hardened.

"It's too late for that."

"Please. I must know you'll be all right despite all my actions."

"Don't worry about me."

"And Christine, I also beg your forgiveness. I don't understand who you are, but I wronged you; my use of magic brought you here against your will. And when I used your healing power, I made you weak and sick."

"My Lady, some good came from this. I have learned not to let people use me. Bon and I love each other."

Garsenda interrupted.

"What other magic? I only know about the love spell, Blodeweth, and the rubies."

"Your father brought a soul-summoning spell from the Outremer. I used it four times. It was supposed to place different souls in people's bodies. It never worked as I intended, and I still don't understand the results. Demons tortured me as punishment for this, and they have made destructive mischief to the people of Mirefoix. I am most heartily sorry for this sin, and tonight I will make a full confession to Father Felip."

Garsenda asked more questions; the Lady told the story about each summoning, what she tried to do, and what happened instead. I was shocked to learn that she had intended to take my body for herself.

I shared what I had learned from talking with Bon, Blodeweth, and Corvinus.

"Each of us, the four summoned souls, was living another life. Each died by fire, and a spirit came after our souls left our bodies and brought us here."

"Where are Blodeweth and Corvinus?" the Lady asked.

"I think Blodeweth killed Corvinus to do shape-shifting magic. She used his bird body to escape. Then she searched for Bon and tried to kill him because he restrained her. I had to kill Blodeweth."

"You? Killed Blodeweth?"

"I had to, or Bon would have died."

"I didn't think you had that in you."

"Neither did I. None of us are blameless."

"I abused power and used you for my own purposes."

I did not contradict that.

"For all that I have done, I am most heartily sorry. Garsenda, if I had treated you as my beloved daughter and heir; and Bon, if I had granted you a house and income in return for your loyal service, perhaps we would have been able to hold Mirefoix. Now Mirefoix is lost. I have decided. Tonight, I will take the vow of Consolamentum and become a Perfect. I will escape the cycle of rebirth and go to heaven. The jinn told me my death would release them from the captivity I inflicted on them by using the spell. They will leave Mirefoix and stop harming my people. I will confess my faith when I go out the gates tomorrow with the other Cathar perfects. De Montfort will burn us, as he has done to others. We will go to eternal life."

There were stunned looks all around, then protests.

"I have decided. It is the only way to save Mirefoix and my soul. De Montfort also demands that you turn yourselves over as hostages. Bon, Garsenda: are you willing?"

Bon responded.

"Yes, Lady."

I was appalled.

"Is there no alternative? Can't we escape through the tunnel into the hills?"

"That would be difficult with so many men posted. If we get away, de Montfort will take out his rage on the people. Garsenda?"

"For the sake of Mirefoix, I will surrender."

The Lady's face showed relief.

"Then I can die in peace, knowing my people will live. Daughter, will you join me in taking the Consolamentum? You would be saved."

Garsenda walked around the table and put her arms around her mother.

"Your way is not for me. The world isn't entirely evil; I have found forgiveness in the words of a friar."

We went to bed late, and sleep did not come. I thought about the Lady's decision. She tried to control everyone around her using magic. She had already paid a terrible price for that, and tomorrow she would give up her life. To my mind, her choice to be burned was horrifying. I tried to understand this from her perspective. To her, death by fire meant atonement for her sins and salvation. In addition, her death would help her people survive. After all that she had done, perhaps this felt to her like the best ending. She would give her life for the people of Mirefoix. Still, it was a mindset I didn't understand. In her situation, I would not insist on a declaration of faith that would doom me to death.

Or would I?

I hardly dared to speak my fears to Bon. De Montfort was brutal. When he conquered Minerve, he burned more than a hundred Cathar Perfects. When he seized Bram, he blinded ninety-nine soldiers in both eyes and the hundredth soldier in one eye. That one soldier led the others in a pathetic procession to Lastours to deliver a warning. He would not let Bon and Garsenda live; as long as they were alive, they would be a threat. But I did not try again to persuade Bon to flee. Even if it were possible, he would not go because of honor. We must face this with courage. He must not have to bear the burden of my fear.

At dawn, the Lady led her group of twelve Perfects outside the walls where de Montfort's men had constructed a wooden palisade around piles of faggots. They bound the Perfects to stakes; they stacked dry firewood below their feet. The Perfects prayed and sang while the soldiers lit the pyres. For most, prayer and song turned to screams of agony.

Bon climbed the city wall above the pyre, and from there, he loosed two arrows. These struck the Lady's throat and chest and brought her the release of a quick death. Immediately, de Montfort's soldiers seized him; they bound his wrists. The horrific smell of burning flesh filled the air, and we heard the sputter of fat. Blackened bodies fell from the stakes.

De Montfort's men brought Bon to the courtyard in front of the cathedral. I followed with Beatritz in my arms. Garsenda was already there; men held her arms behind her back. Bon strained against his bonds. He gazed at me, reminding me with a look that I had promised to remain silent no matter what happened.

Now de Montfort made his plans for Garsenda known:

"Throw this treacherous woman into the well and stone her. She betrayed my man, Sir Dalmas, to his death. She must be punished." Two burly soldiers dragged her to the well while others gathered rocks.

Chapter 73

Garsenda

At first, de Montfort's men pelted me only with curses. There would be no time to confess and receive absolution. For me, this well would be the gateway to Hell.

Christine held Beatritz where I could see her; I hoped my child would survive. Would Christine be able to care for her? That was my one hope. Bon strained to break free from the ropes that bound his arms. I said the words of consolation and prayer I had learned from Brother Matheu. He had promised that God would forgive me for my wrongdoings. There was comfort in that promise. I must face death with dignity.

I begged them: "Please, let me see a priest."

The men jeered. They would not allow me that comfort.

The first stone struck my chest.

Suddenly the door of the cathedral burst open, and Our Dear Dark Lady, the Madonna of Mirefoix, appeared in the cathedral doorway. She wore a robe of white, cinched at the waist. Her veil and cape were sky blue embroidered with gold, and her crown was made of finely worked gold. A ray of sunlight pierced the clouds and gilded her crown and cape as she appeared. A young man with dark skin kneeled before her and cried:

"It is la Moreneta, the Holy Mother! All must bow before her."

The soldiers released me, fell to their knees, and prayed.

The Madonna approached; she extended one hand toward me and the other toward Bon and directed her gaze at de Montfort. "Set them free! They are my beloved children. They have prayed to me all their lives."

De Montfort stood transfixed for a moment. He kneeled before the Madonna and crossed himself. The soldiers let go of my arms and cut the cords that bound Bon's hands. She took each of us by the hand and turned. "Come with me to safety." The crowd of soldiers parted before us; they venerated her. Christine followed. We entered the sanctuary of the cathedral, and Bon closed the doors behind us.

"Quickly!" Mena whispered. We could not maintain the pretense for long. The statue of our dear dark Lady stood in an archway in the nave; I helped Mena remove the crown, veil, and cape that she had taken from the figure of our Lady, and we replaced them on the statue. Mena and her brother ran down the stairs into the crypt to hide. The three of us: Bon, Christine, and I, lit candles and kneeled before the image, giving thanks and praying. I trembled so violently that I had difficulty kneeling.

De Montfort entered and approached the altar. We backed away to make space for him at the foot of the Madonna. He was known for his piety as well as his brutality; he might be willing to believe this deception. He kneeled before the statue and prayed, saying:

"Thank you, Madonna, for permitting me to witness your miracle. Guide me in understanding so I may know God's will."

After what felt like an hour, de Montfort rose to his feet and summoned soldiers. Their leader was a young knight dressed in black in imitation of his master's severity. De Montfort announced his decision.

"God has made His will known to me. I will release you. I banish you from Mirefoix forever. On pain of death, you must never return to this region. Tonight, this man will hold you under guard. Be prepared to leave for Marseilles at dawn. I suggest you make a pilgrimage to Rome to thank the Madonna for her intervention."

I spoke then: "We are grateful for your clemency, my Lord."

"Don't try my patience. Remove yourselves from my sight." De Montfort departed, leaving the knight to carry out his orders. He ordered us to rise, but I struggled. The knight directed his men to improvise a stretcher. They took us to my chamber; the knight lifted me into my bed with surprising gentleness. He tried to speak to me in the lenga romana:

"My men... bring food. I come again... this night." As a northerner, of course, he did not speak our lenga romana. He switched to Latin:

"I have further matters to discuss with you."

Bon asked:

"May we send for the physician?" The knight granted permission before he left.

Rhazes examined me and gave me a bitter but soothing draught. Christine combed my tangled hair and bathed my sweaty face. The guards permitted her to go to the Lady's chamber and open the chest to search for clothes. She returned with a vivid red dress trimmed with pearls. She helped me put it on and laced the sides. I couldn't speak after all that had happened nor swallow the broth and bread she offered.

While Christine tended to me, Rhazes spoke to Bon:

"I would like to come with you. I believe the era of tolerance here has ended."

"We would welcome you. Do you think de Montfort will allow it?"

"With your permission, I will present myself as your servant. I'll bring a cart to the gate. Perhaps they will let us pass without question."

Bon agreed; Rhazes departed to pack what we would need for the journey.

At nightfall, the black-clad knight returned. I sat up in my bed; he brought a chair near and addressed me in Latin.

"I am Jean de Troyes, a vassal of the Duke of Burgundy. De Montfort has charged me to hold Mirefoix. I asked for his permission to marry you. He gave it, but he bade me remember what happened to your last husband."

He suppressed an amused smile. How dared he laugh at me?

"I don't speak the lenga romana; you could help me govern the people, and your presence at my side would make my rule legitimate. I will treat you well. You must swear to obey me as your Lord. You need not decide now, but I must have your answer in the morning."

"Don't you already have a wife and lands in the north?"

"As the fifth among sons, I have no lands. My wife was a woman of cold, dry humors who wept when I brought her to our marriage bed. I released her from our marriage and sent her to a convent. People say that the women of the south have a warmer nature."

He had the ice-blue eyes and flaxen hair of the north. They are cold people. And yet I sensed that he burned for me. I nodded. Bon stiffened; Christine placed her hand on his arm. The knight departed.

"Surely not!" Bon exploded.

I told Bon:

"I will consider it."

"You would give up your child? You would marry this northerner?"

"I am reminded of my sin every hour of every day I see you and Beatritz."

He didn't know how to answer.

"It is my right and my responsibility to rule Mirefoix."

"You know what kind of men these northerners are–" Bon began.

Christine said,

"This is a decision she must make alone. We must not interfere."

Of course, I thought. You want to be rid of me.

Jacotte had finished nursing Beatritz and looked uncertain about what to do. Christine asked:

"Do you want to hold Beatritz?"

I lay down in my bed and turned my face to the wall.

Should I go or stay?

If I went with them, I would see Bon and my child daily. The sight of them reminded me of my sins. I understood now that, even if Christine died, Bon would never love me and take me as his wife.

If I went, the day could come when Beatritz might ask: Who is my real mother? What answer would be adequate? I would have to maintain the pretense that Christine was her mother or else burden her with the truth of my sins. My mother had never loved me as she should. I could not give my child the best love of a mother, either. Perhaps letting go was the most loving thing I might give Beatritz. Maybe I should let Christine be a better mother to her. This was bitter knowledge. My heart was torn with grief. I was a terrible mother whether I clung to Beatritz or let her go.

Which choice was less evil? Which would hurt my child less? I thought of Solomon's judgment and wondered what that wise judge would have advised about my child, torn between two mothers.

I wished for Mena's comfort and counsel, but I dared not send a servant to look for her. If any of the northerners saw her face, they would kill her for blasphemy. If I went, Mena would be alone and unprotected in Mirefoix. She might still be hiding in the crypt without food or water. She had given me a mother's love and risked her life to save mine. I could not abandon her to an uncertain fate. If I went away, I could not protect her.

If I remained bound to Bon and Christine, I might never marry or have children I could claim as my own.

If I went away, I would never see Mirefoix again nor rule it as was my right.

If I stayed, what then? Could I repent of my sin, forget, and make a new life not tainted by guilt?

The young knight's face was smooth and hard as unripe fruit. Perhaps his mind and body were similar. I might bend him to my will in time. He gave practical reasons for marriage. However, his intense gaze told me he admired me. If love could not be mutual, I would prefer to be the one who was wanted. He desired me. Perhaps he would treat me well.

If I stayed, I would be Countess of Mirefoix and the wife of this strange northerner.

If I stayed, my next child would rule Mirefoix.

My time with Brother Matheu taught me the pilgrim way. I would slip away if life became unbearable and take the road to Santiago de Compostela. Perhaps along the journey, I would discover a new life.

I struggled with my decision through the night. As the first red fingers of dawn appeared in the window, I made my choice.

Chapter 74

Christine

The soldiers escorted us to the gate at dawn; Jean de Troyes and de Montfort stood there, and Rhazes waited with a wagon and horses.

Garsenda stepped forward and faced the young knight in black.

"I swear my loyalty to you, and I will marry you." She gave de Troyes her hand. Then she said, in a lower tone: "I have one condition. A day will come when I will ask you for a life, and you must give it to me."

"It can't be a man's life, but I will grant you the life of a woman." He enclosed her hand in his two hands and drew her close. His expression made me hope he might be kind to her.

His soldiers searched the wagon and found our manuscripts, medical instruments, food, clothing, and Bon's weapons. They did not confiscate these. I had hidden the rubies in a place on my person the prudish de Montfort would never search. Jacotte and I scrambled back into the wagon, and Rhazes took the reins to guide it.

Our escort wore the garb of a Knight Templar, a white surcoat with a large red cross. His horse had a glossy coat that shone as if made of gold threads; the Templar's neatly groomed beard was the same shade of gold. Four brown-garbed sergeants accompanied him. De Montfort introduced him:

"This is Philip d'Alluye. He will see you safely to Marseille. From there, you may go where you wish. But never return here."

I found our escort's presence reassuring. These warriors of God had a reputation for fierceness, and he would allow no one to bother us on our journey.

Bon rode alongside the wagon. He and Rhazes spoke of where we might go.

"From Marseilles, ships go everywhere, or we can go east by land," Bon said.

Rhazes said: "There's a famous school of medicine at Salerno. But the House of Wisdom in Baghdad is greater. There are also great centers of learning at Tolosa and Cordoba."

It was good to hear their enthusiasm, but my hopes were different. Perhaps there would be enough silver from the rubies to buy a house and set up a clinic. I had no desire to journey to distant worlds, and I was tired of strange places. Beatritz was my primary concern. It was difficult to keep her clean and comfortable on the road, and I wanted a safe home for her. Once, I visited Aix-en-Provence, north of Marseilles, a city surrounded by fields of lavender; a fountain graced every town square. I wondered what it looked like now. Aix, or a town like it, might be the home my heart longed for.

But home, of course, is not a place. It is people, and I had Bon and Beatritz now. They were my home.

This was a decision we must all make together. I would not be an obedient, silent wife. But I would consider their wishes along with mine.

Sometimes life—or God—demands that we stop doing what is easy for us and instead do what is difficult. We grow beyond the limits of what we are into a larger life. I had accomplished much; life would ask more of me, and I was prepared.

I had built walls around myself in the past and allowed myself to be confined by walls built by others. Walls gave me a familiar and false sense of safety. Finally, I had broken through. Perhaps now I had enough courage to face the dangerous beauties of life.

Of course, we were not finished with the lessons we must learn. Life always brings new challenges. We would leave behind a war-torn world. For each of us, a new path lay ahead. Rhazes would be a respected free man. Bon would use the knife to heal instead of kill. I would be a wife, mother, and healer no longer wounded by healing. We would make a home; all would be well.

A request on behalf of all authors:

If you would like to let authors know you appreciate their work, there are several easy ways you can help!

Buy the book. (Yes, this one is obvious).

After you finish reading your paperback version, give the book to a friend, or donate it to a book sale at a library or thrift store, or leave it in a 'little library' for someone to find.

Rate and review the book on Amazon, Goodreads, or other websites. Books with more reviews show up higher in the algorithms that suggest books to shoppers. Long reviews with detailed praise make authors very happy, but even a one-sentence review can be helpful!

Tell your friends about the book.

Post about the book on social media.

Thank you!

About the Author:

Rebecca loves historical fiction with a touch of magic. She grew up in a small town in Western Pennsylvania, near the steel mill cities of Sharon, PA and Youngstown, OH, feeling out of place and longing for romance and adventure. She sought escape in fairy tales, novels, history books, and travel brochures, and spent most of her free time reading. Her high school nickname was "the walking encyclopedia" (you can spot the nerds early). She loved telling stories, but knew it was difficult to make a living as a fiction writer, so she became a research psychologist. She earned a BA from Carnegie Mellon University and a PhD from Harvard. She was a professor at the University of New Hampshire; she published numerous textbooks and journal articles and traveled and consulted in Europe, Africa, and Asia.

A few years ago she fell in love with southern France, and immersed herself in the history of the 13th century, a time of troubadours, heretics, and heroes—and strong women. Research for this novel included motion-sickness-inducing bus trips to remote Cathar castles, conversations with local history enthusiasts, and lots and lots of books. And, of course, drinking the wines of Occitanie in outdoor cafes.

Other interests include reading, nature walks, travel, early music, and Italian greyhounds. The first thing an Italian greyhound has to learn in her house is that nothing happens before Mommy has her coffee!

She loves to hear from readers! Please visit her author website at www.rebeccawarnerauthor.net

Timeline

1183: Count and Countess of Mirefoix married.

April 1195: Count of Mirefoix left on crusade as par of an imaginary independent army led by the Count of Tripoli, a relative of Raymond, Count of Toulouse.

1197: The Lady received word that the Count had died and she sent Bon, at age 15, out of the Chateau Comtal.

Autumn 1203: Pope Innocent III sent Papal Legates to force Count Raymond VI of Toulouse to suppress Cathar heretics. Count Raymond and many other leaders in southern France refused.

April 1205: Christian crusaders sacked Constantinople.

1206: Dominic Guzman (later called St. Dominic) preached throughout the Languedoc (part of the region of France now called Occitanie). He was unable to bring heretics back to the Church and couldn't persuade southern nobles to hand them over for punishment.

1206: Esclarmonde, sister of the Count of Foix, took the vow of Consolamentum and became a noted Cathar Perfect.

November 1206: After an 11-year absence, the Count returned from the Outremer.

April 1207: Pope Innocent III excommunicated Count Raymond of Toulouse for failure to suppress Cathars, failure to observe Church-mandated truce periods, the appointment of Jews as administrators, and the pillage of monasteries, among other offenses.

Nov 1207: Pope Innocent III called northern French nobles to launch a crusade against heretics of southern France. Despite earlier developments, this took Raymond of Toulouse by surprise.

Dec 1207: Count Raymond of Toulouse asked to meet with papal legates to negotiate. He was sometimes submissive, sometimes defiant.

January 14, 1208: Papal Legate Pierre de Castelnau was assassinated after an unsatisfactory meeting with Raymond of Toulouse. Count Raymond was accused of the murder (although that seems unlikely).

September 1208: A formal call for a crusade was made by Abbot Arnaud Amaury; Cistercians preached the call widely in the north.

December 1208: Raymond Count of Toulouse proposed an alliance with his nephew Raymond-Roger Trencavel, Viscount of Beziers and Carcassonne; Raymond-Roger (unwisely) turned down this. Subsequently, Raymond allied himself with the invaders and this left Trencavel alone as the target of the invasion.

1209: Count Raymond of Toulouse made minor concessions to the Pope; these were not enough. Finally, he capitulated. On June 18, 1209, he was stripped to the waist and flogged at St. Gilles. Count Raymond agreed to join the Crusade against neighboring southern nobles and discriminate against his Jewish and Cathar subjects in return for absolution. This left Raymond-Roger Trencavel to stand alone against the invaders. Trencavel pleaded for peace with the Crusaders, but they attacked his cities, anyway. This was not the first time Crusaders attacked fellow Europeans (that had already happened in Constantinople in 1204). However, it was the first time a crusade was explicitly called against fellow Christians. Crusaders obtained the usual privileges (protection of their property while on crusade, suspension of debts, and absolution from sins). A large crusader army mustered at Lyon in late June 1209 and moved west.

July 22nd, 1209: The massacre at Beziers. The city was burned, and an estimated 12,000 to 20,000 citizens were slain. Narbonne and some other cities in the region choose to open their gates and surrender rather than suffer the same fate as Beziers.

August 1st—August 15th, 1209: Carcassonne was besieged. Viscount Raymond Roger Trencavel went outside the walls to parlay and was seized. In November, Trencavel died in his own dungeon under mysterious circumstances.

HISTORICAL NOTES

Abundant information is available online for most of these topics. I included references only for information that would be hard to locate or for particularly valuable sources.

Apoplexy: Stroke.

Asians in Medieval Europe: Extensive trade routes, both land and sea, connected Europe with East Asia. Most traders probably did not travel the entire distance, but a few travelers did. There are isolated reports of Europeans visiting East Asia, and Asians visiting Europe and the Middle East, mostly later in the Middle Ages (see section about Rhazes below). Marco Polo's accounts of his travels to China include descriptions of Asian physical appearance, including these remarks: "Both men and women are fair and comely" (referring to Changan); and "Their women are particularly beautiful" (referring to the city of Kelinfu). Polo's book may have been based on observations of other Europeans and not his own experiences. Caitlyn Green reported analyses of skeletal data that suggest persons of Asian or African origin may have lived in London as far back as ancient Roman times.

https://www.caitlingreen.org/2016/09/east-asian-people-roman-london.html

Arabic versus Islamic: Not all Arabic people are Islamic, and not all Islamic people are Arabic. During the first Crusade, the invaders did not understand that their opponents were members of many cultural and political groups who were at war with each other.

Baduhenna: A Germanic pagan goddess of war, the forest, and madness, mentioned by Tacitus, who claimed that German pagans engaged in human blood sacrifice.
https://en.wikipedia.org/wiki/Baduhenna

Believer (or *credente*): Cathar believers were followers of the Perfects. Believers were not held to strict vows. They could marry, have children, engage in commerce, eat meat, etc. Many believers planned to take the Consolamentum and become Perfects on their deathbeds to attain salvation without having to live an ascetic life.

Bible: It was heresy to translate the Bible into the vernacular. One of the Cathar practices deemed heretical by the Church was translating parts of the New Testament into Occitan (the lenga romana). Bibles that people could read in their own languages would not be widely available until after the Protestant Reformation and the development of the printing press.

Black Madonna: Hundreds of statues and paintings worldwide appear to show the Madonna as a woman of color. Most are in Western Europe (particularly France); others are found in the Americas, Africa, and Asia. Some may have been intentionally created black; others may have darkened over time because of aging varnish and smoke. Affectionate nicknames such as "La Moreneta," the little dark-skinned one, make it clear that worshippers perceived them as black. In some parts of the world, these images intentionally depict the Madonna as someone who looks like local people. It's less clear why there came to be so many Black Madonnas in places like France. Some speculate that Bernard of Clairvaux's sermons about the Song of Songs, in which a woman sometimes identified as the Queen of Sheba says, "I am black, and I am beautiful," inspired these representations.

Bliaut, surcoat, gambeson, and other clothing: Most of what we know about clothing comes from painting and sculpture. Few cloth garments survive. The cut and fabric of garments changed over time, although style changes were less rapid than those in the modern world. The terms for different garments can be confusing. Some garments are referred to using multiple names, and there are times when the same word refers to different garments or garments worn by both women and men. Social classes wore different types of fiber (e.g., silk versus wool); intense colors were more costly to produce. There would also be some class differences in the cut of garments. The overdress or bliaut for a wealthy woman might have sleeves that ended in an opening so large that the bottom touched the floor, while a less affluent woman could not afford such a wasteful use of material. Fabric was costly, and there was an active trade in rags, which could be used for many purposes, including clothing repair. Fur trim and lavish embroidery would also distinguish the clothing of the wealthy.

Clothing for women: Undergarments for women are a subject of debate. Unlike pictures of men wearing braies, we don't have paintings of women in their underwear. Some authors conclude that women didn't wear any undergarments beneath their shifts. This seems implausible; women having menstrual periods would have needed to wear a pad. The absence of physical evidence does not prove that nothing was worn. Bras with cups dating from the 15th century were found at Lengberg. **(https://medievalexcellence.com/2016/10/25/ the-lengberg-castle-bra/)**

The following video shows layers worn by a 12th-century woman. **https://www.youtube.com/watch?v=4Un5ipTj Dms&feature=share**

The bottom clothing layer would be a simple shift (also called a smock or chemise). This might also be worn while sleeping. Wool hose sewed from pieces, not knitted, came up to the knees and were held in place by garters just below the knee. Shoes were made of leather. On top of the shift would be a kirtle or underdress, possibly made of wool. Lacings on the sides are one example of how such a dress could be made close-fitting. The video shows that the kirtle might have a slit at the neck pinned with a brooch. With a belt added, this layer was sufficient for warm weather or informal wear.

Outer layers were often slit open to show layers beneath, often in contrasting colors.

Hairstyles and head coverings varied. In some periods, it was acceptable for an unmarried woman to let her hair be seen (probably braided), but at most times, married women had to cover their heads, at least partially. The video shows a veil held in place with a circlet. There were many other arrangements for headwear. A hat could be held in place with a strap under the chin (a barbette). A wimple would cover more of the head, including the neck. A coif (the same close-fitted helmet-shaped hat used by some men) might be worn. A fillet was a band, usually worn across the forehead and around the head. Straight pins could be used to attach a veil to some combination of the coif, fillet, or other head coverings. Conical or horned hats with wires to shape them were not in style until a later period than my story.

The next layer would be an overdress, sometimes called a bliaut or surcoat (surcoat also refers to garments worn by men). A bliaut would typically have a fitted body and possibly sleeves that hung all the way to the ground. The overdress might be adorned with fur or embroidery edging along the neck, hem, or sleeves. It might be wool with a lining of linen, silk, or fur. Lacing on the sides could give this garment a closer fit.

A sideless surcoat had long armholes that made a woman's shape visible. It's said that clergy denounced this garment as the "gates of hell." A belt or girdle was worn, tied rather than buckled, and a purse and other useful items might be attached to the belt. Women would also wear a mantle or cloak on top during cold weather. Both women and men wore pattens outdoors when it was muddy (wooden platform shoes, like sandals) to protect their leather shoes.

These descriptions do not include all the possibilities.

The square neckline in the painting on the cover is not 13th century.

Crowfoot, E., Pritchard, F., & Staniland, K. (2001). *Textiles and clothing 1150-1450*. Museum of London.

Clothing for Men: The bottom layer would be braies, something like men's briefs. Wool hose (separate piece for each leg, made of sewed-together pieces, not knit) were attached to the braies. Men's tunics were relatively short, so the hose would be visible. Thin leather shoes, probably tied with laces. Shoes with long pointed toes did not develop until long after my story. The next layer would be an under tunic (an undergarment, possibly also worn while sleeping). On top of this, at least one more layer of tunic. Tunics for men were slightly shorter than those for women, often mid-calf.

For a soldier, the next layer would be a gambeson, a thick quilted jacket often made of linen, closed with ties. A gambeson could be short or long. It added a layer of protection against stabbing and protected the skin from abrasion by mail. (It is redundant to say "chain mail").

A coif might be worn on the head (padded, if a helmet was to be worn on top of it). The next layer for a soldier would be a hauberk or mail shirt. This could vary in length in both body and sleeves and might include a hood.

On top of the tunic (for non-soldiers) or over the hauberk (for soldiers), a surcoat or tabard could be worn. This might be sleeveless. For a non-soldier, a surcoat was also part of everyday dress. For a soldier, the insignia on the surcoat might identify his military affiliation (for Templars, the surcoat was white with a red cross). A surcoat also reduced heat buildup that would otherwise occur from exposure of mail to the sun.

Belts (usually called girdles) were usually tied rather than buckled, and useful objects (for example, a purse) were often attached. All people carried their own eating knives, probably in a sheathe in a sleeve or attached to the girdle. The plate armor that we think of as typical for a knight developed gradually over time and was not worn at the time of my story.

A mantle or cloak could be added for warmth and as a blanket during travel. A man might wear a sword as a sign of rank even when not dressed as a soldier. This list of clothing items is not exhaustive.

This video shows Norman 12th-century clothing.

https://www.youtube.com/watch?v=fJ3VPqxr AOE

Bubonic plague (the black death): This did not become common in Europe until after 1347. This was among the worst pandemics in human history; it may have killed as much as 45% to 50% of the population of Europe. There were also millions of deaths in other parts of the world, particularly in Asia. There were many recurrences of the plague for the next few hundred years. For the characters in my story, the plague and famine of the 14th century have not yet occurred. The 14th century was one of the worst in European history, as Barbara Tuchman (1987) described in *A Distant Mirror: The Calamitous Fourteenth Century*. When many people imagine the Middle Ages, they think of this century. During most of the High Middle Ages (1000-1300), the quality of life for most people was better.

Candles and other forms of lighting: Torches would not have been widely used for indoor lighting. They were smoky and did not burn very long. Instead, people mainly relied on oil lamps, candles made from tallow or beeswax, or lanterns.

Carcassonne: Carcassonne is a World Heritage Site in southern France. Documentaries about castle construction often use it as an example of many possible defensive features. These include multiple rings of curtain walls, round towers, wooden hoards to provide shelter for archers, and murder holes. However, many of these features were added long after 1209. The late 19th-century restoration by Violett-le-Duc is beautiful but inauthentic. The town is now full of souvenir shops and cafes. It's well worth a visit, but here and elsewhere in Occitanie/ Cathar Country, castles and cities do not look as they would have been during the Albigensian Crusades. I imagine Mirefoix as a smaller walled city similar in layout to Carcassonne.

For a look at the city today, see spectacular drone footage:
https://www.youtube.com/watch?v=jt8foZz1b QM&t=25s

Cataract removal: Couching is an ancient method of cataract removal that involves using a needle or lancet to push the lens out; the lens falls into the bottom of the eye. If there was no infection and the patient was nearsighted, some vision could be restored. Celsus described this procedure in 2nd century Greece; it may have originated in India in antiquity. Physicians of the Islamic Golden Age knew about ancient Greek and Roman medicine. Couching is still performed in some developing nations, often with poor results. See Guido Majno, 1975, *The Healing Hand: Man and Wound in the Ancient World*.

Cathar: The heretics in this story would not have called themselves Cathars. At the time, they called themselves "Good Men" or "Good Christians." I use the term Cathar because it is familiar to modern readers. Some popular myths about the Cathars (e.g., that they preserved the bloodline of descendants of Jesus or great treasures of gold) seem implausible to me. According to most sources, Cathars believed Satan created the physical world and that human flesh and sexual reproduction were evil. By this reasoning, the Cathars believed Christ could not have had a physical body and would not have engaged in sex. They did not prize wealth, and their Perfects led ascetic lives. The most plausible Cathar "treasure" would be manuscripts describing their beliefs.

Some authors suggest that Catharism (a dualistic belief system) did not really exist among large numbers of people. Most of what we know about Cathar beliefs comes from detailed records made by Catholic clergy during later inquisitions (See LaDurie, *Montaillou: Cathars and Catholics in a French Village, 1294-1324*). It is conceivable that the inquisitors imagined a detailed heretical theology that did not actually exist in the minds of the people and then got heretics to confess to it. It's clear that the Catholic Church perceived a problem with widespread heresy, even if that heresy was not based on a formal dualist theology. See **https://www.cathar.info/**

Childhood: Philippe Ariès (1960) claimed that there was no concept of childhood in the Middle Ages, that adults did not allow themselves to become attached to children because so many died in childhood, and that children were treated as miniature adults. It's true that children in paintings sometimes resembled adults and wore adult-styled clothing, but I doubt that they had no concept of childhood, and there's evidence that parents grieved intensely when they lost their children.
https://www.representingchildhood.pitt.edu/ pdf/aries.pdf

Clerics: There were three types of clergy. A priest offered sacraments to a parish and had direct contact with laypeople. A monk lived in an enclosed community with relatively little communication with laypeople. Although monks focused on prayer, monasteries often provided services such as lodging for outsiders. A friar was an itinerant preacher; like a priest, he would have much contact with laypeople, but he was not associated with a specific parish. Those higher in the Church hierarchy, such as bishops, usually came from noble families and sometimes led armies.

Consolamentum: The vow that made a Cathar believer into a Perfect (one of the Elect).

Coptic Christianity: The Apostle Mark was said to have brought Christianity to Egypt and neighboring areas around 50 AD. Coptic Christianity was one of the oldest churches, and it was one of several Eastern

Orthodox churches that remained separate from the Roman Catholic and Greek Orthodox Churches. After the Arab and Islamic conquest of Egypt, the status of Coptic Christians varied: sometimes persecuted and sometimes tolerated. There are still many Coptic Christians worldwide.

Count of Foix, Raymond Roger: The ruler of Foix was, along with Toulouse and Trencavel, one of the major figures in the Albigensian crusade. Both his wife and his sister Esclarmonde were Cathar Perfects. The little information I can find is somewhat contradictory in tone. Wikipedia describes him as "famed for generalship, chivalry, fidelity, and affection for haute couture... he was, besides a patron of troubadours, an author of verse himself... a great orator who attended the Fourth Lateran Council of 1215 to defend Raymond of Toulouse...". On the other hand, he was accused of killing many priests and is reported to have told Pope Innocent III that he only regretted not having killed more. Jonathan Sumption (in *The Albigensian Crusades*) mentions that the citizens of Pamiers and Saverdun were "delighted to throw off the harsh yoke of the Count of Foix, and welcomed Simon [de Montfort] as a liberator."

Crusades: At the time of my story, this term was not in use. People said they became pilgrims, "took the cross," or "went to Outremer."

Denier: A small silver coin comparable to a penny.

Donzel: A young man in training for knighthood.

Embalmed heart: The heart-shaped metal box containing the Count's son's embalmed heart is like an actual artifact. Crusaders wanted parts of their bodies to be buried at home. (A German custom, called mos Teutonicus, involved boiling skeletons to remove all soft tissue and sending bones home for burial.)

https://www.dailymail.co.uk/sciencetech/article-3343408/Modern-science-detects-disease-400-year-old-embalmed-hearts.html

Esclarmonde of Foix: She was the sister of the Count of Foix. After becoming widowed, she became a Cathar Perfect in 1204. She was present at the last Cathar/Catholic debates in Pamiers in 1207 and may have been a participant and even an organizer. By some reports, when she rose to speak, a monk jumped up and said, "Go back to your spinning, woman. It is not proper for you to speak at such debates." Her life is brilliantly imagined in Glen Craney's *The Fire and the Light*.

Emotion and Expression of Emotion: There is not much autobiographical writing left to us from the Middle Ages. Even if we had more first-person accounts, we still wouldn't know whether people experienced emotions as we do now. Johan Huizinga suggested that medieval people were emotionally childish and impulsive; Norbert Elias argued that this changed only after people went through a 'civilizing' process over many centuries that involved the development of self-restraint. This view has been questioned by Barbara Rosenwein (2007) in *Emotional Communities in the Early Middle Ages*. There is now considerable scholarly interest in the study of emotion during the Middle Ages. I believe that human nature hasn't changed, and it seems arrogant for modern writers to assume that people in the past were substantially inferior to us. On the other hand: cultural 'display rules' for showing emotion vary across time and geographic locations. Facial expressions and body language may have changed.

Fan Zhongyan: I borrowed the name of a statesman and scholar of the Northern Song dynasty who lived centuries before the time of my story.

Feudalism: Medievalists now regard the term 'feudalism' as problematic. Practices varied across time and location. Most descriptions of feudalism say that land was granted by a king to his nobles 'in fief.' In return, nobles owed the king support, often in the form of military service. Nobles, in turn, granted land to their vassals, who owed them military service, taxes, fees, or labor. In theory, this led to a clear hierarchy with stable oaths of loyalty. In northern France, political organization in the 13th century may have resembled this definition of feudalism. However, in the Occitan, most holdings were wholly owned by the vassal and passed on by inheritance. Occitan vassals swore oaths of loyalty to liege lords, but these ties were often weak in practice. Vassals usually did not owe military service to their lords. Occitan nobles had to rely on mercenaries rather than vassals when they needed to raise armies. The looseness of organization was one of the reasons southern nobles had trouble mounting a defense against the northern invaders.

Fire striker: People would have lighted lamps or candles from an existing flame. If this wasn't possible, they could use a tool called a fire striker (it resembled tongs with steel and flint).

Floor covering: Castle floors may have had rush mats, but probably not loosely strewn rushes or straw, as in stables. Again, this would vary across times and places. Rugs, when available, might have been used mainly to cover walls and tables rather than floors (because they were valuable).

Food: For the poor, pottage was a typical dish. This would consist of grain, peas, and other vegetable foods. Meat or fish could be added when available. As trade increased, spices became available, and food became more varied for the wealthy. For those who could not afford imported spices, onion and garlic gave flavor to food. Many popular modern foods, such as potatoes and tomatoes, were unavailable in Europe until trade began with the Americas. Modern readers may be surprised that almond milk was commonly used for cooking in later parts of the Middle Ages. Most foods were eaten only when seasonally available, but fish and meats were preserved by drying and salting. See more about diet in the separate list in the section **Myths and Misconceptions about the Middle Ages.**

Redon, O., Sabban, F., & Serventi, S. (1993). *The Medieval Kitchen: Recipes from France and Italy.* University of Chicago Press.

Fragmentation and regional variation were common. This applies to political organization, culture, and language. The people of northern and southern France had different languages in the 13th century (the langue d'oïl in parts of the north and the langue d'oc or lenga romana or Occitan of the south). I don't know the extent to which these were mutually intelligible. For the Church and nobility, familiarity with Latin provided a common language across regions. As recently as 1900, residents of neighboring rural towns in France had different dialects, according to Graham Robb (2008) in *The Discovery of France: A Historical Geography*. My characters would have encountered many dialects during their travels (I decided not to make this a problem for them).

Francis (later, Saint Francis): Francis was inspired to devote himself to a life of poverty and began to preach in February 1208; he had his first 11 followers within a year. He obtained papal authorization for his new order in 1209. It is a stretch to portray the fictional Brother Matheu preaching Franciscan beliefs in the Occitan as early as 1209/1210. The specific Franciscan prayers quoted might not yet have been written. Still, I could not resist including St. Francis in my story's mix of 13th-century religious beliefs. Here is a fascinating story: Francis went to Egypt with the Crusader army on the Fifth Crusade. He crossed the battle lines to teach Christianity to the Sultan of Egypt, Malik Al-Kamil, who received him graciously and listened politely. See the book *The Saint and the Sultan* by Paul Moses (2009); the corresponding film is *The Sultan and the Saint*.

Gait: It has been suggested that people had a different gait (walking pattern) in the Middle Ages than we do today, perhaps because of soft-soled shoes, but this has been disputed.

Gambeson: A quilted linen jacket worn under mail for additional protection.

Garderobe: An indoor toilet; waste was disposed of through a chute outside the walls.

Garsenda, Countess of Forcalquier and Provence: She was the inspiration for Garsenda's name. She was a regent of Provence in the early 1200s, a noted patron of troubadours, and the author of at least one known lyric.

Good Christians or Good Men: In the 13th century, the heretics we now call Cathars called themselves Good Christians or Good Men.

Goryeo: The kingdom of Goryeo unified the Korean peninsula and ruled from 918 to 1392, a golden age for Buddhism, art, culture, and trade. I first heard of Goryeo in the historical K-drama fantasy *The Great Doctor* or *Faith*. I imagine Bon's face as that of Korean superstar Lee Min Ho in the role of Choi Young.

Hauberk: A (chain) mail shirt. These varied in design and might have short or long sleeves, and a hood. They were labor-intensive to make and therefore costly. Plate armor did not come into use until later centuries.

Heroine's journey: I enjoy stories where women save themselves – not necessarily by behaving like men. Maureen Murdock's (1990) *The Heroine's Journey* provides ways to imagine how challenges for women can differ from those for men. I couldn't incorporate the entire heroine's journey arc into my narrative, but it gave me something to aim for.

Hildegard of Bingen: She lived around 1098 – 1179. She was one of the great creation-centered mystics of Western Europe. As abbess of a Benedictine abbey, she was also an influential preacher, healer, scientist, composer, theologian, artist, and poet who corresponded with Popes and high-ranking clerics. She is best remembered today for her music.

Humoral theory: Western medicine was dominated by the theory of the four humors, from before the time of the Greek physician Galen in the Roman Empire (circa 216 CE) until the advent of germ theory around the 1850s. Galen said there were four humors or bodily fluids, which have hot versus cold and wet versus dry qualities. Hot versus cold refers to something abstract, rather than physical temperature or spiciness. The four humors included blood, phlegm (not in the modern sense), and two substances with no modern medical equivalent (green bile and black bile). Galen argued that disease arose from an imbalance among the humors. Treatments such as bloodletting, emetics, enemas, blistering, and foods or drugs thought to have warm or cold qualities were intended to restore balance among the humors. Up until the 1850s, such treatments were widely used. Other early systems of medicine, such as Chinese medicine, are also balance theories. Chinese medicine is based on the balance between yin and yang energies (loosely translated as female/male, or cold/hot). Treatments such as acupuncture are believed to change the flow of vital energy or qi through the body; diet and herbal medicines are also used to correct imbalances. Here also, hot/cold means something different from physical temperature or spiciness. Ayurvedic medicine in India is also a balance theory, but it involves three doshas rather than four humors.

Many treatments inspired by humoral theory (aggressive use of bleeding and purging) almost certainly caused more harm than good. Germ theory introduced military metaphors about medical treatment: treatments attack and kill disease-causing organisms. The discovery of antibiotics led to enormous improvements in human health, including reductions in infant mortality. However, there has been a renewed appreciation of balance in health and medicine and the role for spiritual support in medical treatment. Virginia Sweet's *God's Hotel* describes a contemporary American physician's interest in the perspectives of Hildegard of Bingen and humoral theory; Sweet even did a doctorate in the history of medieval medicine.

Temperament or personality was also thought to be related to the balance of the humors. Excess blood (with hot, wet qualities) was associated with a "sanguine" (a cheerful, active, and extroverted personality). Excess yellow bile was related to choleric (irritable) temperament. Excess black bile was thought to cause melancholy, and excess phlegm was supposed to cause a phlegmatic (stolid, calm) temperament. Although these physical explanations are no longer used, assessment of active/passive and positive/negative traits is still included in most personality measures. There are echoes of Galen's ideas in descriptions of people as introverted versus extroverted.

House of Wisdom: An intellectual center in Baghdad, an academy and library that, until its destruction in 1258, was a major center of translation and preservation of documents from Greek, Persian, Indian, and other sources. It was one of many centers of the Islamic Golden Age; great libraries developed elsewhere, as far away as Al Andalus and even Timbuktu. See Joshua Hammer (2017). *The Bad-Ass Librarians of Timbuktu and Their Race to Save the World's Most Precious Manuscripts*, about recent attempts to save these great collections from destruction.

Independent crusader armies: Histories of the crusades usually focus on the most significant armed expeditions launched in response to calls by the Pope. However, many smaller independent armies went to Outremer between the major numbered crusades. The second crusade would have been too early and the third crusade too late to account for the absence of the Count of Mirefoix, so I sent him with an imaginary army raised in 1195 by a relative of Raymond, Count of Toulouse.

https://independentcrusadersproject.ace.ford ham.edu/

Isaac the Blind (Yitzhak Sagi Nahor): This noted Kabbalah scholar lived in Provence from about 1160 to 1235; some believe he wrote the Book of the Bahir, one of the primary texts. A later scholar said that Isaac could sense in the feeling of the air whether a person would live or die and whether his soul was new [meaning that it had not undergone transmigration or reincarnation] or an old soul [that had undergone

transmigration or reincarnation]. I made use of this ability in my story.
https://www.encyclopedia.com/religion/encyclopedias-almanacs-transcripts-and-maps/isaac-blind

Islamic Golden Age: From about the 8th to the 14th century, Islamic culture flourished with significant developments in philosophy, mathematics, natural sciences, medicine, architecture, and the arts (to name just a few).

Jinn/jinni: Singular is jinni; plural is jinn. In popular Islamic culture, and also as mentioned in the Quran, Jinn are spiritual beings usually invisible to humans. Like humans, they have free will and can do good or evil. They have magical powers and can be summoned by humans. My jinn correspond to the air, earth, fire, and water elements prominent in many kinds of magic. See Robert Lebling and Tahir Shah, 2011, *Legends of the Fire Spirits*.

Jongleur: A traveling performer who might juggle, do acrobatics, dance, and play and sing troubadour ballads. The feminine version is jongleuse. Unlike the troubadours, jongleurs were not of high status. Occitan equivalents: joglar and joglesa.

Knighthood: In northern France, knighthood seems to have matched the typical description of knighthood in many historical texts. Sons of nobles trained for knighthood by serving as pages and squires in another noble's castle. When a young man came of age or proved himself, he was formally 'dubbed' a knight in a ceremony that might be preceded by a bath and night of prayer. He would hold a castle or manor for his lord and use the proceeds from the manor to support himself. Often his home was in the countryside, in a manor. He needed an income to pay for servants and equipment (horses, lance, armor, etc.). He owed military service to his liege lord and might be required to bring additional soldiers with him. He would fight primarily on horseback, using a couched lance to unseat other mounted knights. He could also fight dismounted using different weapons. Tournaments were occasions to demonstrate jousting skills. Knighthood worked something like this in northern France during the high Middle Ages. However, in southern France/ Occitania, knighthood does not seem to have had most of these formal features. A knight did not have to come from a noble family; it was more important to have enough funds to own a horse, armor, and arms. Formal 'dubbing' ceremonies, if they existed at all, were rare. A knight's obligations to his lord might be in taxes or goods rather than military service, and allegiances were unstable. Raymond, Count of Toulouse, could not muster an army by calling up knights; he hired mercenaries. Knights might be mercenaries rather than landholders. They often lived in cities rather than in manors in the countryside. There are no accounts of large tournaments held in the south. Militarism was glorified in the North more than in the South. These differences were among the reasons Northerners and Southerners held each other in contempt. See Linda Paterson's (2019) *Culture and Society in Medieval Occitania.*

La Moreneta: I borrowed the nickname given to the Black Madonna of Montserrat from Catalonia, Spain.

Lalibela: The rock-hewn churches of Lalibela in Ethiopia were built as a "new Jerusalem" soon after Jerusalem fell in 1187. The eleven churches are monolithic, carved down into the ground in solid rock, and they form a magnificent complex that is still a popular pilgrimage site for Coptic Christians. It is a World Heritage Site.

Lenga romana: The people in the Occitan called their own language the lenga romana. This name recognized their language's close ties with Latin and other Romance languages; many of their words and personal names sound more Spanish than French. This language is also called Occitan or old Occitan; people still speak Occitan in some parts of southern France. In Occitan the word 'oc' means 'yes.' The language of the south was sometimes called the lenga d'oc or langue d'oc. The language of northern France at the time of my story was langue d'oïl; the northern French word for yes was 'oïl' (similar to the later: 'oui'). The Occitan language is still spoken in a few areas in southern France and the Pyrenees.

Marriage: Marriage was not one of the original Catholic sacraments. Until about 1215, it was sufficient for a man and woman to say: "I marry you" in the present tense. Witnesses and clergy were not required, although a wedding might occur in front of a Church door, and a priest might offer a blessing. This informality led to problems; it could be difficult to know whether a person you wanted to marry was already married. The lack of witnesses often led to doubts about the validity of marriage claims, and lawsuits about marital status were common.

Occitan: My story takes place in the southern area of France now called Occitanie. This was not a unified political entity, but people of the south shared values and cultures different from those of northern France. People probably identified themselves as Toulousain (a person from Toulouse). When my characters speak of 'we Southerners,' this reflects a shared sense of identity based on language, troubadour culture, and the ideal of paratge. The word Occitan is often used to refer to their language and sometimes to the entire region and culture. This term may not have come into common use until a later century.

Love: Did people feel romantic love in the same way during the Middle Ages as we do now? We don't know. The widely shared contemporary assumption of people in the USA and Europe that romantic love should be the basis for marriage is not a cultural universal. Even today, arranged marriages still occur in some parts of the world. Medieval nobles used marriage to create political alliances, and people with property saw marriage primarily as an economic arrangement. Their children would have recognized, although perhaps not always accepted, that parents would choose their marriage partners. Peasants may have had more freedom to choose partners based on attraction (although, even for them, property may have been a consideration). The ideal of courtly love that emerged around 1100 explicitly separated love from marriage. In the love ballads of the troubadours, a knight praised his lord's wife and showed his love through gallant deeds. This love was not usually consummated; it was an idealized and erotic longing made more intense by lack of fulfillment. (In at least some cases, adultery did occur.) The idea of courtly love may have influenced behavior among some nobles through the 12th and 13th centuries, but it was not widespread; it certainly inspired troubadour culture and the development of the Arthur legend. I don't think it tells us much about 'normal' love. Many of the nobility seem to have had loveless marriages of convenience. But there were cases of people at all levels of society who refused arranged marriage and chose love matches. There were cases of nobles who grieved lost partners with an intensity that indicated strong bonds of affection.

The idea that romantic love is a recent development and arises only in Euro-American culture has been challenged; see William Jankowiak and Edward Fischer, (1992), "A cross-cultural perspective on romantic love", *Ethnology: An International Journal of Cultural and Social Anthropology, 31(2),* 149-155. They looked for accounts of anguish and longing, the existence of love songs, elopement due to mutual affection, and other accounts of passionate love. They found these in all major geographic regions. My guess is that, in all cultures, love is experienced in many ways.

Medieval Warm Period: Temperatures rose in Western Europe between about 900 – 1200 CE. New agricultural technologies developed, such as the horse collar and heavy plow. Agricultural output and fishing yields increased. Greater food availability led to substantial population growth, urbanization, and increased trade and prosperity during the High

Middle Ages. By the 13th century, the population had increased to a point where resources again became scarce. Scarcity often leads to the emergence of what Robert Moore called persecuting societies. The Albigensian Crusade was the death blow to the flourishing culture of the Occitan region, but their culture may have already been in decline. By the 14th century, Europe was overwhelmed by famine, the Black Death, and the Hundred Years' War.

Fagan, B. (2008). *The Great Warming: Climate Change and the Rise and Fall of Civilizations.*

Mirrors: Mirrors have existed since ancient times, although access to good-quality mirrors with clear reflections was limited until recently. We live in a world where people are obsessed with images of themselves in mirrors, photos, and social media. I'd like to think that in a world where mirrors were rare luxuries, people might have been less obsessed with and worried about their appearances. (Wouldn't that be a relief?) See Mark Prendergast (2003). *Mirror, Mirror: A History of the Human Love Affair with Reflection.*

Outremer: Outremer refers to the region around what is now Israel, sometimes called the Holy Land. It was the goal of the Crusades to recapture this region.

Paratge: (pronounced something like 'pah ratch chay') This Occitan word has no exact equivalent in other languages. It means a kind of honor that includes virtues such as chivalry, nobility, tolerance, excellence, grace, courage, gentility, courtesy, hospitality, and a sense of what was right. Southern nobles felt the northern invaders did not understand or share this worldview.

https://www.midi-france.info/190403_paratge.htm

Perfect: Writers now refer to Cathar leaders as Perfects; at the time, they were more likely called 'the Elect.' Women, as well as men, could become Perfects. To become a Perfect, a person took the sacrament of the Consolamentum. The vow prescribed an ascetic life and abstinence from sex and foods resulting from sexual reproduction (such as meat and eggs; fish were exempt because they were thought not to come from sexual reproduction). Cathar Perfects traveled in pairs, simply garbed, preaching to believers. Upon their deaths, Perfects who kept their vows were believed to pass directly to heaven. All others were doomed to reincarnate on Earth. They thought the physical world was Hell, created by the devil; reincarnation was a fate they wanted to avoid.

Permit the garrison and people to leave: Seige warfare did not always end in slaughter. By the late 12th century, an (unwritten) understanding of chivalric rules for war had developed, including expectations about surrender by a besieged city or castle. Attackers sometimes permitted people to leave castles or towns unharmed if they surrendered before a siege began. Even after a siege was underway, people could sometimes negotiate terms that allowed them to leave unharmed, taking few or no possessions with them. However, attackers did not always observe these chivalric expectations. Attackers often left buildings and walls intact; crusaders often occupied and strengthened conquered cities. Refugees from captured cities sometimes went short distances and set up new towns outside the city walls. Eventually, some drifted back into the city. Early in the Albigensian Crusades, the invaders did not identify heretics systematically. At Beziers, they killed everyone. When Carcassonne surrendered, all inhabitants, including Trencavel's soldiers, were permitted to leave, and no Cathars were burned. Later, the Crusaders discovered that if they asked people departing from cities whether they were heretics, most Cathar Perfects (leaders) did not deny their faith. Those who refused to recant their faith were burned, often in hundreds, at places like Minerve.

https://www.worldhistory.org/Medieval_Chivalry/

https://www.medievalists.net/2015/01/surrender-medieval-europe-indirect-approach/

Persecuting Society: Jews were persecuted during the Middle Ages, and often entire communities were wiped out. However, persecution of Jews and other groups varied over time. In *The Formation of a Persecuting Society*, R.I. Moore (2007) argued that as elites began to worry about losing their possessions and privileges around 1100-1200, they gradually treated marginal groups worse and worse over time. Southern France/ Occitan was famous for being (relatively) tolerant around the year 1200; in fact, the Albigensian Crusade was launched to punish tolerance of Cathar heresy. In addition, Raymond, Count of Toulouse, was chastised by the Church for favoring Jews; and Raymond Roger Trencavel brought the entire Jewish community when he left Beziers for Carcassonne. Of course, this protection was based on self-interest because Jews served as valued administrators. Just before the Albigensian Crusade, the Jewish community may have experienced somewhat less persecution in the Occitan than in other places and at later times.

Racism in modern sense the (based on skin color) did not yet exist in the Middle Ages. Theories about 'barbarism' and 'savagery' used later to justify the enslavement of Africans emerged during the Enlightenment Period, which was not very enlightened in this respect. There has recently been considerable interest in studying people of color during the Middle Ages. Prejudice and persecution indeed occurred during the Middle Ages, but it was based more on religion than any notion of race.

https://www.npr.org/sections/codeswitch/2013/12/13/250184740/taking-a-magnifying-glass-to-the-brown-faces-in-medieval-art

Pottage: A sort of stew or porridge, often made mostly of vegetables; those who could afford these might add meat, fish, and spices.

Prayer shawls and Jewish clothing: Blue and white striped garments such as prayer shawls for men and veils with a border stripe for women were traditional. The yarmulke was not worn until the 17th and 18th centuries. Jewish men may have worn conical hats, a variation of Phrygian hats from the east, sometimes with a knob at the top, before they became required in some regions. Artists used this hat to symbolize Jewish identity, usually in very negative contexts. In 1215, the Fourth Lateran Council decreed that Jewish people must wear distinctive identifying clothing to distinguish them from Christians. Details and enforcement were left to secular authorities. The Synod of Narbonne required an oval badge as of 1227. This anticipated the use of yellow patches in Nazi Germany. These clothing requirements were part of the emergence of what R. I. Moore called a persecuting society that was gradually emerging during the time of my story. See Sara Lipton's (2014) *Dark Mirror* for further discussion. Muslim rulers also imposed requirements about identifying dress at some times. Under Caliph Haroun al-Rashid (807 CE) in Bagdad, Jews had to wear a patch in the shape of a donkey and Christians in the shape of swine. These identified both groups as 'dhimmi,' religious minorities with some rights and protections.

https://encyclopedia.ushmm.org/content/en/ article/jewish-badge-origins

https://en.wikipedia.org/wiki/Yellow_badge

Raymond VI, Count of Toulouse: (also Marquis of Provence and many other southern French territories, some not adjacent to Toulouse). He is described in many sources as an educated, charming, pleasure-loving man, a better soldier than a diplomat, a poet and a man of culture, and quite a womanizer. He was married six (or possibly only five) times; his wives were from prominent families. You get some idea of his prominence from the status of his fourth wife, Joanna Plantagenet, sister to Richard I (the Lionheart) of England. The fates of his wives remind me of the wives of Henry VIII. Nominally he was a

vassal of the King of France and liege lord to many
nobles in the Occitan, including Viscount Raymond
Roger Trencavel (his nephew). He was related to the
royal family of France and was the most powerful
figure in the Occitan at the time of my story. However,
feudal ties were much weaker in the Occitan than in
the North; Count Raymond could not count on raising
an army by calling on his vassals. Also, alliances were
changeable, particularly in the years immediately
before the Albigensian Crusade. The Count of
Toulouse got in trouble with the Church for numerous
offenses; he either could not or would not suppress
the Cathar heresy, and he was accused of harassing
and raiding church properties and favoring Jews. As
circumstances changed, he made and broke promises;
he was excommunicated and reinstated in the Church
multiple times. As my story begins, first, Raymond of
Toulouse sheltered Cathar heretics; then, he allied
himself with the invading crusader army. This alliance
was a disaster for Raymond Roger Trencavel, his
nephew, who had to face the invading army alone.
After my story ends, Count Raymond changed sides
again and fought against the Crusaders. After
Raymond died in 1222, even though the abbot of St.-
Sernin had absolved him, Count Raymond was denied
burial in consecrated ground. His coffin stood outside
the Priory of the Hospitallers for many years while his
son pleaded with one Pope after another to allow
Catholic burial. According to Jonathan Sumption (in
The Albigensian Crusades), his wooden coffin was
eventually destroyed by rats, and his bones were lost.
Count Raymond of Toulouse is one of four historical
figures depicted in a mural on the ceiling of the
Minnesota Supreme Court (along with Moses,

Confucius, and Socrates) in recognition of his defense of city freedoms. I can't believe no one has written a novel about this remarkable man. (At least, I have not found one in English).

Rhazes (Abu Bakr al-Razi): This 10th-century Persian physician is the inspiration for my character Rhazes; by some accounts, his contributions to medicine were comparable to those of Ibn Sina (Avicenna). Unlike many of his contemporaries, he was skeptical of Galen's humoral theory and used more empirical approaches, including the trial of treatments on animals before use with humans. Joseph Needham reported that a student from China traveled to study with Rhazes, learned Arabic, and made extensive notes; it's another example of how interconnected the world was in the past.

Joseph Needham; Ling Wang (1954). 中國科學技術史. Cambridge University Press. pp. 219, ISBN 978-0-521-05799-8.

For a discussion of his remarkable contributions to early medicine, pharmacy, "medicine of the soul," and surgery, see:
https://web.archive.org/web/20171204104627/http://www.islamicmedicine.org/alrazi3.htm

Riding: Women probably rode astride much of the time rather than sidesaddle.
https://www.sarahwoodbury.com/women-and-riding/

Saint Guinefort: A greyhound was regarded by laypeople in 13th-century France near Lyons as a saint

and a special protector of infants and children.
https://en.wikipedia.org/wiki/Saint_Guinefort

Santiago de Compostela: A major pilgrimage destination in northern Spain, in the Middle Ages and today.

Saracen: Early in the Crusades, European invaders did not understand that the defenders of Outremer included many cultural groups that warred with each other. The Europeans called their adversaries Saracens or Moors. This word reflects the European lack of understanding about how diverse their eastern opponents were (in culture, language, ethnicity, and religion).

Seneschal: A steward of a medieval house.

Simon de Montfort, 5th Earl of Leicester (also called Simon Montfort the Elder): He was a French noble (despite the English title and holdings, which he inherited after the death of an uncle) who emerged as the leader of the Albigensian Crusade after the fall of Carcassonne. He was a ruthless soldier responsible for some of the better-known atrocities committed by the Crusaders. He was also renowned for orthodox religiosity. He was an energetic commander until his death during the second siege of Toulouse in 1218; he was struck in the head by a missile from a trebuchet or mangonel. Tradition has it that this weapon was operated by women. His son, Simon de Montfort the younger, 6th Earl of Leicester, was a leader in the second Baron's war against Henry III of England and played a major role in constitutional development.

Sleep patterns: The idea that we should have a continuous 8-hour sleep may be a modern invention. During the Middle Ages, people often woke in the middle of the night and then went back to sleep. Two-phase sleep (like an after-lunch nap or siesta) reflects underlying biological rhythms. Knowing that two-part sleep can be a normal pattern may help some modern insomniacs realize that waking up at night isn't necessarily abnormal. See Roger Ekirch (2006), *At Day's Close: Night in Times Past.*

Social and Cultural Dynamics: Pitirim Sorokin wrote a massive history of world cultures called *Social and Cultural Dynamics* that may help us understand why the Middle Ages can seem so alien to modern people. He argued that some cultures are more materialistic and others are more ideational. Over time, cultural values go back and forth between these poles. In a materialist culture, reality is nothing but the physical, and reality can be known only by sensory means. In an ideational culture, true reality is spiritual or transcendent; the material world is an illusion. We currently live in a very materialistic culture; culture during the Middle Ages was more ideational. Of course, this is an oversimplification; many people value religion or spirituality today, and there was greed and materialism during the Middle Ages.
https://satyagraha.wordpress.com/2010/08/19/pitirim-sorkin-crisis-of-modernity/

Song Empire: The Song dynasty ruled a region of southern China from 960 to 1279. It was a period of brilliant cultural development and extensive trade.

Southerner versus Northerner prejudices and stereotypes: In *Dynamics of Prejudice*, Bruno Bettelheim and Morris Janowitz (1950) pointed out that ingroup/outgroup stereotypes sometimes sound much like the Freudian id versus the superego. Their discussion focused mainly on racial prejudice and anti-Semitism. Stereotypes about people living in the North and the South also reflect id and superego themes. Northerners may view themselves as having positive superego qualities (e.g., they see themselves as conscientious, hardworking, and thrifty); by contrast, northerners may view Southerners as having negative id qualities (e.g., lazy, wasteful). Southerners may view northerners as having negative superego qualities (uptight, rigid, stingy, cold) and view themselves as having positive id qualities (pleasure-loving, warm, relaxed, refined, hospitable). There could be a kernel of truth in some North/South stereotypes. Perhaps people who live in hotter climates tend to live at a more relaxed pace. But as with other stereotypes, these beliefs become exaggerated until they allow people to view members of outgroups as 'others,' people with different and undesirable qualities. According to Linda Paterson (2002), *Culture and Society in Medieval Occitania*, the people in the north and south of 13th century France had negative stereotypes about each other. Northerners described those in the South as "frivolous, morally corrupt, garrulous, gluttonous, poor Latinists [and] lacking in warlike spirit." The Occitan / Southern ideal of paratge included qualities such as courtesy, nobility, gentility, hospitality, excellence, and tolerance; Southerners thought northern invaders lacked this kind of honor.

Strange Things: I think people in the Middle Ages were very much like us in many ways. And yet, in any thousand years, you can find examples of bizarre things, and the Middle Ages has its share. The bizarre is a fun part of history. Just don't believe everything you read.

A pope was put on trial after he was dead (the *Cadaver Synod*):

https://tinyurl.com/4epd4dfa

At least 85 farm animals faced trial; E. P. Evans, (1906). *The Criminal Prosecution and Capital Punishment of Animals.* For some reason, pigs were often the culprits.

https://tinyurl.com/jj5bafc4

Jousting rabbits, snails, and other motifs appear in some illustrated manuscripts, and I'm not sure anyone really knows why. Perhaps the monks were bored? Some of the wonderful strangeness in Monty Python comes from their knowledge of history.

https://tinyurl.com/wj2zcsub

On the other hand, some other strange things you hear about (such as the chastity belt) are almost certainly myths.

https://www.smithsonianmag.com/smart-news/medieval-chastity-belts-are-myth-180956341/

Surcoat: An overgarment for either a man or a woman. These varied in length and cut and might have side slits.

Swearing: Taking the name of God in vain was considered much more obscene during the Middle Ages than it is now. On the other hand, explicit comments about human body functions were considered less offensive by them. See Mohr, M. (2013). *Holy Shit: A Brief History of Swearing.* Oxford University Press (this is one of my favorite book titles of all time).

Sword of Chinese design: The hilt of Bon's sword has an usual design, The description is based on the sword of the tomb effigy of Jean d'Alluye, interred in 1248, displayed at the Cloisters museum in NYC. The effigy originally covered his tomb in a Cistercian abbey in northern France. The abbey was destroyed during the French Revolution (1789/1799). The effigy was turned upside down and reportedly served as a footbridge across a stream until about 1855 when it was rediscovered and moved to a nearby castle. Other details of the effigy, such as the shape of the shield and chain mail 'mittens,' resemble other relics from this period; but the sword's hilt was unusual, and at least two respected scholars believe the design was of Chinese origin. Jean d'Alluye may have acquired his sword while serving in the Crusades; trade goods from as far away as China were exchanged along the trade routes we now call the Silk Roads.
https://scottmanning.com/content/jean-dalluye-a-crusader-and-his-chinese-sword-in-new-york/

Teeth: Modern people have an overbite; the top layer of incisors hangs over the bottom like the lid on a box (this overbite has been typical only in the last 200 – 250 years). During the Middle Ages, people had an edge-to-edge bite with the top and bottom teeth aligned. The change is probably due to diet. See Bee Wilson (2013), *Consider the Fork: A History of How We Cook and Eat*. Contrary to the myth that people in the Middle Ages had rotten teeth, dental caries was rare during the Middle Ages due to the scarcity of sugar in the diet. People cleaned their teeth with twigs, clothes, and herbs.

https://tinyurl.com/ubxx5p5v

Trade Routes: Ideas, technologies, foods, and so forth were traded long distances over extensive sea and land trade routes. The term "Silk Road" refers to many trade routes, not just one road. Crusaders brought new ideas and trade goods back to Europe; these had an enormous impact on cultural development.

https://tinyurl.com/5auh8yn4

Trebuchet: A siege weapon that propelled large missiles, usually stones, against the walls of a city or castle. Sometimes these had names, like Malvoisin, the bad neighbor, at the siege of Minerve.

Trencavel, Raymond Roger, Viscount of Carcassonne and Beziers and other holdings: It seems that most of the nobles in this region were named Raymond, Roger, or Raymond Roger! Trencavel was greatly admired, courageous, and very young (only 24 years old at his death). However, he was proud and not a skillful diplomat. After he refused an offer of alliance with his uncle, Raymond VI, Count of Toulouse, his uncle joined forces with the invaders. Trencavel tried to negotiate peace with the

Crusader army at Montpellier, but they refused.
Possibly at that point, with an army already massed at
Lyons, nothing could stop the momentum. The fate of
Beziers and Carcassonne was sealed when Trencavel
and his citizens refused to hand over the Cathar
heretics. Through the nostalgic lens of history, this
made them heroes and martyrs of the Albigensian
Crusade. He owed allegiance to Raymond VI, Count of
Toulouse, and later to Peter II, King of Aragon. There
were close ties between Occitan and Spanish nobles,
whose language and culture were similar.

Troubadour: French (masculine) term for a
composer of troubadour lyrics; usually a noble or a
person with patronage from a noble house. They
sometimes performed, but they were more than mere
performers. Poems survive from about 450
identifiable individual composers. Arabic, Christian,
Celtic, and other sources influenced their style. There
were dozens of genres, for example, the alba, song of
the lover as morning approaches; canso, love song;
comiat, song renouncing a lover; crusade song, a song
praising war; planh, a lament for someone's death;
sirventis, a political poem or satire, usually in the
voice of a soldier; and tenso, a debate between two
poets. Most were in lenga romana or Occitan, which
many believed was the most beautiful language of its
day. Rhythm and wordplay get lost in translation. See
Robert Kehew (Ed.), (2005), *Lark in the Morning:
The Verses of the Troubadours.*

You can find many recordings of troubadour
compositions online. My favorite artist is the late
Owain Phyfe and his New World Renaissance Band.
His work includes Ja Nus Hons Pris, a lament written

by King Richard I about his captivity after the Crusades; you can find a recording at https://www.youtube.com/watch?v=sMZ3mSVcSKg.

The instruments used by troubadours came from many cultural backgrounds. These include the Arabic oud (similar to a lute) and the Celtic bagpipe. If you have never heard the vielle or hurdy-gurdy, a popular instrument from the 12th to 15th centuries, you must listen to this performance: **https://www.youtube.com/watch?v=bvNZeh6f8vE**

Trobairitz: There were about 20 known female composers of troubadour music. Their existence is one of several clues that women had more opportunities during this period than at some later times. See Claudia Keelan (2015), *Truth of My Songs: Poems of the Trobairitz*. Accompanying music is known for only one trobairitz composition, A chantar m'er de so qu'eu no volria, written by the Comtessa de Dia. **https://www.youtube.com/watch?v=5Zah4VWPiNE**

Wasting Disease: Tuberculosis, which has been widespread for thousands of years; it was a leading cause of death in the Middle Ages and throughout the world until the 20th century.

Yong Jen: I borrowed the name of Han Suyin's fictional 20th-century Chinese physician from her beautiful novel, *Til Morning Comes*.

Zagwe: The Zagwe dynasty ruled in what is now Ethiopia from 900 to 1270 CE. The empire promoted

Christianity and carried on the artistic and cultural traditions of the Axum empire. The churches carved from rock at Lalibela in the early 13th century are now a World Heritage site; exact construction dates aren't known, so the mention in my story may anticipate their actual existence by a decade or two. In the 13th century, Zagwe's connections with the outside world were relatively limited; they had a close relationship with Egypt.

Common Misconceptions about the

Middle Ages

All peasants were enslaved and they worked all the time: Not true in many times and places. "Peasant" is a broad category often used for all who were neither nobles nor clerics. Early in the Middle Ages, in some regions, peasants were sometimes bound to the land as serfs and engaged only in farming. Over time, some obtained freedom and became merchants or artisans, such as armorers, blacksmiths, brewers, weavers, tanners, etc. Some peasants, artisans, craftspersons, and merchants became wealthy, sometimes even more prosperous than knights or lesser nobility. Two situations led to the growth of freedom and income; a general rise in material well-being from about 900-1250 CE because of the Medieval Warming Period; and the severe labor shortages that arose after the Black Death.

Gregory Clark suggested that medieval peasants may have had shorter work hours and fewer workdays than some persons in early modern industrial societies. **http://groups.csail.mit.edu/mac/users/rauch/worktime/hours_workweek.html**

Clark later said his early estimate that peasants worked 150 days per year was too low; he later suggested that peasants may have worked closer to 300 days a year. That is still less than many modern workers.

https://www.theatlantic.com/health/archive/
2022/05/medieval-history-peasant-life-
work/629783/

It's difficult to compare income across nations and
periods, but by some assessments, medieval peasants
had reasonable income levels:

https://www.today.com/money/medieval-
brits-may-have-had-it-better-poorest-today-
6c9678192.

On the other hand, skeletal remains tell us that many
people did backbreaking physical work.

https://www.smithsonianmag.com/smart-
news/archaeology-inequality-skeletons-
cambridge-180976833/.

**Everyone was poor and starving during the
Middle Ages:** Not true in many times and places.

What was the quality of the diet? Julie Dunn says it
was good for medieval England (we always need to
qualify research findings; they apply only to periods
and regions included in the study):
**https://www.dailymail.co.uk/sciencetech/arti
cle-7040709/Medieval-peasants-England-
lived-hearty-diet-meat-vegetables-cheese.html**

Some authors (for example, Steven Pinker and Max
Rosen) argue that poverty is lower now than at any
earlier time in history. I think that claim is
misleading. Yes, average wealth has risen, but the
distributions of wealth and income are extremely
unequal. Several analyses cited below suggest that the
poorest people in the world today may actually be

worse off than the average peasant in the high Middle Ages.

I agree with Jason Hickel's critiques of Pinker's and Rosen's work (in Hickel's books such as *The Divide*). According to Hickel, a large proportion of modern people, mostly in the southern hemisphere, live in extreme poverty possibly worse than that during much of the Middle Ages. Some other authors concur: "Material consumption in some countries, mainly in sub-Saharan Africa, is now well below the pre-industrial norm.... there walk the earth now both the richest people who ever lived and the poorest" (Clark, *A Farewell to Alms*, p. 3).

For more details see this article from *Science Daily*: "Medieval England twice as well off as today's poorest nations", December 6, 2010.

www.sciencedaily.com/releases/2010/12/1012 05234308.htm

Everyone was malnourished and short: Not true in many times and places.

Genes influence height. However, height is also strongly influenced by nutrition status. When famine and malnutrition are widespread, people do not become as tall as they might otherwise. We can assess height from skeletal remains. Richard Steckel has reported that the average height of European men fell from 173.4 cm (68.26 inches) during the early Middle Ages to 165.8 cm (65.28 inches) during the late industrial period (17th and 18th centuries). He attributes this height decrease to poorer nutrition. In other words, data on stature suggest that European

men may have been better nourished during the predominantly agrarian early Middle Ages than during late industrialization.
https://tinyurl.com/25v8wte2

Everyone believed bathing was dangerous to health; no one bathed or made any effort to be clean; all people smelled bad. Not true in many times and places. The Romans introduced bathhouses to much of Europe. The use of bathhouses continued for centuries and well into the Middle Ages. Medieval books of manners called for handwashing before and after meals and frequent washing of hands and face. Paintings show that some nobility even had bathtubs. Getting enough warm water for a full-body bath was labor-intensive and costly, so a full bath was probably a rare occurrence. But that's a far cry from the often repeated belief that people in the Middle Ages actively avoided washing.

The idea that bathing was actually dangerous to health did not arise until 1348, when King Philippe VI of France asked scholars at the University of Paris to explain why the bubonic plague had occurred. One theory these scholars offered was that hot baths opened pores and allowed the plague to enter the body. This idea became influential and led to a general decline in personal hygiene, which may have been worse in later eras, such as the Tudor period, than during much of the Middle Ages. See Ashenburg, K. (2007). *The Dirt on Clean: An Unsanitized History.* and Smith, V. (2007). *Clean: A History of Personal Hygiene and Purity.*

Rosalie Gilbert states, "Documentation of guilds of soap-producers can be found in Europe as early as 800 AD, although soap as we know it did not come into widespread use in Europe until during the ninth century... By the 12th century, hard soap came into use which was said to be an Arab development later imported into Europe. The best soaps were known as castile soap, having originated in Castile, Spain, and made using olive oil instead of fats."

https://tinyurl.com/3cp7tc23

Everyone threw waste into the streets (and took this for granted). Not true in at least some times and places.

Many of the unsanitary practices that modern people believe were common in the Middle Ages were increasingly regulated as the years passed. A few cities even had sewers, although water and sewage management were less advanced during the Middle Ages than in some cities of ancient Rome. Many towns had regulations about waste disposal and fines for non-compliance.

https://tinyurl.com/ykyepdu4

For a more comprehensive discussion, see Carole Rawcliffe's books, particularly her 2013 discussion of *Urban Bodies: Communal Health in Later Medieval English Towns and Cities*.

Food was bland (or, conversely, spices were needed to cover up the taste of rotting meat). People drank only wine, beer, or ale because the water was polluted. Mostly not true.

Germ theory (and concern about invisible/ undetectable contaminants) did not develop until later. An early version of germ theory was suggested by Girolamo Fracastoro in 1546, but germ theory was not widely accepted until 1850 -1880, following the work of Pasteur, Koch, and others. However, contamination of food, drink, and air that could be seen and smelled was known to be unwholesome, and people tried to avoid it. Rotten meat was known to be unhealthy. Meat and fish were preserved by drying and salting. Of course, food poisoning was common during the Middle Ages. Still, it continued to be common until the passage and enforcement of food safety laws, and the emergence of refrigeration and other food preservation technologies, in the early 20th century. People preferred clean water when available; they understood that spring water was better than most river water.

https://elizabethchadwick.com/blog/the-myth-about-the-medieval-spicing-of-rotten-meat/

https://history.howstuffworks.com/medieval-people-drink-beer-water.htm

People ate everything with their hands and had terrible table manners. Mostly not true.

There were manuals for table manners. Examples of etiquette included: Wash your hands before and after the meal; use your own knife; do not belch or spit; do not stuff your mouth full; do not pick your teeth; use a spoon for broth instead of drinking from the bowl, and do not wipe your mouth on your sleeve (use a napkin).

http://rosaliegilbert.com/manners.html

Everyone had rotten teeth. Not true.

Examination of skeletal remains from the Middle Ages shows little tooth decay, probably because there was not much sugar in the diet. Medieval people cleaned their teeth with twigs or cloths and often used herbs or powders as cleaning agents. **https://slate.com/human-interest/2015/04/dental-hygiene-did-people-in-the-middle-ages-have-bad-teeth.html**

People rarely lived past 30 years of age. Mostly not true.

One estimate of life expectancy for the early Middle Ages is 30 to 35 years.

https://en.wikipedia.org/wiki/Life_expectancy#Variation_over_time

However, this number does not mean people never lived past age 35. The same source says, "... if a Gaulish boy made it past age 20, he might expect to live 25 more years... anyone who survived until 40 had a good chance at another 15 to 20 years" (Lisa Bitel, 2002, *Women in Early Medieval Europe*, 400-1100, Cambridge University Press).

There is a difference between *life expectancy* and *life span*. Estimates of average life expectancy from birth are strongly influenced by infant mortality. When we calculate life expectancy from birth, the age at death for infants (e.g., 0 to 12 months) is averaged with the ages of people who die later in life (e.g., 40, 60, and beyond). When infant deaths are included, the average age at death (and thus average life expectancy) decreases substantially.

Because of widespread contagious disease, infant mortality rates (percent of infants who die within the first year of life) were high until very recent times. Until at least 1900, parents could expect perhaps half their children to die as infants or within the first five years of life. Infant mortality decreased substantially in wealthy nations starting around 1900 CE. Unfortunately, infant mortality rates remain very high in places with extreme poverty.

Life span (an age to which a noticeable number of people live if they survive early childhood) provides a different way to think about people's lives in the past. Life expectancy has increased substantially, but life span has not changed as much across human history. We read about people in ancient Rome or the Middle Ages who reached 70, 80, and beyond. Although many people didn't survive childhood, it was not that unusual for those who survived to reach ages 40, 50, 60, and beyond during the Middle Ages. BBC provides an excellent non-technical discussion of the difference between life expectancy and life span here:

https://tinyurl.com/ybactdnf

Everyone believed the world was flat. Not true for the educated, and most people probably didn't think much about this. Most people probably never thought about this question (and even today, some people insist that the world is flat!). Medieval scholars were aware of ancient writings; Eratosthenes, a Greek scholar, ca. 200 BC, knew the world was round and estimated the circumference of the earth with reasonable accuracy, and medieval scholars knew of his work.

Everyone was ignorant, illiterate, and superstitious; it was a time of little learning or progress. Most people were not literate, and superstitions were widespread; lay religious beliefs involved a lot of magical thinking. Peasants thought a priest was 'good' if he successfully produced rain through prayer (Robb, 2008, *Discovery of France*). Contact with relics was believed to help with concerns such as pregnancy and health. Beliefs about magic, religion, and medicine were mixed together. Medical treatment often included prayer; astrology was used to decide when to do medical interventions such as bloodletting. Many parish priests had minimal education.

However, many higher-ranking clerics were literate and well-educated about Catholic doctrines and writings that survived from ancient Greece and Rome. Some nobles were also well-educated. For example, Richard I of England (the Lionheart) spoke both the lenga romana and Latin and was a troubadour (a composer). (He spent so little time in England that he may not have known much English!)

At the Fourth Lateran Council in 1215, the Church reaffirmed that cathedrals should provide schools even for 'poor scholars.' Over time, the Church played a greater role in promoting literacy and education. Increasing contact with the Islamic world during and after the Crusades reacquainted Europeans with the great writings of antiquity and the scientific discoveries made by Islamic scholars. The use of Arabic numerals is just one of many examples.

People may know that one contribution of scholars in the Middle Ages was the preservation (by copying) of manuscripts from the ancient world (much of this work was done by Arabic or Islamic scholars). There was a Golden Age of Islamic scholarship from approximately 750 – 1258 CE. They established great centers of learning with achievements in mathematics, medicine, and other sciences. Scholars in Western Europe learned much from them.

Impressive technological advances occurred during the Middle Ages, with inventions such as mechanical clocks. There were improvements in water mills, and waterpower was used to raise heavy objects and to power bellows and hammers. The introduction of the heavy-wheeled plow, the horse collar, and three-field rotation increased agricultural yield. The first artesian well was drilled in 1126. Architectural innovations included rib vaults, the first true chimneys, and segmental arch bridges. Additional advances include treadwheel and stationary cranes, the compound crank, the blast furnace, better compass designs, stern-mounted rudders, and the first spectacles. Castles and cathedrals stand as monuments to the skill and intelligence of medieval builders.

https://tinyurl.com/2sjv59vc

Lenses were developed to correct vision, although they were not widely available until later.

https://tinyurl.com/48twrhtr

This example of mechanical ingenuity-- an articulated prosthetic metal hand—came a little after the Middle Ages:

https://tinyurl.com/yeyw9e23

For further discussion see Falk, S. (2020). *The Light Ages: The surprising story of science in the Middle Ages.*

Primae noctis or droit de seigneur gave lords the right to sleep with any bride on the first night after her wedding. Most historians believe this is a myth.

There were elaborate torture devices such as the iron maiden, and chastity belts were used to prevent women from having sex. Mostly not true. Torture was sometimes used to extract confessions. However, chastity belts and many elaborate devices displayed in torture museums did not exist in the Middle Ages. Victorian-era P.T. Barnum types invented them for 'torture museums.' **https://tinyurl.com/4c7y3wae**

All Europeans were pious and obeyed the Church, and Catholicism did not change during the Middle Ages. Not true. Many peasants attended Church rarely and were reluctant to pay to support the Church. For many, their only religious learning would have been prayers such as the Ave Maria and Pater Noster (in Latin because the Church forbade translations of the Bible into the vernacular until a much later period). Many people (perhaps even some clerics) likely repeated Latin prayers without understanding them. In 1215, the Church ruled that people must take communion and confession yearly at the Fourth Lateran Council. They would not have found it necessary to reaffirm this rule if most people had done this all along.

Within the Church, criticism repeatedly arose about wealth, sexual license, gluttony, and other forms of corruption. Sometimes criticisms of the Church were labeled heresies. However, new monastic orders were often established, initially with stricter rules for behavior, hoping that religion could be purified. Examples are the Cistercian and Franciscan orders. Religious beliefs and practices underwent a constant process of challenge, and sometimes they changed.

Before Pope Innocent III launched a crusade against the Cathars, Catholic priests and legates tried to "correct" the thinking of heretics through rational argument and public debate; these were ineffective. This dramatization shows how such a debate might have gone:

Roman Catholic vs. Cathar debate
https://www.youtube.com/watch?v=OaoGQA LGyJo

Apart from the ongoing ferment within Catholicism, and the emergence of Christian heresies such as Catharism, the 13th century was a time of spiritual flourishing in other religions in Europe, for example, what we now call Kabbalah (Jewish mysticism). There were also developments in Sufism during this period. It originated centuries earlier as a branch (or some would say a heresy) of Islam. Many noted Sufi scholars taught in Andalusian Spain during the 12th and 13th centuries.

All knights wore plate armor; it was so heavy they could hardly move. Not true.

Up until about 1300, typical armor worn by a knight consisted of a gambeson (quilted cloth jacket) covered by a mail shirt or hauberk. ("Chain mail" is redundant. It is sufficient to say "mail.") Plates to cover arms, legs, and chest were added gradually, and full plate armor only came into use in the later Middle Ages (around 1420).

https://tinyurl.com/bdzh46xn

The weight a knight in plate armor bore was comparable to that carried by a modern firefighter or soldier. To see how these might compare in action, view *An Obstacle Run in Armour*, a short film by Daniel Jaquet: **https://www.youtube.com/watch?v=pAzI1Uvl Qqw**

This race looks like a 3-way tie to me!

An organization called HEMA (Historical European Martial Arts) recreates fighting styles using various weapons. Their techniques are based on many kinds of historical evidence, including written handbooks and paintings. Of course, they fight with protective padding and are not trying to kill each other! Kicking, striking an opponent with a shield, wrestling, tripping, and other moves were often combined with weapon use. An example of a HEMA tournament: https://www.youtube.com/watch?v=91IIARM5lVs.

Witches were frequently burned during the Middle Ages. Not true.

The publication of *Malleus Malificarum* (Witch's Hammer) in 1486 led to a substantial increase in witch-burning between circa 1500 - 1660. In other words: Most witch-burnings happened after the Middle Ages. (The Middle Ages are often blamed for things that occurred later!) Heretics were burned during the Middle Ages; however, at least in France, heretic burnings were relatively rare before the Albigensian Crusades; they became more common after systematic inquisitions were organized beginning in 1294.

Crusades happened only around Jerusalem.
Not true. The Albigensian Crusade (beginning in 1209) took place in southern France; the victims were Cathar heretics and the nobles who protected them. There were also crusades in the Baltic against European pagans.

All medical practices were completely useless.
Only partly true. Many physicians in the Middle Ages were guided by the humoral theories of medicine described by Hippocrates (ca. 400 BC) and Galen (ca. 150 CE). They believed there were four fluids (called humors) in the body: blood, phlegm, black bile, and yellow bile. They believed that disease arose when there was an imbalance among these (such as too much blood). Many treatments, such as bleeding and purging, should correct this imbalance. Humoral theories did not fall out of favor until around 1850 CE, so we read of people like George Washington being bled on his deathbed. However, there are a few situations where 'bleeding' can be helpful, such as removing excess iron in the blood or reducing some types of swelling.

Physicians thought urine color was informative, and some carried booklets that showed how to interpret different colors. In fact, examination of some characteristics of urine has diagnostic value.

However, not all medieval treatments were useless. Using wine (alcohol) to cleanse wounds is an example of a reasonable practice. Bald's salve (a concoction of garlic, onion or leek, bovine bile, and a few other ingredients) is effective against some bacteria resistant to one or more modern antibiotics (such as methicillin-resistant Staphylococcus Aurea or MRSA). Some researchers are exploring remedies from other historical periods to evaluate their use in modern medicine.

https://www.antibioticresearch.org.uk/1000-year-old-eye-salve-recipe-shows-antibiotic-activity/

Siraisi, N. (1990). *Medieval and Early Renaissance Medicine*. University of Chicago Press.

Marriage was always a sacrament officiated by a priest and regulated by the Church. Not true until later in the Middle Ages. Through most of the Middle Ages, it was sufficient for two people to say "I marry you." Witnesses were not required and a priest did not have to officiate.

Primogeniture (leaving everything to the firstborn son) was universal. Only true in some times and places. In northern France, around 1200, primogeniture was the rule (all property and titles went to the oldest son). Thus, in northern France, large holdings were preserved. However, properties were often divided among several children in southern France, and even women could inherit. As a result, across generations, holdings became smaller or fell under multiple ownership. In The Albigensian Crusades, Sumption mentions a castle owned in 36 parts by different knights. The division of property into small pieces with conflicting claims probably contributed to the problems the disorganized southern nobles had in mounting a defense against the more organized and hierarchical northern French nobility.

Women had no rights. Not true in some times and places. Medievalist Joan Kelly has argued that – regarding attitudes toward female sexuality, economic and political roles, cultural roles, and ideologies about women – women actually fared worse during the Renaissance than during much of the Middle Ages. (Joan Kelly, 1984, "Did women have a Renaissance?" In *The Essays of Joan Kelly*.) Recall also that most witch burnings, with victims who were most often women, took place between 1450-1750, years that overlap the Renaissance and early Enlightenment.

The legal situation for women in Occitania was inconsistent and complex (Linda Paterson, 2002, *Culture and Society in Medieval Occitania*, chapter III). Women could inherit property; they had better legal rights in Occitania about 1000-1200 CE than elsewhere in Europe for many centuries afterward.

https://www.getty.edu/news/what-was-life-like-for-women-in-the-middle-ages/

https://www.worldhistory.org/article/1345/women-in-the-middle-ages/

To support the argument that women had some rights and opportunities during the Middle Ages, people often point out the most notable women, such as Eleanor of Aquitaine, Hildegarde of Bingen, and Joan of Arc. We need many more examples to show that women had greater rights and opportunities during some parts of the Middle Ages than generally supposed. Here's a list (by no means complete) of some less well-known remarkable women from the 10th to 15th centuries (the number in the first column indicates the century):

10	Ende the Illuminator	illuminator
10	Hrotsvitha	dramatist and poet
10	Michitsuna no haha	diarist and poet
10	Lady Murasaki Shikibu	author of 1st novel
11	Trotula of Salerno	physician
11	Anna Comnena	writer
12	Hildegard of Bingen	mystic, author, abbess
12	Guda	illuminator
12	Li Qingzhao	poet and writer
12	Frau Ava	nun and poet
12	Elisabeth of Schönau	mystic
12	Herra of Landsberg	abbess and science writer
12	Heloise	abbess, scholar
13	Garsenda of Forcalquier	ruler and poet
13	Marie de France	multilingual poet
13	Claricia, illuminator	illuminator
13	Lady Eleanor of Montfort	military leader
13	Mechtild von Magdeburg	Beguine, mystic, nun, writer
13	Ben no Naishi	poet
13	Licoricia of Oxford	financier
13	Marguerite Porete	writer and mystic
14	Julian of Norwich	mystic and author
14	Margery Kempe	1st autobiography in English
14	Jeanne de Clisson	pirate
14	Catherine of Siena	writer and mystic
14	Leonor Lopez de Cordoba	first autobiography in Spanish
14	Catherine of Siena	mystic
15	Christine de Pizan	feminist author
15	Gwerful Mechain	poet
15	Laura Cereta	feminist author
15	Teresa de Cartagena	deaf culture
15	Margaret Paston	estate manager

In the later Middle Ages, women could join guilds and practice trades; their participation increased after the Black Death wiped out as much as half of the population of Europe and created a labor shortage. Women could, and in many cases had to, support families through work as artisans and merchants. It became common for widows to inherit their husband's businesses, such as brewing, weaving, copying, or even blacksmithing. The female blacksmith in the movie *The Knight's Tale* is not as unlikely as one might think.

People did not travel far from their homes. Not true. People did travel, sometimes very long distances, often by foot. A pilgrimage might be undertaken to atone for sins or, perhaps, out of a desire to see the world. Persons convicted of crimes were sometimes sentenced to go on pilgrimage as penance.

Sumption, J. (2003). *The Age of Pilgrimage: The Medieval Journey to God*. Hidden Spring.

There were many famous long-distance travelers during the Middle Ages. Here are a few examples.

Benjamin of Tudela left Spain in 1165 and traveled extensively through the Middle East, as far as Arabia.

Popes sent clergy, including John of Plano Carpini (1245) and William of Rubruck (1253-1255), to preach in Mongolia and other parts of Asia,

Marco Polo left for Asia in 1271 along with his father and uncle, who had been to China before; he spent 24 years there. His famous book may have been based on his own observations – or those of other travelers.

Mansa Musa, King of Mali, possibly one of the wealthiest men who ever lived, went on a pilgrimage to Mecca in 1324.

Ibn Battuta, 'the Islamic Marco Polo,' made journeys beginning in 1325 to Iraq, Iran, Arabia, Somalia, the Swahili Coast, Central Asia, India, China, Spain, North Africa, Mali, and Timbuktu.

Zheng He (1403-1424) made extensive voyages of exploration as far as Mogadishu in East Africa.

There must have been countless other pilgrims, traders, and explorers.

Plagues were constant, and most people died from the plague. Not true. The first wave of bubonic plague did not arrive in Europe until 1347. The plague recurred many times. It was catastrophic, killing as much as 50% of the population in some areas. However, many other diseases were widespread. More deaths were due to these other diseases. See John Robb et al. (2021), The greatest health problem of the Middle Ages? Estimating the burden of disease in medieval England. *International Journal of Paleopathology, 34*, 101-112. The Robb article's title is a bit misleading because one of the primary data sources was Bills of Mortality from the 1600s (and that is actually after the Middle Ages), but I think it's plausible that the patterns he found in the 1600s also existed in earlier centuries. Robb et al. reported that tuberculosis, fever, and smallpox were the top three causes of death. Data from Yearly Bills of Mortality from 1657 to 1758 (for London) are posted online at https://www.curiousgnu.com/yearly-bills-of-mortality-1657-1758 as an Excel spreadsheet. In light of some authors' claims about widespread violence during the Middle Ages, I found it interesting that the number of deaths attributed to murder, execution, and 'mistorture' in this list was so small.

There was widespread violence everywhere, all the time. The brief answer is: I don't think so.

An editor's preface to W. C. Brown (2011). *Violence in Medieval Europe* says: "[Brown] argues forcefully that to dismiss the Middle Ages as somehow 'more violent' than the modern Western world is fundamentally to misunderstand that era as well as our own. Instead, he explores a medieval world of differences: different forms of violence, different justifications of it, and arguments about it."

Studying history helps us put our own behavior in a broader context. Consider punishment for theft. We are horrified to read that people were branded or had their hands cut off at some times and places during the Middle Ages. In the 21st-century United States, our solution to problems such as theft and drug use is mass-scale, long-term incarceration; we have more people in prison than any other nation (both in absolute numbers and as a percentage of the population). Some prisoners are raped, beaten, or used as slave labor. I don't think modern people can feel morally superior. There's still a high level of violence, just in different forms. Please do not willfully misunderstand me: I do not advocate that we return to whipping, mutilation, or branding. I'm just saying that we still have major ethical problems.

Some of you will want to skip to the next topic at this point! But if you like data, keep reading. I'm a statistician in my other life, and I like data. (But I don't always trust it!)

Steven Pinker (in *The Better Angels of Our Nature*) argued that we are less violent now than in the past; he presented empirical data as "proof." Many reviewers were enthusiastic about the book; Bill Gates said it was one of his favorites. However, some critics have pointed out that he cherry-picked data and engaged in questionable forms of argument; as a statistician, I agree with most of the points they make. See Sarah Butler's 2018 article, "Getting Medieval on Steven Pinker," in the journal *Historical Reflections*, volume 44, issue 1, pages 29-40; Philip Dwyer and Mark Micale (2022), *The Darker Angels of Our Nature: Refuting the Pinker Theory of History and Violence*; and John Gray's essay at **https://tinyurl.com/2p8kdd73**

Many of the numbers reported by Pinker (and others) may simply be wrong. Death rates are given as the number of deaths (from war or homicide, or other causes) per 100,000 population. However, we don't have accurate counts of deaths; and we also don't have precise information about the total population size. If we are wrong about either, death rate estimates will be wrong, possibly by orders of magnitude. Estimates of death rate also depend on how data are aggregated (by time period and geographic locale).

Keeping in mind the uncertainty of numerical calculations, consider this widely- reproduced public domain graph of global death rates due to war across time, from 1400 to 2000:

https://commons.wikimedia.org/wiki/File:Wa rs-Long-Run-military-civilian-fatalities.png

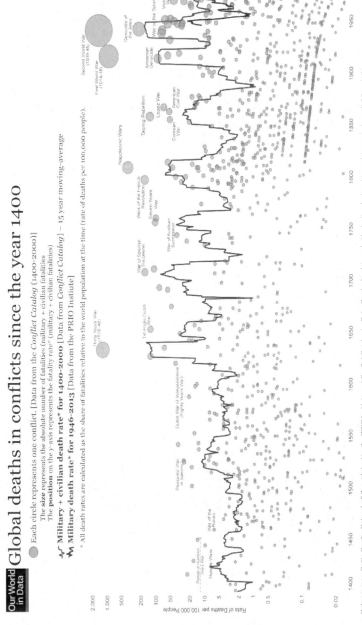

Our World in Data Global deaths in conflicts since the year 1400

● Each circle represents one conflict. [Data from the *Conflict Catalog* (1400–2000)]

The **size** represents the absolute number of fatalities (military + civilian [fatalities])

The **position** on the y-axis represents the fatality rate" (military + civilian fatalities)

〰 **Military + civilian death rate* for 1400–2000** [Data from *Conflict Catalog*] – 15 year moving-average

〜 **Military death rate* for 1946–2013** [Data from the PRIO Institute]

* All death rates are calculated as the share of fatalities relative to the world population at the time (the rate of deaths per 100,000 people).

Data sources: Battle Deaths Dataset v.3.0, published by the PRIO Institute and Conflict Catalog by Peter Brecke for data on battle deaths. And world population data from HYDE and UN

This is a data visualisation from OurWorldInData.org There you find more visualisations on this topic.

Licensed under CC-BY-SA by the author Max Roser.

This graph is in the public domain. The data in this graph do not support a claim that death rates from war were higher during the late Middle Ages than now. (In his book *The Better Angels of Our Nature,* Pinker focused on the last few years as evidence of a recent "long peace".)

Also, note that death rates per 100,000 population are on a logarithmic scale. If you glance at this graph, your eye leads you to think that the WW II death rate was only two to three times the long-term average. If you examine the numeric values on the vertical axis, you will find that the death rate for WW II was actually about 200 times the long-term average. Even people who understand logarithms are sometimes misled by graphs that use log scales.

Now consider some data about homicide. From M. Eisner, 2003, Long-term historical trends in violent crime, *Crime and Justice, vol. 30*, pp. 83-142); retrieved from: **https://ourworldindata.org/homicides**

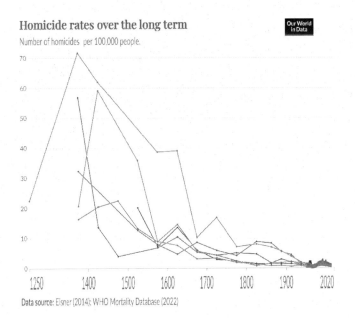

Homicide rates over the long term

Number of homicides per 100.000 people.

Data source: Eisner (2014); WHO Mortality Database (2022)

This graph is in the public domain. At first glance, this graph makes an "oh, wow" impression. Yes, homicide rates were much higher from 1300 to 1500 than now, particularly in Italy. Does that mean people back then lived in constant fear of homicide? I don't think so.

For purposes of comparison, note the following. In 2022, several American cities had murder rates approximately the same as the highest rates in this graph, for example, St. Louis, MO, 69.4 per 100,000; Baltimore, MD, 51.1; New Orleans, LA, 43.6. Data from: https://worldpopulationreview.com/us-city-rankings/cities-with-most-murders

Even 70 homicides per 100,000 people is still an infrequent event (if you convert 70/100000 to percentage terms, it's .07%, in other words, homicide happens to 7% out of 1% of the people).

To add one more point of comparison: If you are a US driver, your lifetime risk of being killed in a vehicular accident is .93% (about 1%). That's a far higher risk than any of the homicide rates in Eisner's graph, but it's a risk most of us accept without worrying about it most of the time. (A. R. Seghal, 2020, The lifetime risk of death from firearm injuries, drug overdoses, and motor vehicle accidents in the United States. *The American Journal of Medicine, vol. 133*, pp.. 1162-1167.)

I don't think the homicide rates in graphs like Eisner's should lead us to believe that all people in the Middle Ages felt personally at risk of being killed all the time. In fact, even though our objective risk may be lower than theirs, we may experience more anxiety about violence than they did because we are exposed to much information about homicide in the media. And people in the Middle Ages did not find high murder rates acceptable – they did not take this kind of violence for granted as an acceptable fact of life.

https://www.historyextra.com/period/mediev al/life-violence-middle-ages-murder-crime/

As noted earlier: people were far more likely to die from diseases than from homicide or war in most parts of the world during most of the Middle Ages. This has been true throughout most of history.

All Europeans were white and Christian. Not true.

There were many large Jewish communities in medieval Europe and often they suffered severe persecution. In the Occitan at the time of my story, there was relatively more tolerance of Jewish communities than in some other times and places in Medieval Europe. Large Islamic cities in Andalusian Spain had close ties with southern France during the high Middle Ages. Some historians have described a Golden Age or "Convivencia" in Al Andalus when Muslim and Arabic people lived in relative harmony with Jewish and Christian populations. However, there were also times when religious minorities were oppressed.

Recently there has been substantial interest in the presence of people of color in medieval Europe. There are at least two types of evidence for their presence. Analysis of skeletal remains from the Middle Ages suggests individuals who came from Asia and Africa as far north as Britain.

https://www.independent.co.uk/news/science/archaeology/chinese-skeleton-discovery-roman-history-society-southwark-cemetery-asian-remains-a7330666.html;

https://www.medievalists.net/2019/09/black-death-burials-reveal-the-diversity-of-londons-medieval-population/;

https://www.museumoflondon.org.uk/discover/bioarchaeological-evidence-black-women-14th-century-london

A second kind of evidence comes from art. Paintings show people of color in Europe during the Middle Ages; they are sometimes shown in costly clothing (evidence that they were not servants).

https://medievalpoc.tumblr.com/

https://www.npr.org/sections/codeswitch/2013/12/13/250184740/taking-a-magnifying-glass-to-the-brown-faces-in-medieval-art

http://www.imageoftheblack.com/

Also see this multiple volume history: David Bindman, Henry Louis Gates Jr., et al. *The Image of the Black in Western Art.*

One last myth: The Middle Ages was a utopian period. Not true. In debunking many negative beliefs about the Middle Ages, I certainly don't mean to imply it was a great time to live, or better than the present. Some alt-right thinkers idealize a distorted version of the Middle Ages. See this essay by Ratner at https://bigthink.com/the-present/time-to-get-medieval-why-some-conservative-thinkers-love-the-middle-ages/) or this book: Kaufman, A. & Sturtevant, P. (2020). *The Devil's Historians: How Modern Extremists Abuse the Medieval Past.* In this distorted view, during the European Middle Ages, white men were in charge, people were obedient to religion, there was little diversity, and women were subservient (and all of these, by implication, are supposed to be good things). Recent research shows that none of these things are true to the extent people once believed.

I would not want to live during the Middle Ages. My utopia would have flush toilets and modern medicine; it would provide access to abundant information. It would have less persecution of women and minorities and less economic inequality and poverty than both the Middle Ages and present times.

Recommended Sources

Best History: Jonathan Sumption (1978), *The Albigensian Crusade*. An engaging narrative based on superb scholarship.

Best Website: https://www.cathar.info/cathar_news.htm

by James McDonald. His web pages have substantial information about the Cathars and the Occitan region. I went on a Cathar Country tour led by James and his wife Sophie a few years ago, and I highly recommend them.

Best Newsletter: https://www.medievalists.net/

Best Lectures: Professor Dorsey Armstrong's Teaching Company course, *Years That Changed History: 1215*. She provides excellent background about what was happening worldwide during this time of enormous cultural and religious change. Topics include the Magna Carta and the Fourth Lateran Council, the rise of Genghis Khan, the Crusades, and developments in Africa and the Americas. Her other lecture series include Medieval World, Black Death, Turning Points in Medieval History, and Great Minds of the Medieval World.

Made in United States
North Haven, CT
22 April 2024

51583202R10274